WHO IS PREACHER?

In November of 1985, William W. Johnstone's western *The Last Mountain Man* was published—and the legendary Smoke Jensen was born. The series became an immediate hit and remains to this day one of his most popular creations.

In 1990, Bill was asked to create a spin-off character. He created a prequel to the Last Mountain Man series called *The First Mountain Man*, featuring another man of the frontier, known only as Preacher—a boy who left home in 1812 and became one of the most fearless men to conquer the American West.

But the question remained: Who is Preacher?

To answer that question, Pinnacle Books has now released—in the volume you hold in your hands—two Preacher western adventures: *The First Mountain Man* and *Preacher*, first published in 1991 and 2006, respectively. With these two novels, you will learn the legend of the first mountain man: Preacher. Solitary, smart, and armed with a long gun, he is as fierce as the land itself.

PREACHER
THE LEGENDARY MOUNTAIN MAN

How It All Began

WILLIAM W. JOHNSTONE

PINNACLE BOOKS
Kensington Publishing Corp.
www.kensingtonbooks.com

PINNACLE BOOKS are published by

Kensington Publishing Corp.
119 West 40th Street
New York, NY 10018

All Kensington titles, imprints, and distributed lines are available at special quantity discounts for bulk purchases for sales promotions, premiums, fund-raising, educational, or institutional use. Special book excerpts or customized printings can also be created to fit specific needs. For details, write or phone the office of the Kensington sales manager: Kensington Publishing Corp., 119 West 40th Street, New York, NY 10018, attn: Sales Department; phone 1-800-221-2647.

PINNACLE BOOKS, the Pinnacle logo, and the WWJ steer head logo are Reg. U.S. Pat. & TM Off.

ISBN-13: 978-0-7860-4483-2
ISBN-10: 0-7860-4483-7

First printing: October 2006

13 12 11 10 9 8 7 6 5

Printed in the United States of America

First electronic edition: April 2018

ISBN-13: 978-0-7860-4248-7
ISBN-10: 0-7860-4248-6

THE FIRST
MOUNTAIN MAN

Book One

1

"When you call me that, smile!"

Owen Wister

He was on the east side of the Absaroka Range, in the timber, heading down toward the Popo Agie. He was in no hurry, and there was no real reason for him to go there. He just had him a hankering, call it. He felt he might run into some old friends around there who, like the lone rider, had felt the calling for companionship.

He hadn't been down there in some time, not since the last rendezvous back in '30, he thought it was. He was pretty sure it was the year of our Lord 1837. Had to be close to that, anyway. If the year was as he figured, he was about thirty-five years old, near as he could figure. And he'd never felt better in his life.

The rider was of average height for his time, lean-hipped and rawhide tough, with tremendous power in his upper body. What women he'd run into over he last seventeen or eighteen or so years in the mountains considered him handsome. He tried to recall the last time he'd seen a white woman. Two, three years at least.

Just thinking about the rendezvous got him all lost in memories—but not so lost that he forgot where he was and to keep a sharp eye out for Injuns. He rode with his Hawken rifle across the saddle horn and had another one shoved into a saddle boot. He carried two .50 caliber pistols behind his waist sash and two more hung in leather on the saddle horn, one on each side. He'd always boasted that he was a peaceful man, but Injuns is notional folks. You never really know how to take them. A man can nearabout always ride into an Injun camp and they'll feed you and bed you down for the night. They'll usually treat a body right well. 'Course, depending on the tribe and the general mood of the day, the rub comes when you try to leave the next morning. They might decide to have some fun and skin you alive. He had seen what was left of a man after that. It was a disheartening sight, to say the least. He didn't expect the other feller cared much for it either.

The lone rider rode easy, ruminating on this and that. He'd seen a white man up the trail about five months back, when the snow was thick, and he'd told him it was Christmas. That had got him to feeling all maudlin and the like, thinking about folks and family he hadn't seen in years and would probably never see again on this side of the grave.

Time gets confusing up in the High Lonesome. The months and years just blend together and don't take on a whole hell of a lot of importance.

He reined up at a creek and swung down from the saddle, getting the kinks out of his muscles and bones and giving his horses a chance to drink and blow. He rode a mountain horse he'd caught and gentle-broke. Called him Hammer for no particular reason. Hammer was a gray, tough as a mountain goat and stood eighteen hands high. His good pack horse was also a gray, just as tough as Hammer and just as smart: he wouldn't tote no more than he felt he could comfortably carry. Overload him and he just wouldn't move. Stand there and look at you with them eyes telling you to get that crap off his back. Smart.

The rider looked all around him careful, then stood still and sniffed the air. He could detect nothing in the cool mountain air except the scent of nature's own growth in springtime. There was no Injun smell. After so many years in the mountains, he had learned that all men have a distinctive scent that can be picked up by others if you just teach your blower to do it.

He stretched out on his belly by the creek and took him a long drink of cold clean water. He thought about taking off his moccasins and sticking his bare feet in the crick and splashing around some, like a kid, but some poor critter downstream that wasn't hurtin' nobody and who just come out of the woods for a cool drink would be sick for a week.

He did take off his moccasins and rub his feet, though. Felt good.

He rubbed his feet dry on the grass and slipped back into his moccasins. He chewed on a piece of jerky and wished long for some coffee, but he'd been out of coffee for weeks. That was another reason for this trip. He had to resupply with salt and beans and coffee and the like. He also had to get him a new pair of longhandle underwear. His was plumb wore out. And his buckskins were thin.

He was known from the Northwest to the deserts of the Southwest as Preacher.

He was far from being a man of the cloth—about as far as a man could get, even though he'd been raised in the church as a boy. When he was new and green to the High Lonesome, Injuns had grabbed him and was planning on slow-roasting him to see how well he stood pain. If he stood it well, they would praise him and sing songs about him. 'Course, those songs would be sort of hard to appreciate from the grave. So he started preaching. He preached all day and all night. The Injuns finally figured he was crazy as a lizard and turned him loose. The nickname stuck.

Preacher had been in the mountains since he was just a boy; he had run away from a good home and reached the mountains a year later. And while he had left the mountains many times to see what was over the next ridge or river, he always returned to the High Lonesome. He had lived with a number of tribes, and gotten along with many of them. He'd had him a squaw from time to time, and a few offspring.

But unlike many of his counterparts, Preacher could see the writing on the wall, so to speak, even though he might have some difficulty reading actual words. The beaver market was glutted. Man was hard-pressed to make a living anymore, and it was only going to get worse. He knew that while most of the other mountain men did not, or would not accept it.

Preacher could do a lot of things besides trapping. He could pan for gold, he could scout for the Army or for wagon trains, he even knew a little about farming—although he kept that to himself.

He cut his eyes to Hammer as the horse raised his head and pricked his ears up. He was over to him in a heartbeat, stroking his neck and talking to him low, so he wouldn't whinny and give away their position. He spoke to the pack horse and rubbed his neck. They stood quiet, but they weren't liking what they smelled one damn bit.

Then Preacher smelled what the horses had smelled, and he heard them coming. Injuns, and their scent was strong. With it came the scent of blood. Fresh blood.

He picketed both horses on graze and pulled the pistols from the saddle horn. He slipped to the top of a rise and peeked through the brush. What he saw below didn't set well at all. Five young bucks and they had prisoners. The Injuns looked to be Arapaho, and Preacher never had got on too well with that tribe. They just didn't much like the white man. Preacher lay still, moving only his eyes, carefully checking everything out. But it appeared five was all there was. But five bucks on the warpath was plenty. He could see fresh scalps on the manes of their horses and on their war lances. And they weren't Injun scalps.

The bucks had two white women and two white men, and from the looks on their faces, they were all plenty scared. And they had a right to be.

A lot of wagon trains were pushing west, to Oregon or California. Wagons had been rolling to Oregon for several years. Nat Wyeth, Preacher thought it was, took the first emigrants over the Oregon Trail back in '31 or '32. Been a lot of them since then, and a lot of them hadn't made it.

Preacher had him a thought that those poor, scared pilgrims was part, or had been part, of a small wagon train that just ran out of luck.

"The Lord will see us through, brother and sisters," a man said. "Put your faith in the Lord."

Missionaries, Preacher thought. Come to the wilderness to bring Jesus to the savages. Damn fools bringing womenfolk out here to preach with them. Injuns don't think like white people. It's not that the whites is right and the Injuns is wrong, it's just that they're two very different ways of life. Whites and Injuns don't think alike. Injuns don't steal 'cause they're bad people. It's more of a game to them, and right and wrong doesn't enter into it. Courage and dying well and bravery mean a great deal to Injuns. They can't none of them abide a coward.

Preacher had tried to tell a few missionaries that the Injuns didn't need or want their religion; they had a religion all their own and the practiced it and lived by it. But you'd have better luck trying to tell a lawyer to shut up than you would with a Bible-thumper.

Preacher watched as one young buck pulled at himself and grinned at the others. He knew then that one of the young women—and they were both lookers—was fixin' to get hopped on right then and there in front of God and everybody else.

Then the buck said as much. Preacher spoke some Arapaho, and heard him tell the woman what he was gonna do. She looked up at him from the log where they'd plopped her, confusion and fear on her face. Then that buck just reached down and run his hand up under her dress. That woman squalled something fierce.

"Here now!" a man blustered up. "You stop that barbaric behavior, you hear me?"

The woman's hands was tied behind her back, but her feet were free. She kicked that buck right between his legs and he went down howling and puking, both hands holding onto his privates.

Preacher winced and he was thirty feet away.

Preacher knew if he was to do anything, it had to be now. He eased the hammers back on his old .50 caliber pistols and laid them on the ground. He took the second brace—hoping the powder was dry on them all—and eased the hammers back on them. Another buck jerked out a knife and whacked an ear off one of the men prisoners. The man screamed and the blood poured. The buck then proceeded to make it clear to the lady—using sign language that an idiot could understand—that if she didn't hike up her skirts and do it real quick, he was gonna cut something else off the man, and it was located a mite lower than his remaining ear.

"Melody!" the man with one ear hollered.

Preacher figured he got the message, too.

The buck she'd kicked in the privates was still on the ground, rolling and moaning and being sick all over the place. She had really put her little foot in him.

There wasn't any other option left Preacher. He lifted his pistols with the double-set triggers and let 'em bang. He had double-shotted these and the first ball hit the buck with the knife in the chest; the second ball hit him in the belly. Both balls from the second pistol hit a brave smack in the face. He was a real mess when he hit the ground.

Preacher grabbed the second brace of pistols and let the lead fly. He couldn't hardly see a thing for the gun smoke but knew he had put four Injuns on the ground and the other one was just getting to his moccasins, still bent over in pain. Preacher jerked his long-bladed knife from its sheath and ran down the short slope toward the scared pilgrims.

He ran right over that skinny Injun with the bruised privates and knocked him sprawling back to the ground. He jumped up, a war axe in his hand, and he was some mad. Preacher told him in his own language what he thought of him, his family, and his horse. The buck screamed and charged. Preacher ducked and cut him from brisket to backbone. That blade was honed to a fine edge and went in easy. The skinny Injun was out of it. Preacher ran back to his guns and loaded up again as fast as he could.

The women were in a shocked silence. The man with one ear looked at Preacher like he was some sort of devil. And, Preacher thought, maybe he did look like one. He hadn't shaved in a month or so and his clothes were made from what he could kill and skin and cure. His hat was so old and floppy it had no shape. Preacher reckoned he did look like a wild man to these city folks.

"Praise be!" Melody found her voice. "The Lord has sent us a warrior!"

"He ain't done no such of a thing," Preacher told her, while cutting her bonds loose. "I just happened to be close by. Now get them others untied and let's get the hell gone from here 'fore more Injuns show up."

The second man put his mouth in motion and stuck his two pennies worth in. "We're all Christians, brother. And we don't hold with strong language in front of ladies."

Preacher spat on the ground. "That's your damn problem. I don't hold with fools comin' into the mountains and stirrin' up the Injuns. So I reckon that makes us even." Preacher cut the others loose.

He helped Melody to her feet and she swayed against him for a moment. She was all woman, that one. And when their eyes met, Preacher could see that she knew he was all man. A high flush came to her cheeks and her smile was tight and her eyes bright, like with a fever. They had a fever all right, but it wasn't brought on by sickness. Preacher released her hand

and she stepped away, each knowing what the other was thinking, and Jehovah didn't have a damn thing to do with it.

"You don't have to worry about the other savages," the man with one ear and bloody face said.

Preacher knew then he was dealing with a real pilgrim. In the mountains, a man *always* worries about Injuns.

Preacher grunted in reply.

"You see," one-ear said, pulling a fancy handkerchief out of a jacket pocket and pressing it to the side of his head. "The other savages fled in a different direction after the attack."

"They didn't flee nowheres," Preacher told him. "They own these mountains; they got no reason to be afraid. All they did was split up to divvy up the booty. But how do you know they didn't plan on meetin' up agin, right here?"

That shut one-ear right up.

"We must get Richard to a doctor," the haughty-acting fellow said.

Preacher laughed at him. "Shore. They's one about two hundred and fifty miles from here. Won't take us more'n a month to get there. What we'll do is get gone from here and then I'll take a look at your partner's head. Clean it out good. I'd pour whiskey on it but I ain't got none."

"You probably drank it all, lurching about in some drunken debauchery," the second female spoke up. She had her color up and was climbing up on her soapbox. "Cavorting about with a loose woman, more than likely a pure, simple, ignorant savage you took advantage of."

"Amen," the mouthy man said. "It's not only the savages to whom we must introduce God."

Preacher chuckled and shook his head. "For shore I drank the whiskey. As to the second part, no. Let's go. When we make camp I'll fix up a poultice for one-ear there. You ain't hurt bad, mister. But you're gonna be tiltin' your hat to the other side of your head for the rest of your life. Now, all of you, move, goddammit!"

2

They were in trouble and Preacher knew that for a hard fact. The Arapaho bucks back yonder had been wearing read streaks on their faces. To an Arapaho, the color red could mean three things: earth, man, or blood. In this case, Preacher pretty well knew it meant blood, and they weren't in the best of positions, either. They were caught with the Shoshoni just to the west of them, the Blackfoot to the north, the Crow to the east, and the Arapaho and the Cheyenne to the south and everywhere in the immediate surroundings.

All in all, it was not a good place to be. Preacher, traveling alone, never gave it much worrying time. He knew how to stay alive in hostile country. But with four pilgrims—that was quite another matter.

And two of them females, no less. That only added to the problem.

"Git up on them horses," Preacher told them.

"We don't have the proper saddles for the ladies," the mouthy man said. "And by the way, my name is Edmond. You know Melody and Richard. This is Penelope."

"Well, I am just thrilled beyond words. Now, get up on them damn horses!"

Nobody moved.

With a snort of disgust, Preacher climbed up the gently sloping bank, slid down the other side, and fetched his own animals, leading them around to the others. They still hadn't made a move toward the ponies.

He swung into the saddle and led an Indian pony over to the group. He looked at Melody. "Mount up, sister. I'll get you outta here. Move, woman!"

Melody didn't hesitate. She stepped up on a log, hiked up her skirts, and swung onto the horse's back. Preacher handed her the reins. "Let's go."

"What about us?" Penelope shrieked.

"Keep your voice down, woman!" Preacher said. "You'd but a hog-caller to shame. If you wanna come with us, put your butt on that pony's back and come on."

"Barbarous cretin!" Edmond said. "You'd leave us, wouldn't you?"

"You see my back, don't you?" Preacher called over his shoulder. "That tell you anything?"

"Are you really going to leave them?" Melody whispered.

"Naw," Preacher returned the whisper. "But they don't know that."

She grinned at him. Preacher winked at her.

"I'm a worker in the house of the Lord, sir," she reminded him.

"You're a woman first," he told her. "And a hell of a woman, at that."

She blushed and tried to adjust her bonnet, pushing some blonde hair back under the brim and almost fell off the pony.

"Hang on, sister," Preacher told her. "You're all lucky them Injuns took saddles from the dead pilgrims for their ponies. You'd be plumb uncomfortable if you was ridin' bareback."

"I can just imagine," Melody muttered.

"I bet you cain't, neither. Here come the others. I figured I'd get them movin'." He looked with approving eyes at the way the men sat their saddles. They could ride. Penelope, on the other hand, was bouncing up and down like a little boat on a great big lake in the middle of a storm. "Grab ahold of that saddle horn, sister," Preacher said. "And hang on. The damn thing ain't for tootin', you know."

She gave him a dark look and muttered something under her breath.

"Must you use profanity?" Edmond said.

"Will if I want to, and I want to, so hush up and stay in line. And don't get lost. Which way's what's left of the wagon train?"

"On the Oregon Trail," Richard said.

Preacher whoaed up and twisted in the saddle. "Somebody's been playin' games with you folks. The Oregon Trail is 'way, 'way south of here. People, you was *lost!*"

"As a goose," Melody said. "I knew that, but nobody would listen to me."

Richard and Edmond both looked embarrassed. Richard said, "I suspected our guide didn't know what he was doing. He drank a lot."

"I know lots of guides who drink a lot," Preacher said. "That ain't got nothin' to do with it. Where'd you folks outfit and jump off from?"

"Missouri," Melody told him. "Our guide told us we would bypass Fort Hall because he knew a better route."

"Damn fool," Preacher muttered. "All right. How far north is the train?"

"I would say about fifteen miles," Edmond said. "No more than that, I'm sure."

"Probably not that far," Preacher said. "Injuns wouldn't travel that distance in these mountains 'fore torturin' and rapin'. If that's what they had in mind."

"Perhaps you could take us on to Oregon?" Edmond suggested.

"I'll take you somewheres," Preacher said, and pointed his horse's nose north.

Night draped the mountains before they could reach the

site of the wagon train. Preacher killed a couple of rabbits with a sling and stopped before dark to build a small fire. While the meat was cooking, he said, "We'll eat, then move on a couple of miles and make camp for the night. It's gonna be cold, so you folks use your saddle blankets for warmth."

"But they *smell!*" Penelope complained.

"You will too 'fore you get where you're goin'," Preacher told her. "Like a bunch of polecats—but you'll be alive. So shut up."

Preacher let the others eat the rabbits while he chewed on jerky and ate a handful of some berries he'd picked. He was used to lean times. These pilgrims looked like they'd never missed a meal in their lives.

He carefully put out the fire and moved them north a couple of miles for a cold camp. Melody was the only one who didn't complain, even though she was just as uncomfortable as the others.

She'll do, Preacher thought. *She's tough.*

Their eyes met in the darkness through the dim light of the quarter moon. She blinked first, then laid her head on the saddle. Preacher grinned and rolled up in his blankets.

Across the small clearing, Edmond had watched the silent exchange through hot eyes, and bristled in anger.

They all saw the buzzards long before they reached the site of the ambush and massacre. Those carrion birds who had not yet feasted on dead flesh soared and circled and wheeled and waited their turn in the sky, while the others staggered around on the ground, too full and heavy to lift off.

"It ain't gonna be pretty," Preacher warned. "I've seen it before. When you puke, don't get none on me. Where are you folks from anyway?"

"Philadelphia," Richard said.

"Shoulda stayed there. This country's too crowded as it is. Can't ride for five days without seeing some damn body."

"It's called progress," Edmond said.

"It's a damn nuisance, is what it is," Preacher retorted.

"Must you swear constantly?" Melody asked.

"Yeah, I must. I'm gettin' in practice for our rendezvous down south. Although it don't look like I'm gonna make it."

"I've read about those affairs," Richard said. "Then you're a real mountain man."

"I am."

"What drove you to this horrible existence?" Edmond asked.

Preacher turned to look at the city man. *"Horrible?* What's so horrible about it? I'm as free as an eagle, wild as a grizzly, mean as a wolverine, tough as a cornered wolf, and quick as a puma. I can out drink, out cuss, out fight, out dance, out sing, ride farther and faster than any man, and tell more lies than any ten men. And I'm good-lookin', too."

Melody laughed at his words.

"You should be ashamed of yourself," Edmond admonished him.

"Why?" Preacher asked. "For bein' what the good Lord intended me to be? You are what you are, I am what I am. It's just as simple as that." He reined up and let the horses drink. "This here's what we call Shine Crick. I know what your guide was up too, now, but he was flat out wrong. He'd been listenin' to lies about a trail through the wilderness just to the west of us. There ain't no wagon trail through there. You'd have to go north over a hundred miles and then cut west. But even then, that would be a tough pull. Windin' way. Get caught there in the winter, and you'd die. You people were listenin' to a fool. What happened to him anyways?"

"When the savages attacked, he ran away," Melody said. "I watched him leave."

"You know his name?"

"Jack Harris," Edmond said. "I did not like him. He was a lot like you."

"Jack Harris ain't nothing like me," Preacher told him. "Jack's a back-shooter and a coward. Brags a lot about how brave he is, but when it comes down to the nut-cuttin', he ain't nowheres to be found."

"He claimed to be a mountain man," Melody said.

Preacher snorted. "He's a hanger-arounder, is what he is. He tell you about the time I whupped him down at Bent's Fort? No, he wouldn't mention that. I whupped him to a fare-thee-well, I did. He ain't liked me to this day."

"What was the fight about?" Richard asked. Although the man was in considerable pain, he'd come up in Preacher's eyes by not complaining about his missing ear and by pulling his weight.

"He insulted my mother. Now, you can insult me all day long—if you do it in a friendly manner—and I'll just insult you back. But leave my dear sainted mother out of it. Or get ready to get bloody."

The wind shifted and brought a horrible stench with it, wrinkling the noses of the missionaries.

"That's . . . the wagon train?" Melody asked, getting a little green around the mouth.

"Yep," Preacher said. "What's left of the bodies, that is. Buzzards'll try for the soft parts first. Belly and kidneys. It ain't a real pretty sight. I've seen yards and yard of guts all strung out like rope. Why, I recollect one time, I come up on this Pawnee village that'd been hit by a band of Injuns that didn't like 'em very much—nobody likes the Pawnee. And I seen . . ." Preacher went into great long gory detail until the sounds of retching stopped him. Penelope and Edmond were off their ponies, kneeling down in the trail.

"What's the matter with you two?" he asked, with a very definite twinkle in his eyes. "Something you ate don't agree with you, maybe?"

* * *

Richard and Melody dropped off their ponies and headed for the bushes when they approached the wagon train. It was evident that the Indians had spent several hours torturing some of the survivors, and many Indian tribes could be very inventive when it came to torture.

"Savages!" Edmond blurted. "They need the word of God even more than I thought."

"Is that right?" Preacher asked with an odd smile. "Savages, huh? 'Ppears to me I read where they was still cuttin' off folks' heads in France and drawin' and quarterin' folks over in England. Big public spectacle. Ain't them religious countries? Would you call that civilized?"

Melody and Richard returned from their hurried trip to the bushes, both of them pale. The stench from the bodies was horrible. Articles of clothing and broken pieces of furniture were scattered all over the area, along with what remained of tortured men and women and older kids.

"Where are the young children?" Penelope asked, her voice no more than a whisper and her face very pale under her bonnet. "There were a dozen or more boys and girls."

"Injuns took them to raise," Preacher said. "They do that sometimes. If the child behaves, they'll live. Some tribes won't harm a child at all. Others will kill them outright. Injuns are notional. Just like white folks, you might say."

"I don't know any white person who would harm a child!" Edmond said.

"Then you don't know many of your own kind," Preacher told him shortly. "You folks start gatherin' up clothing you think might fit you and what food and powder and shot that might be found. Get yourselves some warm clothing."

"Stealing from the dead!" Penelope said.

Preacher turned slowly and looked at her. "Lady, you are beginnin' to wear on me. Do you—any of you—know the trouble you're in? I don't think so. We're smack in the middle of hostile Injun country, and from the paint on them dead bucks, they're on the warpath. Somethin's stirred them up. And it's reasonable to think that they ain't the only tribe that's took up their war axes." Preacher knelt down and began drawing in the dirt. The others leaned over to watch him.

"Now pay attention," Preacher said. "We're here. Dry Crick is behind us here. The South Fork of the Shoshone is to our west. The Oregon Trail is 'way to hell down here. 'Way I see it is like this: we got hostiles on the warpath all around us. We'd be damn fools to try to make it south to the wagon trail." He looked at all of them for a moment, then sighed. "I reckon I'm stuck with you. I can't in no good conscience leave you. Hell, you'd all *die*. Don't none of you seem to know north from south or what's up or down."

"Now, see here!" Edmond protested.

"Shut your fly-trap," Preacher told him. "And don't argue with me. I been makin' it in these mountains for years. You're just a helpless baby in the wilderness. And folks, if you think *this* is wild, you ain't seen nothin' yet. We couldn't make it with wagons where I'm thinkin' of carryin' you, but on horseback . . ." He shrugged his shoulders. ". . . We got a chance. We're goin' into the Big Titties . . ."

"The *what?*" Penelope blurted, high color springing onto her cheeks.

"Mountain range that was named Les Grand Tetones by a French trapper 'cause they reminded him of big tits," Preacher said, ducking his head to hide his grin. The grin did not escape Melody. "It's wild, people. It's the most beautiful and wildest thing you'll ever see. And it's slow goin'. But it's the safest way. We might run into some Bannocks in yonder; but I get on well with the. Likewise the Nez Perce further on west and north. Good people. It's our only shot, folks, and we got to take it. Now look around for a bottle of whiskey."

"My word, man!" Edmond said. "Are you thinking of getting drunk at a time like this?"

Preacher gave him a look of disgust. "No, you ninny. Take

a look at your friend's head. Where his ear used to be. It's fillin' up with pus—infection, to you. I got to open it up, clean it out, and cauterize it with a hot blade. The whiskey's for him, to ease the pain. Even with that, y'all gonna have to hold him down. If we don't do that, he'll die. So shut your mouth and get to lookin'."

Preacher slowly circled the ambush site on foot and concluded that the Injuns who had done this had not been back. No need to, for at first glance there was precious little left to plunder. He began searching the rubble, grateful that the Injuns had not burned the wagons. They had raped and killed and tortured, run off the horses and mules. They'd eaten the oxen, then lay up in a stuffed stupor for a day or so. But this was a sight that Preacher had seen more than once since pilgrims began pushing west. He knew all the secret places where folks liked to stash valuables.

He found a cache of food in one wagon, including several pounds of coffee. Preacher immediately set about building a small smokeless fire out of dead wood and made a pot of coffee.

"Man, we have to bury the dead!" Edmond said.

"You bury 'em if you're in that big a hurry," Preacher told him. "There ain't enough left of most of 'em to bother with. You'd best worry about stayin' alive. The dead'll take care of themselves. I'm fixin' to have me some coffee."

Preacher drank the hot strong brew while the others rummaged around, picking up this and that, stepping gingerly around the torn and bloated bodies.

"You women find you some men's britches and get in 'em," Preacher called from the fire. "Be easier ridin' that way."

"I most certainly will not!" Penelope squalled in outrage at just the thought.

"Either you do it, or I'll snatch them petticoats offen you and dress you myself," Preacher warned her. "I ain't gonna put up with them dress tails gettin' snagged on bushes and such. My life and your lives are at stake here. Damn your modesty."

Preacher looked westward and shook his head. He'd been in the Tetons, but never with a bunch of persnickety pilgrims, and certainly with no females draggin' along.

"Disgraceful!" Penelope said, holding up a pair of men's britches and shaking them.

"Just get in them," Preacher said. "Be right interestin' to see what you ladies look like without all them underthings hidin' your natural charms."

"You are a vile, disgusting man," Edmond told him.

"Maybe," Preacher said, sipping another cup of coffee. "But I'm the only hope you got of stayin' alive. I'd bear that in mind was I you." He looked at Richard, standing with the bottle of whiskey Preacher had found. "Drink it down, missionary. Get stumblin' drunk." He took out his knife and laid it on the stones around the fire. "This ain't gonna be no fun for neither of us."

3

Preacher had to practically sit on the man to get him to take the first couple of slugs. After that, it got easier and Richard got sillier and looser than a goose. He passed out right in the middle of his story concerning the time he peeped in on his sister taking a bath. "Lord, what wonders I did behold that evening," said he, then fell backward, out cold.

Preacher grabbed his knife and went to work. He opened the wound, let it drain, cut away the infected skin, then applied a poultice he'd made. Long before Richard woke up, Preacher had cauterized the wound with the hot blade. Edmond got sick.

"It ain't as bad as it looked," Preacher said. "He's gonna have him a numb of an ear. Leastways his hat won't fall down that side. But he's gonna be hard to get along with for a couple of days. High as we are, wounds heal quick—air's so clean and pure. Won't be for long, the way folks keep showin' up out here," he added.

Preacher prowled around some and found more articles he could use, including some soap and some store-bought britches and shirts that looked like they might fit him. There was a nice lined Mackinaw coat that had only been burned a little bit, and he took that. Best looking coat he'd ever had. And bless Pat, he found him some brand new long handles in the bottom of a trunk. In the same trunk, he found him a fancy razor and new strop and a mug with soap. He was tempted to take some boots off the dead, but he knew he'd worn moccasins for so long his feet would not be comfortable in anything else.

He wandered off down to the crick.

"Glory be!" Melody said, upon sighting him an hour later. "You are a *fine* looking man!"

"Melody!" Penelope admonished her brazenness.

Preacher had shaved, leaving only a moustache. He had bathed from top to bottom—he hoped nobody downstream tried to drink out of that crick for a day or two—and had dressed in the new clothes. He really felt a little self-conscious. He took the whiskey bottle and dabbed some on his freshly shaved face.

"First time in ten years I been without a beard," Preacher said. "Feels funny." He looked at Richard. "He made a sound yet?"

"Moaned a couple of times," Edmond said. "I'm beginning to get concerned about him."

Preacher shook his head. "He's just passed out drunk, that's all. I been that way myself a time or two."

"I'm sure," Penelope said, giving him an acid look.

Preacher just grinned at her. Penelope needed a good man to roll around in the blankets with her for a night or two. He figured that might change her whole outlook.

Of course, he admitted, he could be wrong. It happened from time to time. He was wrong back in '26 or '27, he recollected.

Rather than break their backs burying the dead, they dragged the bodies to a shallow ravine and then caved earth in over them. Preacher, Edmond, Melody, and even Penelope pitched in to drag small logs and then spent the better part of an hour placing rocks over the mass gravesite. It wouldn't prevent digging and burrowing animals from getting to the bodies, but it was the best they could do under the circumstances.

Preacher stood holding a new hat he'd found to replace his old one and listened to Edmond deliver a long-winded eulogy. Five minutes passed. Ten. The sun beat down mercilessly. Fifteen minutes, and still Edmond droned on.

Preacher couldn't take it anymore. "Amen, brother!" he shouted and walked off.

They pulled out the next morning, heading into a wilderness that only a handful of white men—and no white woman—had ever seen. Richard was in some pain, but he never complained. The man might be a Bible-thumper, but he was steadily rising in Preacher's estimation.

The man asked sensible questions, trying to learn about the land and its people, and Preacher answered each question as best he could.

"Is this the Shoshone River we're crossing now?" he asked, as they forded the stream.

"Nope. It's a fork off of it, though. This branch splits off east of what some folks call Heart Mountain. Injuns call it Spirit Mountain. It's sacred to some of them. Bear in mind to keep out of Injun buryin' grounds. That'll bring bad medicine on you. We won't cross the Shoshone this day. Tomorrow, 'bout noon, if all goes well."

"What do you mean by bad medicine?" Melody asked. "You don't believe in Indian superstition, do you?"

"What's the difference in what Injuns believe and what you're tryin' to bring to them? Only difference is the Injuns don't have no book like the Bible. Their religious ways is passed down by mouth. And each tribe has their shamans; they're like you folks, sort of. They believe in the Great Spirit, and life after death. That Happy Hunting Grounds claptrap is white man's bullshi . . . dooky."

Even Edmond and Penelope had pulled closer and were

paying attention and not bitching about this, that, and everything else. For a change.

"Injuns is real good to their kids. Very kind to them. Once you get to know them, and they like you, they're good people. I've lived with them, I've fought them, and I've killed them. And likely I'll do all three things again. And don't you think that most Injun women is loose, 'cause they ain't. An Injun father is just like any father anywhere. You start messin' with his daughter, and he'll kill you.

"You take the Cheyenne tribe, for instance, Tough, mean fighters. Everybody's scared of the Cheyenne. But for all their fierceness, they hold women in high regard. A girl's comin' of age is a big deal in a lot of Injun tribes. And any number of tribes worship dogs and wolves. If one has to be killed for whatever reason, they'll apologize to it. And to a Cheyenne, a dog is damn near a god. They even have a warrior society called the Dog Soldiers."

"It sounds to me that you actually *like* the Indians," Edmond observed.

"Oh, I do. You can't blame them for fighting the whites. Hell, this is their land. It's been theirs for only God knows how long. Thousands of years, probably. If they'd let me, I'd never strike a hostile blow against any of them."

He thought about that for a moment. "Well, exceptin' maybe them goddamn Pawnees."

When they made camp that afternoon, Preacher figured they were within a half day's ride of the Shoshone. As soon as they crossed it, he'd cut south, down toward Togwotee Pass. He sure wasn't going to attempt to take them across the Snake and over the middle part of the Tetons. At least he hoped he wouldn't have to.

While they had been resting back at the ambush site, two horses had wandered back into camp, anxious for human closeness. Preacher had rigged up frames and they were used for pack horses. He'd found enough canvas that hadn't been burned to use as shelters for the pilgrims. While it wasn't any fancy Eastern hotel, it did offer a small creature comfort.

"It's a great, vast, lonesome place, isn't it?" Melody asked, sitting close to the fire as the sun sank past the towering mountains.

"It's big, all right," Preacher told her. "But lonesome? Well, I never dwelled on that too much, though some folks do call it the High Lonesome. I've knowed men who've gone crazy out here, sure enough. And a lot more men who gave up and headed back to towns and people and such. Takes a special breed to make it out here. I knowed one old boy who lost his horse and was afoot during the winter. He fought him a puma to the death. We found 'em both come the spring. Both of them froze stiff to a tree. He had his hand on that big cat's head, like he was sayin' 'It's all right. No hard feelin's. We both was just doin' what come natural.'"

"Did you bury him."

"Not right then. Ground was too hard. We come back about a month later and put them both together in a cave and sealed it shut."

"That was a nice gesture," Penelope said.

Preacher looked at her. "I reckon. Howsomever, we didn't have much choice in the matter. They was both still froze together. It've took an axe to get them apart."

By noon of the next day, Preacher knew they were being followed. Problem was, he didn't think they were Injuns. If they were renegade white men, they could turn out to be worse than Injuns. The mountains weren't exactly overflowing with renegade white men, but there were enough of them to cause trouble every now and then. They'd knock trappers in the head, or even shoot them for their pelts or for food or their boots or coats, for that matter. And, he thought, trying

to cheer himself up, it could be a party of government survey-
ors or explorers.

But he couldn't quite make himself believe that.

He figured they were renegades after the women. Two
beautiful white women could make even a good man go bad.
Especially men who hadn't even seen an *ugly* white woman
in years.

When he called a break and the women stepped behind
some bushes to do their business, Preacher got Richard and
Edmond close.

"We're bein' followed," he told them. "I don't think it's
Injuns, and it ain't the Army—I'm sure of that. They'd have
seen 'way back that we're not a hostile party and they'd have
closed with us. Any good scout would have seen the sign that
women leave and they'd be mighty curious. I think we got us
some renegades on our trail and I think they're after the
women. So keep your powder dry and be ready to fight and
fight quick. 'Cause when they come, they'll do it one of two
ways, they'll either come real sudden like, or they'll hail the
camp and get in amongst us. That's what we don't want. We
can't let 'em get in amongst us. I know you two think of yourselves as highly principled men, but you just remember this:
there ain't no law out here except the gun, the knife, and the
war axe. And if they're renegades, missionaries or not, they'll
kill you both and do it without blinkin' an eye. You got the
women to think about. They got to come first."

"Neither one of us has ever used violence against another
human being," Edmond pointed out.

"Well, you're about to do so," Preacher said, "unless you
want to die. Make up your minds. I don't think we got a lot of
time to ponder it."

"We should warn the women," Richard said. "I feel they
have a right to know about this."

"It's only a suspicion," Edmond said. "Why alarm them
unduly?"

Preacher walked away, leaving the two men arguing. When Melody and Penelope stepped out of the bushes, he walked up to them. "You ladies stay put with the men. Rest awhile. No fires. You understand me?" They nodded. "Good. I'll be back in an hour or so."

He took his Hawken and set out at a ground-covering lope. Preacher could run all day, and had done so several times during his time in the mountains. He'd had more than one horse shot out from under him, by both white men and Injuns, by bullet and arrow, and been forced to run for his life.

He ran for a couple of miles, then scrambled up on a ledge. He squatted down, studying their back trail. Far below and behind them, he could pick out tiny doll-figures moving toward them on horseback. He counted eight riders, and they were not Indians. They had only two pack horses, so they were not trappers. They were not dressed in uniform, so they were not military. That left government explorers or renegades. Preacher had him a strong suspicion they were the latter.

"Damn!" he said. As if he didn't have enough problems without this being added. If that was Bum Kelley's bunch, they were in real serious trouble.

Bum had come out back around '28 or '29 and immediately started making trouble wherever he happened to be. He always had anywhere from ten to fourteen thieves and killers and toughs hanging around him, and the gang ranged from the Utah Territory up into the British-held lands. There wasn't nothing Bum and his bunch wouldn't do, and precious little they hadn't done—and all of it bad.

He wished he had him a spyglass, but then figured as long as he was wishing he might as well wish for a detachment of soldier boys and about half a dozen of his good friends, like Thumbs Carroll, Nighthawk, Tenneysee, and some others. They'd probably all be 'way south of his position, though.

"Might as well wish for the moon," Preacher muttered, and

then picked up his rifle. He paused as four more riders caught his eye, one of them leading a pack horse.

"That's about right," he muttered. "Twelve bad ones and me with a one-eared gospel shouter, a smart-aleck missionary, and two faithful female followers. Lord have mercy on a poor mountain boy."

He picked up his Hawken and loped back to where he had left them. "Mount up," he told them, bending over to catch his breath. "We got big troubles about five miles behind us."

"You ran five miles?" Penelope asked.

"I've run all day, lady, and half into the night 'fore. I'll tell you about it sometime. But not now. Let's go!"

Preacher pushed the group. He knew where he wanted to go. It wasn't no more than a day's ride, and he set a hard pace. They had crossed the Shoshone and now, instead of cutting south as he had planned, Preacher rode straight west, toward a place he'd once wintered. He figured the hidden cave was still there. He had no idea what it would take to make it disappear. Other than God.

He rode into a tiny creek and told the others, "Stay right behind me. Don't get out of this crick. It won't fool them for long, but it will slow them up tryin' to figure out where we left it." He chuckled. "And that, boys and girls, is something that's gonna take them a-while to do."

They rode for several miles, always staying in the creek, until coming to a sandy, rocky flat. "We'll leave it here," Preacher told them, as he swung down from the saddle. "Stand down for a couple of minutes and rest; let the horses blow. I got to do something."

He had saved his old buckskins and now he cut them up to make socks for the horses' hooves.

"Why are you doing that?" Richard asked.

"So's the steel hooves won't scar the rocks and leave a trail," Preacher told him. "Get that old ragged blanket off my pack horse and do the same with it. Quickly, people. Every minute counts."

When the hooves were covered, Preacher led the group to the timber and told them not to move from that spot. Then he led the horses over, one at a time and had each one mount up.

"Stay with me," he told them. "Don't snag a thread on a branch. If you do, holler and stop and pick it off. They'll find this trail, eventually, but let's don't make it any easier for them."

Preacher led them deep into virgin forests, forging his own trail, the needles and leaves making only faint whispering sounds under the hooves. He pointed to a tree, which had strange markings some twenty feet off the ground. "Grizzly. And a big one. He'll stand twelve feet high and weigh damn near half a ton. If a grizzly gets after you, climb a tree. They're so big and heavy they don't climb. Usually," he added with a smile.

Edmond looked up at the scratchings and shook his head, wondering what it would be like to come face to face with a beast that large.

It was a trail-weary and saddle-sore bunch that finally slipped out of the saddle just at dusk. Preacher had set a grueling pace. And he didn't make matters any better when he said, "Cold camp. No fires. Roll up in your blankets now and stay there. Cool clear night like this, the odor of food cookin' or coffee boilin' would travel five miles. This spruce and pine's got an odor to it, too."

"Not even a little fire?" Penelope asked.

"No. See to your horses, rub them down good, and picket them careful on graze."

"Tyrant!" she muttered.

Preacher slept well but cautiously that night, as he usually did in the mountains. He did not awaken at natural sounds. The sounds of a hunting owl seizing a mouse or rat or rabbit would not pull him awake. The lonesome call of a coyote or the talking of wolves would not alarm him. A breaking twig would pull him instantly alert, for deer or elk or most forest creatures would not step on a branch unless they were frightened and running. Man steps on twigs and branches.

The rain woke him several hours before dawn would touch the high country.

He quietly climbed out of his blankets and rolled them in his ground sheet. The others slept on, unaware of anything that was happening around them; they would have to learn the woods, or they'd die.

With it raining, he would chance a small fire for coffee, built under an overhang to break up the smoke. He checked the snares he'd set out the evening before and found two fat rabbits. He skinned them out and carefully scraped the meat from the skin and rolled them up from habit. They made good glove linings. He had the meat cooking before the others began stirring.

Melody was the first up. She completed her morning toilet and joined Preacher by the small fire, both of them waiting for the coffee to boil and the meat to sear.

"We're in trouble, aren't we?" she asked.

"It ain't the best situation I ever been in," he acknowledged. "But it ain't the worst, neither. I get to my secret hidey-hole— and it is a hole—we can all get some rest and figure out our next move. It'll take Bum and them others some time to find us there. They might never," Preacher told her, knowing it to be a lie.

He poured them coffee, both of them cupping their fingers around the tin, warming their extremities, for the morning was cold this high up. The others slept on.

Preacher met her blues across the fire. "Edmond's sweet on you."

"I know. But I don't share his feelings. At all. He's not a bad person, really, Preacher. He's just far out of his element. And he's scared. Like all the rest of us. Except you."

"I'd be scared in a big city like Phillydelphia. Too damn many people for my tastes." He shook his head. His hair was long, hanging well past his ears, for he hadn't cropped it all winter. It helped to keep his head and face warm during the brutal mountain winters. "You don't act like no gospel-shouter I ever seen, Melody. Richard and Edmond, yeah, and Penelope, too. But not you. How'd you get tied up in an outfit like this one?"

"Through a society I belong to. We all thought it would be a grand adventure and we could help bring the Lord to the savages. I'm afraid we didn't think it out very thoroughly."

"You sure didn't. No place for a woman out here. Not yet. Someday, yeah. Someday this country will be ruined with people." The last was spoken with some bitterness.

Melody smiled at him across the flames. "It has to be, Preacher. The nation is growing. People want to build new lives, to explore, to expand. Do you know about the steam locomotives?"

"The what?"

"Locomotives that run by steam. It's true. We've had them for almost six years now. Soon the railroads will be running everywhere."

"Not out here!"

"Oh, yes, Preacher. Even out here. A true visionary by the name of Doctor Hartwell Carver is proposing a transcontinental route."

"A trans-what?"

"Coast to coast railroad tracks. You wait and see. It will happen."

"Stars and garters! I never heard of such a thing. Why, I had a man tell me that no more'n five or six years ago, they wasn't but a hundred miles of track in the whole United States."

"That's true. But I assure you, there are many, many more miles of track than that now."

Preacher shook his head. "Makes a poor man like me feel plumb ignorant."

She smiled. "No, Preacher. Never ignorant. You've just

been isolated, that's all. When was the last time you read a newspaper?"

"I . . . don't remember. I can read," he quickly added. "I went to the fifth grade. But it's been so many years since I read a word I'd have trouble, I 'magine."

"I understand that there is talk already of an expedition to chart a route from St. Louis to San Francisco, although I'm sure it will be several years before that happens. Can you just imagine that? A railroad from St. Louis westward all the way across the nation? It's mind-boggling. Preacher, the government will be looking for men like you to lead those scouting parties. Men like you who know the wilderness that so many of us have only read about. Ignorant, Preacher? No, you're far from being that. You've been to California?"

"Oh, yeah. I seen the blue waters a couple of times. I been to California and Oregon. Hard, mean trip from here. A railroad? That's *impossible!* You can't build no damn railroad through these mountains." He again shook his head. "That's a pipedream, Melody. It ain't possible. You can't hardly get a wagon through. You can't even do that in most spots."

"But you are going to take us to Oregon, aren't you, Preacher?"

"I shore ain't gonna leave you out here alone," he hedged the question slightly.

She smiled and kissed him right on the mouth. Startled Preacher so bad he spilled the hot coffee right on his crotch and he jumped up, hollering and bellering and slapping at himself. The others thought they were under attack and went into a panic. Penelope got all tangled up in her blankets, shrieking like a banshee, and Richard jumped out of his blanket, the back flap to his underwear hanging down. Edmond flew out of his blankets and ran slap into a tree, knocking himself goofy—which wasn't that long a trip.

Melody and Preacher hung on to each other, laughing so hard they had tears in their eyes.

4

"Lost their tracks," the renegade reported back to Bum. "He took 'em into that crick yonder. I don't know whether he went up or down. Down, if he was smart."

"Preacher is anything but smart," Bum replied, knowing he was telling a lie. Preacher was as wily a mountain man as ever tracked a deer, and as dangerous as any puma. He remembered that time down on the Poison Spider Crick when an ol' boy name of Jason Dunbar got to needlin' Preacher about his name. Preacher took all he could stomach and told him to lay off or stand up and get ready to duke it out. Dunbar was a good foot taller than Preacher and out-weighed him by a hundred pounds. But when Preacher got through with Dunbar and finally let him fall, Jason Dunbar didn't have no front teeth left him a-tall, couldn't straighten up for a week, and only had half of his left ear. Preacher had bit off the top half. Preacher had put a thrashing on Jason that was talked about for years afterward.

Bum shook his head. "No, Luke, I done told you a tale. Preacher's smart, he's mean, he's tough, and he's quick. And when we catch him—and we will catch up to him and them folks—he won't go down easy. We'll lose some people. Bridger and Broken Hand Fitzpatrick and Carson and Beckwourth all speak highly of the man. Them boys don't give praise lightly. Bear that in mind."

"Two women out there," another thug said, pulling at himself. "White women. Been a long time since I had me a taste of white women."

"Hell, Slug," another man said. "I ain't even seen a white woman in more'un two year."

"Jack Harris was leadin' them pilgrims straight to us," Bum mused aloud. "How the hell was I supposed to know a bunch of Arapaho was waitin' in ambush?" He cussed and kicked at a rotten branch and it flew into a hundred pieces. "Damn the luck, anyways."

"And where the hell did Jack get off to?" another questioned.

"Runnin' for his life, probably," Bum said. "He's probably settled down and huntin' our trail now. He'll be along. Come on, let's fan out and try to pick up Preacher's trail."

"South?" one of his gang questioned, looking down the little creek.

Bum shook his head. "No. By now, Preacher knows we're trackin' him. He ain't gonna do this the easy way. George, you take a few boys and head south aways just to make sure. Beckman, you take the west side of the crick, Moses, you take the east side. You both work north. Rest of us will wait here so's not to crap up any sign. Take off. Adam, you build us a fire and we'll boil some coffee." He bit off a chew from a twist and looked up the crick. "White women," he muttered. "And them men with 'em is totin' gold, too. I got a good feelin' about this. A real good feelin'."

Several miles from his destination, Preacher halted the short column and once more sacked the horses' hooves. He then led the group up a gently sloping hill to a jumble of rocks on a ledge. A towering mountain loomed high above them, snow-capped all year round.

"It gets right close in here, folks," Preacher told them. "So mind your feet and knees."

He led them into a narrow twisting passageway that was just wide enough for them to pass with not three inches to spare on either side. There was just enough light filtering in from the crack high above them to illuminate their way.

"Eerie," Melody muttered.

With the sacking still on their horses' hooves, the party made very little noise as they moved along. The narrow fissure suddenly opened up into a high, huge, cathedral-like cavern with a bubbling stream running right through it. About a hundred feet long and several times that in width, the other end opened up into a beautiful little valley, about twenty-five or thirty acres of lush grass and a winding little creek.

"I don't think anybody else knows about this place," Preacher said. "Them drawin's on the walls was done hundreds of years ago, I reckon. Lord knows, I ain't never seen no beasties that look like some of them animals yonder. If you was to talk to an Injun about this place, he'd tell you it was the People Who Came Before who done this. Sounds reasonable to me."

"Is the way we came in the only way in?" Richard asked.

"Nope. They's another way. See that waterfall over 'crost the valley? They's another cave under that, leads into a blow-down on the other side."

"A what?" Edmond asked.

"Long time ago, years, must have been a terrible storm struck here. Tore up several hundred acres. Huge trees tore up by the roots and tossed every whichaway. Piled on top of one another and flang willy-nilly about. The cave comes out direct into all that mess. Them chasin' us might look a little ways into that blow-down; but they ain't gonna give it no good looksee. Too wild a place. Now in here where we is, the smoke filters up through them cracks in the ceilin' and disappears somewheres else. I built me a roarin', smokin' fire in here one winter's morning and spent the rest of the day outside. I never seen no smoke nor smelled none. We're as safe as I can make us. Now what I want you folks to do is this: strip the horses and put them out to pasture. I'm gonna take my bow, go out into that blow-down, and kill us a deer or two so's we'll have some meat to go along with the beans and bread that you ladies is gonna make from the flour we salvaged back at the ambush site. They's fish in that stream in the valley that's mighty good eatin'. I'm gonna be gone the rest of the day and maybe the night. Don't worry. I'll be back if a rattler don't bite me, a bear don't tree me, a puma don't jump on me and claw me to death, and Injun don't kill me, or I don't die from phewmona after gettin' soakin' wet duckin' under that waterfall yonder."

"I hate to be macabre," Edmond said.

"Whatever that means," Preacher said.

"But, what happens if you *don't* return?"

"You sit tight until your supplies is just about gone. By that time, if you don't eat all the damn day long, Bum and his boys will have given up and gone. Then you head west. That's the direction the sun sets. If you come to a great big body of water, that's the Pacific Ocean. You'll either be in California or Oregon country."

"You don't have to be insulting," Penelope said.

Preacher stared at her for a moment, then shook his head. He was muttering as he got his bow and quiver of arrows and left the cave and headed out into the meadow, walking toward the waterfall.

Melody stood in the mouth of the cave and watched him until he ducked behind the cascading water and was gone from sight. Penelope was lying down, exhausted from the travels, and Edmond was seeing to the horses.

"He's quite a man, Melody," Richard said softly. "But not the man for you."

She turned slowly and faced him. "Whatever in the world do you mean, Richard?"

"It's easy to see that you're quite smitten with him, Melody. We've all commented on it. But I urge you to think about what you're doing and to try and curb your emotions. The man is a wanderer, a will of the wisp. He'll only break your heart."

"It's purely platonic, Richard," she lied. "Nothing more. I enjoy his company, that's all. He's a fascinating man who has packed ten average lifetimes into one."

"Melody, I don't want to appear ungrateful for all he's done for us. He saved our lives and continues to do so hourly. But the man is only a cut above a savage. I doubt he's had a fork in his hand in ten years. He eats with his fingers. The two of you come from different worlds."

She smiled and patted his arm. "You worry needlessly, Richard. Come, let me change the dressing on your ear. In years to come, no matter where we might be, we'll look back on this episode and enjoy a good laugh."

Preacher got his first deer within moments of entering the blow-down. He quickly but carefully skinned and butchered it, leaving the waste parts for critters of the forest to eat. There would be no trace of the animal come the morning. He put the eatable parts in the hide and using a length of rope he'd brought, he hung the meat high from a limb to protect it. It took him an hour to find, stalk, and bring down the second deer. He heard a rustling in the dense brush and knew that wolves had caught the blood scent and were closing. Three big gray wolves, a male and two females. Preacher tossed them liver, intestines, and other scrap parts, shouldered his load and headed back toward the valley. Lots of folks feared wolves, but most of that fear was groundless. Preacher had never known of a healthy, full-grown wolf ever, unprovoked, attacking a human being. But a starving or hurt wolf was quite another matter. And when any animal is eating a kill or hiding the carcass for a later snack, you best leave that animal alone. And they also get might protective when it comes to their young.

He left the wolves snarling in mock anger and tearing at the meat parts. "Enjoy, brothers," he said.

Preacher rather like wolves. He'd had several as companions from time to time. They had not been pets, for a wolf cannot be domesticated like a dog. And if you're going to be around them, you got to know their ways. They don't conform to human ways; a man's got to conform to *their* ways. Once that's settled, a man can be fairly comfortable around wolves. You just can't never let them get the upper hand. For once they do, it takes a fight for dominance to regain it. And you ain't likely to come out in too good a shape fightin' no two-hundred-pound buffalo wolf.

Preacher figured he was packing close to a hundred and fifty pounds of raw meat, for the deer had both been sleek and fat. It had been an early spring, with lots to eat. But he'd carried more than that for longer periods of time.

He was back in the cave by nightfall and had some steaks sizzling moments later. "We'll smoke and jerk the rest of it," he told them. "Tomorrow, I'll pick some berries and we'll make pemmican."

"What in the world is that?" Richard asked.

"After the meat's dried, that's what we call jerky, I'll pound it into a powder and mix it with pulped and whole berries and the fat I saved from the venison after I cook it down. You mix all that up and it keeps for a longtime. I got some over there in my parfleche. Try some. It's good."

"What is a parfleche?" Melody asked.

"Rawhide case yonder. Hand it here." Preacher stuffed

some pemmican into his mouth and smiled. "I ain't kiddin' y'all. It's really good."

He passed the parfleche around and the others reluctantly tried some of the concoction. They all smiled as they chewed. "It really is good!" Edmond said.

"Y'all gonna bring Jesus to the savages," Preacher said, "I reckon now is a good time to start your learnin'. You got to know something about these folks."

"We were to be instructed in Oregon," Richard said.

"Wagh!" Preacher said in disgust. "Them's coast Injuns. Klamath and Tillamook and Chinook and Spokan and Pomo and Chumash and the like. Hell, they all 'bout either civilized or whupped down by now. I'm talkin' *Injuns,* folks. Scalp-hunters and warriors and the finest horsemen on the face of the earth. Comanche, Pawnee, Ute, Shoshoni, Apache, Blackfoot, Arapaho, Crow, Kiowa, Flathead, Assiniboin, Dakota—that's Sioux to you—and Nez Perce. They's more, but them's the important ones you'll be seein', I 'magine. Most of the ones I just named is hunters and warriors. Only ones I know of that'll grow anything to eat to amount to anything is your Hidatsa, Navajo, Pima, Pueblo, and Papago. Most of them is down in the Southwest. Except for the Hidatsa, and what's left of them is scattered along the northern borders. Mandan and Pawnee will raise a few crops, mostly corn, beans, squash and pumpkin. They trade a lot with other tribes. You watch a Pawnee when you're tradin'. They're slick. Blackfoot, Crow and Comanche won't eat fish. It's taboo to them. Your desert tribes roast snake and insects.

"Richard, you asked me couple of days back about how Injuns cook and what they eat. You'd be surprised. I've lived with Injuns that could whup up a buffalo stew that'd leave you smackin' your lips for days. Injuns ain't like white folks in that they don't waste nothin'. And I mean nothin'. They break the bones and boil the marrow or just suck it out. They clean and scrape out the guts and make sausage cases out of 'em, stuffin' 'em with seasoned meat. They're good with nature's own wild things. They season with sage and wild onions and milkweed buds and rose hips. They peel the prickly pear cactus and add that to stews and soups. It was Injuns that taught me to peel fresh sweet thistle stalks and eat it. Tastes kinda like nuts.

"Injuns ain't got pots like we use, so when they make a stew, they use the linin' from a buffalo stomach. You get you four poles, secure the ends of the linin', dump in some meat and stuff like prairie turnips and wild peas. To make the water boil, the women drop in hot rocks. The pouch will last three/four days until it gets soggy, then you eat the linin'. They don't waste nothin'.

"Injuns use ever' part of the animal they can. The thick pelt from a buffalo's neck can be made into a shield. Animals killed in winter has a special use cause the hair is long and thick. They use 'em for blankets and robes. Rawhide is made into strings and ropes. Buffalo hair is woven into ropes. Buffalo horns is used for everything from spoons to gourds. Injuns used to make knifes out of buffalo bones. Injuns use buffalo hides to make their tipis. And a tipi is not only a home, it's a sacred place to the Injun. The floor means the earth that they live on. The walls, which is peaked, is the sky. They round 'cause that is the sacred life circle, which ain't got no beginnin' or no end. Get it? A circle. And Injuns will always burn something that smells good in their tipis. Sage or sweet grass. It's an altar to them. That's where they pray to *their* gods."

An inference that none of the missionaries missed.

Preacher took one of the deer steaks out of the pan and fell to eating. With his knife and fingers. Around a mouthful of meat, Preacher said, "The tipi belongs to the Injun women of the plains, and don't ever let nobody tell you no different. The women make 'em, they put 'em up, they take 'em down, they haul 'em around. A man lives there only if the woman wants him to. She can chuck his possessions outside and the marriage is over. And he damn well better scat."

"How many hides does it take to make a tipi?" Melody asked.

"Anywhere from seven to thirty. Depends on the size of the lodge. It's a social thing for the women. Kind of like a barn raisin' to you folks. Say a Cheyenne needs a new lodge, the word goes out and the women gather, among them, one woman who is the official lodge-maker. After the woman who's needin' a new lodge feeds them all good, they start sewin' the skins together, usually startin' early in the mornin'. They they'll eat again, and it's back to sewin' and gossipin' and gigglin' and singin' and carryin' on. Takes a day and a new lodge is up."

"Then they have order in their societies?" Edmond asked.

"In a way. The Plains Injuns don't much cotton to someone tellin' 'em what to do." Preacher stuffed the last of his meat into his mouth, chewed for a moment, swallowed, then belched loudly. "You got to belch after a meal. Means the grub was good. If you don't belch, your host might be offended 'cause he'll think you didn't like his woman's cookin'. Always belch after a meal with the Injuns. 'Least the ones I been around.

"Injuns is pretty much free to come and go as they please in the tribe. Contrary to what you probably been taught, the Plains Injuns ain't got no elected nor passed-down leadership. Even a chief ain't got the power to punish nobody. To get to be a chief means that the rest of the tribe respects that man's wisdom, his courage, or even how well he can talk. Every male is a member of the council, and every man has the right to state his opinions. And they all do. It can go on for days!

"I reckon tradition might be the glue that keeps tribes together. I don't know what else could do it. All the tribes is different, but yet they're strangely alike in a lot of ways. When the white man finally gets up a head of steam and starts comin' thisaway, and they will, they's gonna be a lot of blood spilt. On both sides. At first it's gonna be mostly white people who die. But that won't last long. From what I've been able to pick up durin' the past few years, east of the Big Muddy is fairly overflowin' with people. They got to come west. The Injuns ain't gonna adopt the white ways, and the whites ain't gonna adopt the Injun ways. So what we're gonna have—to my way of thinkin'—is a great big bloody mess that's gonna go on for years."

"Then the savages have to be convinced that they cannot stand in the way of progress," Edmond said. "That's where people like us can help."

Preacher looked at him in the dancing light of the fire. He smiled rather sadly. "White man's way is the only way, huh?" He shook his head and poured a cup of coffee. "We shore take a lot upon ourselves, don't we?"

"Civilization and progress must continue if we, as a nation, are to survive," Richard said. "That's the way it's always been, and must continue to be."

"Says who?" Preacher challenged.

"This discussion is silly," Edmond said. "You obviously are not prepared to meet the challenge of a changing world. You miss the point of it all."

"Oh, I get the point," the mountain man said. "And lots of other folks will, too. The point of an arrow."

5

Preacher spent the next morning backtracking the way they entered the cave, carefully erasing all signs of anyone ever having come that way. He spent a couple of hours inspecting the sides of the narrow passageway, picking off hair the horses left as they rubbed the sides here and there. When he was satisfied he could do no more to insure their safety, Preacher rejoined the group in the cave.

"Any sign of them?" Edmond inquired, lifting his eyes from the bible he'd been reading.

"No. But they'll be along. White women's too grand a prize for them to give up on. And they probably figure you're carryin' gold."

"That's ridiculous!" Richard said.

"Really? Them money belts y'all totin' don't fit too well. They pooch out from time to time."

Richard and Edmond automatically put hands to their bellies.

"Yep," Preacher said, pouring coffee. "Gold and women. Many a man has died for that combination. How much you boys carryin?'"

"That is none of your affair," Edmond bluntly stated.

"You're right," Preacher replied easily. "It ain't. But if I'm to put my life on the line for you folks, I figure I at least ought to know what I'm dyin' for."

"This money," Richard said, patting his belly, "must get to our new mission in Oregon. It isn't ours. This is money raised by our organization back East. Contributors' money. This is money that will be used to further God's work.

"You ain't got no poor folks back in Philadelphia could use a helpin' hand? Must be quite a prosperous place," Preacher said sarcastically. "Rich folks aboundin' ever'where. I shore wouldn't fit in."

Richard sighed heavily and Melody laughed at the expression on her friend's face.

"And didn't nobody ever tell y'all that it ain't fittin' for un-married young men and women to go traispin' off unchaperoned? What does you girls' mommas and daddies think about this trip?"

"We left with their blessings," Penelope said. "They know that we are both very trustworthy and level-headed women." She looked at Melody. "One of us is, anyway."

Melody reached over and patted the young woman on the leg. "Don't worry, dear. I'll look after you. I did promise your mother."

Bum Kelley and his boys patiently searched and, as Preacher had predicted, found the trail after Preacher had left the rocks of the creek.

"He's headin' into the wilderness," Beckman said, just a touch of awe in his voice. "You know that country, Bum?"

Bum shook his head. "Can't say as I do. I've skirted it a time or two taking the south route. But that damn Preacher seems to know every rock between the borders and between the Big Muddy and the ocean. And he turned north, right into the Tetons. Damn his eyes."

The outlaws stood on the fringe of the mountain range and gazed at the towering peaks that stood silently before them.

"How old a man is this feller, anyways?" a man called Keyes asked.

"Thirty-five or so, I reckon. He came out here, so the stories go, back when he was about twelve or thirteen years old, and he ain't never stopped explorin'. So he's got twenty or so years of experience behind his belt. And he's as tricky as they come."

"He know you, Bum?" Bobby asked.

"He knows me. And he don't like me."

"Hey!" Slug shouted. "Here comes Jack Harris. I knowed he'd catch up with us."

Jack swung down from the saddle wearily. His clothing was in rags and he looked gaunt. "Put some grub on, boys," Jack said. "I ain't et in days."

A fire was hurriedly built and a thick deer steak jammed on a pointed stick. A blackened coffee pot filled with creek water was soon boiling and the coffee dumped in.

Jack was so worn out he could hardly keep his eyes open. A cup of thick strong coffee perked him up enough to talk, while the cooking steak caused drool to appear on the man's lips.

"What happened back yonder at the wagon train, Jack?" Bum asked.

"Them Injuns came out of nowhere, I tell you. I didn't have a clue they was there. I jumped off the flat and hit the timber at the first yell 'cause I could see we didn't have a chance. The outriders went down first. I don't know what happened after that. I was too busy floggin' my good horse gettin' away from there. I waited two days, I think it was, and went back lookin' for food. But I couldn't find nothin' 'ceptin' some bloody bandages and shod tracks headin' west. You boys' and somebody else's. I just started followin' along."

"Preacher," Bum said. "I recognized that big gray of his through my spy glass. He's got them gospel shouters and the women with him. He knows we're on his trail and he's wary."

Jack was instantly alert. *"Preacher!* What the hell's he

doin' up here? He's supposed to be down on the Popo Agie at the rendezvous."

"Well, he ain't. And he's tooken them folks into the wilderness." He pointed. "Yonder."

"In *there?*" Jack said with horror in his voice. "Northwest to the talkin' smoke?"

"I don't think so. I think he's got him a hidey hole in the lonesome yonder and he's all tucked away, thinkin' he's safe."

"He's pretty damn safe in there, Bum. I don't know that country. Hell, don't *nobody* really know that country. Well, a few does. And Preacher's one of them."

Bum looked hard at the man. "You want to give up?"

Jack jerked the half-raw steak from the stick and went to gnawing. He finally shook his head and wiped the grease from his mouth with the back of his hand. "No. Them two men was carryin' heavy with gold." He belched and farted and tore off another hunk of bloody meat. "And them women, boys, I swear I ain't never seen nothin' so fine in all my days."

"How fine?" a thug named Leo asked, leaning closer to Jack, his thick lips slick with spittle.

"Fine enough to fight a grizzly for."

"Bet they smell good, too," Bull said. "I just cain't hardly wait!"

The ladies had gone down to the waterfall to bathe and wash clothes, using soap they had salvaged from the ruins of the wagon train. Preacher sat on the outside of the cave exit, overlooking the valley. He had carefully cleaned his weapons and placed them at the ready. He knew it was only a matter of time before they would be found. No one is good enough to obliterate all signs of their passing, not if there is a good tracker behind them. And while Bum's people were no-goods, they had survived in the mountains for years, so that made them professional in anybody's book.

Preacher doubted that Bum's boys would have the patience

to explore the blow-down, so the rear entrance was reasonably secure. But one or two of them would be brave enough or curious enough to follow the twisting passageway once it was located—and it would be located, he felt sure of that. So let them come on. They would die in that twisting maze and the silent rock walls would be their coffins.

Preacher had spent that morning rigging dead-falls and other traps in the darkness of the twisting entranceway. He had warned the others not to enter there. To make his point, he had showed them on of his traps, and how lethal it was.

"Hideous," Edmond had said.

"Awful," Penelope whispered.

"Such a terrible thing to do to a person," Richard said.

"I just hope it works," Melody said.

It'll work, Preacher thought, as he honed his already sharp knife to a razor's edge. The first one to hit the traps will make the others awful cautious. But they'll press on. The second trap will stop them cold; maybe for a day. *By that time, we'll be far away and pushing hard.*

"You didn't just stop here for safety's sake, did you, Preacher?" Richard asked, breaking into the mountain man's thoughts.

"What else you think I had on my mind?" Preacher looked at him.

"You knew we needed several days of rest," the missionary said, and pegged it right. "My wound needed to heal and we all needed to lay about and eat and regain strength. But you, alone, would have been a hundred miles away by now. You're risking your life for people you hardly know. You're a very brave and complex man, Mister . . . what *is* your Christian name?"

"Preacher'll do. Yeah, they's some truth in me wantin' to get you folks rested some. When we leave here, we're gonna be pushin' hard, with not much time to rest. They's a small fort down near Massacre Rocks on the Snake. Fort Hall, I believe it's called. Few soldier boys down yonder. But it's gonna be hell gettin' there. If I can get y'all to the fort, that'll put you back on the Oregon Trail and it bein' springtime and all, chances are good a wagon train is there or one will be along shortly."

"And you'll leave us there?" Edmond asked.

"Why should I stay any longer?"

"Melody, if I may speak frankly," Edmond said.

"Fine-lookin' woman. Good woman, too, I believe. Got stayin' power to her. I like her. I'll say that in front of God and ever'body. And it's both an uncomfortable and yet nice feelin'. Been a long time since I experienced anything like it. But our worlds is different. Too far apart. I don't fit in hers and she shore as hell don't fit into mine. So relax, pilgrim. You won't see me again. This is my word, the mountains, the wilderness, the open sky. I plan on dyin' out here. My good horse will stumble, or an Injun's arrow or war axe will find me. I might get concerned by a bear, and we'll have us a high ol' time, a-roarin' and a-yellin' and a-clawed and a-bitin' and a-stobbin' 'til one of us is down." He smiled, showing amazingly good teeth and softened his facial features. "She don't fit in them plans."

Richard smiled. "I believe she might have something to say about that."

"She might think she do. But she don't. Oh, I know the signs, all right. I can see 'em on her face and in her eyes. But once I leave the lot of you at Fort Hall, I'm gone like the wind. I got mountains to climb and rivers to ford. I got valleys to cross where the grass is so lush and high it brushes the belly of my horse. I got to see country I ain't never seen before. I can't do that with no woman taggin' along. Not unless it's a squaw who's used to the hard ways of the trail." Preacher stood up. "You boys stay put. And when the women gets back, y'all start gettin' your possibles together. I'm fixin' to move some things close to that blow-down hole."

"You think those hooligans are close?" Edmond asked.

"I think they're right outside."

Preacher scrambled up the sloping sides of the valley and stepped into a maze of virgin brush and timber. The bench that encircled the little valley was about three hundred yards deep. He made his way carefully to the outer edge and was not surprised to see Bum and several of his gang moving slowly toward the rock face, a tracker on foot, carefully studying the ground. Preacher backed off and silently made his way back to the cave.

"No talkin'," he whispered. "They're outside now. Get your gear together and get gone to the waterfall. You'll see a natural lean-to on the north side of the falls. It's big enough for all of you and the horses. Take my packhorse with you. There's my gear. No fires. Get gone. Like right now."

The men were gone in ten minutes, gathering up their gear and heading out toward the horses. Preacher quickly packed up what he would carry out and set the pack by the mouth of the cave. Then he drank what coffee was left in the pot, packed the pot away, and carefully put out the fire. He went outside and saddled his horse, then sat back and waited, his .54 caliber Hawken at the ready.

He knew it was only a matter of time now, and probably not that much time. He had lied to the others about how safe they would be in the cave in order to give them some comfort and let them relax. It had worked and all of them, even Richard, were back up to snuff and ready for the trail.

Preacher knew that a good tracker would find the cave opening. Whether or not they would search the entire twisting, turning passageway was up for grabs. Preacher had, years back, but he'd also been wary of running into a bear or a mountain lion. He hoped the men out there now would be twice as wary as he was, but they had women and gold on their minds.

He heard a very faint scraping sound and slowly rose, moving silently toward the entrance to the passageway. They had found the opening.

He had rigged the first dead-fall in such a manner that as

dark as it was in that narrow passage, they would probably think it was just an accident.

The second trap would be a hell of a lot more obvious to anyone that it was man-made.

"Dark in there," Bull said, his words not reaching Preacher, who was crouched near the opening, waiting.

"What the hell did you think it would be?" Beckman asked. "A lamp-lit roadhouse? Can you see anything at all?"

"Nothing. Narrow trail, is all. Don't look wide enough for no horse to get through."

Jack Harris shouldered his way into the passage. "It's wide enough. Dirt's too smooth for my likin'. It looks like it's been smoothed out by a branch to me."

"Maybe," Bull said. "There damn sure ain't no puma or bear tracks in the dirt."

"There ain't nothin' on that dirt. See that openin' high up?" He pointed upward to the tiny crack. "It's rained lately here. Drops would have cut the groove in the dirt. He had to hide his tracks, but Preacher was hopin' we wouldn't notice that. I noticed. They's in yonder somewheres, boys."

"Knowin' Preacher is a-layin' in wait in that dark don't make me feel real good, Jack," Beckman said. "You know damn well he ain't no pilgrim."

"He ain't but one man," Jack replied. "Move. Let's search this place. See where it leads."

Preacher had heard only the murmur of voices. He had not been able to make out any of the words. He really didn't need to; he figured they were coming on in.

Bull was the first to inch forward into the dimness of the passageway, moving in a crouch, and advancing very carefully. He was a thug and a murderer, but not an idiot. He knew perfectly well that if Preacher was at the end of this winding, twisting passageway, it would mean a fight to the death.

His fingers touched a rock about the size of a human head. He pushed it aside. That released a tight rawhide thong that whipped out and up, disappearing out of sight and releasing about a dozen other large rocks.

"Slide!" Jack hollered, jumping back as he heard the sound.

Bull jerked back, but not fast enough to avoid getting conked on the head by a rock. The impact laid him out cold on the ground, a swelling knot on his noggin.

"Pull him out of there," Jack said, and he and Beckman tugged at the limp Bull and dragged him out of the passageway, back out into the light.

"Is he daid?" Leo asked.

"I don't think so," Beckman said. "But he's shore gonna have him a headache."

"I think he moved a rock and that triggered the slide," Jack said. "It was a trap."

"You think Preacher done it?" Bum asked.

"Yeah. I do. And they's probably more traps in yonder."

"And Preacher and them others could be long gone," Keyes pointed out.

"Could be," Bum said. "But I don't think so. I think they holed up in yonder for rest. One of 'em's hurt; we've all seen the bloody bandages. The size of 'em tells me it's either a thigh or head wound. Moses, fetch us some long poles to push along ahead of us and wave in the air. That'll set off any traps Preacher might have laid."

All but the last one.

Preacher had taken a small keg of powder salvaged from the wagon train and rigged up a fuse. He had placed the keg between a large rock and the face of the stone wall. When it blew, he felt there would be enough force behind the blast to bring the boulder down and block the passageway.

Preacher could now hear the sounds of sticks whapping the sides of the passageway.

Smart, he thought. *I ain't dealin' with idiots. I'll have to remember that.*

Preacher grinned as the sounds of the sticks striking the earth and the rock walls drew closer. He cocked one of his pistols and let it bang. The sound was enormous in the cave. And he got what he was hoping for.

"Oh, my God!" Beckman hollered in pain, as the wildly ricochetting lead struck him in the leg. "I caught me a ball. Oh, God, it tore up my leg. Get out of there. Git me outta here."

Preacher let bang another ball. He could hear the ugly sound of the ball as it howled from wall to wall, bouncing and careening, looking for a place to strike.

"Get back!" Jack hollered. "Drag Beckman outta there. We got to come up with another plan. It's a death trap in yonder."

"I cain't walk!" Beckman bellered. "Oh, my leg's tore up bad, y'all."

Preacher was reloading as fast as he could, with ball, patch, powder, and ram. He capped his pistols and waited.

"Preacher!" Bum yelled. "You give us the women and the gold and you can walk free. That's a promise, man."

"Go to hell!" Preacher shouted.

"Don't be a fool, Preacher. You're trapped in yonder. Think about it. All we got to do is wait and starve you out. We got the time and you ain't. Them pilgrims ain't worth your dyin' for, man. Give it some thought."

"Ask him if he's got some whiskey to pour on this leg," Beckman said.

Bum gave the man a disgusted look.

Preacher waited.

"One way or the other, we're gonna get you, Preacher," Bum yelled, his words echoing around the twisting passageway. "All you got to do is walk out of there and you're a free man."

"In a pig's eye," Preacher muttered. He knew they'd kill him on sight.

Preacher settled down for a long wait.

6

"So who's got a plan?" Jack asked.

The gang was sitting well away and to the side of the opening in the mountain. They had dug the flattened ball out of Beckman's leg and he lay moaning in pain while Moses rambled around in the woods, gathering up various leaves with which to make a poultice.

"Why not smoke 'em out?" Leo suggested. "It's a cave, ain't it?"

"That ain't a bad idea," Bum said. "As a matter of fact, it's a damn good idea. Let's start gatherin' up all the wood we can tote." He thought for a moment. "No. I got a better idea. We'll build us a shield outta small branches. Lash half a dozen good-sized branches together and stay behind it while we advance. That'll protect us from ricochets and we can get right up on Preacher. When we get close enough we can get right up on Preacher. When we get close enough we can toss burning pitch over into the cave proper and really smoke 'em out."

The thugs all agreed that Bum had come up with a fine plan. The first log shield they lashed together was too wide and got hung up in the first turn in the passageway. Preacher sat back in the cave and listened to them cuss and holler. He chewed on jerky and waited.

When they finally got the right size shield lashed together, it didn't take them long to get close. Preacher had bellied down on the dirt, his .50 caliber pistols in hand. When the men rounded the long curve that would lead them to the cave, Preacher smiled at the sight. The men were holding the shield about six inches off the passageway floor. Preacher fired both pistols, keeping the muzzles about three inches off the ground. Two of the thugs started squalling in pain as the balls tore into one's foot and the other's ankle, shattering bone.

The shield was dropped to the earth and forward movement halted while the two wounded men were stretched out on the earth, to be dragged out into the clearing.

"I'll kill you for this, Preacher!" Slug bellered. "I'll skin you alive, damn your eyes!"

"I'll do worser than that, Preacher!" Bobby screamed over the pain in his shattered foot. "You'll rue the day you shot me, you dirty bastard! You tore offen some toes, damn you. When I git my hands on you, it'll take you days to die, you sorry son."

"Yeah, yeah," Preacher muttered, reloading. "Flap your mouth, boy." He chuckled. He had put three of them out of action so far. He was cutting down the odds right good, he figured.

Preacher popped another piece of jerky in his mouth and waited.

Then the gang got real quiet. He knew they were up to something, and he didn't think it was going to be pleasant.

It wasn't. They started chucking lit torches into the cave. Preacher grinned and began chucking them right back, figuring he might get lucky and set someone on fire.

He did.

"Halp!" Keyes yelled. "My britches is on far. Halp me beat it out, boys. Jesus Christ. Oh, Lord, hit's a-burnin' my leg. Halp!"

Preacher chucked several more burning brands behind the shield.

"Goddammit, Bum!" a man yelled. "This ain't workin' out like you said it would."

"Well, hell's fire, Adam. I never said it would be perfect, now, did I? Oowww! Somebody kick some dirt on my britches leg. Jesus, it's on fire. Hurry up, dammit!"

"Now you know how I feel!" Keyes hollered.

Preacher felt it was time to add even more confusion to the yelling knot of thugs. He had prepared a small bag of powder—a bag-bomb as Richard had called it while watching the mountain man make it—and now he took it out of his possibles pouch and lit the fuse. He tossed it over the top of the log shield.

"Holy Christ!" he heard a man yell. "Run. It's a damn bomb."

The small grenade really didn't do a lot of damage when it exploded. But in the confined space of the passageway, it sounded a lot more dangerous than it really was. It also peppered the thugs with small rocks and pebbles when it blew, stinging and bloodying the men.

Preacher leaned back and laughed at the sounds of panic echoing all around him.

"Damn you, Preacher!" George hollered, then immediately fell into a coughing fit due to all the dust. "Why don't you fight fair, man?"

"Idiot," Preacher muttered. "There ain't no such of a thing as a fair fight."

"Oh, I cain't walk!" Rod moaned. "The bomb done crippled me. Don't abandon me, boys."

"Fool!" Bum yelled. "That's Leo sittin' on our legs. You ain't hurt."

"The whole side of my face is bloody," Adam squalled. "Look at me. Did it blow my face off, boys?"

Preacher scooped up a double handful of dirt and wrapped it up in a piece of cloth. He fashioned a fuse and lit it. He yelled, "Here comes another one, boys!" Then he chucked it over the logs.

Wild panic broke out in the narrow space as the outlaws began screaming and cussing and literally running over each other in their haste to depart the scene. Preacher crawled forward, pushing the burning brands the thugs had tossed into the cave in front of him. He stacked them up all around the front of the lashed-together logs and then hustled back around the bend in the passageway to safety.

"It was a dud!" Jack shouted.

"Long-burnin' fuse!" Preacher yelled.

"You're a liar, Preacher," Bum shouted.

"Look!" Moses shouted. "The barricade's on far."

"Grab some dirt and put it out, boys!" Bum yelled.

Preacher decided he'd had enough fun and lit the long fuse leading to the charge behind the rocks above the barricade. He grabbed his gear and headed out the mouth of the cave. He figured he had maybe thirty seconds to vacate the area before all that powder blew.

He misjudged it slightly. The fuse burned quickly and then touched the powder. The concussion rocked the ground beneath his moccasins when it exploded.

The huge rock and dozens of smaller ones came tumbling down, completely blocking the passage and sealing that entrance to the little valley.

Oue rock bounced off Moses's head and knocked the thug sprawling to the earth, addling him. Jack Harris took a stone right between the eyes and it knocked him cold.

Bum Kelly assessed the damage and threw his hat to the ground and cursed.

In the valley, sitting his saddle, Preacher threw back his head and howled like a great gray wolf. Then he laughed and headed for the waterfall.

* * *

Preacher led his party through the blow-down and headed westward into the Grand Tetons. He figured he had bought them at least two days and maybe as many as four.

Behind him, Bum Kelley and his outlaws had staggered out of the passageway to fall exhausted on the ground. All of them were cut, bruised, and bleeding from wounds ranging from minor to serious.

"Let's start checkin' each other out," Bum finally spoke, heaving himself up off the ground. He swayed slightly on his boots. "Unless you boys want to give up on gettin' the gold and them women."

The outlaws gave him grim looks.

"Not damn likely," Bum muttered darkly. "But I want Preacher worser than I want anything else. I want to stick his feet into a far and burn him slow."

"Yeah," Bobby moaned the word. He looked at the bloody bandage that covered where some toes had been. He was alternately working on a piece of deerskin, making a crude moccasin, and moaning through his pain. "I wanna gouge his eyes out."

"I'm gonna cut him," Beckman said. "And that's just for starters." He looked at his wounded leg and cussed.

Slug was splinting his broken ankle over the damage done by the .50 caliber ball. "I'm gonna rape both them women and make Preacher watch. Then I'm gonna skin him. Slow."

Bum smiled grimly. He knew there would be no stopping these men now. Now it was a matter of honor with them. Preacher had shamed them all and if need be, they would track him right up to and through the gates of hell for revenge.

But, Bum thought, to make matters even worser, as soon as Preacher reached some post or settlement, he would tell the story, and really juice it up. Unless he was stopped, Bum and his boys would be the laughing stock of the territories. He knew the others had the same thought.

They couldn't none of them allow that to happen. They had to close Preacher's mouth. Forever.

Preacher would chuckle occasionally as he built a fire to cook their supper.

"I fail to see what is so amusing about inflicting pain and suffering upon your fellow man," Edmond said.

Preacher looked at the missionary. "Do you have any idea what them ol' boys back yonder will do to you if they catch you?"

"Rob us."

Preacher chucked. "You really are a babe in the woods, ain't you? Well, let me tell you something. If they catch you people, after they get tired of usin' the women, then they'll use you men. You get my drift?"

"I don't believe that!" Edmond said. "That would be— well, barbaric!"

"It sure would. But they'd still do it. Then they'd torture you just to listen to you scream. They've done it all before. Ain't nothin' new to none of them. They been doin' it for years and years."

"Why don't the authorities stop them?" Richard asked.

"Good God, people!" Preacher blurted in exasperation. "Look around you. What authorities? There ain't no law out here. This is wilderness. Can't you people understand that?"

"The *Army* is the authority in wilderness areas, I believe," Edmond said. "When we reach this fort you spoke of, we shall certainly report the reprehensible behavior of those ruffians who attacked the cave."

"Sure," Preacher replied. "People, this land is in dispute 'tween England and the U-nited States. There might not be soldiers their. 'Sides, ain't but about five hundred million billion acres out there. Hell, they oughtta be able to search that in no time a-tall." He shook his head, "Foolish, foolish people."

Preacher fell silent as the little something that had been nagging at him all day finally settled down in the light of his mind. He had known about half of the men behind the voices back yonder in the cave. But yet another voice had been awful familiar to him.

"Jack Harris!" he blurted.

"What?" Richard said, looking at the mountain man. "What about our guide?"

"I *knowed* that voice was familiar. He was one of them back at the cave. I'm sure of it!"

Melody scooted closer to him. "If that's correct, Preacher, then that means that . . ." Her voice trailed off, her face frozen in shock.

"Yeah," Preacher spoke the word softly. "The whole thing wasn't nothin' but a set up from the git-go."

"Whatever in the world do you mean?" Penelope asked.

"Them Injuns spoiled Bum and Jack's plans. They wasn't figurin' on them Injuns attackin'. *They* was gonna ambush the wagon train. That's why Jack took y'all so far north of the Oregon Trail."

Edmond was speechless—which, to Preacher's ears, was a great relief.

Penelope sat on the ground, her mouth open.

"Yes," Richard finally said. "Yes. It has to be. What a thoroughly untrustworthy, black-hearted, and totally reprehensible individual."

"Does that mean he's a dirty, low-down, sorry skunk?" Preacher asked.

"Yes. That sums it up quite well."

"Thought so. Well, it means something else, too: it means they got to kill us all. You see, no tellin' how long Jack's been doin' this. You say Jack hooked up with y'all in Missouri?"

"Well . . . not exactly," Richard said. "Ten days out of Missouri, our guide suddenly disappeared. He'd been out scouting. I think. Well, you can imagine our predicament. We were beside ourselves with worry. We were *lost*. The next morning, Jack Harris rode in. He was so strong-appearing and full of confidence. We practically had to beg him to take on the job of guide."

"Where was your wagon master?"

"Why . . . I don't suppose we had one."

"Just how much beggin' did y'all have to do 'fore Jack agreed to sign on?"

"Well, actually, not very much."

"I thought not. Well, let's fix some vittles and eat up. We got to push hard come the mornin'. There's some damn rough country ahead."

They crossed the Yellowstone and Preacher took them straight west. He took them over the Divide and headed for the Snake. By now, he knew that Bum and his boys would have circled the small range in which the cave was located. They would pick up their trail and be hard on it.

"By the Lord!" Edmond exclaimed one frosty morning in the high country. "This land is exhilarating!"

"Does that mean you like it?" Preacher asked.

"My word, yes!"

"You ain't thinkin' of settlin' here, is you?"

"We've discussed it," Melody said sweetly. "After all, savages are savages, whether on the west coast or here. Of course, we shall have to push on to deliver the monies. But we think we shall return to this wonderful and primitive land."

"Is that a fact?" Preacher's words were glumly spoken.

"Yes!" she said brightly. "Aren't you excited with the news?"

"I can tell you truthful I am purt near overcome."

"I knew you would be . . . darling," she added softly.

Preacher felt like he was standing in quicksand, and slowly sinking. Movement caught his eyes. He looked up. First time in his life he was happy to see a band of Indians.

7

"Relax," Preacher said. "They're Bannocks. I know that brave in the lead. His name is Bad Foot."

"Bad Foot?" Edmond said. "Why would anybody name a child that?"

"Probably 'cause he was borned with a club foot. Sometimes that's the way Injuns name their young. If I knowed y'all better I'd tell you a story about a brave I knowed once called Two Dogs Humpin'."

"Please don't," Penelope said quickly.

"Sounds like a delightfully naughty story," Melody said, her eyes bright.

"I'm sorry I brung it up," Preacher said, getting to his feet and making the sign of 'Brother' to the Indian on the lead pony.

Preacher began speaking to the brave in his own tongue, Snake. Bad Foot grinned and nodded his head and began rubbing his belly.

"They been buffler huntin'," Preacher explained. "And they gonna give us some steaks. We got some mighty fine eatin' comin' up, folks."

"Ask him if he's ever heard of God," Edmond said, digging in his pack for one of the many small Bibles he'd salvaged from the wagon train ambush.

"Ask him yourself. He speaks pretty good English. I's just bein' polite speakin' his tongue."

Edmond approached the Indian cautiously, holding a Bible in his hands. Bad Foot stood smiling at him. Edmond held out the Bible and Bad Foot took it.

"Thank you," the Indian said. "My woman thanks you. She will take it as soon as I return to the lodge. She will use it much more than me."

Edmond's face brightened as he watched Bad Foot finger the pages. "Your, ah, woman is a Christian?"

The others wondered why Preacher was laughing so hard he had to sit down on the ground, holding his sides.

"No Christian. I take all Bibles offered me."

"She studies them? My word. We've got to return and live with this tribe."

"Studies? No study. Can't read. Pages thin. Make good ass wipe."

They stopped early that afternoon. Preacher wanted to get the buffalo steaks on while they were still fresh. Besides, if he was tired, Lord knows what the others were feeling. They camped on the west side of Pacific Creek. Preacher wasn't too worried about Bum and his bunch; he figured they were at least three days ahead of them. They'd eat good this afternoon and just lay around and rest. Give the horses a much needed break, too.

He glanced over at Edmond, who still had his lower lip all poked out over Bad Foot's refusal to return the Bible. Preacher had been forced to step between the two men before Bad Foot forgot he was a peaceful Bannock and went on the warpath.

Before leaving, Bad Foot had grinned at Preacher and pointed at Edmond. He extended the index finger of his left hand and held it straight up in the air, cupping it with his right hand, making and up and down motion.

"What did that savage call me?" Edmond demanded, after the Bannocks had left.

"An asshole," Preacher told him. "Among other things."

"Well! I *never!*" Edmond said.

"I shore hope not," Preacher replied, hiding his grin, and certainly not telling the man everything the hand signals had implied. "Although Injuns tolerate that type of thing better than whites do."

"Whatever in the world are you babbling about?" Edmond asked, irritated.

Preacher shook his head. "Skip it." He looked up at the sky. The weather had been perfect ever since leaving the cave and the little valley, but now it was about to turn foul. Preacher figured they'd be in a hard, cold rain long before dusk.

He set about building the ladies a crude lean-to. If the men wanted one, they could damn well build it themselves. As for himself, he'd just get up under a tree and sleep with his robe wrapped around him, his back to the tree. Richard and Edmond watched him for a few moments, then set about building their own shelter. Preacher eyeballed them for several minutes and concluded their rickety shelter would collapse before the night was over.

Preacher did build a small shelter over the cook-fire and then set about broiling the thick buffalo steaks. He got the shelter up just as the rains came.

The others watched him and marveled at how much a man Preacher's size could eat. He was gnawing on a half-raw steak while cooking the others.

"Learn this," Preacher said. "Eat when you can, drink when you can, and sleep when you can. 'Cause you don't know when you're gonna be able to do any of the three again."

"We've been eating rather well and often on this sojourn," Richard pointed out.

"You ain't never wintered out here," Preacher told him, not quite sure what sojourn meant, but not wanting to appear plumb ignorant. He kind of figured it had something to do with traveling. "Snows can come a-howlin' this time of year. Catch you flat-footed. Makes a fat rabbit look as good as airy steak you ever et."

"Will you please stop speaking like some ignorant savage?" Edmond yelled at him, startling them all. "You have some education. I know you do. Why do you persist in speaking like some addle-brained buffoon?"

"Bothers you, do it?" Preacher adjusted the steaks over the flames. "Why is that, Brother Edmond?"

But Edmond sulled up and sat under his leaky lean-to, refusing to speak.

"You got something stuck up in your craw, spit it out, Brother," Preacher told him. "Anger's a vile thing to keep all bottled up. Might even make a feller sick. You liable to come down with the collie-wobbles or the nobby-noodles or something worser than that."

"There you go again," Edmond broke his silence. "I won't even ask you what those ridiculous illnesses might be."

"They aren't nothin', Brother."

"And stop calling me Brother. I am not your brother. You don't even worship God. How could you be my brother?"

Preacher smiled. "You still got your lips all pooched out 'cause of what Bad Foot done. And who says I don't worship God? I do in my own way. Who says your way is right and mine is wrong? Why, I've even worshipped the Almighty at the Great Medicine Wheel over in the Bighorns. I bet that's something you never studied in your fancy Eastern colleges."

"I've never even heard of it," Edmond muttered.

"High up in the mountains, it is. 'Bout ten thousand feet or more. White stones in a circle, measurin', oh, 'bout seventy-five or eighty feet. Got twenty-eight spokes. And on a river 'bout fifty, sixty miles to the west of there, they's a great stone arrow, pointin' direct at the wheel. Lots of stories 'bout them things, but the Crow say the Sun laid out the wheel to teach the tribe how to make a tipi. I told y'all how the Plains Injuns feel about the sun and the earth. I'm gonna tell you something else: when I stood there in that circle, I got me a strange feelin', I did. Spiritual feelin'."

"Are the Crow dangerous?" Richard asked.

"Depends on how you look at it. They love to steal horses. They're fine horsemen. I know an ol' boy name of William Gordon. Mountain man. He had him a Crow chief tell him that if they killed the white man, they wouldn't come back, and they couldn't steal no more of the white man's horses. So they'll steal from the white man, but they won't kill him. Howsomever, that don't hold true all the time. You get some young buck lookin' to make a name for hisself so's he can impress the girls, he might just take your hair. It don't happen often, but it do happen. All in all, though, I trust the Crow not to kill me. But I sleep with one eye on my horses when I'm in their territory."

Preacher looked at the steaks and said, "They's ready. Come get this food and eat good."

Over supper, Melody said, "The Indians who attacked the wagon train, Preacher—what did you say they were?"

"Arapaho. Strange bunch of people. They stay to themselves mostly, but sometimes they will hook up with the Cheyenne. They ain't got no use for most white people. They's been talk of the Cheyenne and Arapaho comin' together to fight. Both tribes hate the Kiowa. I been hearin' talk that they's goin' to band together and head on the warpath against the Kiowa. Odd, 'cause the Kiowa and the Cheyenne used to be friends. I don't know what happened. The Arapaho will tell you he is your friend, but he ain't—not really. How's your meat?"

"It's delicious," Edmond said. ""And please let me apologize for my earlier outburst. It's been, well, a trying time for all of us."

And it ain't nearabouts over, Preacher thought.

* * *

"I can't figure where he's takin' them," George said. "He's headin' straight west."

"Has to be Fort Henry on the Yellowstone," Bull said. The huge knot on his head had gone away, but the memory of who gave it to him had not. He dreamed nightly of killing Preacher.

"But there ain't no soldier boys there," Bum said. "That's a civilian fort. And that shore ain't gettin' them folks no closer to the Oregon Trail."

"Maybe it is," Jack Harris said. "Preacher knows everybody in the wilderness. They's bound to be some trappers and the like hangin' around Henry. He could get some of them to ride with him down to Forth Hall for protection and then get them pilgrims hooked up with another wagon train headed west. Once that was done, we'd be out of luck."

"How many days you figure they're ahead of us?" Bum asked.

"Maybe two—three at the most. We're travelin' a lot harder than they is. But if we're gonna catch up, we got to push harder still."

"This ain't gettin' us no closer," Bobby said, lurching to his feet with the help of a branch he was using for a crutch. "Let's ride."

Slug, also using a tree limb for a crutch, rose painfully to his one good foot. "I'll follow Preacher clear to the blue waters if I have to," he said, his face tight with the pain from his broken ankle. "I owe him, and this is one debt I damn sure intend to pay."

Beckman hobbled to his feet, grimacing at the pain in his wounded leg. "Let's ride, boys. Hell, even if we get to Fort Henry and they're still around, there ain't no law there. Cain't nobody do nothin' to us. If them pilgrims say we attacked them, it's our word agin theirs. And they's more of us than there is them. If anything's said about our wounds, we'll just say we was attacked by Injuns."

Moses dumped water on the fire and stirred the ashes. Outlaws they were, but none of them wanted to be anywhere near a raging, out-of-control forest fire.

"Get the horses," Bum said. "We got to put some miles behind us."

None of them—Preacher included—knew whether Fort Henry was still operating. Andy Henry had built several forts, beginning back in 1807 when he built a fort on the Yellowstone at the mouth of the Big Horn. Then another fort was built in 1810 near the confluence of the Jefferson and Madison rivers. Blackfeet destroyed that one. Then in 1811-1812 another fort was thrown up on Henry's Fork of the Snake. Blackfeet and hard winters put that one out of business. Back in '23 another, sturdier fort was built and so far as any of the men knew, it was still operating.

They could only hope.

Preacher plunged them across the Snake and into the wilderness of the Teton Range and into Washington Territory. He picked up the pace, knowing by now that those behind him would have figured out where he was going. Problem was, Preacher didn't know if the fort was still standing, much less in business. He hadn't been over this way in several years. There had been several Injun uprisings in that time. He'd asked Bad Foot about it, but the sub-chief had only shrugged his shoulders in reply. Which might have meant anything or nothing.

With an Injun, you just never knew.

The side of Richard's head was still tender to the touch, but the wound had healed nicely. Edmond had gotten over his mad with Preacher, Penelope was still a bitch, for the most part, and Melody, seeing her advances thwarted, had taken to not speaking to Preacher. Which suited Preacher just fine. He didn't have time to fool with some love-struck female.

If he had any kind of luck, in a couple of weeks he'd be done and through with the whole damn bunch of them and the entire misadventure would be behind him.

With any kind of luck.

They rode right into a storm and had to seek shelter from the cold driving rain that had bits of ice in it. The ice, driven by high winds, cut like tiny knives on bare skin.

"These late spring storms can be pure hell," Preacher said, almost shouting to be heard over the howl of the wind as it came shrieking down off the mountains. "We might wake up in the mornin' and they'll be a foot of snow on the ground. You just never know this high up."

"It sounds like the wailing of a million lost souls," Edmond said. "I've never heard or felt anything like this."

"That's a right good way of puttin' it," Preacher agreed. "Never had thought of it like that."

"But if we can't travel," Richard said, shouting the words, "neither can those behind us."

"Don't bet on it," Preacher told him. "This storm might be local. It might not be doin' nothin' fifteen miles to the east of us. Sorry."

Preacher managed to throw up a windbreak and get a fire going. But all in all it was going to be the most miserable night the pilgrims had yet spent on the trail. Preacher took it in his usual manner: calmly and philosophically. He knew there was no point in bitching about it; wasn't nothing he nor anyone else could do about it.

The rain soon changed to snow and in a very short time, the land was covered in white. The snow, whipped by the high winds, soon reduced visibility to near zero.

"Don't no one stray from camp!" Preacher yelled. "You got to relieve yourself, you just step behind the nearest tree. You stray from camp in this, and you'll get lost sure as shootin'. You'll be froze to death 'fore we could find you."

For once, no one argued with him. The pilgrims were scared, and looked it.

About midnight, the lean-to that Richard and Edmond built gave up and collapsed. Preacher, wrapped up in a ground sheet and buffalo robe, his back to a tree and his hat brim tied over his ears with a scarf he fastened under his chin, opened one eye and chuckled at the antics of the men as they thrashed around in the cold and snow.

One thing about it, the mountain man thought, all four of these people will be a sight smarter about the wilderness when this is over. If they survive, he added. Then he closed his eye and went back to sleep, snug in his robe.

Neither Richard nor Edmond was in a real good mood come the morning.

"I have a head cold," Edmond complained. "I am in dire need of a plaster for my chester and some hot lemonade."

"Jesus Christ!" Preacher muttered.

"I simply must have a cup of hot tea," Richard said. "Do you have any left, Penelope?"

"I'll make us some. I have a few leaves left."

Preacher had been ruminating on their situation. "Y'all don't need to hurry none," he told them. "We shore ain't goin' nowheres. We'd leave a trail a drunk blind man could follow."

"That means the hooligans behind us will gain on us," Richard said.

"They'll gain," Preacher admitted. "But I left the trail and turned gradual north early yesterday mornin'. I didn't figure none of you would notice, and you didn't. Then I cut back south for a few miles, then headed west again about noon. That's when I led y'all into that little crick. If y'all had paid attention, you'd have noticed that crick cut back south. A lot of cricks and rivers do flow that way," he added drily. "Howsomever, Goose Crick does run north. It's a weird crick. But that ain't got nothin' to do with us." He pointed. "That mountain right there, it's got about fifteen different names, but the

Injuns call it Mountain That Takes Life. They say it's evil. I 'magine what happened was some sort of sickness killed a bunch of them years back and they just figure the mountain is evil and won't go near it. That's where we're goin' soon as the sun melts this snow. Reason I'm tellin' you all this, is that I took us 'way, 'way off the trail. Now with the snow, if we just sit tight and don't build no big fires, Bum and them others won't have no idea where we is. They'll just think we kept on the trail westward and that's the way they'll go. They might even make the fort—if it's still there—two or three days ahead of us."

"Well, what would be the advantage of them doing that?" Richard asked.

Preacher smiled. "'Cause we ain't gonna go to the fort. Soon as the snow melts, I'm takin' y'all southwest to Fort Hall."

8

Bum and his party of no-goods pressed on, never leaving the westward trail. They had lost the trail, but were all convinced that Preacher was heading for Fort Henry on the Yellowstone. It was the only logical thing for him to do. South was very rugged country.

A dozen miles to the south, Preacher and his pilgrims sat it out until the snow was completely gone. By that time, everyone was well rested, including the horses. Preacher had listened to Edmond bitch about his head cold until he knew if they didn't get on the trail, he was really gonna give Edmond something to complain about. Like maybe a poke on the snoot.

"Pack it up," Preacher told them. "We got about a hundred miles to go."

Preacher led them straight south, toward Teton Pass. His plan was to take them through the pass, then cut more to the west, leading them through the Caribou Range, staying north of the great dry lake some called Gray's Lake, cross the Blackfoot Mountains, then on into Fort Hall. That was his plan, but in Indian country, plans were subject to change.

Once clear of Teton Pass, Preacher cut southwest and pushed his party hard. They were becoming used to the trail, and Richard had become a fair hand. Preacher began ranging far out in front of them whenever he felt it safe to do so—safe was his being fairly sure Richard would say on the trail Preacher forged and not get the others lost. He tried to stay apart from the group as much as possible, for Melody had once more begun speaking to him and batting her blues and shaking her bottom at him. Damn woman was about to drive him nuts.

Bum and his bunch had found themselves smack in the middle of a Blackfoot uprising. A friendly Bannock had told them the Army was warning all people to leave the area north of the upper curve of the Snake. And the Bannock also had told them, that everybody was gone from Fort Henry until the Blackfoot had been settled down. They'd been gone for several weeks. He knew that for a fact, 'cause he'd been there.

"Tricked us," bum said. "He cut south during the snow, and holed up until it melted 'fore pullin' out. That has to be it."

"Then we're out of luck on this run," Jack said. "No way we can make Fort Hall 'fore they do."

Bum thought about that while he was warming his hands over a small fire. "You know where Red Hand is?"

"Yeah. But you ain't thinkin' of trustin' that crazy renegade, is you?"

"I don't see that we got a whole lot of choice in the matter. With his bunch, and with us maybe pickin' up eight or ten other ol' boys, we could take on any wagon train. We could hit them anywheres between Fort Hall and Oregon Territory."

"I don't like it. Why would Red Hand even want to join up with us?" Bull asked.

"For prisoners and booty. We could make a deal with him. He will keep his word on certain things. I've worked with him before and always been careful not to try to rook him. We can pick our spot once they leave Fort Hall, 'cause there ain't no Army forts along the way until you get to Oregon Territory, and I think them's all British, far as I know. And them silly people don't worry me none. Hell, they'll stop and drink tea right in the middle of a damn battle."

"Them women we been chasin' might get killed," Keyes pointed out.

"And they might not. 'Sides, all the gold them Bible-toters is carryin' will make up for the women."

"True," Moses said.

"So what do we do?" Slug asked.

"Git our butts outta Blackfoot country first thing. When that's done, we head south to find Red Hand and his bunch and to find us some more ol' boys that we can trust. When we talk to him, we don't mention nothin' 'bout the gold or the women we're after. Luke, do Preacher know you?"

"No. I ain't never laid eyes on the man."

"Then you'll be the one to ride into Fort Hall and find out what wagon train them pilgrims is leavin' with. We'll be camped 'bout fifteen miles southeast of the fort, down close to the Portneufs. That's where Red Hand hangs out. Let's get the hell gone from here. I don't wanna tangle with no damn Blackfeet."

"Two days from the fort," Preacher told the group. *And then I'll be shut of you,* he silently added. *Praise be!* "We'll stop at a crick just 'fore we make the fort and you ladies can bathe and whatever and change back into them dresses you toted along. Howsomever, it's gonna be right difficult for y'all to ride properlike in them saddles."

"We want to pay you for all your troubles," Edmond said.

Preacher fixed him with a bleak look. "I did what I done cause it was the right thing to do. So don't you be tryin' to hand me no money. I don't want your damn money." *I just want to get shut of you and I hope I don't never see none of you again.* "I feel bounden to see you hooked up with a wagon train, and I'll do that. Then I'm gone."

"Where will you go, Preacher?" Penelope asked. Now that salvation—in the form of less cretinous people—was near, she felt it wouldn't hurt to be at least cordial to the man. To a degree.

"Don't know. Furrin's about played out. I can see that while most of the others can't. But I'll tell you what I ain't a-gonna do. I ain't a-gonna guide no gawddamn wagon trains full of pilgrims."

He would live to eat those words. Without benefit of salt, pepper, or anything else. And a lot sooner than he could possibly know.

Preacher had tucked them all in a natural depression off the trail. The fire was built against a huge rock so the rock would reflect the heat back to the group. They were running out of supplies, and Preacher had not wanted to risk a shot bringing down a deer, and had not been able to get close enough to one to use an arrow. He had managed to snare a few rabbits, and that was what they were having this evening.

"A paté would be wonderful," Penelope said, holding a rabbit's leg.

"Yes," Edmond agreed. "Or one of your mother's wonderful meat pies."

Preacher rocked back on his heels and gnawed at his meat.

"I dream of being warm again," Melody said. "The luxury of sitting in a chair, snug and warm by the stove, and reading poetry, while the elements rage outside the window."

"Stimulating conversation over tea and cookies," Richard said.

"Luxuriating long in a hot, soapy bath," Penelope said. She gingerly took a dainty little bite of rabbit.

Preacher broke the bone and sucked out the marrow. He muttered under his breath.

"I beg your pardon?" Edmond inquired.

"Nothin'," Preacher said, reaching over and slicing off a hunk of rabbit. He tensed only slightly as an alien sound came to him. He shifted position and continued to eat. But he had moved closer to his saddle and the extra brace of pistols. The move also put his back to a large rock. The others did not seem to notice.

Preacher glanced over at the horses. They had stopped grazing and were standing very still, their ears all perked up.

Preacher ate the last of his meat and then picked up a handful of snow that remained on the shady side of the small boulder. He rubbed the snow on his hands to clear away the grease and used more snow to wipe the grease from his mouth. He dried his hands on his britches and wiped his mouth with his jacket sleeve. Free of the odor of grease, he took a deep breath. He picked out the tangy odor of old woodsmoke. There was no way he could tell by smell what tribe the Indians were from, but he'd bet ten dollars they were Blackfeet. And there wasn't no fiercer fighters anywhere—unless it was Red Hand and that bunch of half-crazy renegades that run with him. But this was just a tad north for Red Hand, although Preacher had once run into Red Hand a hell of a lot further north than this.

This bunch was slipping up from behind Preacher. To the front was clear, as was to his left. He stretched and scooted back another foot or so, putting himself in the shadows. Using as little movement as possible, he slowly eased both his pistols from his sash and cocked them. The pilgrims were busy discussing poetry and the latest fashions back East.

Preacher figured this was a mightly small bunch of Injuns. If they'd had any size to them a-tall, they'd have already attacked and done the deed. These were probably young bucks, out to take some hair so's they could impress the girls back at the village.

"Richard," Preacher said in a soft whisper.

The man cut his eyes to Preacher while the others kept talking, unaware of any trouble.

"Real easy like, now, without you sayin' a word, you put your hand on the butt of your pistol and be ready to jerk and cock and fire."

"What? What?" Edmond said. "What's this about discharging a weapon?"

Penelope jumped up. "Are we under attack?" she screamed.

Melody looked up just as braves came leaping into the camp. She jumped to her feet and let out a shriek that would put a mountain lion to shame.

Preacher put two bucks on the ground and crippled a third when he fired his pistols, both of them double-shotted. He grabbed up his second brace and let them roar. His left hand gun was a clean miss and his right hand gun misfired.

Richard fired, the ball catching a brave in the stomach and stopping them cold. The missionary stood rock still for a second, looking at the gore he'd caused, then vomited down the front of his coat.

Preacher was on his feet, his long blade knife at the ready when a buck came screaming at him, a war axe in his hand.

Preacher side-stepped the blow from the axe and cut the buck across the back, from his shoulder down to his buttocks, the big blade slicing deep. The Indian screamed and rolled on the ground, coming to rest near Penelope. He reached out and clamped one hand around her ankle. Edmond picked up a rock about the size of a grapefruit and smashed the buck on the head, cracking his skull.

Preacher jumped for his Hawken and cocked it, leveling the .54 caliber rifle just as a brave leaped at him. At point-blank range, he fired. The ball struck the Indian in the center of his chest and turned him in mid-air. He was dead when he hit the ground.

"Reload, goddammit!" Preacher yelled, dropping the rifle

and hurriedly trying to charge his pistols. "Edmond, see to the horses."

A brave leveled his bow and Melody screamed at Preacher. Preacher threw himself to one side and the arrow whizzed past him, embedding into a tree. Preacher charged the lone brave and clubbed him with his pistol, smashing his head on the way down.

Edmond never made it to the horses. He was on the ground, unconscious, and a Blackfoot was grappling with Richard. Richard was holding onto the buck's wrists.

"Kick him in the parts, Richard!" Preacher yelled.

The Blackfoot kneed Richard in his groin and the man went down, moaning.

Melody grabbed up a burning brand from the fire and jammed it against the Indian's arm. He screamed in pain and slapped her in the face, knocking her down. Preacher leveled his pistol and fired, the ball striking the brave in the head and doing terrible damage to the man's face, tearing away part of his jaw and slamming the man to the ground.

A young buck, armed with only a war axe, took a vicious swing at Preacher. Preacher clubbed him with the butt of his Hawken just as another brave jumped onto Preacher's back, screaming his defiance. He tried to ride Preacher down. Preacher flipped the brave off his back. The buck hit the ground, rolled, and came to his feet just in time to receive the full length of Preacher's knife in his belly, the cutting edge up. Preacher jerked the knife upward, the heavy blade ripping through stomach and into lung and heart. The Blackfoot was dead before he stretched out on the cold ground.

The fight was over. If there were any more Blackfeet, they decided their medicine was bad this night and vanished back into the timber.

Edmond was getting to his feet with the help of Penelope, and Melody was trying to get Richard to his feet. Richard wasn't having any part of that. He lay on the ground in a fetal position, moaning, both hands holding his privates.

Preacher reloaded his pistols, then his rifle. He walked over to Edmond and looked at the man. The missionary had a lump on his noggin but other than that was unhurt. Melody's face was red and swelling where the brave had smacked her. She'd have a pretty good bruise there come the morning.

Penelope pointed to the dead Indians. "What are we going to do with them?"

"We're not doin' nothin' with them," Preacher told her. "We're packin' up and getting' the hell gone from here. Injuns will come back for them." He shook his head. "Injuns must really have their dander up to attack at night. They don't usually do that."

"Why?" Edmond asked, fingering the knot on his head.

"Most tribes believe that if they're killed at night, the spirit wanders forever. Some believe that if the body is not recovered and properly buried the spirit wanders." Preacher inspected each of the dead braves. All young men. "Mosquitoes," he said.

"I beg your pardon?" Richard said, finally able to get to his feet. He was still all hunched over.

"Pack up. I'll tell you while we pack. We got to get gone from here, people. Them Blackfeet'll be back. Bet on that. Get busy. Move." Preacher began rolling his blankets. He said, "Each tribe has several warrior societies. These here Blackfeet are in the middle society. That's reserved for young men between the age of nineteen and twenty-three. They're called Mosquitoes. The one they're in before that is called the Doves. Them's all boys between fifteen and eighteen. That's how they learn to be warriors. These bucks got so excited about attackin' us, they forgot their teachin's."

Preacher started saddling up, leaving the others to finish packing.

"How far do we ride tonight?" Melody asked. "I'm really very tired."

"I don't know that I *can* ride," Richard said.

"You'll ride. And you'll all ride just as far as we dare push it," Preacher told the group. "Unless you'd rather be dead. People, I don't think this was just a chance attack. Something's got the Blackfeet all riled up and they're on the warpath. We all best close up the distance 'tween us and the fort. Now stop flappin' your gums and get to work. I got things to do myself that might buy us some time."

Preacher went to work dragging all the bodies to the center of the camp and lined them up neatly. He put their war axes on their chests and tidied up as best he could.

"Whatever in the world are you doing?" Richard asked, eyeballing the work.

"Showin' them Blackfeet that'll shore come back here this night that these here bucks fought bravely and we all respect them for it. We'll leave the rabbits cookin' on the spit and some of the supplies we got left we'll set out for them. I'll arrange it so's they'll know it's an offerin'. Injuns set a mighty lot of store by that. It might not help us, but then again, it might. You just never can tell about Injuns. It's best to cover all your bets out here."

He looked at the fat rabbit cooking on the spit. Preacher smiled and reached out and tore off a hunk and popped it into his mouth. He chewed thoughtfully for a moment. "We don't want them to think we're too respectful, though."

9

When they finally stopped and made a cold camp, Preacher figured it was about near midnight. And he had him a group of tired, butt-weary pilgrims. They were all asleep moments after crawling into their blankets.

Preacher checked his pistols and his Hawken and wrapped up in his buffalo robe, his back to a tree. He would sleep there, and sleep very lightly. Just before he closed his eyes, Preacher reminded himself that he'd better stock up on copper caps for his rifle at Fort Hall.

He slept well, but lightly, and was up long before the others. He made a small fire and used up the last of their coffee. With the distance they'd traveled during the night, Preacher figured to see the walled stockade called Fort Hall by late that afternoon.

Providing the Blackfeet didn't make another appearance.

Richard rolled out of his blankets and joined Preacher by the small fire. "Not far now, right, Preacher?"

"As the crow flies, just about two hours. It'll take us eight or ten. Did I teach y'all anything out here, Richard?"

Richard smiled and poured a tin cup full of coffee. "More than any of the others will probably ever admit. At least to you. This is the last of the coffee?"

"That's it. Enough for everyone to have a cup and then some. We're sitting right on the western slope of the Blackfoot Mountains. The Snake makes a big curve not too far ahead. We'll cross it and then about ten miles further, they's a crick where the ladies can bathe and get all gussied up. I know a spot where they's plenty of privacy. After that, it's the fort."

Richard studied the man for a moment, peering at him over the rim of his cup. "You'll be glad to be rid of us, won't you, Preacher?"

The mountain man sighed. "Tell the truth, yeah, I will. We been lucky, missionary. I can't tell you just how lucky we've been. Y'all must have God ridin' on your shoulders. This ain't no place for pilgrims."

"Maybe God sent you to us?" Richard suggested.

"Doubtful," Preacher said with a shake of his shaggy head. "I ain't set foot in a church in nigh on twenty-five years."

"Of course you have, Preacher. All this," he waved a hand at the lonesome splendor, "is God's work. His cathedral. My word, but I can feel His presence out here more strongly than I ever experienced it in my life."

"Are you a minister?"

"Yes, but not a practicing one. I graduated seminary. But administration is my field. Edmond is the one who was called."

"How much money are you carryin', Richard?"

"We're each carrying several thousand dollars."

Preacher whistled softly. "That's a fortune. Don't let no one on the train know you're totin' that much. But now you're gonna have to use some of it to get outfitted. You know that, don't you?"

"We have a fund for that purpose. Don't worry."

"I'll help you choose the mules, if they got any at the fort. Some folks prefer oxen, but I'll take a big red over an ox any day. It'll be easier goin' for y'all over the others. You ain't tryin' to haul no heavy family heirlooms. As I'm sure you seen comin' out here, the trail is littered with possessions folks tried to bring along and was forced to leave along the way. Once you leave the fort, Richard, y'all is on your own. They's damn little 'tween here and the blue water. Miles and miles of nothin' but wilderness and Injuns and bears and puma and danger. But you folks has toughened up considerable. You'll make it, I'm thinkin'."

"After we leave the fort, how far to the next settlement?"

"Fort Vancouver, 'less they's others built that I don't know about. Long, long way. I keep hearin' 'bout a mission of some sort that was built up near where the Snake and Columbia meet. In the Blue Mountains. But I ain't talked to nobody yet that's been there and seen it. So don't count on it."

The others began rising stiffly from their blankets, and Preacher noted with some amusement that they were a bedraggled-looking bunch. A lot of the haughtiness had been drained right out of them. The wilderness can do that to folks who try to fight it. You can't fight the wilderness. You got to work with it. You got to know the rules and stick by them. But men and women and whole families was pushin' west, and they was bringin' their civilized Eastern ideas out into the wilderness. That's why so many people was already buried alongside what was being called the Oregon Trail.

And they'd be hundreds, maybe thousands more buried along the way 'fore it was all said and done, Preacher figured.

Preacher noticed that the hands of the ladies was all cut and dirty and the nails broken. But that was all right, it showed the females had toughened and that's what it took to make it out here. And they'd get tougher 'fore they reached Oregon Territory. They'd either get tougher mentally and physically, or they'd die—and that was all there was to it.

Preacher watched as the ladies poured coffee and sat down quite unladylike by the fire. They just plopped down on their rear ends. He hid his smile as Penelope reached out and tore off a leg from one of the rabbits he'd snared during the night and was now cooking over the fire. It wasn't quite done, but she didn't seem to pay that no mind.

Melody, too, ripped off a hunk of meat and fell to gnawing, eating with her fingers. Even prissy-pants Edmond was eating with his fingers just like he'd been doin' it all his life and it was the natural thing to do. And maybe it was, Preacher thought. None of us was that far removed from the dog-eat-dog ways of our ancestors, and it sure didn't take a body long to fall back on those ways.

He'd miss these folks; he admitted that to his mind. It had been right pleasant to have folks to palaver with—at least part of the time. And Preacher was some sorry he hadn't taken Melody into the blankets for a night or two. But that would have only complicated things and he'd probably have never gotten shut of her if he'd done that.

She'd make someone a good wife; but that someone would not be Preacher.

She lifted her blues and looked at him across the fire. She reached out and cut off a hunk of meat and offered it to him. He nodded his thanks and took the offering.

Preacher ate the rabbit and then abruptly left the fire and walked to his horses, holding the bit of his good riding horse under his coat to warm it 'fore he tried to put it in Hammer's mouth. How'd you like to have an ice-cold hunk of steel jammed into your mouth?

He spoke to his horses for a moment, then saddled up Hammer and fixed the frame on his pack horse. He glanced back at the forlorn-looking group. "Fifteen minutes, people. Then we ride."

The day turned warm and pleasant, the miles passed quickly and uneventfully, and by the time Preacher led the group up to the creek several miles from the fort, he figured the water would be plenty warm enough for a bath. For the others, not for him.

"Y'all go on," he told them. "I'll stand watch."

Before the women did anything, they shook out their dresses and hung them up on bushes to get some of the wrinkles out. Then they peeled right down to the skin and hit the water, rag and soap in hand.

Preacher hadn't heard such gigglin' and carryin' on in his life. Richard and Edmond wasn't no better. They was duckin' and dunkin' each other and altogether the whole bunch was actin' like a gaggle of schoolkids.

Be a hell of a time for a bunch of Blackfeet or Arapaho to show up.

The pilgrims showed up about forty-five minutes later lookin' a whole hell of a lot better than the last time Preacher had seen them. The men was all duded out in suits and white shirts and ties and the women was gussied up to the nines. Then damned if the men didn't grunt and strain and work to arrange the women proper on the saddle, with one leg hooked around the horn.

"Ain't that uncomfortable?" Preacher asked.

"I will not ride into the fort astride this mount like some common whore," Penelope said.

"Nor will I," Melody echoed.

"If we have to make a run for it, y'all are gonna fall off smack on your behinies," Preacher told them.

"We shall cross that river when, or if, the need arises," Penelope informed him.

"Oh, my God!" Preacher pointed, jumped about a foot off the ground, let out a wild whoop and ran for his horse. "Injuns!" he squalled.

Penelope and Melody jerked up their skirts and undercoats—exposing some right shapely ankles and knees and a lot of milky white skin that was further up and wasn't never seen by no man—and was astride their horses before Preacher could reach Hammer. Preacher lay down on the ground and kicked his feet up in the air and hoo-hawed with laughter.

"Fooled you!" Preacher said, wiping the tears from his eyes. "That was a right good sight to see, ladies."

"You, sir, are no gentleman!" Penelope said.

"Eh, eh, eh," Preacher chuckled, getting to his feet. "No, I reckon I ain't. I been called a lot of things, but never no gentleman. I . . ." He looked up the little valley. "Oh, *shit!*" he hollered, leaping onto Hammer's back. "Come on, people, rake them cayuses! Here comes a whole passel of Injuns. Move, dammit, this ain't no joke."

"Now, see here, sir!" Edmond protested. "I must insist that this sophomoric behavior you are displaying cease immediately. It's crude and disgusting. You are frightening the ladies and I—" He looked behind him as a wild savage yell reached his years. His eyes widened. "Son of a bitch!" the missionary bellowed, and kicked his pony in the slats.

About a hundred braves were thundering toward the creek, their war cries and the pounding of hooves filling the warm spring air.

"Stay on the trail!" Preacher hollered. "It'll lead you straight to the fort." He made sure the others were ahead of him and wheeled Hammer, cocking his Hawken and bringing it to his shoulder. He compensated for the distance and squeezed off a round. The ball struck a lead rider and knocked him off his pony and under the hooves of the other hard-running horses. If he wasn't dead when he hit the ground, the hooves finished him.

Preacher gave Hammer his head and the horse took off like shot from a cannon. Hammer didn't like the sound of those wild screamin' Injuns no better than Preacher. And the pack horse, light-loaded now, after weeks on the trail, was keeping up all his own. He didn't like what was coming up behind him either.

Preacher tied the reins on the horn, turned in the saddle, and pulled his other Hawken from the boot, booting the empty rifle. "Give me a nice steady run, old hoss," Preacher said, "So's I'll know when to pull this trigger."

The horse seemed to understand and steadied down.

Preacher let the muzzle wag up and down a few times, to get the rhythm of it, then fired.

He hit a horse right in the head and the animal dropped, creating the biggest pile-up Preacher had seen in many a year. "Sorry, hoss," Preacher muttered. "I musta lost the rhythm."

He turned around in the saddle, but not before he saw a dozen or more Injuns all crippled up and sprawled around both sides of the trail after their mounts piled up.

"The fort!" he heard Edmond shout, after a couple of miles of hard riding.

Preacher put the reins in his teeth and pulled out both .50 caliber pistols and let them bang to warn those in the fort that trouble was coming hard on the hoof.

The gates swung open and they were inside.

"Yee-haw!" Preacher heard the call just as he was jumping from his horse. He grinned and turned around to face a grizzled mountain man, looking to be much older than he was.

A huge bear-like man, dressed all in skins and fur, lumbered toward Preacher. "Preacher, you old hoss, you! You bring all this trouble down on us?"

The defenders of the fort—more civilians than soldiers—were on the ramparts, blasting away at the attacking Indians. Most of the Indians were armed only with bows and arrows and the guns of the defenders were swiftly driving them back. But all knew that come the night, it would be a much different story, for the Indian was a master at stealth.

"Wagh!" Preacher shouted. "Greybull, you old bear, you. How come you ain't down on the Popo Agie?"

The two men bear-hugged each other while the pilgrims looked on. The battle raged around them and these two were behaving as if nothing were happening.

Greybull held Preacher at arm's length. "Did you find these poor lost children in the woods?" he asked, glancing at the four missionaries.

"Wagon train attack over crost the Tetons," Preacher said. "The Good Lord delivered them into my hands."

Greybull glanced at the nattily dressed men. "You shoulda throwed 'em back. What are they?"

"We are under attack, gentlemen!" an Army officer shouted at the men. "We must defend this post."

"Aw, keep your britches on," Greybull told the young man. "This ain't nothin'. Wait 'til the night comes. Then you'll see trouble lookin' you in the face."

"Wild Indians do not attack at night," the young officer said.

Greybull and Preacher grinned at each other. "He's new out here," Greybull explained. "He knows ever'thing there is to know 'bout Injuns. Just ask him. He gradeeated from Sandhurst."

"Do tell. What's a Sandhurst?"

"Some fancy soldier school. Teach 'em how to walk nice and give orders in a military manner."

"I say, sir," Richard butted in. "My companions and I survived an attack on our wagon train. We—"

"What happened to your ear, sir?" the officer asked.

"Injuns cut it off," Preacher told him. "He was defenden' the honor of these ladies here."

"Oh, I say now," the officer beamed. "That was gallant of you, sir. I'll have the post surgeon take a look at it."

"No need," Preacher told him. "It's all healed up now. I fixed it good."

"Indians are breaking off, sir!" a soldier yelled from a lookout tower. "They're fleeing."

"Fleein'?" Greybull asked.

"They'll be back come the night," Preacher told the young officer. "Mighty young soldiers boys," he remarked, looking all around him. "Why, there ain't a one of them dry behind the ears."

"The Injuns are fleein'?" Greybull muttered.

Penelope batted her eyes at the young officer and he about melted down into his boots.

"Where's the regular Army?" Preacher asked. "Hell, these ain't nothin' but kids!"

"We are British troops, sir," the officer said. "And I am in command. Lieutenant Jefferson Maxwell-Smith at your service. The troops who were garrisoned here were transferred west to Oregon Territory."

"Any of you even been in a war?" Preacher asked.

"Only a few minor skirmishes like the one we just repelled, sir."

"You didn't re-pell nothin', boy. Them Injuns'll be back come the night. You best double the guards and keep a sharp eye out, or they'll be comin' over these walls."

"Indians do not attack at night, sir." Jefferson Maxwell-Smith stood his ground.

"You in for a big damn surprise, boy," Preacher told him. "Whether they attack at night depends on en-tarly on how they feel their medicine is workin'. If they medicine is good, they'll attack."

"You are wrong, sir."

"They flee-ed," Greybull said. "The Injuns flee-ed. I got to 'member that. Tell Dupre about how the Injuns flee-ed."

"Incredible!" Maxwell-Smith said, looking at the huge mountain man.

"They gonna be fleein' back here in about three, four hours," Preacher said. "Come on, Greybull, let's us flee over yonder to the sutler's store for a drink of whiskey."

"Shore won't be time for drinkin' tonight," Greybull said. "Not once them Injuns flee back at us."

"Come, ladies," the lieutenant said to Penelope and Melody. "Let's see about making your comfortable in quarters. I assure you, you are quite safe here. The savages have gone and will not return."

"They flee-ed," Greybull said.

"Yeah," Preacher said. "Right over that damn hill yonder to make more medicine."

10

At the sulter's store, a dark and crowded low-beamed building, the men each ordered a cup of whiskey and settled down at a table.

"So how you been, Preacher?" Greybull asked. "I ain't put eyes on you . . . how long? Two years?"

"Sounds about right. I think it was over on the Powder, wasn't it?"

"I believe so. 'Bout the time Lazy Bob got scalped by them renegades of Red Hand."

Preacher drank his whiskey down and chuckled. "They jerked Lazy Bob's hair off his head so fast they didn't even check to see if he was dead. He run into Red Hand 'bout a year later and scared that Injun so bad Red Hand turned around and run screamin' off into the woods."

Preacher got Greybull another cup of snake-head whiskey and sipped on his first one. "Bring me up to date on the Injuns' uprisin'."

"Don't nobody seem to know what kicked it off, but the Blackfeet is damn shore on the warpath. We got three wagon trains backed up here and the wagon masters done quit on two of them. The one bossin' the third one is about to quit. One train already tried to get through this spring. Didn't none of them make it. I led the party out to what was left of it. Turrible sight to see."

"You scoutin' for the Army now?"

Greybull shrugged his massive shoulders. "Got to do somethin'. Beaver's about gone. I noticed your packhorse ain't carryin' no heavy load of pelts."

"Shore ain't," Preacher said morosely, looking down into his cup. "You like scout work?"

"It beats starvin' to death."

"I reckon."

"What you plannin' on doin', Preacher?"

"I ain't made up my mind. But I ain't gonna work for that damn kid lieutenant bossin' this garrison. Greybull, that youngster ain't got no sense."

"He's got some growin' up to do, fer a fact. And out here, he'll either do it quick, or get dead."

"Yeah. But how many others is gonna get kilt with him?"

There were a lot of Flathead Indians and some Mandans living close to the fort, but they had long since been tamed and posed no threat to anyone. The Methodist church had sent missionaries several years back, in April of '34, with Nat Wyeth's second expedition. The mission of the church was to find the Flathead Indians and to live with them and wrest the heathen nation from the clutches of Satan. It had proved to be a major undertaking.

Preacher knew several of the Flatheads and squatted down to palaver with them about the Blackfoot uprising. Both the Flatheads and the Nez Perce were, for the most part, friendly to the white man, and neither tribe cared for the warlike Blackfeet.

"It will be very bad before it is better," a Flathead told Preacher. "The young man directing the soldiers is brave, but foolish."

"We agree on that," Preacher told him.

"The Blackfoot say they are going to drive the Bostons out of this area."

Both the Nez Perce and the Flatheads called the trappers and mountain men Bostons, since many of the pelts were sold to Boston-based companies.

"They ain't done it yet."

Preacher walked the sturdy walls of the fort, and they were stoutly constructed. That was due to the efforts of one Nathaniel J. Wyeth, who back in '34, after being treated very rudely by Fitzpatrick and Sublette (of the Rocky Mountain Fur Company), moved on to the Snake River Bottom and walled in what is called Fort Hall. The timbers were cottonwood, very close set, and stood fifteen feet high. He built bastions, a log storehouse, and many cabins. That troops were here was a surprise, for the garrisoning of troops at company forts, while not rare, was not customary.

Well, even green troops were better than nothing. Although not by much, in Preacher's mind.

He walked outside in the waning light and shook his head at the slap-doodle manner in which the wagons were placed. "Idiots," he said. "You can't tell a pilgrim nothin'." He stalked around the wagons until he found the one remaining wagonmaster and confronted the man. "Tell them pilgrims of yourn if they wanna live through the night, they'll circle their wagons, stock inside the circle, and keep weapons at the ready and a sharp lookout this night. You ought to have had sense enough to know that. How many wagon trains you ramrodded?"

"This is my first," the man said stiffly.

Preacher spat on the ground. "Then whoever hired you was a goddamned fool!" He walked back inside the fort.

He found the young lieutenant and the young man's manner had changed noticeably toward Preacher, probably due to talking with Richard and Edmond.

Preacher put a hand on the young officer's shoulder. "Son," he said, even though he was probably no more than ten or twelve years older, "I got to say this to you. You might feel hard towards me afterward, but I still got to do it. What you know about Injuns is mighty thin; 'bout as thin as frog hair. You'll learn. But that ain't helpin' you none now. Them Blackfeet's gonna be back. If their medicine is good to them, it'll be tonight. Forget all that 'bout Injuns not fightin' at night. Sometimes they do, sometimes they don't You're thinkin' war as a white man. Injuns don't think like us. Injuns think like Injuns."

"I'm . . . beginning to understand, sir. I feel rather like a fool, not listening to Greybull from the start. I'm afraid my behavior has been boorish to say the least."

"I don't know what that means. But I do know this: we got to get ready for an attack. And we ain't got a whole lot of time to get set."

"Tell me what you want done, and it shall be done."

"Fine. This is what we'll do . . ."

Preacher left the lieutenant readying his troops, while he and Greybull concentrated on the outside, where both of them intended to be when the attack came. And both of them felt an attack was not far off.

They helped hitch the teams and pull the wagons into a box, with the rear of the box against the walls of the fort. "Fill all your buckets and barrels," Preacher told the pilgrims. The Injuns will be sure to use fire arrows to set the canvas ablaze."

"Our children?" a woman asked.

"Inside the fort, if they'll go. If not, under the wagons we got in the center of this box. I can't believe y'all come all the way from the Big Muddy to here without no Injun fights."

"The wagonmasters all said we were very lucky," a pioneer stated.

Greybull shook his shaggy head. "Damn sure was that," he muttered.

Like Preacher, the mountain man was loaded down with weapons, and after the wagons were in place, he and Preacher went off into the gathering gloom of evening to find a good spot from which to fight and to check their weapons.

"The lieutenant's took a likin' to you, Preacher," Greybull said, once the two had settled down near a wall. "I bet he'd hire you on if you'd ask."

"I ain't made up my mind," Preacher said. "I ain't never worked for nobody but me in all my life. I don't know how I'd be taken' orders from fresh-faced kids."

"It ain't so bad. The lieutenant the kid replaced was a real horse's butt, though. You'd a-killed *him,* for a fact. I damn near did."

"What was his problem?"

"I just told you. He was a horse's butt."

"Oh."

"I say, gentlemen," Lieutenant Maxwell-Smith said from above them.

The mountain men looked up. The young officer was standing on the rampart looking down at them.

"Git down, Smith," Preacher told him. "Your noggin makes a dandy target all stuck up there. In case you ain't noticed, they's timber all around us. Speak through the gun slits."

"Oh. Yes. Quite right." He ducked down out of sight. "The missionaries you rescued speak highly of you, sir. But I must fill out a report concerning the wagon train attack and those ruffians following you. What is your Christian name?"

"I ain't got one. Preacher'll do just fine."

"But are you a man of the cloth?"

Greybull started giggling. "Not likely, Lou-tenant. I been knowin' him over twenty years and never knowed him to go to church yet." He scratched his head and frowned. "'Course, they ain't been no churches out here 'til recent. That might have something to do with it."

Jefferson Maxwell-Smith walked away, muttering under his breath.

"You didn't say nothin' 'bout no one followin' you, Preacher," Greybull said.

"Bum Kelley and his gang. Jack Harris has hooked up with 'em, too."

"Wagh! That no-count."

"That ain't all," Preacher told Greybull about his suspicions of Jack deliberately leading the train north so Bum and his gang could ambush it.

Greybull was thoughtful for a time. "That'd be a low thing for any man to do, Preacher. But Harris is that low, I reckon. Reckon, hell, I know he is. Yeah. It has to be like you say. Ain't no way even a fool like Jack Harris could get that far north of the trail."

Then, as night touched the wilderness around the fort and the wagons, Preacher set Greybull to chuckling when he told him about the antics in the cave.

"He's got to kill you, Preacher. Bum and all the rest of them bad apples. It's a matter of honor now. They'll never give up. And I hope you ain't forgot that Bum has been in cahoots with Red Hand and his renegades more'n one time in the past."

Preacher bit off a chew of twist he'd bought at the store. "I ain't forgot."

Both men tensed, then glanced at one another as the unnatural sound of silence settled around the fort. Nothing moved in the forest. No birds called.

"Here we go," Greybull muttered.

"I'll warn the pilgrims to get ready," Preacher said. "See if you can get some soldier boy's attention and tell them to pass the word and get set."

"Will do."

Preacher found the wagon master. "Get your people in place. The Injuns will be along shortly."

"I've never been in an Indian attack before," he admitted.

Preacher studied him closely in the faint light. The man was scared and showed it. "Where in the hell did you ever get the experience to be called a wagon master?"

The man sulled up and stuck his chin out. "I drove a freight wagon out of Pittsburgh," he said defensively. "I traveled all over Pennsylvania and Ohio. It's plenty wild back there, mister."

"Oh, I know it is," Preacher said. "I can just imagine. Injuns on the warpath at every turn of the road. Get your people ready to fight."

He got back to Greybull and made himself comfortable on the ground. "How many men's the kid got under his command?"

"Forty. All green 'ceptin' the senior sergeant. Just got to the coast by ship not six months ago. I think they come the long way around. Some of 'em still look sick."

They watched as several dark shapes flitted from stump to tree several hundred yards out.

"Workin' in close and then they'll jump us. You reckon they'll try to breech the walls?"

"That's the word I get. They gonna try to burn it down. They want the fort and the soldiers and the Bostons gone from this country. And all these wagon trains comin' in sudden really got em mad."

"Well, they better get over it. Them holy-shouters I brought in told me folks was fixin' to pour into this country like ants to honey."

"You don't say?"

"I do. Thousands of people." He shuddered at the thought. "Gonna be a lot of folks killed, too. I just can't understand how these folks come all the way from the Muddy and didn't get set upon by Injuns."

A fire arrow lit the night as it soared up and then came

down, missing a wagon by only a few feet. Several men jumped up and started to move to the flames.

"Let it burn out! Get down!" Preacher called. "Don't show yourselves. And save your powder and lead."

"Was we that stupid when we come out here, Preacher?" Greybull asked, never taking his eyes from the area in front of their position.

"No. 'Cause times was still wild where we come from. We growed up more cautious than these pilgrims. And do you know what else I learned from them soul-savers?"

"What?"

"They's people in the big cities back east puttin' crappers in their *houses!*"

"You mean like a chamber pot?"

"No. I mean like a regular room where they go to take care of business."

Greybull blinked. "You mean to tell me they shit in their house?"

"Right next to where they sleep."

"I can't believe it!"

"That's what them folks told me. I think it's disgustin'. Who'd wanna do something like that?"

"Shorely not me. Why, I never heard of nothin' like that in my life. And I bet they's some of them same people that say folks like you and me ain't civilized 'cause we live in the mountains. Tsk, tsk, tsk."

"Look sharp now, Greybull. They's workin' closer. See that stump over yonder? It wasn't there two minutes ago."

"You're right. You want the honors?"

"I believe I will." Preacher pulled his Hawken to his shoulder, took careful aim, and let her bang.

The "stump" grunted when the ball struck him. A war axe went flying up into the air and the brave fell forward and lay still.

"Here they come!" Greybull roared, and the fight was on.

11

The Indians became darting shapes in the night, utilizing every bit of cover as they worked their way closer to the fort and the wagons. So far, although two dozen shots had been fired from the defenders, Preacher was the only one to have scored a hit.

"Don't fire until you're sure of a target!" Preacher yelled. "Goddammit, save your powder and shot. This ain't St. Louis. You can't go to the store and buy more." He dropped back down beside Greybull. "Damn pilgrims anyways. I'd hate to be saddled with guidin' them fools."

Another fire arrow lanced the night and this one landed on the canvas of a wagon, igniting it almost instantly. Greybull drilled the Indian who fired the arrow and the brave doubled over, mortally wounded from the .54 caliber Hawken.

Men and women ran to put out the fire and the Indians showered them with arrows. One woman was struck in the throat and died horribly, the life gurgling out of her, and a man went down screaming with an arrow in his stomach. Children were laying under their parents' wagons, many of them screaming in fright.

"Welcome to life on the frontier, folks," Preacher muttered

without malice. "I 'spect it ain't at all like the big adventure it was painted to be."

"They're using ladders to breech the north wall!" a young soldier shouted.

"Did you tell the kitchen people to have lots of boilin' water ready?" Preacher asked his buddy.

Greybull chewed and spat. "Yep."

"Well?"

"The lieutenant said he wouldn't do nothin' like pourin' no boilin' water on folks. Said that was agin the rules of war."

"Until that boy grows up, we're gonna be in trouble, Greybull."

"Yep. Must be two, three hundred Blackfeet out yonder."

Both men were lifting their rifles to their shoulders.

"At least," Preacher said.

"Wait a minute," Greybull said, lowering his rifle. "What the hell's that chantin'?"

Preacher listened for a moment. "Them back over that ridge is singin' their death songs. But . . . why? And why the rush to attack us? Ain't none of this makin' no sense, Greybull."

From out in the darkness, far away from the light of the burning wagon, came the angry shouting voice of a Blackfoot. Greybull and Preacher listened intently to the hard words.

"My sweet Jesus," Greybull whispered. "Is he sayin' what I think I'm hearin'?"

"Yeah," Preacher told him, his words hard and grimly offered. "He damn shore is." Preacher tapped on the logs of the wall. "Can anybody hear me in yonder?" he called.

"Right here, Preacher," a trapper he knew slightly said. "I heard them words, too."

"Get to usin' an axe, Jim. Get some men choppin' and make us a space big enough to get folks through and do it quick. And get the lieutenant over here."

"Right, Preacher."

Only a few heartbeats passed before the voice of Maxwell-Smith came through the logs. "Yes, Preacher?"

"Now listen to me, Lieutenant," Preacher said, steel in his words. "I ain't gonna say this but once. Don't let no Injun come over the walls. Don't touch none of them. We got to get all these pilgrims inside the walls and keep the Injuns out. Now you get them goddamn pots filled with water and keep it hot. When they try to come over, you dump it on them. You got all that, Lieutenant?"

"I hear you, Preacher. Boiling water poured on the flesh of those poor wretches out there. But can you give me a reason for the barbaric behavior?"

"Them's their death-songs they's singin' out yonder, boy. The white man's done brought smallpox down on them. Whole villages has been wiped out. And them out yonder got it too. They want to die in battle—but not before they infect us. Now, is that good enough for you?"

"I'll get right on it," Maxwell-Smith said, his voice filled with horror.

"You do that." He turned to Greybull. "Them on the other side'll be through in two jigs. Soon as the hole's cut, I'll start workin' them pilgrims over here. We got to do this fast." He handed him his Hawken. "Little extry firepower, Greybull. I'm gone."

The wagon was almost burned down to smoldering char as preacher made his way into the knot of men and women.

"They're through!" Greybull called.

"Get to the wall," Preacher told the first bunch. "Grab what you can and run like hell. Move, people. *Move!*"

"What's the meaning of this?" the wagon master confronted him. "I give the orders out here."

"Not no more, partner," Preacher told him. "If you want to live, you do what I tell you to do."

"I don't take orders from you . . . you smelly, shaggy reprobate!"

"Then you can go right straight to hell," Preacher replied. "I ain't got the time to fart around with someone as dumb as you." He shoved the man out of the way.

The wagonmaster grabbed him by the shoulder and spun Preacher around, his fist drawed back for a blow. He never got the chance to throw it. Preacher put him on the ground, butt first, and a hard left and right to the jaw. Then he went about his business of gathering up those pioneers who would go into the fort.

And not all of them would.

"I don't believe you!" one man said. "And I'm not leaving my wagon out here for the savages to plunder and burn."

"Then stay here," Preacher said, and pushed past him. It was cold on the mountain man's part, but he was doing what he felt was necessary, and he didn't have much time. And he also knew what smallpox could do. He'd had it and survived it, as had Greybull. They'd been with some Mandans when it struck their village, and it was a horrible sight to witness.

About half of those in the wagon train chose to leave their wagons and run for the fort. Preacher held several sets of parents at pistol-point while Greybull and two young soldiers forcibly took their young children from them and ran for the fort.

"I'll see you in hell for this!" and man shouted.

"You'll be there 'fore me," Preacher told him.

Then the enraged Blackfeet struck the fort and there was no time for anything except survival as the infected and sick and dying Indians threw themselves against the thick walls of the fort. They came out of the night in silent waves of fury and hate.

The first wave was repelled by shot. On the heels of that one came another with makeshift ladders. Boiling water was poured on them and they ran shrieking into the night, burned horribly.

Those pilgrims who had refused to leave their wagons fared

not well at all. It did not take the Blackfeet long to overwhelm them, and the Indians were in no mood to take prisoners for slavery or barter.

The screaming of those being tortured played hell on the nerves of the defenders inside the fort.

"What are they doing to them?" Edmond asked nervously, standing beside Preacher on a rampart.

"Injuns can get right lively with their torture," the mountain man replied. "And if they're a mind to, they can make it last for days. Each tribe has its own favorite way of torture, and there ain't none of it very pleasant."

"What happened to the tame Indians who were living around the fort?"

"They run off 'fore the Blackfeet got here in force."

Flames from the burning wagons illuminated the night, highlighting the bodies that littered the ground around the walled fort. Moaning from the wounded mingled with the screaming of those being tortured. A man from the wagon train came stumbling out of the night, his head on fire and his hands tied behind his back. His shrieking was hideous.

Preacher lifted his Hawken and shot him dead.

"My God, man!" Edmond said.

"I put him out of his misery," Preacher said. "They'd gouged out his eyes and set his hair on fire. You ever seen a man who's brains was cooked?"

"Ah . . . no."

"It ain't a nice sight."

An arrow whizzed between them and fell to the earth on the grounds inside the walls.

"When we whup them," Preacher said, "and we will do that, eventually, we got a real problem. Those of us that's had the pox has got to go out there and burn them bodies to kill the germs. You been scratched, Edmond?"

"Yes. All of my party received the cowpox."

"Good. Y'all can help then. Hudson's Bay sent supplies of

smallpox vaccine to all its forts. The lieutenant said his people had been vaccinated."

Greybull came hunched over to them. "From what I been able to pick out of the night, the Blackfeet's lost a lot of people. Whole villages wiped out. A Mandan just slipped through and he sayin' that all along the Missouri there ain't nothin' but death. His whole tribe was wiped out. He says that folks is runnin' away from it, headin' west, and that's how it got here so fast. He says that people of his tribe is killin' themselves right and left. Said the talk is it started over at Fort Union. Brought in by someone on a keelboat."

Preacher nodded his head. "Listen to that," he said, as the chanting and singing grew louder, coming to them from out of the night. "Them Blackfeet's gone crazy. They're workin' themselves up into a killin' rage."

"Can't say as I blame them," Greybull replied. "I'd rather die quick than linger in pain for days with the pox, havin' the skin rot off me."

Edmond shuddered. "You are rather graphic in your description, sir." He paused. "A thought just occurred to me. Those savages we encountered the night before we reached the fort. Do you suppose . . . ?"

"Yeah, they probably had it, or suspected they did. But you all been vaccinated, so you ain't got nothin' to worry about. What you got to worry about is right out yonder."

The singing and chanting stopped. The sudden silence gathered all around them.

"What does that mean?" Edmond asked.

"It means they comin' straight at us," Preacher said. "Like right about now!" He lifted his Hawken and blew a hole in the chest of a running brave.

The ground on all sides of the fort was suddenly transformed into a mass of charging Blackfeet, some of them carrying makeshift ladders. They threw ladders against the log walls and began climbing up. Buckets and pots containing hot water were dumped on the Indians, scalding them. They flung themselves off the ladders, screaming in pain, running away into the night. Men were firing straight down from the ramparts, the heavy caliber rifles and pistols inflicting horrible damage on the Indians at close range. The cool night air became thick and choking with gunsmoke and the stench of death.

Although outnumbered by at least twenty to one—and probably more than that—the defenders of the fort held the high ground, so to speak, and fought savagely, once again breaking the Indian attack.

Lieutenant Maxwell-Smith made his way along the ramparts to Preacher. "While it is quiet, I am going to stand half of my men down for a rest and some tea."

"Good idea. They damn sure earned a rest," he complimented the young officer. "We just might have broken their spirit this last charge. Them Blackfeet might think their medicine has turned bad and fall back to ponder on it some."

"I'll have the men in the towers keep a sharp eye out."

Preacher watched the young man leave and said, "I think he learned something about the frontier this night."

Edmond mopped his grimy, sweaty face with a handkerchief. "I know I certainly did."

Most of those inside the fort managed to catch an hour or so of sleep that night. The Indians made no more charges against them. They settled back to harass them with arrows and an occasional gunshot, for many of them did not have rifles, and those that did were not very good shots, not having sufficient powder and shot to practice.

The sun rose to a sight of mangled bodies on all sides of the fort. More than a dozen of those men and women who had refused to leave their wagons had been stripped naked, tortured, then tied to a wagon wheel and burned alive. Even the children had been killed, a sure sign of the Indian's rage over the white man bringing his deadly diseases to them.

"I 'spect we can salvage 'bout half them wagons," Preacher opined. He glanced at Richard, looking out grim-faced at the carnage that lay before them. "Any clothing found out yonder will have to be handled careful-like, with a stick, and boiled 'fore anyone uses it."

"Yes. Have the Indians gone?"

"I don't know. I doubt it. Mad as they is, I don't 'spect they'll give up too easy." He was studying the body of a Blackfoot that lay on the ground at the base of the walled fort. "Cut his claws off," Preacher muttered, just as Greybull walked over to them. "You noticed that, Greybull?"

"What?"

"Them Blackfeet done cut their claws off 'fore this battle. Strange."

"Claws?" Richard asked. "Claws? Like in animal claws?"

"Thumbnails," Preacher explained. "Blackfeet men let their thumbnails grow until they crook like a claw. Something else, too. See them dead ponies out yonder? Look at the symbols painted on the necks. Them's the ponies of war party leaders. We just may have broke this bunch. They've pulled 'way back now, busy electin' new chiefs and leaders."

Preacher glanced to his left. Lieutenant Maxwell-Smith was standing silently, watching him and listening intently. The young officer had learned many things during the past twenty-four hours. One important thing was that these disreputable-looking mountain men knew what they were talking about when it came to Indians and how to fight them, and if he was going to survive out here among the savage heathens, he'd better shut his mouth and listen and learn.

"You done just fine, Lieutenant," Preacher told him.

The young officer smiled through the grime that covered his face, most of it residue from the black powder of pistols and rifles. "Thank you, Preacher. For a lot of things." He smiled again, and it made him look very, very young. "I'm afraid that Sandhurst did not adequately prepare me for life on the American frontier."

"This is a land and a people that nobody else can learn you, Lieutenant," Preacher said. "It's just so damn . . . *big* out here."

"Yes," the officer said, stepping closer and speaking quietly. "I was quite awed by the vastness of it; I still am. England pales by comparison. Although I wouldn't want the men to hear me say that."

"Let's get a report from the men in the towers," Greybull said. "Then we got to make plans about draggin' off and burnin' them bodies out yonder and roundin' up all the pioneers' stock that run off."

"We got to see who all ain't been vaccined against the pox and get the company doctor to fix 'em up."

"I'm ahead of you there, Preacher," Maxwell-Smith said. "I've already canvassed the group and the doctor is preparing to scratch people now."

"Good, good!" Preacher clasped the man on the arm, and was not surprised to find it heavily muscled. "Let's go see what the lookouts can tell us."

"They're still out there," the only senior sergeant in the garrison reported. "Over those ridges. See the faint smoke?" He pointed. "But none of us can detect any movement in the woods near the fort."

"You wouldn't be able to," Preacher said. "And I ain't castin' no doubts on your soldierin' abilities by sayin' that. Injuns is the greatest fighters and hiders and ambushers in the world. Settlers down in the southwest tell a story about an Apache who found himself out in the desert with no place to run and the army comin' hard up the trail. That Injun wasn't twenty feet from what passed for a road. Well, he just laid down on the sand and didn't move and he blended right in. Problem was he didn't figure on two patrols, back to back.

When he got up the second patrol was toppin' the rise and they shot him dead.

"Out here, be scared when you see Injuns. Be twice as scared when you *can't* see them."

Maxwell-Smith said, "It's going to be a very warm day, gentlemen."

"Yeah," Preacher said. "And them bodies is gonna bloat and stink before long. And we can't allow no buzzards in to tote that infected flesh off and spread the pox. We got to kill ever' one of 'em that lands. See 'em circling high up? They'll be comin' in for breakfast right shortly. Ever seen a buzzard a-tearin' at human flesh, Lieutenant?"

"Thankfully, no. I have yet to witness that disgusting sight."

"I have," the grizzled sergeant said. "In India. I hate the filthy buggers."

"No need for that," Preacher said. "They're just doin' what God put 'em on earth to do. They don't know no better. I don't much care for rattlers, but I don't hate 'em. Human bein's now, that's another matter. We got a brain, and God give us the power to think and reason things out. But there ain't no earthly reason for a human person to do bad things. I ain't got no use for human trash. None a-tall. I'd just as soon shoot 'em as have to look at 'em. And have, more'n once."

"Law out here in the wilderness is, ah, primitive, to say the least," Maxwell-Smith said.

Preacher cut his eyes to him. "What it is, is final."

12

By noon, the health hazard was becoming a real concern. The day had turned out unusually warm and the bodies were beginning to bloat and stink.

Not one Indian had made a sound that the defenders could hear, shown himself or fired a ball or arrow.

The defenders had stayed busy killing the buzzards that had swooped in to dine on the dead.

Finally, Preacher made up his mind. "I got to go out there," he said to Greybull.

"Either you or me," the mountain man replied. "And I think it ought to be me. I'm takin' money from the soldier boys to scout."

"It better be me. You're as big as a damn grizzly bear and as clumsy as a armadiller. You'd stumble around out yonder and them Blackfeet would be sure to catch you and I don't want to have to spend the rest of the day and night listenin' to you holler. You beller like a damn constipated hog."

"Mayhap you be partly right," the huge mountain man said. "Even if they catch you, you so damn ugly and miserable-lookin' they'd prob'ly feel sorry for you and run you off 'fore you frightened their horses and caused their wimmin to go barren."

"You can make yourself useful whilst I'm gone by gatherin' up some ropes and gettin' ready to drag them bodies off aways so's we can burn them. I know if I don't tell you what to do, after I'm gone you'd just sit around lookin' like a fat dumb child and do nothing."

"Them Injuns is over that ridge, Preacher," Greybull pointed and continued the insults. "That's south. As foolish as you are 'bout directions, I want you keep that double-humped ridge to your skinny rear end at all times. That way you might find your way back here by this time next week."

"Thankee kindly for the consideration. It's nice to know somebody cares."

"Oh, I don't care a twit for you," Greybull told him. "I'm just tryin' to keep you alive long enough so's you'll pay me that fifteen dollars you borrowed from me ten year ago over on the Platte."

"It was more like two dollars and it was on the Missouri, you ox. And I paid you back at the rendezvous the next year. You was so drunk you don't 'member."

"Git outta here 'fore I throw you over the damn walls!"

The mountain men grinned at each other, for the moment satisfied with their insults. Preacher checked his pistols and his Hawken and dropped down from the ramparts, walking over to Lieutenant Maxwell-Smith.

"I'm goin' out yonder to eyeball the situation," he told the officer. "I got me a hunch the Blackfeet's done pulled out, figurin' their medicine is bad for this fight."

"I thought the savages always returned for their dead?"

"They usual do. But in this case, they probably got so many dead and dyin' all around them they just don't care no more. There ain't enough livin' to take care of the dead. We'll see. I'll be back." Preacher wheeled about and walked to the rear of the post. The other trapper, Jim, wounded in the shoulder by an arrow, lay on a pallet near the rear gate.

"How's your wing?" Preacher asked him, squatting down beside the man.

"Pains some. But I been hurt worser. If the Injun who handled that arrow had the pox, I reckon the infection was on the point."

"Probably. You been scratched with vaccine?"

"Last year. Made me sicker than shit, too."

"I do know the feelin'. I wintered with the pox some years back. You heard anything movin' out back?"

"No. And I been listenin' careful and peeking out through the logs, time to time. Ain't seen nothin', neither. I think they's gone, Preacher."

"Me, too. I'm goin' out for an eyeballin'."

"You watch your topknot out there, boy. These Blackfeet don't care no more."

"I gleaned that right off. See you."

"Don't step on that damn stinkin' swole-up body layin' next to the logs. It might blow up."

Preacher cracked the gate and squatted for a time, moving only his eyes, searching the hills and timber very carefully. The dead Blackfoot by the gate was all puffed up and smelled really bad. From the looks of him, he'd taken a full vat of boiling water and it cooked him proper. He had died hard, but not as hard as lingerin' at death's door with the pox.

Preacher dashed out and made the timber. There, he squatted down and listened just as hard as he looked. In the distance, the birds had returned and were singing. That was a good sign. He worked his way up a ridge, moving carefully. He almost stepped on the body of a pilgrim the Injuns had dragged off and tortured. Looked like they had kept him alive for several hours while they had their fun. From the looks of him, the pilgrim didn't appear like he'd thought it a damn bit funny.

Preacher stepped over him and moved on to the crest of the ridge. He found another body there. It was an eastern woman and she'd been used hard 'fore they cut her throat and scalped her bare. She'd been a blonde, and that was a much sought-after trophy for a war lance.

She lay on her back, bare legs spread wide, her eyes open and bugged out in shocked death. Preacher tried to close her eyes but the lids were stiff and would not close. He gave up and moved on.

He came upon a Blackfoot, badly wounded and dying. The brave was so weak he could not lift his war axe at Preacher's approach. The Blackfoot cursed Preacher, heaping great insults on Preacher and his entire family, including his horses, his dogs, and his bastard children, if any.

"Left you here to die, did they?" Preacher asked, when the brave ran out of steam.

The Blackfoot curled his lip and snarled at Preacher.

"No need to feel hard at me," Preacher told him. "I didn't shoot you. If I'd shot you you'd be dead."

"Finish it," the brave gasped, speaking English.

"All right," Preacher said, and bashed him on the head with the butt of his Hawken.

It was done with no malice. If Preacher had been found bellyshot as bad as the brave, with his guts hangin' out the hole in his back, knowin' there was no hope, he'd want someone to do the same to him. Preacher was a lot of things; mainly he was a realist.

He stayed in the timber and brush, moving carefully and silently, and skirting a little meadow, he worked his way up another ridge.

The sight before him brought him up short.

Row after row of dead or dying Indians lay in the shallow meadow. Preacher squatted down by a tree and eyeballed the gruesome sight. He had never seen anything like it in all his years. There must have been five hundred or more Blackfeet all laid out in rows, most of them dead. But Preacher knew the defenders of the fort hadn't killed near that many. Most of the dead and dying had just been too weak to go on; they'd used up everything they had during the night fighting and staggered back to this place to die. Probably the place had been all picked out beforehand.

Damnest thing he'd ever seen.

He made his way back to the fort and hailed the front gate. "Preacher!" he called. "I'm comin' in. Lieutenant, you got to see this sight. It's something you can tell your grandbabies about, for sure."

Lieutenant Maxwell-Smith took ten men with him, leaving the senior sergeant commanding those troops back at the fort. Greybull walked with Preacher back to the little valley of death.

Maxwell-Smith removed his tunic and laid it over the body of the raped and dead woman.

"Dumb move," Preacher told him.

"What do you mean, sir?" the young officer said, his eyes flashing. One simply did not say something like that to an officer in front of his men.

"She'd been hopped on half the night by Injuns dyin' with the pox. Pox germ stays alive a long time, so I'm told. Now you got to fetch your jacket back with a stick and boil it out good 'fore you even think about puttin' it back on." Preacher turned his back to him and walked on.

Maxwell-Smith arched one eyebrow and slowly smiled very ruefully, indeed. "Yes. Quite right. Come on, men," he said to his troops.

They stood on the crest and looked down into the small valley. "Incredible," one of the enlisted men said.

"We best start gathering up brush and pile it on the bodies Preacher said. "Greybull, you want to take a couple of the men and start some backfires so's we don't set the whole damn forest ablazin'?"

"I'll do 'er."

"Some of those savages are still alive out there," Maxwell-Smith pointed out.

"They won't be for long," Preacher told him.

"Preacher," the officer said softly. "I won't permit you to burn people alive."

Preacher stared at the man for a moment. "I was plannin' on shootin' the ones near death, Smith. Believe me when I tell you they'd want it that way."

"I won't permit that either."

"You ever seen pox close up, Smith? The flesh rots. Go down there and take a good look."

There was anguish in the young officer's eyes. This was a decision that no man should be forced to make; Lieutenant Jefferson Maxwell-Smith was going to have to make it. And do it quickly, for the stench from the little valley was already getting strong.

"Do what you think is right," Preacher finally told him, after several moments of silence, while the two men stared at one another. Neither of them had blinked. "I'll leave Greybull here with you and I'll go back to the fort and start burnin' the bodies back yonder. Just 'member this: you been scratched, but that don't mean you can't catch you a small dose of the pox. You work careful, now, you hear?"

"I hear you, Preacher," Maxwell-Smith said, his tone low.

Preacher went back to the fort and organized volunteers to help drag off and burn the bodies of the dead. They tied rags around their mouths and pulled on gloves. Those that did not have gloves wrapped rags around their hands in an attempt to avoid flesh contact with the dead.

Those at the fort would not know it until months later, but this epidemic of smallpox killed nearly two thousand Mandan and nearly six thousand members of the Blackfoot tribe. The Blackfoot's power on the plains was greatly reduced and they were never again the power they once were. From the Missouri River westwood, thousands of Indians died from the white man's disease. In the year 1837, doctors were aware that injections of the cowpox virus would immunize people against smallpox. The Hudson's Bay Company had sent great amounts of smallpox vaccine to its traders, and many Indians were saved because of that vaccine. Most of the Indians who refused to be inoculated died.

At the fort, Preacher and the others worked swiftly to drag off the bodies of the dead and burn them, while others stood guard, attempting to frighten away, or as was usually the case, killing the many buzzards that angrily fought to tear and rip at the dead and bloated and infected flesh.

Women kept huge vats of water boiling constantly, for every bit of clothing had to be boiled and sterilized. The smallpox virus could survive for months in the most unlikely of places. Knowing that, nothing could be left to chance.

Before the epidemic would run its course, entire tribes would be wiped out, or very nearly so. Some of the Indians attempted to combat the disease by rolling in fire, giving everything they had to medicine men, taking sweat baths. Many killed their own families in desperation, killed their horses, and killed themselves by the most gruesome of methods, often shoving arrows, knives, or other sharp objects down their throats. Of the Mandans, only a handful survived. All in all, more than fifteen thousand Indians would die. That is more than would die fighting the Army and the settlers during the rest of the century, before the western frontier was finally tamed.

It was a grim-faced, haggard and haunted-eyed young British officer, who, along with his men, dragged back into the fort just before dusk. Preacher did not ask him what he had done back in the valley of death. He did not have to. He had heard the shots and seen the smoke.

"Bad," Greybull told Preacher. "That boy growed up a whole lot this day."

"So did the pilgrims," Preacher replied. "It's been tough on them buryin' them folks they come westward with. It's been hard on me buryin' the young children them foolish parents kept out of the fort. But I can't get the thought outta my head that they's a lot of grievin' Injun mommas and daddies that it's just as tough on."

"It's gonna be a terrible thing when the whites really get to crowdin' in this country," Greybull opined. "It's got to the point now where a man can't hardly ride four or five days without seein' a white family. I tell you, Preacher, the ruination of the high country is fast comin' on us.

"Makes a man just wanna sit down with a jug of good rye whiskey and get drunk, don't it?"

"That might not be a bad idea."

"They's a small problem, Greybull. 'Cause they ain't no more whiskey to be had here at the fort."

"What?"

"It's true. The company doctor used it all easin' the pain of them that got wounded."

"That's disgustin'!"

"But true."

Several rather matronly-looking ladies marched up to the two mountain men and stood glaring at them, hands on hips. "Into the fort," one told them.

"Go waggle your bustle and flap your mouth somewheres else," Preacher told them.

One of the ladies, just about the same size as Greybull, grabbed him by one ear and marched him off toward the front gate, with Greybull hollering and bellering loud enough to wake the dead.

"Don't crowd me," Preacher warned the group, which was growing in number.

"Get in there and strip down to the buff," another of the ladies told Preacher. "We got fresh hot water and lots of soap waiting for you."

"I'll take my bath in private, thankee," Preacher told her. "Now be off with you."

"Move," she told him.

Preacher noticed there was a wicked look in her eyes. He really got nervous when Melody appeared in the group, holding a towel and a bar of strong lye soap. She smiled at him.

"Git away from me," Preacher warned them all.

About nine hundred pounds of determined female, and in most cases, dubious pulchritude moved closer.

"You're a rake and a reprobate," one lady told him. "And most likely those terms are mild, but you are going to take a bath, and take it now."

"You'll play hell givin' me one."

Four of the larger ladies moved in and grabbed him by legs and arms and bodily lifted him off the ground and toted him inside the walls of the fort.

"Unhand me, goddammit!" Preacher roared.

"Right down to the buff," Melody said, then started laughing.

13

"Them women took my damn clothes!" Greybull roared as he sat in a wooden tub filled with hot water. The water had already turned black. "I ain't got nary a stitch on."

"Well, what the hell do you think they done to me!" Preacher bellered. "I ain't sittin' in this tub with no suit of clothes on myself."

"That big fat one wanted to know if I needed some help in awashin' myself! Damn women is shore gettin' pushy nowadays. Next thing you know they'll have the vote, too!"

"That'll never happen," Preacher said, finding the bar of soap and working up a lather.

Melody walked up behind him and dumped a bucket of hot water on his head. Preacher jumped up with a roar.

Melody eyeballed him from knees to neck. "My, my!" she said approvingly.

"You brazen hussy!" Preacher hollered. "You 'bout as much a missionary as I is President of the U-nited States."

Laughing, she strolled away, humming and swinging the bucket. Among other things.

"That women's got her bonnet cocked your way, Preacher," Greybull warned. "You bes' make tracks quicker'n a 'coon can wash his supper. At least as soon as you get your clothes back. And sit down. You ain't no sight to behold in your altogether."

When a nearby gaggle of women started pointing at him and giggling, Preacher sat back down in the tub. He was red with embarrassment from his nose to his toes.

"I reckon I was some dirty," Greybull said, looking down at the dark water which had dead fleas floating in it. Lye soap was hell on bugs.

"I ain't never knowed you when you wasn't."

"Preacher?"

"What?"

"When I come out here, feller by the name of Jim Madison was President. Who is now, you reckon?"

"Last I heard, when I was in St. Louis four or five winters ago, it was a man name of Jackson. I reckon he still is. But I can't rightly say."

"That woman that's got her eye on you—she really a missionary?"

"I don't much think so. I never seen no Bible-thumper that sassy. Where in the hell is our clothes?"

"The burned 'em," Greybull said mournfully.

"Burned 'em! Why didn't they just boil 'em good? I ain't had them clothes on more'n a month."

"I'd had them skins of mine on considerable more than that," Greybull admitted. "I reckon they was kinda greasy. You feel all right, Preacher?"

"Oh, hell, yes, Bull. I'm fine. I'm sittin' here nekked as a jaybird, a gaggle of females done burned my clothes, and a half-crazy woman is makin' improper advances toward me. I never felt better."

"That ain't what I meant."

"Oh. Yeah, I'm all right. I wasn't even scratched the last time I was around the pox and I didn't catch it. I reckon oncest you got it two or three times you can't take it no more.

I just want to get gone from this place. If you got any sense, you'll come with me."

"I made my mark on a company paper. I signed on to scout for the Army. I think the lieutenant is gonna ask you to help out with the wagon train, Preacher. That foolish wagonmaster was kilt last night."

"The lieutenant can go kiss a buffalo. Lord God in heaven and all his angels, man! You think I wanna lead them pilgrim-people through the wilderness? Do I look like an Israelite? I'd be a stark ravin' lunatic 'fore we got there." Preacher threw back is head and roared, "Where's my gawddamn clothes?"

The trapper with the busted shoulder had a brand new set of buckskins a Mandan woman had made for him. He gladly gave them to Preacher to shut him up. Said all that bellerin' was causin' his shoulder to ache.

Preacher, clean from the top of his head to his toes, thought he'd best save the skins for the trail. He put on some home-spuns the ladies gave him to wear for what time he would remain in the fort. And that wasn't going to be very long if Preacher had anything to say about it.

Everybody was breathing as shallowly as possible, for the stench of death was still very strong around the fort. Workers kept the funeral fires blazing throughout the night. Lieutenant Maxwell-Smith and the sergeant stayed busy recording the names of the pioneers who died in the fight, and any addresses of relatives back east.

The next day, Preacher and Greybull went out to gather up the loose stock and drive them back to the fort, while the survivors set about trying to piece together wagons from the wreckage. Of the more than fifty odd wagons that had been gathered around the fort, the men managed to put together twenty wagons that looked like they might be able to stand the trek westward to Oregon Territory.

Maxwell-Smith called Preacher into his office and asked him to have a chair.

"Don't want one," Preacher said with a straight face. "Ain't got no reason to tote one around."

"Sit, sir!"

Preacher sat.

"Tea?" Maxwell-Smith offered.

"Whiskey'd be better. But I reckon coffee will do. I ain't never developed no real taste for tea."

"As you wish." The officer asked his orderly to bring them refreshments. He and Preacher sat and stared at one another until the coffee was poured and the tea was steeping.

"What you got on your mind, Lieutenant?"

"You are aware, sir, that you are in British-held territory."

"The land's in dispute. I reckon it'll soon be in American hands."

"Don't count on that, sir. You colonists might have a fight on your hands."

"Y'all tried that a couple of times, as I recall. Seems like you'd learn after awhile."

The lieutenant's smile was very thin, indeed. "Be that as it may, sir, I am in command here. Solely in command. I give the orders, to both civilian and military personnel who are at this fort."

Preacher stood up. "I'll be gone 'fore you can blink."

"Preacher, sit down, please."

Preacher sat.

"I need your help, Preacher."

"I ain't guidin' no damn wagon train."

Maxwell-Smith leaned back in his chair and smiled. "I can promise you more pay than any guide ever received before you."

Preacher slowly shook is head. "I ain't got no use for riches. What am I gonna spent 'em on? Hell, man, I know where they's gold nuggets big as your toe. I got a sackful out there in my possibles bag. They's enough gold in that bag to last me the rest of my years. I ain't got the patience to guide no bunch of hollerin', squallin' runny-noised kids and whinin' complainin' women, and foolish men. You got Greybull on the payroll. Give the job to him."

"We have to keep him here. What is that man's Christian name?"

"I ain't got no idea. He got his name cause he nearly drowned in the Greybull just west of the Bighorns."

"I beg your pardon?"

"Twenty year or more ago. 'Round '15 or '16, I think it was. He got drunk and fell off his horse. He's been called Greybull ever since. Names ain't very important out here, Lieutenant. It's what's inside a man that counts."

"By that you mean personal courage, the keeping of one's word when given, never shirking one's duty, and of course, helping those in need." The last was spoken with a slight smile.

"Ah . . . yeah, something like that." Preacher had the feeling he was being pushed into a box canyon. This young officer might not know doodly-squat about the wilderness, but he sure was good with words.

"*I* am in need, Preacher. Those poor pioneers out there are in need."

Preacher held up a hand. "Whoa, now. Just back up. I didn't tell them folks out yonder to head west. They done that all by theyself. Didn't nobody force them to do nothin'. Them folks ain't my responsibility. And the truth be known, they ain't yours, neither."

"So you would just have me send them off westward, into a large unexplored land that is fraught with danger. A land that no man knows—"

"I know the damn country!" Preacher exploded. "Unexplored? Why hell, they's been trappers and traders and the like all over that country for years now. Why I—" He closed his mouth. *Just diggin' your hold deeper ever' time you flap your gums,* he thought.

"Precisely, Preacher!" Maxwell-Smith said. *"You* know the country they have to travel through. You're the best. You're a legend, Preacher. I marveled about your exploits in England. You—"

"All right!" Preacher said. "That's enough grease. You slop anymore lard on me and I'll be so slippery I won't be able to sit a saddle. I'll guide your damn wagon train." He shook his head. "Lord have mercy on a poor mountain boy like me."

"It's the pox!" Luke reported back to Bum. He had not entered the fort, only watched from far off and talked to some Mandans he met on the trail. "The Blackfeet took the disease and then attacked the fort. They died by the hundreds. But not 'fore they kilt more'n half of them movers and tore up a whole bunch of wagons. Them folks is busy piecin' together wagons, so they gonna keep on their journey."

"Did you see Preacher?"

"Yeah. And the missionaries. They made it through and is all right, 'pears to me. What's Red Hand say about this plan of yourn?"

"He's thinkin' about it. Gone back to his camp to talk it over with his bunch." He eyeballed Luke suspiciously. "You didn't bring nothin' back with you, did you?"

"Huh? Oh! No. I never got close enough to catch nothin'. And them Mandans I talked to had already been scratched for the pox." He looked over at the new men that had joined the group since he'd left. "I know Burke and Dipper. I figured they'd hook up with us. Who's them others?"

"Jennings and Penn rode with the Hawkins' gang up in the northern territories. They're good boys. Halsey and Wilson busted out of jail back in St. Louie in the winter. Olson's a farm boy from back east. He's wanted for murder."

"Who'd he kill?"

"His parents. I think he's a good man."

"Sounds like it. I got more news. They's another wagon train comin' in later this month. The commandin' officer at the fort sent some of his men to make sure it got in all right. They's some talk about the guide a-fixin' to quit the train. What's left of the pilgrims at the fort is gonna wait and hook up with this new train."

"Who'll be guidin' it?"

"Don't know. But Greybull's there. I seen him. Hard to miss a man his size."

"Greybull's scoutin' for the Army. I know that to be true. Trappin's about played out." Bum smiled. "Preacher. Has to be Preacher."

"Doin' what?"

"Guidin' the damn train, idiot! Ever'thing is workin' out just right. We'll get the gold, the women, and have Preacher to torture."

"So we'll just stay right here and keep low and by the time the trains link up and get ready to pull out, the boys will be healed up for the most part."

Bum looked at him. "Sometimes you can make sense, Luke. Not often. But sometimes."

Luke grinned like a fool.

Preacher carefully inspected each wagon. If he found something wrong, he ordered it fixed. From Fort Hall to Fort Vancouver was a long, hard, dangerous pull, with Indians being only a part of the problem. There were rivers and streams to cross, and many of them would be running over their banks this time of the year. There would be broken bones and sprained limbs and squabbles among the movers.

And Bum Kelley and his gang.

There would be wagon breakdowns, wheels would come loose and have to be repaired. Tongues would break and harnesses would rip. Kids would get sick and probably one or two would get lost in the woods. A couple of these silly females were pregnant and that meant they would probably birth along the trail.

And Bum Kelley and his boys would surely be cookin' up something unpleasant to spring somewheres along the way.

He would have to see that additional canvas was brought along 'cause sure as shootin' some pilgrim wouldn't have his lashed down proper and come a high wind it'd go sailin' off to China. Better lay in a stock of nails and shoes for the animals and make damn sure there was plenty of powder and shot and lead and copper caps and spare bullet molds. There would be weapons aplenty, with the ones taken from the dead pioneers.

And he wished he knowed where Bum Kelley was plannin' on stagin' his little surprises; and whether he had throwed in with that damn no-good Red Hand.

Preacher paced the lines of wagons and went over them again. The men and women and children watched him in silence, the kids big-eyed. He knew what he looked like to them, all dressed out in skins, from his feet to his jacket. He looked like some grim-faced wild man, with pistols and knives ahangin' all over him as he prowled up one side of the line and down the other, never speaking to anyone.

He stopped when he came to Richard and Edmond's wagon. The wagon was loaded with new supplies but none of the quartet was anywhere around. One of the teenage boys in the train was sitting on the seat. "What you doin' up there, tadpole?"

The boy, maybe fourteen at the most, red hair and freckle-faced, grinned at Preacher. "Mister Richard employed me to drive the wagon through the wilderness, sir."

"Did he now?"

"Yes, sir, he did. And the money will come in handy when we get through the wilderness and start to homesteading."

"I reckon so. Your parents don't object to you doin' this, do they?"

"Oh, no sir. Not a bit."

"You figure on handlin' that team of mules all day, by your-self, do you?"

"I'm going to try. We had mules back in Missouri. Big reds. Just like the ones I'll be driving here." He frowned. "The ladies don't know how to drive a team. I never heard of any-thing as silly as that. But Misters Richard and Edmond said they would spell me from time to time."

"That's right considerate of them. What are they goin' to be doin'?"

"Riding their mounts, sir. I believe they said something about assisting you."

Preached choked on his 'baccy and coughed for a spell. He spat and said, "They's plannin' on doin' *what?*"

"Assisting you, sir."

"Ass-istin' me doin' what?"

"Scouting, sir, I suppose."

Preacher looked at the lad, blinked a couple of times, and walked off, muttering "Sweet Baby Jesus. Them two couldn't find their ass-ends if they britches was on fire."

He spied Melody heading his way and ducked between wagons. Preacher sighed. It was hard to believe that about six weeks back, he was headin' down to rendezvous without a care in the world. Now he was saddled with a wagon train load of pilgrims, with more coming in, a gang of outlaws on his trail, and dodging a love-struck female who could raise the temperature of a room by ten degrees just by walk-ing into it.

He had even offered Greybull two of his gold nuggets to take the train westward.

"Not for that whole en-tar poke of yourn," the big moun-tain man told him. "And I'm sorry 'cause I'll prob'ly never see you no more after you pull out."

"What are you talkin' about, you big ox?"

"Why, hell's far, that blue-eyed, honey-haired missionary

lady's got marriage on her mind. And you're the man she plans on hitchin' up with. She's gonna have you out hoein' gardens and pluckin' petunias, and totin' her little bag whilst she shops and the like."

"Have you lost your mind? I ain't gonna marry nobody, you mule-brained, goat-headed giant!"

"Yep. I can see it now," Greybull said somberly and sorrowfully, but with a definite twinkle in his eyes. "You clerkin' in some store, strainin' your eyes sortin' ribbons and socks and drawers and the like. You be goin' home to the little lady after work—only by this time she'll prob'ly weigh about as much as a buffalo, and have seven or eight kids a crawlin' around on the floor, a-squallin' and a-dirtyin' their diapers and a-hollerin' for their daddy and—"

The pioneers stood in shocked silence, wondering what was going on as Preacher chased a laughing Greybull around the fort, the smaller man waving a tomahawk and cussing at the top of his lungs.

14

Preacher had done everything he knew to do to make the wagon train ready for the trail. Oddly enough, he felt good about what he had done. Even Greybull and another trapper, Jim, had noticed the subtle change in the mountain man.

"You've changed, Preacher," Jim pointed out. "I can't put no finger on it. But they's something different about ye."

Greybull smiled. "I think it's 'cause he knows they's love at the end of the trail."

Preacher sighed and held his tongue.

Even though several weeks had passed since the pox had struck the Blackfeet and their bodies had been burned, the smell of death still hung faintly over the area, for not all bodies had been found and burned.

"The patrol that just come in says the second train is 'bout five days out." Greybull wisely changed the subject, not wanting to be again chased around the fort by a tomahawk-wielding Preacher. "Twenty-five or thirty wagons. With them three wagons that rattled in last week, you'll have near 'bouts sixty wagons to guide through the wilderness."

"The soldier boys say anything about the guide and the wagonmaster?" Preacher inquired.

"Only that they picked the guide up in St. Louie and the wagonmaster is original from back East somewheres."

"Wonderful," Preacher muttered. "More pilgrims a-comin' to the promised land."

Maxwell-Smith walked up in time to hear the last couple of comments. "This train started out with more than forty wagons," the officer said. "They survived half a dozen major engagements with hostiles along the way. That tells me that they are at least trail-wise."

Preacher nodded. "Mules or oxen?"

"More ox than mules," Greybull said. "That means they won't be totin' no heavy supply of grain."

"But they'll be slower," Preacher countered. "On the other hand, Injuns don't steal oxen as a rule. I reckon it'll all balance out. Mainest thing is gettin' these pilgrims through with their hair."

Preacher turned to Maxwell-Smith. "You had any word on Red Hand?"

"Nothing," the British officer replied. "And I was specifically warned about that renegade."

"That worries me," Preacher admitted.

"You think Bum may have hooked up with him?" Greybull asked.

"He's done it before," Trapper Jim answered for Preacher. "I'd like to see the end of both of them. And soon."

But Preacher's thoughts had again shifted to the monumental task that lay before him. He said, "Best you can expect from ox is twelve to fifteen miles a day. Mules can give you eighteen to twenty. We're lookin' at near 'bouts the end of summer 'fore we reach Fort Vancouver. Is losin' ten percent of these people along the way off the mark, 'Bull?"

"I wouldn't think so. Prob'ly more'n that 'fore it's all said and done."

"Twenty percent of 'em," Trapper Jim said.

"I want the post surgeon to check these new people over

good," Preacher told Maxwell-Smith. "My bunch is clean of cholera and I want it to stay that way. Has he got enough laudanum to give us a goodly stock?"

"Yes. Since the trains started coming this way, he's tripled his orders from the Company." He held out several pages. "And this is not going to help matters any."

"What's all them words say?" Greybull asked.

"A financial panic has struck the people back East," Maxwell-Smith said. "Newspapers are calling it the panic of '37. And according to this newsletter, thousands of people are making plans to come westward."

"Shit!" Preacher summed up his feelings with that one bitter word.

"There is more," the British officer said, "and none of it is good. Andrew Jackson has retired from office and nearly all the major New York City banks have closed their doors. A massive financial depression has enveloped the land. Farmers can't sell their agricultural products, farm surpluses are clogging the markets and farmers are being forced off the land because they have no money. A massive movement is on for the free lands of the Pacific."

"That's the end for us," Greybull said. "Folks that ain't got no money shore can't buy pelts. You was right in what you said two year ago, Preacher. You said the end was in sight and we'd all better brace for it. Them that laughed at you is eatin' mighty bitter words now."

"Bein' right don't make me feel good, though," Preacher said. He looked at Maxwell-Smith. "What else is writ on them pages? I know that ain't all. Your jaw is hangin' low enough to touch your boots. So let's have it all."

"Sickness. Back East there are epidemics of typhoid, dysentery, tuberculosis, scarlet fever, and malaria. New Orleans is very nearly quarantined. Cholera is being brought over from Europe and is trekking westward with the human movement."

"Ain't they nothin' good a-tall in them pages?" Preacher asked.

"I'm afraid not, Preacher."

Someone among the wagons started singing, the voice lilt-ingly Irish.

> *"Will you go lassie,*
> *go to the braes of Balquihidder*
> *where the blackberries grow,*
> *mang the bonny highland heather . . ."*

"I've tried to tell these folks about this northwest trail," Preacher said. "Tried to talk some sense into they heads. But they don't wanna listen. Ol' Joe Walker blazed one trail back in '32 or '33. I went over it with him. That one was hell, boys, pure hell. This one is only slightly better."

"Fools and dreamers," Greybull said quietly. "But, hell, wasn't we the same when we pushed out here, Preacher? I was at Pierre's Hole back in '32 when one of the first bunch of colonizers came a-staggerin' in. John Wyeth was one of them. But he tried again and I was tole he made it. You'll get them through, Preacher. I kinda wish I was goin' along."

"Please feel free to take my place," Preacher said dryly.

Preacher laid around the fort for the next several days, waiting for the second train to roll in. Then he would carefully inspect the wagons and give the people a good eyeballin'. 'Sides, them folks would be trail-worn and sufferin' bad from the wearies. They'd need some rest.

He didn't have to work at avoiding Melody now. She'd changed her tactics and had latched onto Lieutenant Maxwell-Smith, hoping to make Preacher jealous. The lieu-tenant squired her about, with her hangin' on his arm, shakin' her bustle and battin' her eyes at him.

Preacher only made matters worse by tipping his hat at them every time they met and saying, "Mighty handsome couple you are. Yes, siree. You shore do complement each other. Mighty handsome couple." Then he would go away chuckling.

"You tryin' to get the lou-tenant kilt?" Trapper Jim asked one afternoon, after Preacher had tipped his hat and Melody had bared her teeth at him like a mad puma.

"The boy needs some excitement in his life." Preacher jerked his head toward a man over by the company store. "You know that hombre over there?"

"Cain't say that I do. He drifted in last evenin'. Name's Luke."

"Trapper?"

"No traps or pelts on his pack horse. I don't much cotton to him, Preacher. He's a tad shifty-eyed to suit me."

"What's he ridin'?"

"Big gray with a reworked brand. 'Course, that don't mean nothin'. As many folks that's been kilt tryin' to come west, that horse could have belonged to anybody."

"Yeah," Preacher said, but he was unconvinced. After Jim had wandered off, Preacher walked over to the store to eye-ball the man called Luke. He stood on the rough-hewn log porch and stared at the young man.

Luke smiled at Preacher. He did not receive a returning smile. "You want something?" Luke asked in a nervous voice. Preacher was known from the Big Muddy to the blue waters as a man a body had best not mess with.

Preacher didn't immediately reply. He was busy studying the clothes the young man had on. He had a feeling he'd seen that jacket somewheres before. Yeah, he knew he had. But where? Then it came to him. At the ruins of the ambushed wagon train. He'd tried that jacket on himself and found it too tight across the shoulders.

'Course that didn't mean the feller had done anything wrong. Preacher had taken clothes there himself. Only a damn fool leaves useable clothing to rot in the weather if he is able to put them to use—but not to sell or barter. A man had to draw a line somewheres.

Luke's right hand drifted to the pistol tucked down behind his belt, a movement that did not escape the eyes of Preacher.

Then something else returned to Preacher. Edmond had knowed the man who owned that coat. He had found his body and put the coat on over his tortoured flesh before they dragged off the bodies and caved the earth over them.

That meant . . .

"Goddamn grave robber," Preacher told the young man.

"What'd you mean, Preacher?"

"How'd you know who I was?" Preacher demanded.

"Uh . . . I asked and somebody told me."

"Who?"

"I . . . ah, disremember 'xactly."

"You're a damn liar!"

Lieutenant Maxwell-Smith and Melody came strolling by about that time. They both was gonna have to buy new shoes if that second wagon train didn't soon get here and they all could get gone.

"Here, now!" Maxwell-Smith said. "What's going on here?"

"Look close, Melody," Preacher said. "You recognize the jacket this grave-robbin' scum is wearin?"

"Why . . ." She peered at the frightened Luke. "That's the suit coat we buried poor Mister McNally in! Edmond put it on the poor man himself."

"That's right," Preacher said grimly.

Luke grabbed for his pistol and Preacher kicked the young man on the knee, knocking him off balance. Preacher stepped forward and busted Luke on the side of the jaw with a big hard fist. Luke went down, addled to his toes.

Preacher jerked the pistol out of the man's britches and looked at it. The name Blaylock was carved in the butt, along with Boston, Mass., 1832.

Greybull had come at a running lumber and jerked the now very badly frightened Luke to his feet, holding him by his neck with a huge hand.

"Where'd you steal this, boy?" Preacher said, holding up the pistol.

"I ain't stole nothin'. It's mine. My pa give it to me."

"What's your pa's name?"

"Wilbur Mason."

"From where?"

"Mary-land."

Preacher smiled, "Do you know what's carved here, boy?" He traced the words with a blunt finger.

"Yeah! My pa's name."

"Where was your pa back in '32?"

"In the ground dead. Fever got him and my sister."

"Then how come this pistol's got the name Blaylock carved on it? Along with Boston, Mass., 1832."

"I . . ." Luke shut his mouth and shook his head.

"I thought you told me you couldn't read words?" Melody asked the mountain man.

"I lie on occasion," Preacher told her. "And I didn't say I couldn't read. I said it'd been a long time since I had, that's all."

"What else have you lied about?" she pressed him.

"This ain't the time to go into that." Preacher looked at Luke. "You ride with Bum and his trash, don't you? You come in here to spy for him, didn't you?"

"I don't know no one named Bum Kel . . ." Luke's eyes darted from person to person like a child caught with his hand in the cookie jar as he realized he had, more than likely, just stuck his head into a hangman's noose. He knew the British had issued death warrants against Bum and anyone who rode with him.

"Then how did you know his last name?" Maxwell-Smith asked.

"I heared it one time," Luke told them. "But I don't ride with no gang. I ain't done nothin' wrong 'ceptin' take this here coat offen a dead man. Critters had pulled him out from under the cave-in and the brush and had been eatin' on him. I took his coat 'cause I needed it and then I buried him proper.

Took me the better part of an hour to dig the hole. I even spoke words over the grave."

"You're a lyin' son!" Trapper Jim said, walking up and eye-balling the young man. "I know you. You're Luke Chatfield. You're wanted for murder back in the Ohio Territory."

"It's a state now," Melody said. "Admitted and recognized in 1803, I believe! How long have you been out here?"

"I was borned here," Jim said. "My daddy was half grizzly and half wild tornader and my momma was a Pawnee."

Preacher looked at him. "Wagh! Pawnee!" Preacher grinned. "I knowed there was something I didn't like about you."

Luke was tossed into the post stockade and would be taken—sooner or later—to the northern territories for trial. Bum was a gutsy outlaw, but all suspected he was smart enough not to attack a fort under the protection of the Crown. Not for someone as unimportant and blatantly worthless as Luke Chatfield.

Luke had given up protesting his innocence the same day he was tossed in the stockade. Now he was offering to make a deal in return for his neck.

"What do you think?" Maxwell-Smith asked Preacher.

Preacher shrugged. "He's gonna tell you that Bum has hooked up with Red Hand and they's gonna ambush the wagon train somewheres between here and Fort Vancouver. Big deal. As far as him takin' us to where they's camped, forget it. When he don't return on time, they'll know he's either dead or captured and shift camp. But it would be nice to know the size of Bum's gang and how many renegades Red Hand has with him."

"And what do we offer him in return for that information?"

"We don't hang him."

15

Luke took the offer without hesitation. "Bum's got about twenty men, and he's lookin' for more. Bum wants the gold them missionaries is carryin' and he wants the white women. Red Hand's got near'bouts forty bucks with him."

"'Way more'n enough to give us hell out yonder on the trail," Preacher said after they left the stockade building. "Red Hand's people would hay-rass us at night, stealin' and killin' stock and cripplin' the wagons. They'll try to drag us down slow and then move in for the kill."

"And your plan is . . . ?" Maxwell-Smith asked.

By now this had become a challenge to the mountain man. "I'm takin' the wagon train through to Oregon Territory. To hell with Bum Kelley and Red Hand."

"I really wish I could let you have some men, Preacher. But I don't have the authority to do so."

"I'll get them through. They'll be some that don't make it. I'll lose some to accidents, some will probably fall to diseases, and Bum and Red Hand will get some more. But most of them will get through. Or I'll be buried along the trail with them."

Preacher fixed up one wagon and with Lieutenant Maxwell-Smith's permission, commissioned Trapper Jim to drive it through. The wagon would be filled with gee-gaws to trade with the Injuns they would encounter along the way. Preacher stocked the wagon with bolts of calico and Hudson's Bay blankets. He laid in a stock of metal knives and a trunk filled with three-pound carrots of tobacco. He put in several dozen one-pound metal kettles and lots of cheap but flashy trinkets.

The second wagon train finally rumbled up to the walls of the fort and Preacher stood and watched as more kids than he'd seen in many a year poured out of the wagons. Seemed like they never would stop coming, all of them yelling and shouting and giggling and runnin' around like a bunch of idiots.

"I sure hope some of them is midgets," he said to Greybull.

The huge mountain man slapped Preacher on the back. "I got to go a-scoutin' ol' son. We'll say our hail and farewells now, I reckon."

"You be careful out there, you moose," Preacher said, shaking hands with the man. "Stay with your hair now, you hear?"

"You ride easy in the saddle, Preacher. And try not to get hitched up with that honey-haired filly."

The men grinned at each other and Greybull was gone, walking to his horse to begin his lonely and dangerous job. Preacher stood in the open gates of the fort and watched him until he was swallowed up by the wilderness.

He wondered if he would ever see the man again.

He'd wondered those thoughts many times. He wondered them when Jed Smith went off on his last adventure back in '30. Commanches got him.

Preacher shook such thoughts from his head and set about locating and acquainting himself with the guide and wagon master of the train.

"There appears to be a small problem," Maxwell-Smith said, stopping Preacher along the way.

"Well, hell, when ain't there been?" Preacher said. "What's wrong now?"

"The guide just quit. Said he was going back to St. Louis."

Preacher dismissed that with a wave of his hand. "I don't

need no second opinion in gettin' this train acrost the wilderness. How about the wagon master?"

"He seems to be a good, solid man. He's staying on."

"Let's go meet him."

He introduced himself as Swift and Preacher immediately sized him up as a man who would brook no nonsense from anyone. Swift was a well-built man of middle age with quick intelligent eyes. Preacher knew that he was also being sized up by the wagon master.

"You've been over the trail?" Swift asked.

"More'n once."

"How bad is it from this point on?"

"You ever been to hell?"

"Can't say that I have."

"You're about to get a goodly taste of it. You got any sickness with you?"

"No. At least nothing more serious than blisters and sore muscles. My bunch are all in good shape. I insisted that all people be scratched before we left."

Preacher's first impression of the man had been correct. Swift knew his business.

"We've got sheep, goats, milk cows, and extra mules and oxen," Swift said. "We hooked up with a small train three days ago. We are thirty-one wagons and more than a hundred and twenty people."

"Most of them kids," Preacher remarked.

Swift smiled. "Correct, sir. But I've found them to be well-behaved and they've become trail-wise. You'll find none of them dashing off to become lost in the woods. One did, back in Wyoming. We never found him. That settled the rest of them down."

"It usual takes something like that to do it, so I been told. Sorry you had to lose the kid. I got things to say, and I be honest with you, Swift. I been a mountain man for all my life—since I was twelve year old. I come out to this land—*this land*—fifteen year after Mackenzie. I wasn't the first. But them that was first, they left. I stayed. Blackfeet probably wouldn't hate the white man so much if Lewis hadn't shot one he caught stealin' rifles . . ."

A crowd of people from the fort and both wagon trains had gathered around, listening to this buckskin-clad, shaggy-haired, wild-looking man of the mountains.

". . . But they ain't nobody blamin' Lewis. He done what he had to do. But the Blackfeet still tell the story about how, not too long after that, one of Lewis' own party accidental shot him in the ass. Lewis had to be toted around on a litter for some time. Blackfeet still get a big laugh when they tell that story.

"Now I'm gettin' to what it was I was original gonna tell you, Swift. I know the trail. I been over it and back. But I ain't never guided no wagon train filled with females and squallin' kids. I ain't got no patience with young'uns. So I'll stay shut of the train as much as possible.

"One more thing and then I'm done. Don't cross me when I tell you something to do. If I tell you to gather the wagons, you give that order right then and there. If I tell you we're stoppin' early in the day—I got a reason for it. And I warn you now that we got a bad bunch of outlaws on our trail and they've hooked up with some renegade Injuns who's headed by a Blackfoot called Red Hand. And so's I won't have to answer a bunch of gawddamn foolish questions, Red Hand was named cause they's a big birthmark on his hand that's red." Preacher caught Penelope's eyes and said, "Kinda like them two dogs I was tellin' y'all about."

"Well!" Penelope tossed her curls and marched off.

"I beg your pardon?" Swift leaned forward. "Did I miss something?"

"Naw. Where was I? Oh. That's about it, I reckon. You folks have put some hard miles behind you, and you've got some hard ones ahead of you. You folks get busy checkin' out your wagons and the like. We'll start whenever you people have rested and resupplied. Until then, don't bother me. I don't have the patience for a bunch of damn fool questions from a pack of pilgrims that shoulda stayed to home in the first place."

Preacher nodded his head at Swift, then wheeled about and stalked off without another word.

"What an ill-tempered, sharp-tongued, savage man!" one woman observed of the mountain man.

Maxwell-Smith smiled and said, "Be thankful you have him to guide you, madam. There is no more qualified man in all the western lands. However, he does take some getting accustomed to."

Melody looked at the young lieutenant and rolled her eyes at what had to be the understatement of the year.

Preacher squatted on his heels and with a stick, drew a crude map in the dirt for Swift and a handful of men from the newly arrived wagon train.

"We're here, on the Snake. Once we leave here, we'll dip south just a mite, then start anglin' some north and west. What's left of the Blackfoot is north of us. Also north of us, but that don't mean a whole lot, 'cause Injuns is roamers—they apt to pop up anywheres so don't never take nothin' for granted—also is the Nez Perce, the Flatheads, and some Crow and Shoshone. Over here," he jabbed the stick, "is the Bannocks and here is where you'll find the Paiutes. The Yakimas is all over this area here.

"Don't worry about the Paiutes. They's pretty peaceful Injuns. War ain't very high up their list of things to do. In their society there ain't no glory or honor in fightin' and killin'. When a Paiute hears a bunch of whites is comin', they been known to hide their kids in brushpiles or run off in a panic.

"Shoshone ain't quite that kind to the white man. I get

along with them alright, though. I ain't never had no problem with the Washos neither. Tell the truth, I ain't expectin' much in the way of Injun troubles. This is probably gonna be the largest wagon train most Injuns west of here has ever seen. Injuns ain't foolish; they ain't gonna attack nothin' that they think is gonna beat them back or cause a lot of deaths and injuries. Them that attacked us here at the fort did so out of rage and desperation. It's Bum Kelley and Red Hand that's gonna be causin' us the problems."

"My people will be ready to go in two days," Swift said.

Preacher stood up. "That's when we'll stretch 'em out, then."

On the morning of the pull-out, Preacher rolled out of his blankets while the stars were still bright overhead. He saddled Hammer and rigged up his light-loaded pack horse—most of his things were in the wagon—and tied the reins to the back of the wagon driven by Jim.

Richard and Edmond had made their appearance in their new trail gear the day before. Preacher had been wondering about those two, so he was not surprised when they showed up all in buckskin. They'd arranged for one of the Flathead women who'd returned to the fort to make the skins.

Damnest lookin' sight Preacher believed he'd ever seen in all his days.

Melody and Penelope had come up with sidesaddles—only God knew where—and they had announced that they would be mounted at least part of the way.

"Don't make no difference to me if you ride a camel," Preacher told them.

"You don't have to be rude," Melody told him.

"I ain't," Preacher replied. "Just truthful."

"Don't you think the new attire of Richard and Edmond makes them look quite dashing?" Penelope asked.

"I can say truthful that I ain't never seen nothin' to compare it with."

"Oh, good!" Melody clasped her pretty little hands together. "They were afraid you might laugh at them."

"Cry might be a better word," Preacher muttered.

"Beg pardon?" Melody asked.

"Nothin'."

Melody found Preacher as he was squatting down drinking coffee and chewing on a biscuit filled with salted fatback. It was still dark and the morning was pleasant.

He looked up at her. Both women had been doing a lot of sewing and each had put together several fashionable riding outfits. She sat down beside him.

"I'm so excited I could just fairly burst!"

"Yeah, me too."

A very large, muscular, and smart-aleck teenage boy about fifteen or sixteen that Preacher had taken an immediate dislike to let out a wild yell of excitement.

"Idiot," Preacher muttered. "If he does that on the trail somebody's gonna shoot him. And it might be me."

"Avery is just full of himself, that's all. He's been flirting with all the girls. Why, he even made eyes at Penelope."

"Better watch him around the sheep, then," Preacher muttered.

"Beg pardon?"

"I said did you get enough sleep?"

"Oh, yes. How far is it, Preacher?"

"In miles, I ain't got no idea. We'll be weeks on the trail. We'll do good to average, ten or twelve miles a day over much of this country. They'll be days we'll push fifteen, days we'll do four or five. They'll be days we'll never leave camp 'cause of the weather."

"You always look on the gloomy side of things, Preacher."

He cut his eyes to look at her. "I look at the way things is, Melody. Not the way I want them to be." He tossed the dregs of the coffee to the ground and stood up in one smooth, effortless movement. "Get your kit together. We'll be pullin' out at first light." He turned to leave.

"Preacher?"

He stopped and looked back at her.

"Why do you dislike me?"

Preacher stared at her in the semi-gloom. Many campfires were now being lighted, the pioneers stirring from their blankets, ready to begin the second phase of their long journey to the promised land. The smell of coffee brewing filled the early morning air. "I don't dislike you, Melody," Preacher spoke the words softly. "Matter of fact, I like you more'n I have any woman 'fore in my life. And mayhaps that's the problem. This is my world, Melody. The mountains and the valleys and the plains and the wild things. Yours is all different. I don't fit in your world, and you don't fit into mine. So there ain't no point in startin' nothin' that neither of us can finish. It's not that I won't change. I *can't* change. I'm as much a part of this land as the mountains I live in and the winds that blow through the passes. This is where I'll die. You folks back East, you read all about the carryin's-on of Kit Carson. Melody, I was out here *years* 'fore that squirt showed up.

"I was the *first* white man to see much of this country. It was me that opened up many of the trails that folks are now usin'. I wasn't alone in doin' it, but I was there. I can't leave this country for no length of time. It just keeps pullin' me back. It calls to me, Melody. Sings to me. It's a part of me and I'm a part of it. I can go for weeks without hearin' the sound of a human voice. And I love it, Melody. I love it. I don't need people the way you do. Hell, I don't even *like* most people. They want ever'thing that I don't see no need for and ain't got no use for. I got my good horses, a fine saddle, my guns, and a good knife. What else do I need? Nothin'. Not a thing. You desire a roof over your head. Woman, I can't hardly sleep under no damn roof. Not for no length of time. It hems me in. Makes me nervous when I can't look up at the stars.

"You're a fine woman, Melody. I believe that. A looker, too. You 'bout as easy on the eyes as any female I ever seen. But I ain't the man for you. I got to say that I'm prideful you like me. Any man who wouldn't be is a pure damn fool. So lets us be friends. No more than that. 'Cause it can't be, Melody. You and me . . . just can't be."

He turned and walked away.

Richard stepped out of the shadows, moving quietly in his fringed buckskins. Melody turned to face him.

"You heard, Richard?"

"Not intentionally, Melody. I was bringing you a cup of coffee and a biscuit when I heard you talking. I didn't want to interrupt Preacher. He was telling you the truth, Melody. Heed his words."

She took the tin cup and the biscuit with thanks. "I've never had a man affect me the way he does, Richard. And I've never said that to anybody."

"Melody, I had a pet wolf once. I raised it from a cub. Found it when I was summering on my grandfather's farm in the country. I loved that wolf. But I had to let it go. I cried like a baby, but I still turned it loose. It belonged to nature. It was a wild thing—just like Preacher. This is where he belongs, and he knows it. Just like that wolf longed to be free. I truly believe that wild animal loved me, in its own way. But it loved the land more. I finally saw that and let it return to its rightful heritage."

Richard saw that Melody was crying, silent tears streaming down her cheeks. He stood for a moment, then turned away and walked back to their wagon.

Preacher was in the saddle, restlessly walking Hammer up one side and down the other of the wagon train. Faint streaks of gray were slowly highlighting the eastern horizon.

He stopped by the gee-gaw wagon. Trapper Jim sat on the seat, the reins in his big, work-hardened hands. "Are ye filled with excitement and wonderment at the journey ahead?" Jim said with a twinkle in his eyes.

"Where'd you hear that?

"One of the movers said it about fifteen minutes ago. I like to have fell offen this seat."

"What I'm filled with is coffee and biscuits and fatback. You et?"

"A right good meal. One of the movers hailed me and fed me. Right nice folks. Preacher, I had me a run-in with that boy called Avery. Last evenin'. He's gonna cause us some woe, I'm feared."

"I got the same thoughts. What'd he do?"

"Sassed me right smart. I was of a mind to box his ears. But ifn I'd a-done that, I'd probably had to kill his pa. He was a-watchin' close. Shootin' the man wouldn't a been no way to start off a trip."

"It would have spoiled this evenin', for sure," Preacher agreed. "Yeah . . ." he sighed. "The boy's gonna be trouble. I gleaned that right off. Swift thinks so too. He told me he come close to banishin' the wagon from the train but he just couldn't do it in the middle of hostile country."

"You might have to do it, Preacher. Some of the other movers wanted to call a meetin' here at the fort and discharge the family. Since others talked 'em out of it."

"I guess we'll cross that river when it comes time." Preacher lifted the reins. "Be shovin' off in a few. Talk to you later."

"I'll shore be creepin' along," Jim said with an easy grin. "All filled with wonderment and excitement."

Preacher laughed and moved up the line. "Get the kids that's ridin' into the wagons!" he yelled.

Preacher moved up to the rear of another wagon. "Replace that rope on your grease buckets, Sanders," he told the man standing beside the oxen. "You'll love it 'fore the day is gone."

At another wagon, he said, "Secure your canvas back here, Smithers. A good gust of wind and she'll rip and sail clear to the blue waters."

Wagonmaster Swift was mounted on a fine-looking black. He blew his bugle and called, "All know that those not yet ready to take their place in the line of march must fall to the dusty rear for this day. Get in place!"

"All fires out!" Preacher yelled.

Preacher eyeballed Lieutenant Maxwell-Smith, all decked out in his dress uniform, as he rode out of the fort on his pony, a-bouncin' up and down on his silly little saddle like the British is trained to do.

"Count your young 'uns," Preacher yelled.

"Drovers to the livestock in the rear," Swift yelled, and tooted on his bugle again.

"That damn bugle is gonna get old 'fore this journey is done," Preacher muttered.

Edmond and Richard rode up, all splendid in their new buckskins and wide-brimmed hats. Preacher noticed that Bible-thumpers they may be, but they were both armed with a brace of pistols and rifles in the boot.

As dawn split the skies, Edmond took off his hat, waved it over his head, and yelled, "Onward to our western destiny!" He jerked on the reins, his horse reared up, and Edmond fell out of the saddle, landing on his butt on the ground.

"Lord, give me strength," Preacher said.

Book Two

1

"If God will only forgive me this time and let me off I will leave the country day after tomorrow—and be damned if I ever come into it again!"

John Colter at Lisa's Fort
on the Yellowstone River, 1810

"Did he ever return, Preacher?" Swift asked, after Preacher had told him about John Colter and his promise to God.

The men were riding together, ranging ahead of the slowly plodding oxen.

"Nope. He died in St. Louie a few years later. He was a hell of a man, though. I never knowed him, but nearly everyone speaks highly of him. He was captured twice and tortured by the Blackfeet, and both times he broke loose and escaped. One time he ran nekkid for miles after they'd tortured him. Finally hid out in a river. I'd like to have known him. I think he was probably a hell of a man."

"What are you going to do after the train is safely placed in Oregon Territory, Preacher?"

"Head back just as fast as I can. You?"

"I'm going back to take another train through. There is

good money to be had doing this sort of work and I like the open skies of the trail."

"Lots of folks want to come out here, eh?"

"Thousands."

"Plumb depressin'."

They were on the south side of the Snake River. Across the river to the north lay the Snake River Plain, lava beds, and totally inhospitable terrain. They would not cross the Snake for several weeks, and that was if nothing went wrong.

For the first several days, it would amount to a shakedown. The movers would adjust to life on the trail and each would find their place in the long train. Those in command could pinpoint the trouble-makers and the whiners and complainers. All would soon know if the repairs made back at the fort would hold.

The first several days passed uneventfully, the weather was near perfect, and the wagon train soon settled into a routine. In four days, Preacher figured they had covered about thirty-five miles. He could ask for no better than that.

Preacher was not worried about Bum and Red Hand attacking this close to the fort. They would wait until the train was a good hundred miles out, then they would make their move. And they were about; Preacher had ranged out far and picked up their sign. Bum and Red Hand had gone on ahead, to pick out their ambush site, leaving scouts behind to watch the train for weak points. Soon they would start harassing the train.

Preacher was up early the morning of the sixth day out, earlier than usual. He had quickly put a stop to the sentries' habit of discharging their rifles at four o'clock in the morning to awaken the encampment. The first time they did it he damn near shot a man.

"Toot on that goddamn bugle to wake folks up," he told Swift. "I don't want no guns goin' off in my ear at four o'clock in the morning."

Preacher wasn't sure why he awakened so early, but many

of his hunches had kept him alive in the wilderness, and he never questioned them.

Preacher moved silently past the sleepers, most of whom slept under their wagons, for the bed of any wagon was filled with precious possessions the movers had carefully packed, from woodburning stoves to coffee grinders to violins. They took whatever they could, for supplies were very scarce and very expensive on the coast.

Preacher stopped and gazed out at the blackness of night. Storm clouds had moved in during the night, and the stars and moon were unseen this early morning.

But something was out there in the darkness. Something that had triggered the mountain man's survival instincts and brought him out of a sleep. He wasn't sure, but Preacher had an idea that Bum or Red Hand was about to make a move. Probably to slip in, cut a throat or grab a child, and leave without disturbing anyone's sleep.

There! Preacher's eyes focused on a very slight movement in the gloom. Was that object—whatever it might be—there the night before? No. He stood motionless just outside the circled wagons, standing beside one of the nearly six-foot-high rear wheels, nearly two feet higher than the front wheels. The front wheels were smaller to allow for sharp turns.

The object that Preacher had spotted moved ever so slightly. Preacher smiled and quietly pulled out his long-bladed knife from its sheath. Preacher opined to himself that he'd been playing at this game longer than that fellow out there in the night . . . and doing a better job of it.

He was still alive, wasn't he?

Preacher motionlessly stayed his position, holding the big-bladed knife close to his leg, to prevent any glimmer of light from reflecting off the polished metal, the heavy blade held edge up for a gut cut.

The man Preacher watched moved closer to the encircled

wagons, moving expertly and soundlessly on moccasined feet. Preacher caught the glint of faint light off a blade.

Come to do some dirty work, eh? Preacher thought. *Well, just come a little bit closer and you'll find your work is gonna be a tad more difficult than you figured.*

The man made the circle of wagons with one final and swift dash. Preacher could smell the grease and smoke on the half-naked flesh of the renegade Indian. The buck took one more step and grunted in surprise as his eyes picked out the shape of Preacher, standing not two feet from him.

It was the last sound the Indian ever made. Preacher whipped his knife and laid the razor-sharp blade under the Indian's jaw, cutting off any further sound from the savaged throat. He grabbed the Indian by the hair and soundlessly lowered him to the dewy ground.

Not one mover had heard a thing, even though an entire family of husband and wife and two kids was sleeping under the wagon not five feet from the death scene.

Preacher stood for a moment, waiting to see if the renegade had come alone or had some help waiting for him in the night. After several moments, Preacher concluded the buck had been working alone. He relaxed some.

Preacher squatted down and contemplated on whether to scalp the renegade. He decided against it. These movers might think him to be a terrible savage if he done that. Most of them thought that anyways. Preacher wiped his blade clean on the Indian's leggings. He left the body where it was and walked off toward the center of the encirclement for some coffee. He smiled, figuring it was gonna be right interestin' in a few minutes. Just as soon as Swift tooted on his bugle.

Preacher almost scared the crap—literally—out of the man whose job it was to keep a small fire burning and the coffee hot for the sentries when he approached him as silent as a ghost and said, "Howdy."

"Lord God!" the mover said, whirling around, his rifle at the ready. "You took ten years off my life."

"You wouldn't have had ten seconds left you if I'd been a hostile," Preacher told him. "Dwell on that for a time."

Preacher squatted down and took a tin cup and poured it full of strong coffee. "I figure it's near'bouts four o'clock. You got airy watch?"

The mover reached into a vest pocket, clicked open the lid, and consulted his timepiece. "Five minutes 'til four," he said. "My woman made panbread last evening. It's there." He pointed. "And there's some jam to spread on it."

"Kind of you," Preacher said, helping himself. "Where y'all from?"

"Ohio. Lost my farm when the depression struck. Couldn't sell my pigs. I went bust. Had to do something and this seemed like the thing to do."

"Goin' to the promised land, eh?"

"Beats watchin' my woman and kids starve."

"I reckon. What's your name, pilgrim?"

"Prather."

"Well, Prather, let me give you some advice about guard work. Don't stand in one spot for very long. Move around. And when you're stationary, stay in the shadders. Move your eyes, not your whole body. We got people after us that can come into a camp like this, cut a throat, and be gone and won't nobody know they's done it 'til the body's found."

"I do not believe that, sir."

"Is that right?" Preacher did not take umbrage at the words. One of the many things he'd learned about these eastern people was that they thought they could flap off at the mouth and not be held to account for their remarks. "Well, I reckon in about two minutes you gonna have to be eatin' them words. We'll see." Preacher chuckled.

"I see nothing amusing," Prather said.

"Neither will them folks sleepin' warm in their blankets

under that wagon yonder, I 'spect. But it might just teach them a hard lesson."

"You're a strange man, Preacher."

"I been called worse." Preacher ate his panbread and drank his coffee. "Just about now," he said, as Swift tooted on his bugle.

"Holy Christ!" a man yelled and his wife began screaming and the kids rolled out from under the wagon.

Preacher guffawed and slapped his knee. "Hee! I called it right, didn't I, Prather?"

"There's a body of a savage over here!" the mover yelled. "And his throat's been cut."

Preacher looked at Prather. "Don't ever call me no liar again, pilgrim. I don't like it. It's bad business out here in the wilderness. I cut that Injun's throat. Cut it 'fore he could cut yours or grab some child or jerk the hair off a woman. You got a lot to learn about this country, mover. You folks think you're goin' to a city that's got boardwalks and streetlamps and the like?" He laughed. "You're all in for a surprise, you are."

Preacher rose and walked over to the wagon, stepping over the tongue and pointing to the dead Indian. "Red Hand's got a dozen different tribes in his bunch. All of 'em bad poison. But this one's a rogue Kiowa. See that raggedy sash hangin' over his shoulder? That means at one time he was a Principal Dog. One of the ten bravest men in the tribe. Or wanted Red Hand to think he was. If he was a Dog, he musta done something terrible to get kicked out of the whole damn tribe."

"How could he get this close without one of the sentries seeing him?" a woman asked.

Preacher smiled at her. "You traveled twelve hundred or so miles and still don't understand, do you, ma'am? The Good Lord alone only knows how you folks made it this far." Preacher shook his head and walked away.

"Here now, sir. What about this dead savage?" a man called after him.

"You wanna bury him, hop to it. Was it up to me, I'd just roll him 'bout fifty feet away from the wagon and leave him lay. Some of his own will come fetch him. If they don't, the buzzards or varmits will take care of him."

"That's disgusting, sir!" a woman called.

"Practical, is what it is," Preacher called over his shoulder, and kept walking.

In the years ahead, when thousands of movers would attempt either the Oregon or California Trail, they would not be so kind to their own dead. Between 1837 and the late 1860's, more than half a million people would try those trails. It is not known exactly how many died, but twenty thousand would not be an unlikely number. Many times wagonmasters simply would not halt the train for a lengthy funeral, and the bodies were buried in very shallow graves—if they were lucky—or simply stretched out alongside the trail for the elements and the varmints. Old diaries have writings in them telling of the callousness toward the dead. People rolling or riding, or in most cases walking across the trail have written of witnessing human hands and feet and even heads sticking up out of the ground. And still they came, but the Great Adventure illusion had long been shattered. It was either broiling hot or bone-chilling cold. Across the plains the dust would pile three or four inches thick inside the wagons. Animals and humans alike dropped dead from exhaustion, or lack of water, or disease. Wheels splintered and wagons collapsed on people, crushing them to death, or shattering bones so badly that the movers had to be knocked on the head, held down, and the limb crudely sawed off before gangrene set in.

And still they came, by the thousands. In what is now Wyoming, the ruts of their passing wagons are still there, visible after a century and a half, hundreds of miles of them. Silent ghosts of the past. Of humankind's insatiable urge to move, to settle, to strive for a better life.

They rode and drove and walked through dust storms so violent they could not see the wagon in front of them. Cholera struck them hard, due in no small part to crowded camp-grounds where bacteria thrived on mounds of garbage and excrement. Cholera killed by horrible degrees: violent dehydration, uncontrollable diarrhea, vomiting, sweating, death. When cholera struck on the trail, many times those afflicted were abandoned by their fellow movers and left to die alone in the vast stillness of what many called the Big Lonesome.

And still they came.

Those who took the route to California faced hardships not known on the northern route to Oregon Territory. They faced deserts seemingly so cruel many thought they had been guided straight to Hell. Tongues became so swollen from thirst people actually tore their lips off in panicked frenzy. Christianity received a lot of converts on the way west.

Starvation took its toll. Canvas rotted or was ripped away and when the oxen or cattle dropped dead, they were skinned and the hides used as a roof over the ribs of the wagon—until hunger drove the people to tear down their roofs and eat the hides.

On occasion, some of the graves were dug up by scalawags in a train coming close behind and the bodies robbed of rings. On very, very rare occasions, some reverted to cannibalism and dug up the bodies and ate them.

But still they came.

2

"He ain't a-comin' back," Bum said to Red Hand. "Preacher got him. Bet on it."

The renegade Indian looked into the distance and was silent for a moment. Red hand was no friend of Preacher; their paths had crossed on more than one occasion, with Red Hand coming out the loser each time. Red Hand knew from bitter experience that the mountain man called Preacher was a savage fighter and could be totally ruthless toward his enemies.

Red Hand turned to face the outlaw Bum Kelley. "He was a Dog Warrior. One of the best in my band. I sent him to test Preacher. To see if he had lost any of his skills. He has not." The Indian smiled. "Now you send one of your men to kill Preacher on the trail while he scouts."

Bum knew he was being tested by the renegade whose own people had banished him from the tribe. If he didn't send someone after Preacher, Red Hand and his men would just leave. And he needed the force of Red Hand's group if any attack against the train was to succeed.

Bum had picked up two more men who were running from the law in California. Waller and a man named Seedy. He suspected Luke had sold them all out back at the fort. Not that the fool had that much to tell anybody.

"You're right," Bum told Red Hand. "That's what I'll do, for a fact."

"When?" the Indian demanded.

"Today."

Red Hand smiled. "Good. Good! Then when your man does not return, we shall be even, won't we?"

Goddamn strange Injun logic, Bum thought, but managing not to lose his smile. "That's right, Red Hand. We'll be even."

Bum walked to the fire and poured coffee from a battered and blackened pot. He looked at his men, one at a time. Finally he settled on one man. "Rod, pack you a kit for several days and go kill Preacher. Take him out on the trail, away from the train. If you don't kill him, don't bother comin' back here. You understand that?"

The outlaw nodded his head and walked to his horse, saddling up. He knew perfectly well that if he didn't kill the mountain man, he wouldn't be alive to even think about returning. With men like Preacher, you only get one chance. Sometimes not even that many.

He put some panbread in the pocket of a coat he'd taken from a dead man back up the trail, and swung into the saddle. With rifle in hand, he rode away from the camp without a look back.

"He won't be back," Moses said quietly, looking into his coffee cup. "And you know it."

"Maybe he'll get lucky." Beckman said, rubbing his leg. Damn wound still bothered him. "And kill that goddamn Preacher."

"You're dreamin' ifn you believe that," Slug said. "Rod was sent 'cause that damn Injun didn't come back, that's all. You know how Injuns think."

"You reckon Red Hand will go back down yonder and bury that buck?" Leo asked.

"Hell, no," Bum said. "This bunch don't pay much attention to their tribes' customs. 'Sides, we don't know for sure that he's dead."

"He's dead," Beckman said flatly. "And we all know it. He went on a fool's mission with Preacher prowlin' around the train. And don't sell Trapper Jim short neither. He can be as mean as a cornered puma."

"Shut up," Bum warned him.

"Preacher's just a man," Bull said. "He's just one man, that's all."

"Why," a mover asked Preacher as the train rolled along. "would one Indian attack an entire wagon train?"

"Yes," another asked, walking alongside Preacher's horse. "Why? That's foolish."

"If he'd been lucky, if his medicine had been good and he'd brung back a scalp or a woman for them to hop on, he'd a been a big man in his bunch," Preacher told them. "Injuns slip into each other's camps all the time and steal horses and people. They been doin' it for hundreds of years. Slippin' into an Injun camp is tough, slippin' into a wagon train full of pilgrims is easy."

"Unless someone like you is around."

"That's a fact." Preacher stood up in his stirrups. "Little bit of a river up ahead. We got to cross it. It won't be no problem les' it's over the banks, and I don't think it is. See you boys."

He rode up to the head of the train and walked his horse alongside the mounted Swift. "Hold the wagons here, Swift, so's the animals won't smell the water and act up with it so near. I'll ford this river and check it out. You can rest your folks some while I'm gone."

As rivers go, it wasn't supposed to be much of a river. But there had been a lot of rain that spring, and the winter had been terrible harsh, with a lot of snow, so the rivers were running over their banks.

"Well," Preacher said to Hammer, "we gonna be here for a couple of days, ol' hoss." He rode back to the train to break the bad news to Swift and the others.

"Is this the best place you know of to cross?" Swift asked.

"Yep. Banks is too steep for miles up or down. And I've been up and down for miles." He looked at Swift. "Come on. Have a look-see. Then you can decide whether you want to build rafts or try to rope and float them across."

"I say," Richard said, as he and Edmond rode up. "May we accompany you men?"

Swift shrugged his shoulders. "Suits me. Let's go."

The river was high and full and running very fast. "Rocks?" Swift asked.

"No," Preacher told him. "Like I said, Injuns been usin' this spot to cross for hundreds of years, and whether you believe it or not, they's some of the best engineers in the world."

"What do you mean?" Edmond asked.

"Most of the roads in the U-nited States started out to be Injun trails. Then the white man come along and widened them for wagons. White man makes the mistake of thinkin' that Injuns is dumb. Injuns is far from bein' dumb. They just don't think like we do. Gimme your ropes, boys." He tied them together, using knots neither Richard nor Edmond had ever seen (many trappers had worked on keelboats and Preacher was no exception) and then tied one end to a sturdy tree. Preacher smiled and said, "See you directly, boys," and plunged Hammer into the waters. He held his rifle high above his head to at least keep the powder dry on one of his weapons.

Hammer scrambled up the bank on the other side and Preacher jumped off, securing the other end of the rope to a large tree. "Get your people to buildin' them rafts!" Preacher shouted across the water. "Start emptyin' wagons. We got to make 'em lighter. We'll build rafts and float their possessions acrost."

Swift waved his hand and turned his horse. Preacher pick-

eted Hammer and swiftly began drying out and reloading his
pistols and his spare Hawken. This was no time for wet powder,
not with Bum and Red Hand liable to pop up at any minute.
And Preacher knew Red Hand and how the renegade thought.
Red Hand had lost one of his people, so that meant that he
would expect Bum to send one of his men in. Injun logic.

No way that any of those hooligans and ne'er-do-wells in
Bum's gang would have the courage to try Preacher alone and
face to face, so he would have to be doubly cautious at all
times, for an ambush or a sneak shot in the back.

He quickly dried and readied his weapons, then called to
Richard and Edmond. "First raft over, send my kit with it. I
ain't a-crossin' again."

"Will do, Preacher," Richard shouted, and turned his horse
sharply on the slick bank. The horse started to slip as it struggled to keep its footing and failed, sliding slowly down into
the river, Richard frantically waved one arm, the other hand
gripping the saddle horn.

"Well, if you're that anxious to join me," Preacher shouted.
"Come on acrost." he shook his head. "Gawddamn pilgrims."

While Richard retired to the bushes to strip down and dry
off, Preacher built a fire and a lean-to for that night's shelter.
Swift stayed on the other side, getting operations ready over
there. It was not a complicated move getting wagons across
swollen rivers, but it was a dangerous one.

"Does the river have a name?" Richard asked, stepping out
of the bushes with leafy branches held in strategic places
about his body.

"Called the Raft," Preacher told him. "Just down the trail a
few miles is what's called the California Trail. Some take that
route. But she's a dangerous one. Swift done right in stickin'
with this trail."

The sounds of axes working hard reached the two men. Men of the wagon train were busy chopping logs to build rafts.

"Do you suppose this river was named the Raft because somebody once had to build a raft to cross it?" Richard asked.

Preacher paused for a moment, a quizzical expression on his face. "I can't rightly say. But that's as good a reason as any, I reckon."

"You say the route we're taking is the correct one, Preacher. But several back at the fort urged us to change our plans and take the California Trail. Why is that?"

Preacher smiled. "Sure, they did. But it wasn't done with no charity behind the words. The Hudson's Bay people is tryin' to keep as many settlers out as they can."

"Why?"

"Fur, Richard. They don't want to see pilgrims comin' in and settlin' up the fur country. But when they told y'all this route was a bitch-kitty, they wasn't lyin' about that, ol' hoss. But it ain't near'bouts as bad as the California Trail. If we was to take the southwest trail, it leads a body through rocks, sagebrush, greasewood and smack into that gawdawful Great Basin. And that's over five hundred miles of hell. Dry, dry, Richard. Salt and baked clay. Mountains all around it that act like a damn white-hot mirror. Then you reach the Humboldt. It don't flow, it oozes. You eat dust instead of drinkin' water. Then, if you was to make it 'crost that, and that's doubtful, you got the Sierra Nevadas to 'crost, and them mountains is tough, boy, mighty tough."

Richard excused himself and slipped back into the bushes to pull on this nearly dry longjohns, then his buckskins. "And the way we're going?" he called.

"It's bad, hoss. It's bad. Injuns, rivers, storms. A lot of the time you people is gonna spend with an axe in your hand, clearing a way through for the wagons.. They ain't no roads, Richard. Y'all got to cut your way through. But 'fore then, 'fore we turn to cross the Blue Mountains, you gonna see some of the wildest country you ever gazed upon. The south rim of the Snake. That's about three hundred miles of rough. Then you cross the blues. After that, you got about two hundred and fifty miles that you got to raft down the Columbia—and ride out some wild damn rapids, or about two hundred and fifty miles that you can attempt to wagon through the Cascades. Only then will you see the Willamette Valley. And they'll be some in this train who won't see it. Believe that."

"So we have weeks still ahead of us?"

"Yeah. Weeks. If you're lucky. We have trouble and get caught in them Cascades in the fall, we gonna be real unlucky. You get caught up there when the snow comes, you liable to end up eatin' each other. And it's happen sooner or later. Some damn fools will get trapped. Bet on it."

"I would *never* resort to cannibalism!"

"You ain't never been hungry," Preacher said softly. "I've come up on folks that was tryin' to make it 'crost in the winter that was pawin' through the snow like an animal, eatin' grass and roots and bark offen the trees. If you can find grubs, eat them, they ain't bad and some even say they's good for you. I don't care for them personal."

"Those people you found . . . did they live?"

"None of the first bunch I found did. Two of the second bunch did. The others was too far gone for me to help. And the damn fools brung their kids with 'em. Turrible sight to behold, let me tell you that. And stupid, too."

"They were trying to improve their lives by moving west, Preacher."

"Well, they didn't," Preacher said shortly. "I don't like buryin' kids. Ain't right. Crazy folks to set out in the middle of the summer headin' for the blue water. You just can't tell some folks nothin'."

Richard decided to drop the subject.

"Hello the shore!" A woman's voice reached them.

Preacher looked up—Melody. She waved. Preacher grunted.

"Are you all right over there?" she called.

"Just peachy," Preacher muttered, and ignored her.

"Yes, we're fine, Melody," Richard shouted.

Then Melody started jumping up and down and pointing. She acted like she wanted to scream but no words would come out. Preacher glanced at her and without a word, grabbed his Hawken and jumped for the bushes.

"What is the matter with people?" Richard said, looking across the water at Melody, leaping all around.

"Indians!" Melody finally found her voice.

"Where?" Richard called.

"Behind you!" Melody shrieked.

"We ain't neither no damned Injuns," the voice came from behind Richard.

He turned around and stared at three of the most disreputable looking men he had ever seen in all his life.

"Well," the spokesman said, jerking a thumb at the man to his right. "He is. Dupre's a Frenchy and I'm called Beartooth. I'm a pure-dee frontiersman."

"I bet you can't spell that word," Preacher said, stepping out of the bushes.

"Wagh!" Dupre shouted. "Hell, no, he can't spell it. He just learned to pronounce it a week ago." He jumped off his pony and ran over to Preacher, grabbing him in a bear hug. The two men jumped around for a few seconds, each pounding on the other's back.

"Ummmm," Nighthawk grunted, watching the antics of the two.

"Beg pardon?" Richard asked him.

The Indian sat his pony and stared at the missionary.

"He don't say much," Beartooth said. "But he'll come when you call him to eat. How you been, Preacher?"

"Tolerably well, thankee. You lookin' prosperous."

"Looks don't always tell the story. Furs about played out,

Preacher. We didn't make enough to write home about. If I had a home to write to, that is."

"When did you learn to write?" Dupre asked. "I been readin' what newspapers we could find to you for years."

Beartooth said, "Yeah, but you read 'em in French, you igit. I don't know what the hell's goin' on. I think you do it deliberate." He looked back at Precher. "You a-guidin' wagon trains now, Preacher?"

"Just this one. I sorta got roped into it, you might say. After the fight at Fort Hall."

"What fight?" Dupre asked.

"Y'all heard about the epidemic?"

"Naw," Beartooth said. "We've been clear to the Cascades this winter. Sold our pelts over to Fort Vancouver and then headed east."

"Pox wiped out the Blackfeet, near'bouts. Y'all light and set. We'll palaver later. We got to start gettin' these wagons of pilgrims acrost this stream here. If you was a mind to, you could help me."

"What fight?" Dupre asked.

"What's in it fer us ifn we do hep out?" Beartooth asked.

"Food cooked by a woman's hand."

"That's good enough for me," Dupre said. He looked at Richard's nubby ear. "What happened to you, pilgrim?"

"It's a long story," Richard replied.

"Ummm," Nighthawk said. "Eat first. Talk later."

3

While they waited for the first wagon, aided by raft and ropes, to begin the crossing, Beartooth said, "You watch when you get up close to the Blues. Them damn Cayuses is on the prod for some reason. We had us a good fight a couple of weeks ago. Seems like of late, when the Injuns we been friendly with for years has turned meaner 'an a grizzly. Them Cayuses is all riled up about that new mission that was built last year, I think it was."

"I heard about it," Preacher said. "It's really there on the Oregon Trail?"

"Just north of it. Right where the Walla Walla forks. Man by the name of Whitman built him a church there and is preachin' the gospel to the savages. But them Cayuses ain't takin' to it real well."

"Wagon coming!" Edmond shouted across the water.

"What the hell's he expect us to do?" Dupre asked. "Swim out there and pull it in? How do you put up with these pilgrims, Preacher? They don't 'pear to know nothin'."

"I'm a patient man, boys," Preacher said with a straight face. "I come upon these poor lost children and the Lord told me to help them . . . in a roundabout way. And you all know that I have the disposition of a saint and have never turned my back on a child of God in need of help."

Richard was listening, pure astonishment on his face.

"Ummm!" Nighthawk said, and rose to his feet, wandering off into the bushes.

"What you is is a lie," Beartooth told him. "You the most cantankerous, ornery, sulled-up, and mean-spirited man I ever met. I bet you got you a skirt on that train, that's what I think."

"Wagon coming!" Edmond shrieked, panic in his voice.

Preacher looked up. "Crap!" he said, for the raft had broken free of the ropes and was turning round and round in the swirling waters.

The mountain men jumped into the water and grabbed the ropes, straining with all their might to hold the raft. Richard, who was showing more savvy every day on the trail, grabbed the loose end that Dupre tossed him and quickly secured it to a tree.

Preacher, Dupre, and Beartooth muscled the raft around and got the other end secured. Nighthawk jumped his pony into the water and trailed another rope across the small river so the fording could continue.

"This rope's been cut," Dupre said, after climbing out of the river and shaking himself like a big dog.

The mountain men and Richard gathered around and looked at the rope.

"Cut halfway through and the strain done the rest," Preacher said. "But who? . . ." He lifted his eyes and looked across the river. The young troublemaker, Avery, stood on the other side, smirking at him.

"Everything all right over there?" Swift shouted.

"Yeah," Preacher called. Up to now, all the kid had done, and that was aplenty, was nonsense stuff. Just pranks, but mean pranks. He hadn't actual hurt anybody. But this was different. This could have resulted in a family losing everything they had and maybe even loss of life.

"Preacher, you know who cut this rope?" Nighthawk said, stringing together more words then than he had all day.

"I got me a pretty good idea. That smart-aleck boy standing right yonder. He's gonna get somebody killed 'fore this trip is over. I got me a good notion to hogtie him and dump him in the back of his daddy's wagon for the ret of the trip."

"Wagon coming across!" Swift hollered.

Preacher waved it on then turned to Richard. "Richard, you cross over and you and Edmond keep your eyes on that Avery boy. He's gonna get somebody bad hurt or dead if this keeps up."

"You don't know that he did it, Preacher. Although I certainly wouldn't put it past him."

"Let's just say he's a likely candidate. Go on. Let's get some wagons acrost this stream. And tell Swift to send a team over next. We can't muscle these damn wagons up this slope."

The men worked all the rest of that day and managed to get ten wagons, teams, and personal possessions across the river. As nightfall approached, Preacher called a halt and the mountain men sank wearily to the ground.

"This is too damn much like work to suit me," Beartooth complained. "I'm so hungry I could eat a raw skunk."

A woman placed a heaping plate of meat and potatoes and dried apple pie in front of him. Beartooth grinned up at her and fell to eating.

"'Bout the only thing that'll shut his mouth," Dupre said. "Tell us 'bout the fight and the sickness and them that's after you, Preacher."

After they finished the first huge plates of food, Preacher told his friends all that had happened, right from the beginning, when he had found the missionaries.

"Mayhaps we could hire on this here train," Beartooth said later, after thanking the woman for bringing him his third plate of food. She had looked at the bearded, shaggy-headed, and buckskin-clad man and walked away, shaking her head in disbelief. "Tell you the truth, we could use the money."

"I don't know that they could pay much," Preacher leveled with him. "These folks are all purt near broke. What money they got, they have to dole it out careful. They got to have a poke to get by in the promised land 'til they get a crop in."

The three mountain men looked at each other and reached a silent agreement. "Aw, hell, Preacher," Dupre said. "You know we ain't gonna ride off and leave you in this mess alone. We'll just tag along for the vittles if that's all they can pay."

"What you gonna do when the grub runs out?" Preacher asked with a grin.

The mountain men had all been observing carefully the silent play between Melody and Preacher. Mostly on Melody's part. She had pitched a fit to get over to be near him. Beartooth said, "Well, we'll be like you, I reckon."

"How's that?"

"Live on love!"

They worked for another full day and a half before all the wagons, teams and possessions were across the river. The rest of that day was spent reloading the wagons and getting them trail ready.

"We been lucky that no Injuns ain't fell up here on us," Dupre said, as the men sat over a small fire on the morning of the pullout from the banks of the river. "Or some of Bum or Red Hand's people. Preacher, you get the idea that someone is a-watchin' us?" Few others were awake except the sentries.

"Yeah. I get me a tingly feelin' in my back when that happens. And I've had one since yesterday."

"Not Indians," Nighthawk, the big Crow said. "White man. Wears long coat. Fine thread."

"Well, damn your mean eyes," Beartooth told him. "Wasn't you gonna tell us?"

"Am not your mother," the Crow said.

Preacher grinned at the Crow. "One man, Nighthawk?"

"Yes. Very careful man. Afraid, I think."

"Now how could you possibly know that?" Edmond said, after listening for a moment.

"By the way he moves," Dupre told him. "His tracks will show if he's skittish. He's from Bum's bunch, then."

"Yeah," Preacher said, slurping at his coffee. "Dupre, you guide these pilgrims on this day. I'm gonna lay back and watch the train go. Then do some huntin' on my own."

"You take my hat and give me yourn. We'll swap horses too. That ought to throw them off."

They were both dressed in buckskins and were nearly the same size, Dupre being only slightly taller than Preacher.

When Swift tooted on his bugle, Nighthawk, Dupre, and Beartooth very nearly jumped out of their moccasins.

"Sweet Baby Jesus!" Dupre hollered, grabbing his Hawken and jumping up. "What the hell's that all about?"

Preacher rolled over on his back and busted out laughing. Springing to his feet and wiping his eyes, he said, "That's how they wake people up. He'll toot it again to signal the train's shovin' off."

"I can think of a place where he can shove it," the usually taciturn Nighthawk said, settling back down. The Crow spoke perfect English when he wanted to.

"'Fore I joined the train they woke the people up by firin' their rifles in the air," Preacher informed his friends.

"These folks do have a sight to learn about the wilderness," Beartooth allowed.

Preacher and Dupre exchanged hats and Preacher slipped away from the campsite and into the woods long before dawn cut the sky. Nighthawk had already led Dupre's horse away and picketed it. Preacher sat on the ground, his back to a tree, and dozed until Swift honked his tooter and the train slowly pulled away.

While the train was getting under way, with people shouting at oxen and mules, mothers squalling for their kids, and the wagons creaking and grumbling and rattling away, Preacher circled and came up on the spot where Nighthawk figured the outlaw to be. The Crow wasn't off by a hundred yards.

Only problem was, he was gone.

Preacher could see that his horse's droppings were still very fresh, so the man—whoever he was—hadn't been gone more than a few minutes. He had made a cold camp, and had eaten some biscuits.

"Sloppy eater," Preacher muttered.

Preacher ran back to his horse and swung into the saddle. Mounted, he backtracked and picked up the outlaw's trail. The mountain man rode with his rifle across the saddle horn, all senses working hard.

Preacher soon found that the man he was tracking was either very sure of himself, or just downright stupid. At no time did he find where the man had reined up just to listen and look around him. He just plowed on ahead. In the wilderness, that was a damn good way to get captured by Injuns and get slowly and very painfully dead.

Preacher found where the man he tracked watered his horse and himself, propping his rifle up against a tree, some yards from the stream. No way he could reach it with a single jump. This feller was downright ignorant.

The man he tracked left the cover of timber and brush and moved his horse onto the trail the wagons were taking . . . and making as they went. Preacher swung in behind him, walking his horse. He was in no hurry to kill the man.

It wouldn't be long before the train would hit the south rim of the Snake River—actually they were already in it, but the going was still relatively easy for the route, though that wouldn't last long. If Bum and his people were going to attack, they would either do it before the train hit the rugged south rim, or wait until they were between the rim and Blues.

Preacher figured it would be the latter. Probably in the Blues itself so's any patrol that come up on the ruins would blame it on the Cayuses. Preacher personal knew Chief Tamsuky of the Cayuses, and got along with the tribe for the most part. He couldn't figure why they had turned violent. That Bible-thumper who build the mission must have really riled them up.

Preacher whoaed his horse and studied the tracks. The man he followed had been joined by at least three more riders, all of the horses shod.

"Ain't this sweet," Preacher said, dismounting and squatting down, the reins in his hand.

The riders had stood and talked for a goodly time. Preacher found where someone had knocked out the remnants from a pipe, and found the butt of a soggy stogy.

The riders resumed their trek west, and Preacher followed, soon discovering that the three new men were just as confident or stupid as the original rider. Their sign told him they never stopped to check their back trail or just to sit their saddles and listen. Stupid. Just plain stupid.

Preacher grew more cautious. He was now up against four outlaws instead of just one. Stupid and careless they might be, but one man against four was lousy odds anyway a feller wanted to cut it.

Preacher found a place to cut a ways south and into the timber, then a game trail that went due west, keeping him several hundred yards to the south of the wagon trail. He walked his horse now, staying in the grass that muffled the sound of his horse's hooves.

He picked up a sound that was not of the wilderness and reined up, sitting very still. He listened hard. There it was again, clearer this time.

Voices came to him. But so faintly he could not make out any of the words. He swung down from the saddle and checked his pistols, then took a third pistol from its saddle holster and stuck that one in his sash, to the rear. He would have to make every shot count, but Preacher was used to doing that. He had left his bow and quiver of arrows back in the wagon that Trapper Jim was driving.

He moved out, walking as silently as a ghost as he made his way through the timber and brush. The voices lost their muffled tone and he could pick out words, now.

". . . help me kill that damn Preacher and Bum'd shore welcome you into the gang, for sure."

"I been hearin' about that man for ten years," another voice came to him. "I'm sick of it. It'd be worth killin' him just to get folks to shut they fly traps a-talkin' about him."

Preacher smiled and listened. He held his Hawken in his right hand, hammer back, and a .50 caliber pistol in his left hand, likewise cocked and ready to bang. The pistol was double-shotted, the twin balls capable of inflicting terrible damage upon a human body. The Hawken was a war-hoss of a weapon to fire one-handed, but Preacher was a war-hoss of a man and he'd done just that many times.

"What's so damned important about some lousy wagon train?" another man questioned. "Hell, them folks ain't got nothin' worth stealin'."

"This one do," Rod told him. "'Sides, it's got some of the finest-lookin' white women this side of the Muddy. How long's it been since you cast your eyes upon the nekkid flesh of a beautiful woman?"

"Lord, Lord," yet another man said, "I'm gettin' all swole up just thinkin' about that."

"We'll just keep taggin' along after the train," Rod said. "Bum and Red Hand ain't that far behind us. 'Tween the four of us, we ought to be able to take out Preacher and them other nasty lookin' men that jined him by the Raft. Then, with them gone, the wagon'll be easy. They ain't nothin' but a bunch of pilgrims and women and kids."

"What other men?"

"Three trappers come up on the train back at the river. They don't look like much to me," Rod explained.

Preacher grinned at that. Nighthawk and Beartooth and Dupre had roamed the mountains together for years. They were three of the toughest men Preacher had ever known. Besides Jedediah Smith and himself, Beartooth was the only other man Preacher personal knew who had actual killed an attacking grizzly with just his knife. There might have been others—and probably were—but Preacher didn't know them.

If these four piss-poor rogues squatting down there by the trail thought they were the match for any mountain man Preacher knew they were sadly and badly mistaken.

"White women," one of the men breathed. "I can't hardly wait. After we get through with them, we can swap them to the Injuns for horses and pelts."

"What about the kids?" another asked.

"Bum and Red Hand says we kill them. You boys got any problem with that?"

"Naw. Just grab the babies by the ankles and bash they brains out agin a wagon wheel or boulder. I've done it lots of times with Injun brats. But ten, twelve-year-old girls make for good hoppin' on."

"You know," one of the outlaws said, "I got me an idea. See how you like it, Rod. We could take them young girls down into California and sell them to slavers. I know people who'll pay top dollar for a fine-lookin' girl. 'Specially blondes. They really bring a good piece of change."

"That ain't a bad idee," Rod said. "But that's up to Bum and Red Hand. I'll shore suggest it, though."

Nice folks down there, Preacher thought. Real gentlemen types. I ain't gonna have no trouble sleepin' after puttin' lead into these rabid coyotes.

Preacher moved closer still, his moccasins making only a faint whispering sound as he moved. He could now pick out shapes. But he wanted to get closer. This was going to be mainly pistol work, and he was still too far away by many yards for his short guns to be as effective as he would like.

"You say they's missionary people on this train, Rod?"

"Yeah. Two of the finest-lookin' females you ever seen. Make your mouth water just gazin' upon them. Hell, we been chasin' 'em for five hundred miles. That's how fine they is."

"I got to see this. I cain't hardly *wait* to see this."

Preacher warbled a bird's call. None of the four men so much as looked around.

Stupid worthless trash, Preacher thought. Outlaw scum can't even tell the difference between a man's call and a real bird. Mine echoed, you idiots.

"Hell, let's ride!" and outlaw declared.

"Hell, let's die!" Preacher shouted, and opened fire.

4

Preacher's yell startled them all. When he shot a big lard-butted, pus-gutted ruffian in the belly with his .54 Hawken, that really got their attention. The outlaw folded up like he'd been kicked by a mule and hit the ground, squallin' and bellerin', both hands holding his tore-up belly.

Preacher fired his double-shotted pistol and the muzzle exploded in fire and smoke. Both balls struck Rod in the face, and suddenly the outlaw no longer had a face. He fell back dead without uttering a sound.

Preacher dropped his Hawken and jerked out a pistol. It misfired and he found himself facing two pistols ready to discharge. Preacher leaped back into the brush just as the outlaws fired. He rolled fast, then came to his feet, holding his last charged pistol.

One of the two remaining outlaws threw good sense to the breeze and came hollering and crashing and cussing into the brush after the mountain man. Preacher opened him up from belly to gullet with his knife. He wiped the blade on the dying man's jacket and charged his weapons. He took his time, working fast but carefully. The dying man watched him and used some of his last breath.

"He's here, Jason!" he managed to gasp. "He done me in, I say. Oh, it hurts something fierce."

Preacher glanced at him and winked. "Have a pleasant journey to hell, child-raper."

"Damn your cold black heart!"

But Preacher was gone, slithering away soundlessly, working his way north of the last man on the trail, who, by now, must be getting real nervous.

"Who are you?" the last outlaw shouted. "Some brigand? Hell, join us. They's no point in anymore shootin'."

Preacher was standing about twenty yards from the man, by a tree. The man he'd belly shot with the Hawken was jerking and crying on the ground. But his cries were becoming weaker.

"It's Preacher!" the outlaw Preacher had opened up with his knife hollered weakly. "I knowed I'd seen him somewheres afore. Kill him for me, Jason. Avenge me, boy. Avenge your old partner!"

Preacher lifted his freshly charged and cocked pistol. "Yeah, Jason," he said. "Why don't you do that?"

Jason whirled, his face pale with fright and with a very nervous trigger finger. His shot went wide. Preacher's did not. Preacher coolly fired, the ball striking the young man in the chest. He screamed, dropped his pistol, and went down, both hands holding his bloody chest, covering the mortal wound.

Preacher charged his pistol, stood for a moment listening, and only then slowly walked over to the young man, guessing him to be in his early twenties. He stood over the man, his tanned and rugged face as set and hard as his eyes. "Gonna be a big tough outlaw, huh, boy? Didn't quite work out the way you had it planned, did it?"

"The old Devil take you!" the young man gasped. "Damn you to the pits of hell for killin' me."

Preacher snorted. "Well, if it wasn't me that put a ball in you it'd been someone else, I reckon. You got a ma you want to speak any last words to?"

"Hell with her and you."

Preacher shook his head in disgust. "You're a real no-good, ain't you?"

"It's gettin' dark!"

"It's gonna get a hell of a lot darker, boy. And you can trust me on that."

"I hate you!"

"Man shouldn't go to meet his Maker with hate in his heart. That's just another mark agin you, lad."

"I still hate you."

"Whatever." Preacher turned away and began gathering up the outlaw's horses. And they were good horses too. That's one thing you could count on about outlaws—due to their way of life, they had to have horses with a lot of bottom to them, so they always stole only the best.

"You ain't gonna leave me to die alone, is you?" the young man called.

"I thought you hated me?"

"I do. But I want somebody here when I pass."

"I'll stay. But I ain't gonna get too close. I might get a hot-foot when you expire."

But Preacher was talking to a dead man. He closed the lad's staring eyes and with a sigh, dragged him and the one with no face off the trail and into the timber. Then he went to see if the one he'd carved on was still alive. He was, and moaning.

"I hate you," the man said in a surprisingly strong voice. His eyes were very bright with pain.

"This is gettin' to be like an echo," Preacher told him. "You keep sayin' bad things about me, I ain't gonna say no words over y'all's restin' spot."

"You gonna bury us?"

"Yeah. I'll pile some rocks over you so's the varmits can't worry you. You got airy person you might want to know about your fate?"

"Damn bitchy wife and a shackful of squallin' kids back in the Missouri bottoms around New Madrid."

"You should have stayed to home."

"Fine time to tell me that." He closed his eyes, jerked once, then passed.

Preacher piled them all into a natural depression and tossed rocks and small logs over their bodies until he had them covered best he could . . . or wanted to. He took off Dupre's hat and said, "Oh, Lord, here these misbegotten, worthless, trashy, no-count, and misguided souls is. Do whatever the hell you want to with them. Amen."

He sat down and built a hat-sized fire and boiled some water for coffee. While that was heatin' up, he went through the possessions he'd taken from the outlaws' pockets. Between the four of them, they had three dollars and fifteen cents cash money.

"The glamorous life of an outlaw," Preacher said, and pocketed the money.

Their sleeping blankets were all ragged and full of fleas, so he tossed them aside. But their saddlebags were filled with pocket watches and rings and brooches and all sorts of jewelry, also some gold teeth, which they'd pried out of the mouths of the dead they'd robbed. A real nice bunch of people, these four.

Preacher took the ill-gotten booty and threw it all into the timber and brush.

He sat for a time, drinking his coffee and letting his nerves settle down. He knew there was no point in kidding himself, Bum and Red Hand were not going to give up simply because he had killed another of their gang. The quick way one of the gang—now lying dead—had recruited others showed him how easy it was to find those inclined to rob and rape and murder. The wilderness was not only attracting decent men and women and their families to settle and work the land and be good citizens, it was also attracting the thieves and murderers and the like.

And it would only get worser, Preacher figured.

Preacher carefully put out his fire, poured water on what remained, and stirred the ashes with a stick to make sure it was completely out. He squatted for a time, his mind busy on the problems facing the wagon train. He did not have one idea in all of billy-hell how he was going to get all those wagons through and past the south rim and then across the Snake. These pilgrims just didn't know what faced them.

Preacher knew that the missionary, Whitman, had tried it— and he guessed succeeded—the year before. But he'd been forced, so Preacher had heard, to abandon his wagons and transfer everything to pack animals. But these folks Preacher was guiding wasn't about to give up their possessions—it was all they had.

Well, he thought with a sigh, he'd just have to find a way. That was all there was to it.

"That's some fine-looking horseflesh there, Preacher," Dupre said, inspecting the animals Preacher brought into the encampment. "Their riders decided to walk the rest of the way and just given 'em to you, hey?"

"Something like that," Preacher replied, giving Dupre back his hat and settling his own on his head. He took the plate of food handed to him by a settler woman and sat down on the ground to eat. Nobody asked him anything until he had finished filling his stomach. Mealtime was serious business and there wasn't no point in chit-chatting until a man was done eating.

When he'd set his plate aside and hottened up his coffee, Preacher leaned back against a wagon wheel and told the others what had happened."

"The wilderness is fillin' up with scalawags," Beartooth opined. "I knowed when towns started up they'd be fillin' up with foot-padders and back-shooters and the like."

"What towns?" Preacher asked.

"Over in Oregon and Washington Territory. Why, I seen one town this last trip had more'un two dozen buildin's. Dupre said one of 'em had a ladies' dress shop that was spelt with two p's."

"Why?"

"Damned if I know." Beartooth scratched his woolly head. "How many p's is it 'posed to have?"

"Boys," Preacher said, "how in the hell are we gonna get these wagons acrost the south rim and over the Snake?"

"I talked to Tom Fitzpatrick not long ago," Dupre said. "He told me how he thought it could be done. He said Tom McKay had done it last year, but they had to leave the wagons at the Snake River Gorge. I think they's a way, but it's gonna be a rough one."

"What happens when we reach the Dalles on the Columbia?" Beartooth asked. "That is one evil place."

"We portage it," Preacher said.

"With the wagons?" Nighthawk broke his silence. "It's never been done."

"It's either that or float them," Preacher said.

"I reckon we could build rafts to ferry the people."

"With the wagons on them?" Nighthawk again spoke. He shook his head, "Ummm."

"Look," Dupre said, freshening his coffee. "Let's get these folks through the south rim and out of the gorge first." He looked over at Preacher.

Preacher nodded his head in agreement. "We'll take 'er one day at a time. I don't know of no other way to do it. Hell with it. I'm going to sleep."

"My God!" Swift exclaimed, as he stood with Preacher and the other mountain men, looking at the brutal terrain of the Snake's south rim.

"Get the winch out," Preacher told the wagonmaster. "The heaviest ropes. We're gonna be here for several days gettin' all these wagons acrost this mess. Get your strongest men to work the winch and put others unloadin' the wagons and totin' the possessions up that trail. We ain't gonna do it by standin' here jawin'. Let's go to work."

"How many of these steep rocky trails lie ahead of us, Preacher?" Richard asked.

"Oh, 'bout a thousand or so," he replied, then walked off.

"And he ain't kiddin'," Dupre told the missionary.

"Just be glad some trappers found a way around Hell's Canyon," Preacher called over his shoulder. Laughing, he walked on.

"What's that all about?" Swift asked.

"A place you don't even wanna look at," Dupre said. "Let's get to work."

And work they did. It was either that, or turn around and take the California Trail, which no one in the party wanted to do. Using ropes and muscle and winches, and sometimes doubling the mules and oxen, one by one the wagons reached the summit of the peak . . . only to discover another seemingly insurmountable, boulder-strewn steep mountain trail was what faced them.

So they squared their shoulders, rubbed sore and aching muscles, and faced the task. The men and women worked all that day, and managed to make three miles.

Richard and Edmond had lost their city flabbiness. Their waists and hips were leaner and their chests and arms and shoulders much more muscular. Now they didn't look so stupid strutting around in their buckskins.

No one sang songs around the fires that night. Directly after supper, nearly everyone except the sentries rolled up in their blankets and were snoring in two minutes.

"You gotta hand it to them, Preacher," Dupre said. "If this bunch here is gonna be the breed comin' from the East, we gonna be all right, to my way of thinkin'. I'm right proud of these pilgrims."

Preacher nodded his head in agreement, but he was still deep in thought.

"Spit it out, Preacher," Beartooth said.

"We're goin' over the Cascades," Preacher said.

Nighthawk looked across the dying fire at the mountain man. "Still got the fast water to cross."

"Rafts. We'll take the wagons apart. I'm talkin' about right down to the box. We'll make the box waterproof with tarps and tallow. From this moment on, save the candle drippin's. We'll use that to fill the small cracks and holes in the beds of the wagons. That way, should a raft get ripped apart, the wagon beds will still float."

"You a genius, Preacher!" Dupre said. "Hell, I'd a-never thought of that. But why not just stay on the rafts and head on down the Columbia?"

"Bum Kelley and Red Hand, and them warrin' Cayuses. We'd be sittin' ducks a-bobbin' around in the river. 'Sides, if the Cayuses is up in arms, the Snakes and others will be, too. I've made up my mind. We go over the Cascades."

"It's a hard two hundred and fifty miles through them mountains," Beartooth reminded his friend.

"And nobody every took no wagon train through them, neither," Dupre added.

"Well, boys," Preacher said, standing up and stretching. "The likes of us has been the first to do a lot of things. We've climbed up through mountain passes that no other white man ever done before us and gazed upon land that was wild and pure. We've seen the eruptin' steam holes in the high-up country and we've crossed the wild deserts to the south of us. We've drunk our fill from cold pure streams where no white man ever bellied down afore us. We're the ones who blazed the trails and forded the rivers and laid it all out and made it easier for them others we knowed would come a-snortin' and a-blowin' after we blazed the way. How many nights has we laid up in our buffler robes whilst the snow blowed all around us and was the first white men to be sung to by the wolves and the coyotes. We were, boys. Us. The very first mountain men. Nobody else 'ceptin' us. And there ain't never gonna be no one else like us. Bet on that. How can there be? We already done it.

"It was us who was the first to make friends with the Injuns—them that would let us—and the by-God first to do near 'bouts *everything* else that's been done by white men out here. We was the first. So the way I look at it, why, hell, boys, this little adventure we lookin' at now won't be nothin' compared to what already lays behind us."

"Damn, ain't that purty?" Dupre said. "You shore do talk nice when you're a mind to do so."

Beartooth was so moved he wiped a tear from his eye.

"Ummm!" Nighthawk grunted, getting to his feet to head for the bushes. Speaking of getting moved.

5

"He ain't comin' back, Bum," Slug told the outlaw leader. "And them Injuns is gettin' jumpy. They ain't likin' movin' so far out of their territory."

Bum nodded his head. He was rapidly getting a gut full of the mountain man called Preacher. But the thought of calling off the chase never entered his mind. He could not, however, afford to lose the support of Red Hand. Without Red Hand's braves, they would have no chance against the wagon train.

Bum knew Slug was right: Rod was not coming back. But that didn't necessarily mean he was dead. He might have developed a yellow streak and went the other way, rather than face Preacher alone. But Bum didn't think that was what happened. Rod just got careless and Preacher finished him.

Bum went to see Red Hand. He had been working out a plan in his mind and now was the time to see if it would work.

"I wouldn't blame you if you took your people and run back to the Portneufs," Bum told the renegade. "That's a mighty mean man we're chasin'. Lots of folks is scared of Preacher. So you take your boys and run away, if you're a mind to."

Red hand drew himself up tall and glowered at the outlaw. "Red Hand does not *run away* from an enemy." The Blackfoot spoke the words contemptuously. "Why would you think I would even consider such a cowardly act?"

"Well, I don't know. Just come to me, that's all. You gettin' so far away from home country, I reckon. And we ain't been doin' so good agin Preacher."

"You worry about the cowards among your own group," Red Hand told him. "And do not ever again question my courage or the bravery of my people."

"Fine," Bum said, ducking his head to hide his smile. "That suits me, Red Hand."

The Blackfoot stalked away, his back stiff from the insult against him. Bum went back to his own group. He squatted down by the fire and poured coffee.

"How'd it go?" Beckman asked.

"Red Hand wouldn't quit now no matter what happens or how far we have to travel. He's in it all the way."

"When do we hit the train?"

"Between the Blues and the Wallowa. Right along the Powder, I'll toss it to Red Hand and before it's over, he'll be thinkin' he suggested it."

"Why don't we hit them on the Columbia?" Moses suggested. "You know they got to take the river."

"Maybe not. Preacher ain't never done nothin' the easy way; so I been told. I got it in my mind that he's gonna try to take them acrost the Cascades."

"That'd be plumb stupid!" Bull said. "Ain't nobody ever took no damn wagon acrost them mountains. Ain't nobody ever goin' to, neither."

"I don't know of no one who ever tried it," Bum said. "But if anyone can do it, it'll be Preacher."

"So when do we ride for the Blues?"

"I'll give Red Hand an hour or so to get over his mad, then talk to him. I 'magine we'll pull out in the mornin'. We'll get there in plenty of time to lay out an ambush site and get all rested up."

"I liked Rod," Keyes said. "He was a good man."

"Obviously not good enough," Seedy said.

The traveling got rougher for those in the wagon train. The terrain was terrible and the mosquitoes worse. Great thick hordes of them fell on the wagon train and soon everybody was slapping and cussing and scratching from the bites. The weather was just as miserable as the terrain. One day it was ninety degrees, the next day it was cloudy and cold.

Bands of Digger Indians would line up on either side of the trail, to stand in silence and watch the wagon train. Many of them begged for food.

"Don't give 'em nothin'," Preacher warned the movers. "If you do, they'll wart you forever. Them's the sorriest tribe anywheres. They'll take crickets and roaches and make a stew of it. They eat rats and the like. Most disgustin' bunch of people I ever met in all my days."

"But they're *hungry!*" Penelope said.

"They won't do for themselves," Beartooth said. "They beg and steal. They'd rather starve than work. Ignore 'em, missy. They just ain't worth your pity."

The wagon train rolled on, following the Snake over rough and rocky ground. The wagon train stopped early that day, due to several broken wheels. The ground was so rough one woman fell off the seat and busted her head wide open. The wound was not serious, but like all head wounds, it bled freely for several minutes, giving the pilgrims a good scare.

"Everybody off them wagons and walk!" Preacher passed the word up and down the line.

"My wife is with child, sir!" a mover yelled in defiance.

"Shoulda thought of that 'fore you started, fool!" Preacher muttered in disgust.

They crossed Goose Creek the next day, straight up and straight down. Most movers lost articles out of their wagons. The ground was the worst they had experienced thus far.

That night, Preacher told Swift and a few of the others, "We can expect trouble up ahead. Place called Rocky Creek. It's about twenty miles from where we're camped. Since the first big band of movers come through last year, trouble-huntin' Injuns have been hangin' around there, and they're a mean bunch. Pass the word that nobody wanders off once we're there."

When Swift was gone to pass the word, Preacher said to his friends, "We're gonna push it tomorrow. We're gonna put fifteen miles behind us. That way we'll make Rocky Crick by mid-mornin' of the next day and put it behind us."

"You figurin' we'll have trouble there?" Trapper Jim asked.

"Yeah. Somethin's got these Injuns all stirred up. I don't wanna camp nowheres near the crick."

"What kind of Injuns will these be?" Richard asked.

"Northern Paiute, probably. Maybe some Bannock. Ain't no tellin' really. A lot of them renegades and just plain trouble-hunters. Renegades will put aside centuries-old tribal hatred and band together for protection." Preacher refilled his cup and sat back down. It was a nice evening, for a change. They were camped near a creek and everybody had bathed and washed clothes and were lounging about simply relaxing after a grueling day on the trail. Kids were playing within the relatively safe confines of the circled wagons. Mothers kept a good eye on them nonetheless.

The mountain men smiled and winked at one another. They alone knew that what they were doing had never been done before. A few wagon trains had punched through to the Columbia, for sure, but no one—*no one*—had ever taken a wagon train over the Cascades.

These mountain men would be the first to do so, something that mountain men enjoyed. Being the first.

"This is an excellent stretch of trail through here, Preacher." Swift remarked about noon of the next day. "I feel we could make better time."

"We could."

"Then why aren't we?"

"I don't want us to have to camp on Rocky Crick, that's why. We'll do about fifteen miles and then shut it down. That way we'll hit the crick and be long past it come time to circle for the night tomorrow."

"I hardly think these savages would attack a train of this size," Swift persisted.

"I've had my say," Preacher told him, then lifted the reins and rode ahead. "Damn igits!" Preacher muttered. "Can't see no further than the end of their noses."

He whoaed Hammer up short. Not a hundred yards ahead, sitting smack in the middle of the trail, was a mother grizzly and two cubs. She had not yet caught his scent and Preacher backed Hammer up and beat it to the train.

"Hold it up," he told Swift. "And don't be tootin' on that damn bugle, neither."

"What's the matter?"

"I said, hold up the goddamn train!"

Clearly miffed, Swift rode back and stopped the long wagon train. Beartooth rode up. "What's the matter?"

"Mama griz and two cubs sittin' in the middle of the trail. She'll weigh a good eight, nine hundred pounds. We'll let them alone and they'll move directly."

Young Avery rode up on one of his father's horses. "I'll go up and shoot her," he said.

"You'll do no such of a thing," Preacher told the hulking teenager. "Who'd care for them young of hern?"

The man-child shrugged his shoulders. "Who gives a hoot?"

"We do," Beartooth said. "Larn this now, boy: you don't kill something for the sake of killin'. You kill for survival or for food. You eat what you kill. You don't kill something just 'cause you—"

Avery sneered at the man and spurred his horse, heading at a gallop up the trail.

"Smart-mouthed little son of a bitch!" Beartooth cussed the young man.

Preacher touched his moccasins to Hammer and the big horse leaped forward, easily overtaking Avery. Preacher reached out and slapped the young man clean out of the saddle. Avery hit the ground and bounced on his butt a time or two.

"Pa!" he squalled.

"Get your butt in the saddle and get back to the train," Preacher told him.

"My pa'll whup you!" Avery said, climbing back into the saddle.

"Doubtful," Preacher told him. "Move."

"I'm fixin' to kill me a bear!" Avery said. "And you can go to hell."

Preacher jumped his horse forward and knocked Avery out of the saddle with a hard right fist to the smart-aleck's mouth. the blow was a brutal one and it smashed lips and brought blood leaking down onto the young man's shirt. Beartooth galloped up at that point and settled a loop around Avery's shoulders just as he was getting to his feet. Beartooth jerked on the rope and Avery went down again.

"Larn you some manners, squirt!" the burly mountain man said. He turned his horse and began dragging the youth back down the trail, to the train.

Preacher grabbed the horse's reins and led him along.

Avery was cussing just like a full growed man—which he very nearly was—and struggling to get to his feet. Everytime he did, Beartooth would jerk on the rope and down he would go again.

"By the Lord, you'll pay dearly for this!" Avery's pa, a man called Wade, yelled furiously upon witnessing his pride and joy being dragged down the trail at the end of a rope.

"Shut your trap or I'll dab a loop around your shoulders," Preacher told him.

"You step down from that horse and I'll give you a thrashing you're not likely to forget for the remainder of your days," the man said.

"Wagh!" Nighthawk shouted.

"There's to be a tussle!" someone in the train yelled.

"You a damn fool!" Dupre told the man. "Preacher'll clean your plow 'fore you can blink, pilgrim."

"I fought Cornish all my days," the mover told him, as Preacher slowly dismounted. "I'm not worried."

"Back away, mover," Preacher cautioned the man. "Your boy got what he deserved, and no more. It's nothin' to be fightin' about."

"You and that snot son of yours have been nothing but trouble since Missouri," a woman yelled from the train. "We should have voted to abandon you before reaching the Rockies."

A great majority of those gathered around loudly agreed with her statement.

Avery's father was rolling up his shirt sleeves and flexing his muscles. He did a little footwork in the trail to limber up.

Preacher was paying no attention to him. He had walked over to Swift to report what had taken place between Avery and the mountain men.

"Preacher," the wagonmaster said, "you'd best be wary of the man. He's a rough fellow. He ran taverns back East."

"Is that right? What do you 'spect I best do: run off somewheres and hide?"

The wagonmaster smiled. "Look at him carefully, Preacher. The man's a brute."

"He's big'un all right. I bet he'll make the ground tremble when he hits it . . . on his butt."

"My boy's been cut and bruised!" Wade hollered. "And he says you struck him in the mouth and face, Preacher. By the Lord, you'll pay for this. Turn and face me, Preacher. Receive your trashing like a man."

"Hee, hee, hee!" Beartooth giggled. "Pilgrim says he's a-gonna thrash you, Preacher. His one or two friends on the train say he's a mighty tough man. I'm afeared for your safety, Preacher."

"I just can't watch it," Dupre said. "The sight of blood makes me dizzy-headed."

"Hell, that's your natural condition," Preacher told the Frenchman.

Wade was drawing a line in the trail with the toe of his boot. Preacher watched the man, amusement in his eyes.

Nighthawk was watching Wade, puzzlement in his dark eyes. White people sure did some odd things.

"Be you warned that to step across this line means you are ready for the fight," Wade said.

"Is that what it means?" Preacher said with a laugh, as he took his pistols from the sash and handed them to Swift. "Now I 'spect you gonna tell me they's rules to this here fight?"

"That is correct, sir," Wade said. "Mister Swift will keep the rules and shout out when to break."

"When to do what?" Beartooth asked.

"To give a man time to recover from a knock-down," Wade told him. "Each man will retire away from his opponent once the other man is down. The fight will continue until one man yields or is knocked unconscious."

"Is that the way they do it back East now?" Preacher asked.

"That is correct. Now toe this line," Wade said.

"Yeah, Preacher," Dupre said. "Step up here and receive your thrashin'."

Preacher suddenly screamed like a panther and leaped at the bigger man. One foot shot out and slammed against Wade's face, knocking the man down to the dirt.

Preacher looked down at Wade, looking up at him, a startled expression on his face. "Now tell me again, where it is I re-tire to?" the mountain man asked.

6

Wade slowly got to his feet, an angry red splotch on the side of his face where Preacher had kicked him. He was trembling with rage. "You, sir, are no gentleman," he ground out. He lifted his fists and began dancing around.

"Oh, my!" Preacher said. "Now I know what you want to do." He jumped over and before the mover could throw a punch, Preacher grabbed Wade's wrists in an iron vise. Wade, red-faced in embarrassment, tried to break fee. He could not break loose from Preacher's powerful grip.

Dupre, Nighthawk, Trapper Jim, and Beartooth began clapping their hands in unison as Preacher danced the man all around the trail. "You dance good, Wade. This is fun. Somebody get a fiddle and a squeeze box. Let's have us a party."

"Circle round and dipsy-doo, up on your toes and turn real slow," Beartooth chanted. "Twirl your partner around there twice, back again and ain't that nice."

"You goddamn heathen, unhand me!" Wade bellered. He struggled in vain to break fee of Preacher's grip.

Dupre grabbed the first women he spied and began dancing around the trail. Others soon joined in. Someone found a fiddle and another man took out a squeeze box. Still others began clapping their hands. Up the trail, the grizzy sow lifted her huge head and grunted at the strange sounds. She moved her cubs off the trail and into the timber and stashed them safely in thick brush. Then Usrus horribilis went lumbering down the trail to investigate the strange noises in her woods. All nine hundred pounds of her.

Nighthawk was doing a little jig on the trail with several little boys and girls dancing with him.

Richard and Edmond, while taught to mightily forbid dancing as the devil's own work, were getting into the action, patting their boots to the rhythm. Melody and Penelope were shaking various parts of their anatomy to the beat.

"Turn me loose and fight, you bastard?" Wade shrieked.

"I'd rather dance," Preacher hollered. "Ain't this fun?"

"No!" Wade screamed.

"Kick him, Pa!" Avery yelled. "Trip him down on the ground!"

A mover just couldn't resist the opportunity. He leaned out from his wagon seat and conked Avery on top of the head with the handle of his bullwhip. Addled to his toes, the rash young man sank to the ground, both his eyes crossed from the blow.

"Yee-haw!" Preacher yelled, dancing around and around with his very reluctant partner.

The grizzly sow reached the top of the hill and looked down at the goings-on below her. She had never seen anything like it. She wasn't afraid of it—it is not known whether grizzlies are afraid of anything—yet something in her brain told her that this should be avoided at all costs. But not before she told the strange animals below here that this was her territory and to get the hell gone.

She reared up, standing about nine feet tall, and roared.

Horses, mules, cows, dogs, sheep, oxen, goats, and about forty cats panicked. The horses and mules reared up and fought their harnesses. The cows bellered and squalled. The goats and sheep bleated. The dogs barked. The cats howled.

The oxen did their best to turn the wagons around, right there in that narrow trail, and everything got all jumbled up.

The grizzly sow took one more horrified look and ran at full speed back to her cubs. She gathered them up and headed for another, more peaceful part of the timber.

Preacher had danced Wade to just the right spot. He released the man and give him a little shove. Wade went tumbling down the embankment and did a belly-whopper in the Snake River. Preacher looked around him, found Avery, and jerked him up and tossed him over the side. Avery rolled down the hill and slammed into his father, just beginning his climb back up the embankment. Father and son went together into the Snake.

"You son of a bitch!" Wade squalled at Preacher, standing on the trail, laughing at them.

It took the better part of an hour to get the livestock settled down and untangled. When Wade once more appeared, in dry clothing, and wanting to fight, Wagonmaster Swift told him that if he threw down one more challenge, he'd tie him to a wagon wheel and deal out twenty lashes from his whip. He had the power to do just that, and Wade knew it. Wade gave Preacher a dark look, which Preacher ignored, and returned to his wagon. Swift tooted on his bugle and the wagon train moved out, with everybody except Wade and Avery feeling better.

Wade's long-suffering wife had to struggle to hide her smile.

Preacher halted the wagon train about five miles from Rocky Creek. He ordered the sentries doubled and the wagons pulled in tight. Then he walked the circle of trains, visually inspecting each wagon. "Get dead leaves and twigs and the like and scatter them in front of your wagons. Make it several feet wide and put them three or four yards out. You wake up with something cracklin', shoot it. 'Cause it ain't gonna be nobody friendly."

"I got me a feelin'," Dupre said.

"Yeah, me, too," Preacher agreed. "I think we gonna have troubles this night."

Injuns is all turned ever' whichaway," Beartooth said. "Snakes down in Ute country. Paiute moved up north. Blackfoot and Arapaho wandering around down here. Cayuse on the prowl. It don't make no sense to me. We seen some Hidatsa over west of here. Whole bunch of them, wasn't there, Nighthawk?"

"Too damn many," the Crow said. "And they weren't huntin' food, neither. I think they flee the fever back East."

"I keep hearin' talk of an uprisin'," Preacher said. "'Bout tribes buryin' the hatchet and bandin' together. I reckon it's true." He leaned forward, cutting off a chunk of meat fairly oozing with fat. "Any Dog Soldiers with them?"

"Couldn't tell for certain," Beartooth said. "I hope not. I hate them damn contraries."

The Hidatsa Dog Soldiers did everything backward, hence they were called contraries. But they were fierce fighters and much feared.

A mover walked up and squatted down. "I thought the wild red savages always beat on drums before they attacked?"

Dupre and Beartooth grinned, Nighthawk looked disgusted but said nothing. "Some do back at the village," Preacher said. "Before a fight—gets 'em all worked up into a lather. But I ain't never seen no Injun totin' no drum in battle a-whuppin' on it. Although if you was to tell a contrary he couldn't, he would." Preacher laughed. "Wouldn't that be a sight to see?"

Thoroughly confused, and really wanting to ask what in the world a contrary might be, the mover sighed and stood up, returning to his family.

Very soon after supper was eaten and the dishes washed, the movers began settling down for sleep. Trapper Jim brought over a fresh pot of coffee and the mountain men relaxed, drinking the hot, strong brew.

"When you think they'll hit us?" Jim asked.

"You feel it too, huh?" Dupre asked.

"Yeah. My guess is just as soon as the people get good asleep. I don't think they're gonna wait too long."

"That's a good thought," Preacher said. "We'll just drink this here coffee and then take up positions. Our backs is in pretty good shape, backed up to the bluffs. East is clear enough. West and south'll be the way they'll hit us." He drained his cup. "I reckon it's time to go to work."

Preacher found Swift. "Get the folks out of their blankets," he told him. "We're a-fixin' to get hit by Injuns."

The wagonmaster cocked his head and listened for a moment. "But I don't hear a thing, Preacher."

"That's right, Swift. You don't hear nothin'. Now think about that."

The two men stared at one another for a moment. Swift nodded his head. "I'm learning," he told Preacher. "Takes me awhile, but I'll get there."

Preacher clasped him on the shoulder. "Good man. Now get them movers up and ready."

"I see something out there," a woman told Preacher as he walked by her wagon. "Several somethings. They're not trying to hide."

Preached angled over to her and stood gazing out into the night. He called out in Snake.

"One third of your horses and mules," the harsh voice came back to him, speaking in English, "And one third of all your supplies. Then you may pass through."

"Forget it," Preacher returned the shout. "And don't tell me you're hungry. They's game aplenty out there this summer. We ain't botherin' you, so there ain't gonna be no tribute paid."

"You will die then. All of you."

"Sing your death songs."

The Indians shouted out some very uncomplimentary and very uncomfortable suggestions to Preacher.

Preacher heard Beartooth's laugh. "Your horse wouldn't like that either, Preacher."

"You have that stinking cowardly Crow puke Nighthawk with you?" the Indian shouted.

That prompted a long stream of invectives from Nighthawk. He told the Snake where to put his bow and arrows, his horse, his wife, his kids, his mother, his father, and all his friends.

"Wagh!" Dupre said. "Talk about a tight fit."

A bow string twanged and the arrow thudded into the bed of a wagon near Preacher.

The shapes that the woman had seen had long disappeared as the Snakes prepared to attack.

"Only cowards attack women and children!" Beartooth shouted. "None of you are fit to be called braves. I say you is all stinking coyote vomit."

"Bear-Killer will not die well, I am thinking," the Snake's words came out of the darkness.

Preacher had hunkered down. His eyes had found a shape on the ground that was unnatural to the terrain. He lifted his Hawken and sighted it in, squeezing the trigger. The powerful rifle boomed and the shape lifted itself off the ground for a few seconds, then collapsed, shot through and through.

Preacher quickly reloaded as arrows filled the night air. One mover screamed as an arrow embedded in his thigh. A child began crying and its mother tried to soothe the child into silence with calming words.

Nighthawk's rifle crashed and another Snake went down, shot through the stomach. The brave began screaming in pain as he rolled on the ground, his innards ruined.

"If we can get three or four more," Preacher told the man who crouched beside a wagon wheel, "them bucks will break it off. I don't think they's many of them out there."

Preacher was thoughtful for a moment. "Pass the word:

everyone with two rifles get ready to stand and deliver. We'll all fire at once. Injuns is notional. That much firepower all at once might change their minds. Keep your second rifle at hand in case it just makes 'em mad and they charge."

The mover looked at Preacher.

Preacher shrugged his shoulders. "Life's full of chances."

Within two minutes time, all the men were ready. "Now!" Preacher shouted, and the night roared and flashed with fire and smoke and lead balls.

The movers were lucky this night. Their blind fire had hit several warriors. The Indians, never with enough ball or powder, figured that any group with so much shot and powder that they could waste it made their medicine very bad. Shouting threats and insults, they pulled back into the night.

Nighthawk laid on the ground, his ear to the earth and listened. "They're riding away," he finally said, standing up. "Heading south. That bunch is through for this night."

Preacher walked over to the man with an arrowhead sunk more than halfway through his thigh. "You got any drinkin' whiskey?" he asked.

"In the wagon," the mover said through gritted teeth.

"Get it," Preacher told the man's wife.

The woman returned quickly with a jug of rye and handed it to Preacher. "Thankee kindly, ma'am," he said. Preacher took him a long pull and then handed the jug to the wounded man. "I could say that this is gonna hurt me worser than it does you, but I'd be lyin'. You take you three or four good swallers and tell me when you're ready."

The mover's adam's apple bobbed up and down as he swallowed the raw brew. "I'm ready."

Preacher nodded at Dupre and Beartooth and the mountain men grabbed the mover's arms. Preacher got him a good grip on the shaft of the arrow and pushed hard. The man screamed as the arrow tore out the back of his leg. Preacher quickly broke off the shaft and pulled it out, then reached behind the man's leg and jerked out what remained.

The mover had passed out.

Preacher poured some whiskey on the wound, front and back, and told the woman, "Nighthawk'll take over now. Let him fix his potions and poultices and don't interfere. Injuns been usin' things like marigold and goldenseal and dandelion and nipbone and others for centuries. And they work."

"What do you suggest for a bruise?" Edmond asked, pulling up his sleeve and showing a badly bruised arm.

"I won't ask how you got it. You pick you some bruisewort in the mornin'. That'll fix you right up."

"Some what?"

Preacher smiled. "Daisy flowers. Crush 'em up and lay 'em on the bruise. Works, ol' son."

"Pickin' handfuls of daisies on the banks of the Snake," Beartooth sang and did a little dance. "This'un I don't like, that'un I'll take."

Dupre looked at him. "I swear you too young to be getting senile. But you shore been actin' goofly here of late. Did you fall off your horse and bang your head?"

"Nope. I just feel good, that's all. And you best feel good too. 'Cause when we cross the Snake in a week or so, and start headin' north, feel-good time is gonna be over."

"I allow as to how you may be right." The two men linked arms and went off singing, "Pickin' daisies on the banks of the Snake . . . This'un I don't like, that'un I'll take . . ."

Then the two mountain men did a little dance step and made up some lines that caused several of the women to squeal and cover their faces with their aprons.

Nighthawk sighed and shook his head.

7

Preacher halted the train about a mile from Rocky Creek and he and Dupre, Nighthawk, and Beartooth rode up to the crossing. No Indians were in sight, but the four of them knew that accounted for nothing in this country.

"Quiet," Preacher observed. "But a peaceful kind of quiet."

"Right," Dupre said dryly. "Like that bird singin' yonder that ain't no bird."

"I gleaned that right off," Beartooth said. "So they're waitin' for us in them rocks over yonder crost the crick. Now, I consider that to be downright nasty, sneaky, unfriendly, and not a-tall to my likin'."

"Yeah," Preacher said with a grin. "Not nothin' like any of us would do."

"You got you an idee," Beartooth said. "'Ever' time you grin like 'at, I know you got something sneaky wigglin' around inside you headbone."

"I do for a fact. Let's ride on back and get things set up. We'll give them renegades something them that live through can tell their grandkids."

"Real easy like and not in no hurry," Preacher told Swift, "I want you to pick out twelve of the best shots in the train and get them ready to load up, six in each wagon. Three to a side. I want them to have at least three rifles loaded up and pistols at the ready. Beartooth and Nighthawk is on the south right now checkin' to see if we're bein' spied on. Rig the canvas so's it can be jerked up from the inside. Have Jim drive one wagon, and a damn good man on the seat of the other. We're gonna turn this ambush around."

The warbling of a bird reached them. Preacher smiled. "That's Nighthawk tellin' me it's clear. When you get your men picked out, load ever'body up on the south side of the wagons so's the Injuns won't see what's goin' on."

"Where will you be?" Swift asked.

"Me and Beartooth will be in front. Dupre and Nighthawk to the rear. What we'll do, you and me, is have a big argument on the banks with me yellin' that we can only take two wagons acrost at a time. Then we'll move 'em out."

Swift looked doubtful. "I hope this works," he finally said, with a shake of his head.

Preacher grinned at him. "Me and Beartooth's gonna be in the front. What are you complainin' about?"

Preacher walked back to where the two wagons were being prepared. With only the flaps facing southward lowered, men busied themselves off-loading the wagons' contents, making room for the marksmen. The mountain men double-shotted their pistols and checked their rifles.

"Me and Nighthawk found signs that show some lazy-butt Diggers has joined this bunch," Beartooth said. "This bunch mostly is tribal castouts. For a Digger to throw somebody out of the tribe means they really must have done something awful."

"I ain't never heard of a digger ever throwin' nobody out," Dupre said. "Most of 'em's too damn lazy to take the time for a meetin'."

Preacher told Swift, "Make your people ready for an attack. We can't circle here, so keep everybody in the wagons, or right near them. Guns ready."

"We're ready," Trapper Jim called.

"Come on, Swift," Preacher said. "Let's us walk down to the bank and have a quarrel."

The two men stood on the banks and shouted at each other for several minutes, with a lot of finger-pointing at the other side of the creek. Finally, the wagon master threw up his hands and stalked off.

"Bring 'em on," Preacher shouted. "Beartooth, bring my horse down here, will you?"

"You think they bought it?" Beartooth asked, when Preacher had swung into the saddle.

"I hope so." He cocked his Hawken and Beartooth did the same. "We're gonna have to fire these things like pistols," he told the big mountain man with a grin. "So get a good grip on yourn. I'd hate for you to lose it and you have to go wadin' in the crick after it. Your feet's so dirty the water'd be ruint for miles downstream."

"Wagh!" Beartooth said. "You ain't token a bath in so long even the fleas is a-leavin' you. I oughtta shove you offen your horse so the poor animal could take a decent breath. It's a wonder he ain't dropped stone dead from havin' to smell you."

They insulted each other while the wagons were lumbering down the trail to the creek.

"I reckon we'll play this here game out like we see it oncest we're crost," Beartooth said. "Watch your top-knot ifn you have the leave the saddle, ol' son."

"Same to you, Bear-Killer. Here they are. So here we go."

They stepped their horses into the creek and began the crossing, staying close to the first wagon, driven by Trapper Jim. They felt the attack would begin as soon as the second wagon was fully out of the creek and past the top of the embankment. The renegade Indians would, in all likelihood, be content with slaughtering those in the two wagons rather than face defeat or taking heavy losses by waiting until the entire train was over.

"In the rocks left and right," Beartooth whispered. "Unless a rock has taken to growin' a hand."

"Yep. That's a careless Injun. Tell you what, just as soon as the last wagons crost, we kick these hammerheds into a gallop and get past them boulders. I'll swing left and you swing right—that's the side your furthest leg is on," he added with grin, "and we'll come up 'hind 'em."

"I would tell you to keep low in the saddle," Beartooth responded with a smile, "but you so damn scrawny and poor as it is, if an Injun gets an arrow in you it'll be pure luck. Never seen a man afore that has to stand in the same spot twicest to make a shadder."

"Don't worry none 'bout takin' no arrow-points, Beartooth. They's so much lard and blubber on you it won't do no damage to amount to much."

They stepped their horses onto the bank and started up the slight incline.

"The only place Beartooth might take an arrey is in his butt," Trapper Jim called. "Way it hangs out over the sides of that saddle makes a right temptin' target."

"I don't know why I 'ssociate with the likes of you people," Beartooth said. "Way you continue to heap insults upon the poor head of this humble child of God."

"Wagh!" Preacher said, then spat. "You bring it all on yourself. Any man who'd winter with a squaw as ugly as that female you took up with back in '31 is beyond redemption. I thought you'd took up with a bear first time I come up on you two. What was her name? She Who Frightens The Sun?"

Beartooth grinned. "She cooked good and was right cosy in the robes, though."

"I 'spect she were that. 'Course you had to kill nine deer to get enough skins for her dress. First time that woman reared up in front of me I jumped ten feet in the air. I thought I done come up on a Sasquatch."

"I allow as to how she were a queen compared to that Assiniboin you took for a bride back in '28."

"I *had* to marry up with her," Preacher said. "It was either that or they was gonna kill me. I'm tellin' you, her father was desperate to get shut of that girl. He didn't name her Squalls a Lot for nothin'. First time she hollered at me the whole damn tipi fell down."

The second wagon reached the crest of the bank and Preacher let out a wild whoop and Hammer took off like he'd been shot out of a cannon.

Preacher cut left and Beartooth cut to the right just as the rocks on both sides of the trail were suddenly swarming with rogue Indians.

The canvas on the wagons was jerked off and the riflemen inside leveled their weapons and cut loose with a volley. These Indians never had a chance. Taken completely by surprise, they were cut down and their blood began staining the rocks and boulders by the creek.

Preacher left his horse and slammed into a buck, knocking him to the ground. He sprang to his feet with a knife in one hand an a pistol in the other. Preacher shot him at nearly point-blank range with the Hawken and the ball passed right through him, the impact knocking the brave off his moccasins. Preacher used his rifle like a club, cracking the skull of a buck who came screaming at him.

Dropping the Hawken, Preacher jerked out two pistols—double-shotted as usual—and took two more out with them, the balls doing fearful damage to the braves.

A brave jumped at Beartooth and the huge man grabbed him by the neck and hurled him against a boulder, breaking the warrior's back with a horrible cracking sound.

Nighthawk turned as a renegade Sauk—identified by his distinctive necklace of grizzly bear claws—cursed Nighthawk for a mangy Crow dog. Many of his tribe had been pushed west by the ever-moving and encroaching whites. Nighthawk lifted a pistol and drilled the Sauk through the heart, then ran to help his friend, Dupre, who was struggling with two Indians who wore Sioux markings.

Nighthawk clubbed one with the butt of his pistol, smashing the man's skull. Dupre threw the other one to the ground and shot him in the head.

Trapper Jim had left his wagon seat, a pistol in each hand, and two dead Indians lay at his feet.

"It's over!" Preacher shouted. "Stop firin'. It's over."

Men coughed nervously and rubbed at eyes that watered and smarted from the thick gray smoke from their black powder weapons. The mountain men went about the grisly task of finishing off those warriors who were badly wounded.

"Stay in the wagons," Preacher told the movers. "This ain't nothin' you need to get involved in. It's just something that has to be done. Reload all your weapons. That'll give you something to do." He shook his head, but he was proud of the movers. They had conducted themselves well.

Nighthawk knelt down beside a badly wounded, gut-shot Cayuse and spoke in his own language. "You are dying. Do you want me to hasten death?"

"I want you to do nothing, Crow puke," the defiant warrior told him. "Except leave so I do not have to look upon your stupid, ugly face. I do not want that to be the last thing I see in this life."

Nighthawk rose. "Then I shall certainly abide by your wishes, Cayuse vulture shit."

He walked away, leaving the buck to die alone.

"You ever see so damn many tribes in one spot?" Dupre asked, as the mountain men met back on the trail. "I counted eight tribes. They's a dead Cree over yonder."

"Worries me," Preacher admitted, as Swift yelled from the other side.

"When do we cross?" the wagonmaster yelled.

"Bring 'em on over!" Trapper Jim shouted, waving at the

man. He climbed back on the seat and pulled his wagon on ahead, the second wagon following.

"Worries you?" Nighthawk said, pointing to a dead Indian. "That's a Crow over there. I knew him as a good man. It's hard for me to believe that a Crow would join up with such a band of puke and maggots."

The men gathered their horses and got off the trail as the wagon train began its crossing of the creek. No one asked if the mountain men were going to bury the dead Indians. By now, they knew they would not. But they did help drag them out of sight so the womenfolk wouldn't have to look at the mangled and bloody bodies.

The wagons lumbered across slowly, the creek crossing going well until a wheel came off and dumped some of the wagon's contents into the now muddy water.

"Don't try to drive them wagons around it," Preacher hollered out the warning. "They's rocks on one side and a drop-off on the other."

"Rig a skid!" Swift shouted. "Helpers down here, boys. Let's step lively now."

Melody walked her horse across the creek to sit side-saddle and watch the proceedings. She wrinkled her little nose at the smell of death that hung heavily around the ambush site, and very pointedly ignored Preacher.

"That woman wants to share her blankets with you, Preacher," Dupre said.

"She's a looker," Beartooth said.

"I'd sooner bed down with a coyote," Preacher said. "I done told that woman fifteen times to leave me be. It's like tryin' to get shut of a hongry bear when you're totin' fresh-kilt meat."

"Why don't you bed her down and then just ride off?" Dupre suggested.

"If I done that, she'd be followin' me around forever, totin' a bedroll. I can just see it now. All the rest of my days, I'd have this female followin' me acrost the plains and the mountains.

No matter where I might wander, she'd be right behind me, callin' out, 'Come back, Preacher. Preacher, come back,' Lord, I'd be the laughin' stock of the West." He shook his head as his friends broke out in laughter.

Melody cut her eyes to the group of mountain men, unaware of the Indian who was only a few yards from her. He had not moved during the ambush. He lay between a rock and a small bush. He was one with the earth, conspicuous to anyone who might glance his way and actually see what lay before them. But the Indian knew that while whites look at many things, most of them actually see very little.

All around him movers strained and grunted and swore as they finally got the wagon with the broken wheel out of the creek and up the grade. No one saw the lone brave. He was going to die, and he knew it. It didn't matter. He had sung his death song hours before. He moved only his eyes as he planned out his final few minutes on this earth. Up swiftly, one short jump, and the honey-haired woman on the horse would be dead. No matter if the others killed him. That was not important.

But the horse didn't like the strange scent in his nostrils. He kept fighting the bit, wanting to leave this place, the smell of the warrior making him nervous.

Preacher looked at the skittish horse, wondering if there was a snake over there. Something was sure making that horse nervous. Melody was having a hard time controlling the animal, and Preacher knew she was a good horsewoman. Something was very wrong. He left the group and walked toward Melody, reflex making him cock the Hawken as he walked.

The Indian sensed it was now or never. He knew the legendary mountain man called Preacher, and he was proud that it would be a mighty warrior who killed him. That was good. The mountain men would tell the story and Indians would hear it. Songs would be sung about how he died. He made his move, springing off of the earth and leaped toward Melody, a war axe in one hand, ready to bash her brains out.

The horse walled its eyes and trembled, then reared up in fright, took one big jump, and Melody fell off the side-saddle rig and hit the ground, landing on her butt in a sprawl and in a cloud of dust. She cut her eyes, saw the Indian in mid-air, and let out a shriek that was startlingly close to the sounds that Squalls a Lot used to make.

Preacher cooly lifted the Hawken one-handed and fired it like a pistol, the heavy ball striking the warrior just under his throat and tearing out his back. The ball seemed to stop the warrior in mid-flight. He did not utter a sound. He was dead when he hit the earth.

Melody jumped up, ran to Preacher, and flung her arms around his neck. "My hero!" she said, then passed out cold.

"Oh, Lord!" Preacher said. "I ain't never gonna get shut of this female."

8

Preacher handed Melody over to a gaggle of females and
retreated back to his horse.

"Preacher, come back!" he heard Melody call weakly.

"Hell, it's started already," he muttered, and put Hammer
into a trot. Beartooth climbed into the saddle and rode out
after him, catching up with him about a half mile from the
creek.

"You're a marked man, Preacher," he told him. "I hear
weddin' bells in your future."

"What you're hearin' is your dried-up brains rattlin' agin
each other."

"We'll come see you from time to time." The mountain
man wasn't about to let up. "See how you're gettin' on, havin'
to live with walls all around you."

"You best build you a wall around that mouth of yourn,"
Preacher told him. But he knew the ribbing was far from over.
The boys hadn't even got started yet. Preacher knew he was in
for it now. He cut his horse toward a stand of timber. "This
looks like a good spot to light and sit and have some coffee.
It'll take them movers hours to get crost that crick and this far."

"I'll start a fire and boil some coffee," Beartooth offered.
"You best go over to that little puddle yonder and wash your

face and hands and slick back that shaggy mane of yourn. Your ladylove'll be along shortly."

Preacher told him where to go, how to get there, and what to do when he arrived.

"Wagh!" Beartooth said with a laugh. "That shore would be uncomfortable ridin'. Speakin' of ridin', here comes them two Bible-thumpin' friends of yourn."

"I say," Edmond said, dismounting. "We've taken a vote and decided to rename the creek back there."

"Is that right?" Beartooth asked, unable to get the grin off his bearded face.

"Yes," Richard said. "We are going to erect a sign and call it Hero Creek. In honor of Preacher."

"Have mercy!" Beartooth said. "Hero Crick. You hear that, Preacher?"

Preacher muttered under his breath.

"What's that you say, Preacher?" Beartooth pressed.

"I said I ain't no gawddamn hero. That's what I said."

"Oh, but I say, Preacher, you are indeed. Why, Miss Melody would have been killed if it were not for your brave and heroic actions and quick thinking," Edmond said.

Beartooth rocked back and forth in front of the small fire. "Hee, hee, hee!" he cackled. "Gen-u-ine hero, that's what we got in our midst, yes sirrie. I be a frontiersman like Dupre read to me about, and you be a hero. Lord, what a pair." He howled with laughter and rolled around and around on the ground.

"I fail to see the humor in this," Richard said. "I must admit, I am at a loss."

Preacher looked at the two Easterners. How to tell them that what happened not an hour past was something that occurred with almost monotonous regularity in the wilderness. It became a hard fact of life that had to be faced. No one thought anything about heroics.

Preacher shook his head. "Richard, you and Edmond ride back to the wagons and guide them to this spot. Right here."

Richard stuck out his chest. "It would be an honor, sir! Come, Edmond."

They ran for their horses.

"I bet he gets 'em lost 'tween thar and here," Beartooth opined.

"I don't hardly see how he could. The trail's fifteen feet wide and a blind man could follow it. 'Sides," he said with a smile. "He's got Jim and Dupre and Nighthawk to sorta help him along."

"We gonna be crossin' the Snake in 'bout three, four more days, Preacher. You been givin' that any thought?"

"A lot of thought. They's wagons that's crossed it, but not very many and not with the water so high. I'm thinkin' we're gonna have to raft and rope . . . and pray, if you're of a mind to."

Beartooth grinned. "Oh, everything will be all right, Preacher . . ." Beartooth noticed Preacher's hand inching toward a rock and got ready to jump. "I just know it will, since we got us a hero along!"

Preacher hurled the rock and Beartooth jumped. But he was just a tad too late. The rock caught him smack in the ass and Beartooth howled like a mad puma. Then he rolled to his feet and chased the much smaller and much more agile Preacher all over the place, until finally Beartooth collapsed on the ground.

"Ox," Preacher said, falling down beside him and relaxing on the cool ground, shaded by the stand of timber. "You and Greybull gettin' to be 'bout the same size. Fat."

"I ain't neither fat. I'm stocky built and have lots of muscles, that's all."

"Between your ears, mostly."

"Preacher?"

"I ain't moved."

"It ain't never gonna be like it was before, is it?"

Preacher was silent for a moment. With a heart that was

heavy, he said, "No, it ain't, Bear. That's over. Or will be soon. It's our fault; we done it."

"How you mean?" Beartooth rolled over and up on one elbow.

"Don't fall on me, you moose. You'll squash me flat as a flapjack. How do I mean? Hell, we're the ones who trapped out all the streams, ain't we? Just to satisfy some fancy lady or foppish man back East. We talked about it 'fore. Lots of times. But we kept on doin' it. We ain't got no one to blame but ourselves . . . as far as the fur, that is. The people comin' out here like swarms of locust? Well, that was bound to happen. We're a nation of movers, I reckon. And I opine we ain't seen nothin' yet. They'll be towns a-springin' up right and left and folks a-buildin' fences and roads and dammin' up cricks and rivers. Why, you know what Richard told me? He said that folks has dug a big wide ditch, a canal, he called it, that's three hundred and fifty miles long and filled the damn thing up with water so's people can float boats on it."

Beartooth reared up and blocked out the light. Preacher rolled out of the way. "He's a-lyin' to you, Preacher. They ain't nobody that damn stupid."

"He ain't lyin' neither. They call it the Erie Canal. And it cost millions and millions of dollars to build."

"Who paid for it?"

"Why, hell, I don't know. The government, I reckon."

"Where'd they get the money?"

"Do I look like a damn professor? How should I know?"

"Life's getting' too complicated for me, Preacher." Beartooth flopped back down and the ground trembled for a moment. "I think I'll just find me a good woman who can put up with me, build me a little cabin in the mountains, and re-tar."

"You ain't a-gonna do no such of a thing and you know it. Neither am I. We gonna be ridin' the mountain 'til the day we die."

"Greybull's a-scoutin' for the Army. I heard tell that Pugh was hangin' on, tryin' to make a livin' trappin' up north of here. Him and Lobo and Deadlead. Thumbs Carroll is some-where on the Platte. I don't know where Powder Pete and Tenneysee and Matt and Audie is."

"I thought Lobo was a-livin' with a pack of wolves that he adopted—or they adopted him?"

"He goes back to 'em from time to time. He tried to teach one to talk for five years. I think he finally gave up on that. Wolf hiked his leg and pissed all over him.

"That'd be discouragin', I reckon."

The group rolled on without further mishap. The only ad-venture they encountered was the daily grind of surviving the oftentimes monotonous trek westward.

The second day after the failed Indian ambush at Rocky Creek, the train rattled and lumbered over twenty-two miles of trail. It was the most miles they'd ever done in one day on the Oregon Trail. The next several days were also uneventful. The following day would not prove to be so peaceful. They had to cross the Snake.

The mountain men stood on the south side of the river, gazing across its rushing waters to the north bank.

"Here's where we test the mettle," Dupre said.

"It ain't as bad as I've seen it," Preacher said. "The islands is visible and they're big enough to hold wagons to rest. I reckon a far-thinkin' man could make some money by oper-atin' a ferry here."

Within a few years, someone would.

"Well, let's get ropes strung and start gettin' the people acrost," Beartooth said. "I'm just hopin' we don't lose nobody here."

"If we do, maybe it'll be that damn Avery," Dupre said. "But I don't figure we'll be that lucky."

He'd been caught spying on ladies as they went to the bushes. Swift had warned the young man's father that if it happened again, he was going to lash his son. The father had said that would be done only over his dead body.

"That can be arranged," Preacher told the man.

They lost the first wagon that attempted to cross. Currents grabbed it and carried it downstream, smashing it against rocks. The team was saved, and most of the possessions had been off-loaded.

"We got two of the wheels," Preacher told the devastated man and woman. "We can build you a cart and a travois."

"A what?" the woman asked.

"I'll show you later. It ain't hopeless, people. It just looks that way," he added.

It took three days to get the entire train across the river. No more wagons were lost, but several had been damaged due to ropes coming loose or breaking under the strain. And half a dozen wheels would have to be repaired. One child fell into the river, but a very alert Richard grabbed the screaming girl before she could be swept away and lost.

"Now you can be a hero," Preacher told him. "I gladly give up the title."

"You take all the fun out of it," Beartooth told Preacher. But he stood a safe distance away as he said it.

"How much stock did we lose?" Preacher asked Swift.

"We were very lucky. We only lost a few head. And no milk cows. They'll be a tragedy here someday, I'm thinking. That's a wicked crossing."

Preacher's smile was grim. "You ain't never seen the Dalles on the Columbia."

The train rolled on, now taking a more northerly course as they put the Snake behind them. No one missed it. Indians came down out of the mountains to watch them, standing or sitting their ponies and silently watching the long train as it pushed north and west.

"Relax," Preacher passed the word for the first time the Indians appeared. "Them Nez Perce. They ain't gonna bother you if leave them alone." I *hope,* he silently added. He rode over to stand in front of a mounted sub-chief and made the sign of friend.

"I speak your language," the Indian said. "So it is as we were told. The white man comes like ants to honey."

"Looks that way," Preacher told him. "And I ain't likin' it no more than you."

"Preacher has never lied to us so I will be truthful to you. The Cayuses are making war talk. And Red Hand has joined with a large band of whites and now waits in the Blues. Is it you they are after?"

"Yeah. How many is they?"

The sub-chief shook his head slowly. "Plenty. Twenty-five, maybe thirty, maybe more of the white outlaws. Red Hand has gathered a large force to follow him. Bad Indians whose tribes ran them from the village. Killers all. Maybe seventy-five of them. White haters. You are going the way of the trappers—through the Blues?"

"Right through them. Blues to the west and the Wallowas to the East."

The Nez Perce nodded his head gravely, his eyes expressionless. "May the Gods ride with you, Preacher." He made the sign of friend, and he and his party were gone.

Preacher rode back to the train and reined up beside Dupre and Nighthawk. "If that Nez Perce can count, we're lookin' at maybe a hundred or more of Red Hand's and Kelley's people."

"In the Blues?" Nighthawk asked.

"Yep. You 'member where the Powder makes that big wide curve? That's a bad crossin' there. We'll be tied up the better part of two days. That's where they'll hit us. Bet on it."

"When we're all split up, half on one side and half on the

other," Dupre said. "Red Hand and Bum might be worthless, but they ain't stupid."

"You got it," Preacher looked thoughtful for a moment. "Well, we can't do nothing to change it, so's let's concentrate on just gettin' there."

That was beginning to be a problem. The wagons had put hundreds of tough miles behind them, and they were all beginning to show signs of wear. Wheels were shattering nearly every day. Tongues were breaking and the pace of the trek had slowed considerably.

Preacher did not push them. He made daily inspections of the wagons and knew that the movers had to set their own pace. He could only guide them, not make them move faster.

They pushed on, crossing Canyon Creek and several days later, camping near Lucky Peak. From there, Preacher turned them westward for a time and plunged deeper into the wilderness.

"You reckon they's some boys gone be up here at the fork?" Preacher asked Dupre.

"They wasn't when we went out that way. But that was some months back. If they is, they gonna be plumb shocked to see this bunch come a-rattlin' in."

"And be busy callin' us nine kinds of fools for bringin' 'em, too," Beartooth added.

Richard came a-foggin' up, lathering his horse. "Preacher! A child is gone. Little Patience Lander. Swift has halted the train for a search."

"Had to happen," Preacher muttered, and turned his horse, riding back to the hysterical mother, standing with a group of other women by the wagons.

This was brush and low hill country, perfect for ambushes and for Indians to sneak in and steal a horse, cut a throat, or grab a child. But neither Preacher nor any of the other mountain men believed Indians grabbed the little girl. None of them had seen any sign of Indians since Preacher talked with the Nez Perce several days back. But that possibility could not be discounted.

"We're gettin' real close to Cayuse country," Dupre reminded him.

"Yeah, that is a fact," Preacher said. "Let's start circlin' for sign. We'll find her." The mother's wailing had grown louder. He turned to Swift. "Somebody calm that female down 'fore she works herself into the vapors."

Preacher left his horse and set out walking, slowly working in an ever-widening circle. He took the terrain to the northeast. Bogus Basin lay only a few miles away, near the edge of the Salmon River Mountains.

The thing that bothered Preacher most was that some of Red Hand's people might have been spying on them and seen a chance to grab a kid and done it. The young age of the girls wouldn't make any difference to a renegade—white or red. They'd mount her and then kill her.

Behind him he heard someone shout wildly, "Lord, Lord, everybody. Mary Ellsworth's gone into hard labor. She's gonna birth anytime now."

"Wonderful," Preacher said. He paused, his eyes picking up on a track. He knelt down and studied it, his skin growing clammy. Moccasin tracks. He carefully inspected the find. Four sets of Injun tracks and one set of little girl prints. They had her. If it was a Cayuse or even Blackfoot, they wouldn't harm the little girl. They'd adopt her into the tribe. Her life would be hard, but she'd be alive. They might beat her, but they wouldn't rape her. But Preacher had him a hunch these were renegades from Red Hand's bunch.

That put a whole new light on it.

9

He looked back. He was a good mile from the wagon train—too far for a shout and he didn't want to fire a shot into the air. Since this was brush country, and it had been dry, the renegades would have stashed their horses several miles away—not wanting to raise a dust—and approached the wagon train on foot. So now it was a race against time.

Preacher broke into a trot, staying with the tracks. And the Injuns were running now; he could tell that by the longer strides. One of them was making a much heavier print, so he was carrying the child.

I tole and tole and tole them women to keep their eyes open for their kids, Preacher thought. *Don't never take your eyes offen them. Dammit!*

But he knew this wasn't the woman's fault. The girl had probably been riding on the sideboard—called a lazyboard—or on the tailgate and Red Hand's people just popped out of the brush and snatched her off 'fore she could set up a squall. They snuffed a gag into her mouth and set off on a run once they got clear of the trail.

Preacher was gaining on them. He caught a glimpse of brown skin not that far ahead of him. He had his Hawken and his brace of pistols. Three shots and four of them. He'd have

to make every shot count, and then, when the bastard totin'
the child set her down to make a fight of it, Preacher would
have to be close enough to cut him.

He wanted desperately to look behind him, to see if Beartooth or Dupre or Nighthawk or Trapper Jim might be closing,
but he knew he couldn't risk it. He had to keep his eyes to the
front.

He was only a few hundred yards behind them now. He had
heard their running footsteps a couple of times. Approaching
a huge boulder, Preacher took a chance and jumped, landing
on top of the boulder and kneeling down. He pulled his
Hawken to his shoulder and sighted one in, compensated for
the distance, and squeezed the trigger. He saw the renegade
throw up his hands and fall face down into the dirt. The three
Injuns left paused for a second, then took off running.
Preacher was off the boulder and running hard, knowing the
shot would bring the others at a gallop.

The Lander girl must have worked the gag out of her
mouth and really put her teeth to work on the renegade, for he
let out a fearful holler and Preacher heard the slap as he
struck the child.

The one Preacher had killed, he noted as he ran past him,
was a Hidatsa, and the buck carrying the girl looked to be the
same. Preacher hollered out, "Beater of little girls! Does your
nightmare-in-the-blankets taste run to little boys, too?"

The brave stopped and turned around, his face a mask of
war-painted hate.

Preacher didn't let up, he continued running toward the
three Indians, now all stopped, hurling insults. "No wonder
you are all lovers of men. No woman would look up such ugliness for fear of being struck barren."

The Hidatsa threw the girl to the ground and Preacher shot
him stone cold dead with one ball from a pistol that caught
him in the heart and knocked him down.

"Run to yonder horsemen, girl!" Preacher shouted. "Run like the real red Satan was after you personal. Fly, child!"

One of the other renegades, a Crow, Preacher noted, lifted his rifle. Preacher hit the ground, rolling behind some rocks and working frantically to reload his pistol. The ball from the Indian's old Kentucky rifle whanged off the rocks as Preacher rammed home shot and powder and patch. Now his pistols were both double-shotted.

He chanced a look behind him and saw where Nighthawk had swept the girl up in his arms and was riding back toward the wagons at a gallop. Dupre and Beartooth were slowly circling Preacher's adversaries, cutting them off.

The two remaining renegades had disappeared, dropping to their bellies in the brush, hoping to slip away, and Injuns being what they were, the chances were good they'd do just that.

Dupre and Beartooth were staying in the saddle, scanning the area around them from that better vantage point.

"You all right, Preacher?" Dupre called.

"Dandy. Watch your butts, boys. There ain't nothin' more dangerous than an Injun who's in a trap."

"I told Hawk to tell them others at the train to stay put. We'd take care of this. He's comin' back."

Preacher had a pistol in each hand, the hammers back. He heard only the faintest of brushing sounds on the other side of the boulder. He quickly backed up and hunkered down amid some smaller rocks. He heard the rustling sound again and put it together. The buck was trying to snake up the other side of the huge rock. Preacher smiled as he heard a rifle boom. Dupre or Beartooth had spotted him, and that was that for another of Red Hand's crap and crud.

Preacher slipped from the rocks just as the last renegade rounded the boulder, a war axe in his hand and a look of raw hatred on his face. He screamed at Preacher and the mountain man put two lead balls into his chest, the impact knocking the buck back and flinging him dead against the boulder. He slid down, his blood smearing the stone.

"That's it," Preacher called.

"For the time bein'," Beartooth added.

When they returned to the wagon train, Richard met them with a grin on his face that a charge of blasting powder couldn't have removed. "It's a girl!" he said proudly. "Mary Elizabeth just gave birth to a girl!"

"Wonderful," Preacher said. "Something else for me to have to worry about."

"Naturally, we'll have to camp here for a day or two until the mother regains her strength," Richard said.

"Oh, naturally. It wouldn't do to move on. Not a-tall. It makes sense to stay here close to them four dead bucks out yonder in the brush. Seein' as how some of their own might decide to come after them for burial and spot us here restin' and decide to attack. That makes a lot of sense to me."

He walked off, muttering to himself. But the wagon train stayed put for two days.

While they waited, Preacher thought about the re-crossing of the Snake, not that many more days ahead of them. He just didn't know how it could be done without taking days to build some rafts and ferry the wagons across.

"Got to be," Dupre agreed. "There ain't no other way to do 'er."

Preacher looked at Jim and Nighthawk. They both nodded their heads in agreement.

"And I got my doubts these wagons will hold together over the Cascades," Dupre added. "You give any thought to that."

"I been givin' lots of head-ruminatin' to that. I been usin' parts of my brain that I ain't put to work in years. Makes my head hurt, too. Let me put it to y'all this way: if we can beat back and put a good enough whuppin' on Bum and Red Hand in the Blues, we could chance a run down the Columbia. But that's a mighty big if, boys."

"There might be some ol' boys camped on the Boise that'd lend us a hand," Beartooth said.

"*If* and *might* don't feed the bear, boys." Preacher sighed and took a slug of coffee. "I agreed to see these people through, and that's what I'll do. Or they'll bury me out here in the wilderness."

"We'll get them over the Cascades, then," Nighthawk said. "I know trails. But . . .?" He smiled and shook his head.

"Yeah," Preacher said glumy. "But."

When the train reached the crossing where the Boise juts off from the Snake, there was evidence that trappers had been there, but only one man remained, a trapper who'd taken an arrow in his leg and it had gotten infected. He was near death when Preacher found him, propped up against a tree, waiting stoically for death to take him.

"You don't look so good, Ballard," Preacher said. He struggled to maintain his composure, for the stench of the rotting leg was very strong.

"I feel a damn sight worser than I look, Preacher," the dying man said. "And you can bet on that." He cut his eyes to the wagon train, just them coming into view. "I heard y'all comin' for a long time. Didn't know what the hell it might be."

"How come you didn't let them take your leg, Ballard?"

"I ain't never knowed no one-legged trapper. Be kind of hard to sit a horse, wouldn't it?"

"Might be. Never gave it much thought. They's missionaries in the train. I can get some of them to pray over you, if you'd like."

"It'd beat the sound of my own voice, I reckon. That's all I been hearin' for a week. I thought I'd be long dead 'fore now. Why don't we make an e-vent of it. We can have singin' and shoutin' and preachin' and prayin'. If I set my mind to it, I reckon I could expire durin' all the festivities."

"I'll see what I can do."

"He wants *what?*" Edmond asked.

"A party and some prayin' and a jug."

"That's grotesque," Richard said. "The man needs salvation."

"What he needs is what he wants," Preacher told them. "I'll get the jug, you get to prayin' and the like."

"I'll conduct this with dignity," Edmond told the dying mountain man.

"I ain't interested in no dignification," Ballard told him. "How dignified can I be with my leg all swole up the size of a tree and pisen all in my body? Gimmie that damn jug, Preacher."

Ballard took him a long pull and sighed. "Mighty tasty. Now git some of them women to singin'. I'll get myself all ready to pass."

"Is he serious?" a mover asked Beartooth.

"Shore. I once knowed a man who rode a hundred miles with two arrows in his stomach. By rights he should have died days 'fore he did. But he wanted to pass in the company of friends. So he hung on 'til he reached a camp. He fell off his horse, looked at us, said 'Howdy,' and died."

The mover looked at the mountain man, not at all sure he was hearing the truth. He had learned that mountain men do, on occasion, tell lies.

"Lift your voices some, sisters," Ballard said. "And you might lift them skirts up some and show me a shapely leg, if you've a mind to. I ain't seen a white woman in nigh on two years."

"Mind your manners, sir!" Edmond admonished him.

"Go to hell, boy," the dying mountain man told him. "Preach or pray. But get to doin' something."

A group of ladies began singing.

"That's better," Ballard said. "That shore sounds sweet." He took another long pull from the jug. "Pretty women, soft singin', and good whiskey. I can see the gates of Heaven openin' up now."

"What you see is storm clouds," Preacher told him. "It's a-fixin' to rain."

"Not 'til I pass," Ballard told him. "You mind them damn Cayuses, Preacher. Something's got 'em all stirred up. You got airy stogy on you?"

Preacher found the butt of a cigar and stuck it in Ballard's mouth and got a burning twig from the fire and lit it.

"Now I'm a contented man," Ballard said. "You look after my good horse, Preacher. Give my rifle and my pistol to someone who needs them. And bury me deep so's the varmints won't get me."

"I don't know of no varmint who'd want you, lessen it'd be skunk."

"Well, you might be right there." Ballard puffed on his stogy for a time, waving it in the air every now and then in time to the singing of the ladies.

Preacher had lifted Ballard's buckskin shirt and seen the deadly lances of blood poisoning from his gangrenous leg shooting all the way up to his chest. That the man had lived this long was nothing short of a miracle.

"They's some laudanum on the train, Ballard. You want me to fetch it?"

The mountain man shook his head. "No. Hard to believe, but most of the pain is gone. I think the pisen and the rot done killed it. I ain't been able to feel nothing below the waist in two days. Can't piss neither. So my kidneys ain't workin'. All in all, it's gonna be a blessin' to pass."

"Been me, I'd had one of them ol' boys shoot me 'fore they left," Preacher said.

"I axed 'em to. But they said they just couldn't do it. It was a pisen arrow, Preacher. You ever known of Injuns to use pisen arrows?"

"Yep. A few. You just got unlucky, Ballard."

"You got that right. I'm gonna let them ladies sing about one more song, and then I think I'll pass." He shook the jug. "Well, maybe two songs."

"Oh, Lord God, our Savior!" Edmond thundered, his voice drowning out the singing. "Look down with pity upon this poor wretch of a man who lies dying before You . . ."

"Make it one song," Preacher urged. "Believe me."

Ballard took a mighty slug of the hooch and wiped his mouth with the back of his hand.

"He isn't much, Lord," Edmond intoned, "and I know his life has been filled with debauchery of the vilest kind . . ."

"Yes, it has," the ladies said in a sing-song voice.

"It has?" Ballard asked. "Pray tell me, Preacher, what do them words mean?"

"It means you've enjoyed strong drink and whores."

"He got that right," Ballard said solemnly.

". . . And his soul is dark with sin, Lord . . ."

"Is that feller tryin' to get me in or out of Heaven?" Ballard asked.

"Dark with sin," the ladies sang.

"He's a savage, Lord! Just like the heathens he's lived with, and laid up with their savage women and lusted in their red flesh, Savior," Edmond's voice rippled the leaves. "Wallowing in the blankets and stroking the hot naked flesh of sweating women."

A couple of the ladies took to fanning themselves quite vigorously.

"I do recollect that Kiowa squaw that I took to one long winter. Married 'er, I did," Ballard said. "She and the boy were killed by Blackfeet whilst I was runnin' my traps. Then there was a Fox woman that was mighty fine, mighty fine." Ballard took him another long pull. "There was two or three more along the way, that I recall. But I ain't been no ladies man, that's for sure."

"Save this poor creature, Lord!" Edmond shrieked and Ballard and Preacher both jerked.

"He's just getting' warmed up, Ballard," Preacher warned. "I'm a-tellin' you."

"I can't take much of this. I wanted some quiet prayin' for my soul. Not no revival. Listen, Preacher. They's a bunch of missionaries done build them a church just north of the Blues," Ballard said. His voice was getting weaker. "They got the Cayuses all stirred up. Even some of the real small tribes is smearin' on war paint. Be careful."

"We'll do it, Ballard. You rest easy on that."

"I think I'll just give up the ghost, Preacher."

"Whenever you're ready, Ballard. I'll plant you deep. That's a promise."

"Preacher?"

"Right here."

"I can't lift the jug, ol' hoss. Ain't this a pitiful way for a man to go out?"

"I don't know of no real good way."

"You do got a point."

Edmond was shoutin' salvation and damnation to those gathered around.

"See you, Preacher," Ballard said.

"See you, ol' son."

The mountain man closed his eyes and died.

10

Preacher, Beartooth, Dupre, Nighthawk, and Jim wrapped the dead mountain man in his robes and carried him deep into the brush and timber.

"Do you want any of us to accompany you?" Richard asked.

"No," Preacher told him. "We'll do this private."

"I think I understand now," the missionary said.

Preacher looked at him and smiled. "Yeah, Richard, I think you do myself. You've come a far ways, and I ain't talkin' about distance in miles traveled."

"Thank you, Preacher."

Preacher studied him for a moment. "You come on and you go with us, Richard. I think you've earned that."

The men dug a deep hole and planted Ballard, covering the grave with rocks. Richard said a very short and quiet prayer, and it was over.

"When I go to the Beyond," Nighthawk said, "I want to be buried Indian way. Remember that, all of you."

"Damned heathen," Beartooth said with a grin.

"Makes me closer to the Gods," the Crow said. "Much better than having to dig out of the earth."

Richard was thoughtful as they walked back to the wagons. "He does have a point."

Edmond was still preaching when they returned.

"Long-winded feller," Preacher remarked. "But the folks seem to be enjoyin' it. Never took to no lengthy sermons myself. I recollect my pa sayin' that he figured more souls was won in the first five minutes of a sermon and more souls was lost in the last five minutes."

Richard was in quiet agreement with that.

"Too much talk about gods and spirits makes head hurt," Nighthawk said.

"Let's take a long look at this crossin'," Preacher said. "'Cause it sure ain't gonna be easy."

It took five days of brutally hard work to build the rafts and get across the flood-swollen river. There were a lot of cuts and bruises and badly strained muscles, but fortunately no broken bones.

Within a few more years, the Hudson's Bay Company would have one small ferry boat operating there. The movers would pay three dollars a wagon to cross. By then, most of the area Indians would be "tamed"—with only an occasional uprising and massacre of the settlers—and the Indians would swim the river with the stock, moving them along. But that was years ahead.

On the afternoon of the first day past the river, Swift galloped up to Preacher. "Two families have pulled out, Preacher. They say they're going to stay right here. They're not going any further."

The news came as to no surprise to the mountain man. He'd been expecting something like this for weeks. "They's actin' like damn fools by doin' it, but I ain't gonna waste no time jawin' with 'em. Leave 'em be."

"Man, they'll die out here!"

"That's their problem. I didn't sign on to hold nobody's hand. 'Sides, they got a chance of survivin' here. They's cabins all over the wilderness. Life'll be hard for 'em, but they could make it."

"That's all you've got to say on the subject?"

"There ain't nothing else to say, far as I'm concerned."

The wagon train rolled on, leaving two families behind, standing silently by the side of the trail, waving at those who continued on. Preacher did not look back.

He had it in his mind that the movers weren't about to stay out here in the wilderness. They'd had a gutful of it and were planning on headin' back East to civilization. How they planned on getting back across the rivers and the like was anybody's guess. He could be wrong about their plans, but he didn't think so. And it was just as well, for this country was no place for cowards or the faint-hearted. The wilderness seemed to bring out the best in some and the worst in others. It oftentimes appeared to Preacher that the sometimes savage vastness seemed to know the cowardly or timid who came into it. The silent earth they were buried in was the only homestead they ever occupied.

After the brief rains that fell the day Ballard died, the sun returned and it came with a vengeance, baking the land in midsummer's heat. The trail was dust that coated wagons, animals, and people. And the stretch they were coming up on was void of water.

"Top your barrels," Preacher told them at a creek. "Fill everything that'll hold water. Your animals come first. You drink after them. Swift, we'll be headed straight north once we make this next thirty or so dry miles." He took a stick and drew in the dust. "Here's the Snake, and this here's the Burnt River. I'm takin' us right between 'em." He moved the stick north. "Once we get up here, that's close to Lookout, we'll rest. We'll be about thirty-five miles from where I figure Bum and Red Hand is gonna hit us."

"Maybe they'll have given up by then?" Swift said hopefully.

"Don't count on it," Preacher told him.

They moved on through the heat and the choking dust. That afternoon, they buried the Ellsworth baby. No one among them knew why the baby died. She had appeared to be a perfectly healthy baby.

"Damn fools!" Preacher said. "Fools to start a two thousand mile journey through the wilderness with a woman that's with child."

The mother's wailings could be heard as she stood over the small mound of earth, being comforted by other women. Richard had told Edmond that he, not Edmond, would conduct the brief service. Edmond protested, but Richard prevailed.

"Maybe they didn't have no choice in the matter," Dupre said.

"This family did," Preacher said sourly. "They sold a good business back East to become movers. Ellsworth told me he wanted a great adventure. I asked him why he didn't wait 'til his woman birthed? He just looked at me and walked off. Damn fool!"

"We stayin' the night here?" Beartooth asked.

"No," Preacher said. "We'd use too much water and we ain't got it to spare. We got to push on."

"Gonna be hell gettin' that mother away from that grave," Jim said.

"Yeah," Preacher's reply was short.

Preacher walked away, back to his horse. He cinched it up tight and swung into the saddle, riding up to Swift, who was unsaddling his horse. "Put it back on, Swift."

"What?"

"Your saddle. We're pullin' out in a few minutes."

"Man, you can't be serious! Mary is sick with grief. She's flung herself across the grave."

"Well, unfling her. Pour some laudanum down her throat and knock her dopey and put her in the wagon. Swift, I ain't tryin' to be no mean, heartless man. But we got to move. We stay here, and we use up the water. No matter what you tell these people, half the water'll be gone come the mornin'. And we won't be no closer to more water. Now get the goddamn people to their wagons. Toot on that bugle and do it!"

"I refuse to be so cruel! The mother has a right to her grief."

"Her grievin' ain't gonna change a damn thing. The baby's dead. She's with Jesus, Swift. There ain't nothin' in that hole in the ground."

"We're staying right here for the night."

"Then go to hell, Swift. You either get these people movin', right now, or I'm gone, and I won't be back. I told you from the git-go, I tell you to stop, we stop, I tell you we go, we go. And you agreed to those terms. Now I'm tellin' you, Swift. Get this train rollin'!"

Swift looked up at Beartooth, Nighthawk, and Dupre rode up. He looked up at Jim, saddling his horse. "What's he doing?"

"Gettin' ready to pull out with us," Preacher told the man.

"You'd all leave us? Swift looked at the unflinching gazes of the mountain men.

They sat their saddles silently, staring their answers at the wagonmaster.

"My God, but you're a cruel, heartless pack of brutes!"

"To your wagons!" Preacher shouted. "Let's go. Move it, people."

"No!" the grieving mother screamed.

"I said, get to your wagons and goddammit, do it now or I leave you here!" Preacher roared.

Slowly, with undisguised ill-feeling toward him in their eyes, the settlers began moving toward their rolling homes. Mary screamed and Ellsworth fought his wife. She kicked him, she slapped him, she bit him and she cursed him and fought him from the grave to the wagon. He manhandled her into the wagon and her other children held her down.

"Pour some laudanum in her," Preacher told Richard. "Force a whole bottle down her. Knock her out, get her drunk, and tie her in." He looked at Swift. "Toot that bugle, wagonmaster. Toot it loud and toot it now."

Preacher sat his horse by the side of the trail and watched the wagons roll past, following Nighthawk, Dupre, and

Beartooth. He wanted to be damn sure they all headed out. The hot looks he received bounced off him like raindrops off his fringed buckskins. When the last wagon passed, followed by the livestock, Preacher rode back to the head of the column.

"You shore didn't win no new friends back yonder," Beartooth observed.

"No. But I kept some old ones alive."

They plodded on, through the dust and the heat and the dryness, each step drawing them closer to the mountains where Preacher was certain Bum and Red Hand were waiting. When they made camp that evening, Preacher saw to it that the water was carefully rationed. They had just enough water left to make the next crossing. They had twelve waterless miles to go before they came to Burnt River. Once they left there, it was just over thirty dry miles to the Powder.

Preacher walked the camp. Very few people had anything to say to him. That in itself did not trouble him. Preacher was a hard man in a hard land, and to survive out here, that was what it took. These pilgrims would soon discover that, or they'd die. That was the bottom line.

Preacher went back to his own kind and sat down by the fire, accepting a cup of coffee from Jim.

"We'll lose some when them renegades hit us," the trapper said. "This won't be no little skirmish. Bum and Red Hand will throw everything they've got at us."

Preacher sipped at his coffee and then nodded his head. "I've done all I know to do. I've seen to it they's plenty of powder and shot. I've warned 'em what they can expect. I can't do no more."

"You know," Dupre said, waving his hand at the encircled wagons. "This is what we're all gonna end up doin' 'fore it's all said and done."

"What?" Jim asked.

"Either guidin' trains through or scoutin' for the Army. That's all that's left."

"Wagh!" Beartooth said.

"Ummm!" Nighthawk said.

"He's right," Preacher spoke softly. "What else can we do? Think about it. Another two, three years, the fur will all but be gone. Them's that's plannin' on trappin' forever is kiddin' theyselves. Can't none of us tolerate no towns or houses for any length of time. I can't see none of us clerkin' in no store. We damn shore ain't gonna get married and settled down and scratch in the ground raisin' crops—at least I ain't. So you tell me what that leaves us."

"You must make plans on returning to civilization and law and order," Edmond said, strolling up.

Trapper Jim said a very ugly word that summed up the feelings of all the mountain men.

"In the not too distant future," Edmond said, ignoring the profanity, "I can envision this trail being a wide and well-traveled road. Engineers will come in and build bridges across the rivers. There will be towns along the way. The railroads will cut through the mountains and link coast to coast . . ."

"Plumb depressin'," Preacher said.

"That's the most terriblest thing I ever heard of!" Beartooth said. "Them people best stay home. What's all them people gonna do out here?"

"Bring civilization and law and order," Edmond told him. "Raise families and build towns and schools and churches. Make a decent life for thousands of people. All sorts of factories will be built . . ."

"To make what?" Jim asked.

"All sorts of goods for the newly arrived settlers. It's the law of supply and demand. It's called progress, gentlemen. You can either be a part of it, or it will coldly push you aside.

You cannot stop progress, gentlemen. It's futile to try."
Edmond turned and walked away, back to his wagon.

"What's fu-tile?" Beartooth asked.

"I don't know," Preacher said. "But it sounds bad to me."

"Railroads!" Beartooth said. "There ain't nobody gonna build no damn railroad through the mountains. It can't be done."

"Melody told me they's people back East taken to travelin' in balloons," Preacher said.

The mountain men stared at him. "Now, Preacher . . ." Dupre said. "You have told some whoppers in your time, but . . .?"

"It's true. They make a big bag and then fill it with hot air and soar up to the clouds. They ride in baskets that's got little stoves in 'em. They keep the bag filled with hot air by burnin' wool and straw and the like."

"That ain't natural," Beartooth said. "If God meant for men to soar, He'd birthed us with wings."

"How high up do they soar?" Nighthawk asked.

"I don't know. I ain't never seen one. More'n a mile, I reckon."

"What happens if the bag busts?" Dupre asked.

Preacher shrugged his shoulders. "I reckon you'd have to fall back to the earth. What the hell other direction would you go? Up?"

"Why, that'd be the same as jumpin' off a damn mountain?" Jim said. "Who'd be foolish enough to do that?"

"Then folks back East, I guess. There ain't nobody ever gonna get me up in no damn oversized picnic basket."

Jim looked around him at the rapidly quieting camp. "Folks back East just ain't got good sense."

Preacher glanced at him. "Took you this long to figure that out?"

11

When they had run the long dry miles and finally came to Burnt River, Preacher told them to rest and water up. Nighthawk had already switched his saddle to another pony and was ready to pull out for the Powder, to see what he could learn.

"You be careful, Hawk," Preacher told him. "That's a mean, nasty bunch up yonder."

"And also very sure of themselves," the Crow said. "Red Hand is an arrogant fool, and Bum Kelley is worse. I will be back in two days." Preacher nodded his head and stepped back, watching him leave.

"We got trouble," Dupre said quietly, appearing at Preacher's elbow. "One of the movers is about to go mad, I'm thinkin'."

Preacher was not surprised, and he had a pretty good idea who it was. A very soft-spoken and timid little man from New Hampshire. His wife was timid and their kids were timid. Never heard a peep out of any of them. Preacher had been watching the man as the deep wilderness closed around them. Day by day, he talked more to himself in a mumbling sort of way. He wandered the camp after dark, twisting his hands and rubbing his arms nervously.

"Winston?"

"That's him. Swift is over there talking to him now. The Big Empty got to him, I reckon."

"Let's go have a look."

The man's eyes were wild looking. His hands were shaking and his face was pale as a fresh-washed and sunshine-dried sheet. He also had a pistol shoved down his belt.

"Winston!" Swift said. "Where is your family, man? Talk to me."

"What about his family?" Preacher whispered.

"They's missin'. All of them."

Swift looked around. His eyes were not friendly. He still hadn't gotten over Preacher's insistence they move on so quickly after the Ellsworth baby's death. "No one's seen them since this morning. Winston was late getting started. The stock drovers said he didn't catch up with them until we'd been on the trail more than an hour."

"Watch that pistol of his," Preacher said to Dupre. He walked around to the rear of the wagon and looked inside. It was the awfulest mess he'd ever seen. Looked like a pack of Injuns had gone berserk. He picked up a shirt that caught his eye. It was covered with blood. "Damn!" he whispered.

Carrying the shirt, he walked around to the front of the wagon and opened the lid to the jockey box and looked in. A small hatchet was on top of the various tools. The axe head was bloody, with several strands of hair stuck to the edge. Preacher held the axe to the light. The hair was of different colors.

"Take his pistol, Dupre," Preacher called.

The mountain man reached down quickly and jerked the pistol from Winston's belt. Winston offered no resistance. "What'd you find, Preacher?"

Preacher walked around the wagon and held up the blood-stained shirt and the bloody axe. "This."

Winston screamed and jumped up. Swift popped him a good lick that put the crazed man on the ground, stunned but not out. "The voices told me to do it. They've been talkin' to me for days and days now. I could resist them no longer. I had to do it, I say, I had to."

"Where'd you do them in, man?" Swift asked.

"Back at last night's camp. After the train pulled out this morning."

Preacher turned to Trapper Jim. "Saddle us some horses. And rig up three pack horses. We'll bring the bodies back when, or if, we find them. It'll be long dark 'fore we get there, but it's got to be done. Dupre, you ride with me."

The mood of the settlers very quickly grew dark, and some men were talking about a rope and the nearest tree limb.

"Chain Winston to a wagon wheel," Preacher told Swift. "We'll be back sometime tomorrow."

The mountain men rode easily back down the trail. There was no need to hurry, the victims weren't going anywhere. Neither man was all that anxious to find the bodies of the woman and her two daughters, for they were both pretty sure that by now the varmits had been at the bodies. It had been a horrible and shocking event, but not so appalling to the mountain men. They had seen it all before, more than once. The loneliness of the wilderness was something that not everyone could endure. The vastness of it all and the silence worked on some people. The savage land, void of accustomed amenities, had driven many people mad. They had all known trappers who had gone berserk and killed friends while they slept. This was not a land for the weak-hearted; no place for those who could not live without newspapers and comfortable chairs and lamplight and walls.

The mountain men, leading the pack horses, rode through the twilight and into the night, finally reaching the site of the previous night's campgrounds.

The vultures and the varmits had been at work all that day, but enough was left for identification. While Dupre kept the carrion eaters away with firebrands, Preacher rolled the torn and partly eaten bodies into canvas and lashed them onto the nervous and skittish pack horses. They rode back up the trail for a few miles before making camp for the night.

They hung the canvas-wrapped bodies from limbs to keep the varmits from them and made camp away from the now odious carcasses. They were back at the wagon train by noon of the following day.

Winston was bug-eyed and slobbering. He had soiled himself and was a pitiful sight chained to a wagon wheel. During the night he had gone completely around the bend and had been reduced to a babbling idiot, or so it appeared.

Avery's father had built him a noose and was talking hanging.

"You can't hang no madman," Preacher told him. "He ain't responsible for what he done."

"We do what you tell us to do when it involves the trail," Swift told Preacher. "But I set the law of the train."

Preacher could not argue the words. That was the rule of any wagon train. He walked away and joined his friends, sitting on the ground away from the still-circled wagons. Beartooth handed him a cup of coffee.

"Dispatched each one with a blow to the head," Dupre said. "I reckon them poor little girls only had a few moments of fright. But we'll never know."

"Did he abuse them?" Jim asked.

"Hard to tell," Preacher said. "They was all some et on. I'd rather think he didn't."

"Them pilgrims has been workin' theyselves up into a frenzy," Beartooth said. "I think they're gonna hang him."

"T'ain't up to us to interfere," Preacher replied. "If it was up to me, I'll turn him loose. Injuns won't bother him. He'd survive for a time. But on the other hand, he might get his hands on another axe, or a club or rock, and do in somebody else who's comin' up behind us. Personal, I'm just glad the decision ain't up to me."

"There ain't nobody been doin' much sleepin' 'ceptin' the

kids," Jim said. "They been palaverin' all night, all broke up into little groups." He glanced over toward the wagons. "Here we go, boys. Looks like they fixin' to take them a vote now."

"They'll be more than one," Preacher opined.

The mountain men drank their coffee and waited by the fire. Their opinions were not asked. The settlers argued and shouted and fussed and talked for the better part of an hour. A dozen times men and women alike left the group to walk over to the bodies and throw back the canvas, looking at the bodies of the woman and two girls.

Finally, Swift walked over to where the mountain men sat, drinking coffee. "We've voted. We've decided to take him with us and turn him over to the proper authorities."

Preacher shook his head in disgust. "Man, *what* authorities? There ain't no law out here. We ain't got no in-sane asylums. There ain't no jails. I don't know what the billy-hell you people got in your minds that you're gonna find when we reach Fort Vancouver. But it ain't no town like y'all think of. Either hang the poor wretch or turn him loose. Injuns won't bother a crazy person. They stay shut of them. Hell, they might even adopt him and look after him. You can't tell about Injuns. But they ain't gonna harm him, and that's a fact. You want to take him with you, fine. But he's your responsibility, now and forever. The chief factor at the post ain't gonna take him off your hands. He ain't got no way of takin' care of the poor bastard. He don't *wanna* take care of him and he ain't *gonna* take care of him. Winston is your responsibility. He ain't ourn. He's yourn."

Swift walked back to the group. Winston was howling like a chained dog.

The mountain men ground some more beans and brewed a fresh pot of coffee and smoked and chewed and waited.

The group argued and shouted and seemed to be unable to reach any decision.

"Oh, Lord," Dupre said, looking up. "Here he comes again."

"We're taking him with us," Swift informed the men. "We've voted and that's the way it's going to be."

Preacher shrugged. "Suits me. Have fun guardin' him and hand-feedin' him and bathin' him and wipin' him after he shits. 'Cause you folks sure got it to do."

Preacher walked to his camp under a tree, laid down, and went to sleep.

Since most of the movers thought it inhuman to chain a mad-dened person like an animal—even though that was exactly what was happening in the young nation's asylums, and would continue that way until well into the next century—Swift was persuaded to merely bind the man securely with ropes.

Of course, Winston escaped.

Preacher, laying warm in his blankets, as well as Beartooth, Dupre, and Jim, heard the man after he slipped his bonds and made his way out of camp.

"You gonna stop him?" Dupre whispered.

"Not me," Preacher said, speaking in low tones. "It's a hard thing, and these pilgrims don't wanna accept it, but the man will be better off thisaway. I seen the insides of one of them in-sane asylums one time back in St. Louie. Most pitifulest things I ever did see."

"Winter'll probably kill him," Beartooth said.

"But you never know," Jim spoke up. "Folks like that got some sort of natural survival about 'em. That fool over yonder in the Bitterroot's still there. And he's as silly as a gaggle of geese. Been over there for goin' on fifteen years, I reckon."

"I clean forgot about that feller," Dupre said. "But you sure right. Wonder if he still lives in a tree?"

"He was two . . . no, three year ago. 'Cause I seen him with my own eyes. He liked to have scared the crap outta me." Trapper Jim chuckled softly. "I was ridin' along, just a-fol-lowin' the St. Joe and en-joyin' the view when all of a sudden this fool comes a-runnin' and a-hollerin' and a-squallin' out of the woods and a-wavin' a stone axe. My good horse damn near bucked me out of the saddle, pack horse tore loose and run off about a half a mile, and I damn near made a mess in my britches. That crazy man was nekkid as the day he was borned and his hair was a-growed down to his waist. Turrible lookin' sight. Don't speak words that make no sense to nobody. Injuns is scared to death of him. I talked to Mark Head last year and he told me he seen Ol' Crazy clear down to the Red Rock one time. Ol' Crazy do get around."

"Mark ain't got much more sense than Winston," Preacher said. "That boy takes too much chances." He chuckled. "I was at the rendezvous, back in '33 or '34 when ol' Bill Williams scolded Mark for cuttin' buffalo meat across the grain."

"I heard you fit Mark once," Dupre said.

"We had us a round one time. He told me shortly after he left the Sublette party back in '32, I think it were, that he'd been in the mountains for ten years. I gleaned right off that the boy was a greenhorn and he was storyin' and I told him so. Although not that kindly. He was a good scrapper even then. But I whupped him and then we was friends and still is. If he ain't dead."

"He ain't," Beartooth said. "Least he warn't last year. He fit a grizzly over on the Grand River. The grizzly won but Mark he lay still as a log and ol' griz figured he was dead and wandered off. Them two or three others that was with him thought shore he was gonna die. But he didn't."

"The boy's too brash for my tastes," Preacher said. "I don't care to ride with him. Brave is one thing, reckless is another story. He'll come to no good end, you mind my words."*

"Reckon when some sentry is gonna look into the wagon and see that Winston's done slipped away?" Dupre questioned softly.

*Mark Head was killed around 1847. Shot in the back outside of Taos, New Mexico.

No sooner had the words left his mouth when a shout shattered the quiet night. "Winston's gone! He's slipped his ropes and fled. See to your women and children. The madman is among us."

"Oh, hell!" Preacher said, throwing off his blankets. "Somebody's sure to get shot if we don't sing out."

"He's gone!" Beartooth hollered. "So y'all just calm down."

Swift ran over, looking rather foolish wearing his long handles and nothing else. "You saw him leave?"

"Sure," Preacher said. "I'd say it was a good hour ago. He had enough sense to take a pack and a poke with him. So he ain't as crazy as you might think."

"Why didn't you stop him?"

"'Cause we're better off without him, that's why. Now go away and let me sleep."

Swift sputtered and stuttered, so angry he could not speak. He finally stalked away into the night, yelling for a search party to be formed.

"Some of them is gonna get lost sure as we're layin' here," Jim said.

"You wanna volunteer to lead 'em out there in the night?" Preacher asked.

"Nope."

"Then shut up and go to sleep."

12

Preacher lay in his warm blankets but did not return to sleep. He figured that in about twenty minutes, someone would yell that someone else was lost, and he'd have to get up anyway.

"George Wilson is lost!" came the shout, just reaching the campgrounds.

"Oh, hell!" Preacher said, throwing back his blankets. "I knowed it."

"Paul Davis is alone and lost in the wilderness!" another mover shouted.

"Naturally," Dupre said, standing up and putting on his hat. He nudged Beartooth in the rear end with the toe of his moccasin. "Get up, lard-butt. The rescuers and the searchers done got theyselves lost in the woods."

"Well, why don't they just sit down on the ground and wait 'til mornin'?" Beartooth grumbled.

Jim stuck his pistols behind his sash. "No, they got to go blunderin' around in the timber in the dead of night lookin' for a fool who's probably five mile gone from here by now."

"Oh, hush up and come on," Preacher said. "Them folks'll be shore enough lost if we don't go in there and take 'em by the hand and lead 'em out like lost children in the wilderness. I wish to hell they'd all stayed to home."

"Caleb Potter is lost in the woods!" a man shouted.

"Everybody just stay where the hell you is!" Preacher shouted the words into the night. "Just sit down on the ground and wait for us to find you and fetch you back. Good God Almighty!"

"You don't have to be rude," a woman told him.

"Oh . . . hush up, woman!"

"Well!" she said indignantly, and flounced away.

It took the mountain men hours to round up all the movers and lead them back to the wagon train. Some of the men were badly shaken by the night's events. Even to men accustomed to the woods, getting lost in the deep timber at night can be a shattering experience.

"Here's Winston's tracks," Jim called, kneeling down. "He's token straight out north and he ain't lookin' back."

"I wouldn't neither," Preacher said. "All he's got in that numb mind of his is puttin' distance between himself and the wagon train. Is everybody accounted for?"

"Far as I know," Dupre said. "Seems like these folks would know that things look different at night."

"Most of these folks come from towns and cities. You notice that the farmers amongst 'em didn't get lost. Come on, I want some coffee."

The train stayed put for another day, until Nighthawk returned from his scouting. The Crow swung down from the saddle and handed the reins to a boy. He walked to the fire and poured a cup of coffee.

"We're in for it, all right," he finally spoke. "Looks like every renegade west of the Little Missouri has gathered up there in the Blues."

Nighthawk was not known to exaggerate, and that placed him as a rarity among mountain men.

"That many, Hawk?" Preacher asked.

"I would say about one hundred and fifty Indians—many

tribes represented—and probably fifty or more white and half-breed or quarter-breed outlaws."

Beartooth whistled softly and shook his shaggy mane. "Lord, have mercy. I've heard worser news, but I can't rightly recall where or when it was. Where in the *hell* did Bum come up with that many whites?"

"Lots of ol' boys come driftin' out here over the past couple of years, wantin' to be trappers and such," Preacher said. "I reckon lots of them was wanted for some crime back in the organized country. They soon found out that trappin' these mountains was damn hard work. It was easier to find they own kind and go back to stealin'." Preacher smiled and the others, including several movers and Swift, noticed it.

"You find placing our women and children in danger amusing?" one mover asked.

"I find it plumb ignorant that you brung 'em out here to begin with," Preacher said, pouring a tin cup brim-full of hot, black, and very strong trail coffee. "But you did, and they're here. So that's beside the point. Red Hand and Bum, they don't like me very much. Red Hand, well, he hates whites. All whites. He hates Bum Kelley, too, but he'll work with him 'cause one's just as sorry as the other. It'd be grand for Red Hand if he could take my hair. He'd be a big man. Same for Hawk here, and Beartooth and Dupre and Jim. This show-down's been comin' for years."

"And you're looking forward to it?"

"You might say that. I ain't lookin' to get my hair tooken. But when somebody just keeps a-proddin' at me, I sorta get my hackles up and start to thinkin' about ways to prod back. Y'all better understand this now: they gonna be hittin' us all the way to the blue waters. They really gonna hit us in the Blues, probably on the Powder. They want your womenfolk, and they covet your possessions. I heared them trash I kilt back aways talkin' about seizin' the girls, ten, eleven, twelve year old, and sellin' 'em to slavers. So you folks talk and make up your minds that they just might be a lot of killin' from here on out. Get your stomachs set for it. Break out your molds and lead and start makin' balls. You gonna need 'em," he added grimly.

They spent another day and night in camp, the movers melting lead and casting balls for their weapons. A new spirit seemed to overcome the movers, and the mountain men could sense it. The settlers had come far, and no band of wild rene-gade Indians and white trash was going to stop them—not this close to their final destination.

"When the train pulls out in the mornin'," Preacher said to Beartooth, "I want you and Dupre and Hawk to guide them through. I'll be doin' a little pre-ambulatin' about on my own. This is gettin' right personal to me now."

"Sounds like you gonna be havin' fun whilst the rest of us is left behind," Beartooth said.

"I am gonna make life some miserable for them trash north of us. I'm gonna roar like a grizzly, howl like a wolf, and snarl like a mad puma."

"Wagh!" Dupre slapped his knee. "Them doin's shine mighty right with me, Preacher. You talk about ol' Mark Head bein' rash; what do you call one man goin' up agin two hundred or better?"

"I call it takin' the fight to 'em," he replied, with a twinkle in his eyes. "Preacher-style!"

Melody and Penelope, with Richard and Edmond in tow, stopped by the camp of the mountain men just as dusk was settling. It was obvious they wanted to talk to Preacher by the way they kept looking around and fidgeting like kids.

"T'ain't here," Beartooth told them. "He left out hours ago. He'll meet us on the Powder."

"Whatever in the world makes him do something that brash?" Penelope asked.

"He go count coup," Nighthawk said with a grunt and a hidden twinkle in his obsidian eyes that only his friends knew was there. "Take plenty scalps. Hang on horse's mane. Impress pretty girls."

"I happen to know that you can speak perfect English, Nighthawk," Richard said. "And you can read and write and do sums. You were raised and educated in a white home. Now will you stop grunting like a heathen and speak properly?"

"No," the Crow said. "Like talk this way. Talk like white man make tongue tired."

"Oh, for pity's sake!" the missionary said. "I give up."

"Good," Nighthawk said.

"Why has Preacher gone away into hostile territory?" Edmond asked.

"He just told you," Dupre said, jerking a thumb toward Nighthawk. "Can't you hear good?"

Edmond drew himself erect and in a very condescending tone, said, "My good man, I will have you know that my auditory faculties are excellent, I assure you."

"Your *what?*" Jim asked, pausing in the lifting of coffee cup to mouth and staring at the man.

"My hearing!"

"Why didn't you say so? Preacher's gone to hay-rass Bum and Red Hand's people."

"Alone?" Melody gasped.

"No," Beartooth said. "Course he ain't alone. He's got his hoss with him. Damn, woman, you didn't think he'd *walk* up yonder, does you?

"I meant—"

"I know what you meant," Beartooth cut her off before she got started.

"Don't you worry none about Preacher, Missy," Dupre

said. "Preacher's an ol' lone wolf. He's at his best operatin' by hisself. He'll be all right, missy."

"But . . ." Melody protested.

"He *likes* it, ma'am," Jim said. "Preacher's part grizzly, part wolf, part puma, and part rattlesnake. And he's mean when he's riled up. Lord have mercy, Missy, but he's mean. He ain't gonna cut them folks up yonder no slack when he goes on the warpath. He's the best they is, ma'am. I ain't never seen nobody that'd even come close to Preacher in the wilderness. You hear all sorts of talk about Carson and Bridger and Johnson and Brown and Simpson. And the talk is true for the most part. But them's explorers and guides and so-called adventurers and trappers and the like. Preacher's all of them things, too, but what counts most is he's a *warrior.* After Preacher gets done with his slippin' around up yonder and his throat cuttin', they's gonna be some, white and Injun alike, that's gonna pull out. They ain't gonna want no more of Preacher. You'll see, ma'am. All of you. Right about now, Preacher is gettin' ready to make war. And when he starts, it's gonna be right nasty."

Dupre nodded his head in agreement. "Shore is. I'd give my possibles sack full to be there, too. Hee, hee, hee," he chuckled. "Ol' Preacher gonna be sneakin' up on some right about now. They gonna be pourin' a cup of coffee, feelin' all safe and snug and the last thing they ever gonna know is how a knife blade feels cuttin' they throat. Hee, hee, hee."

Melody shuddered.

Preacher lowered the Indian to the cool earth. The dead renegade had him a right nice war axe, so Preacher took that. Standing in the darkness, he hefted the tomahawk. Had a dandy feel to it. Later on, he'd see how it was for throwin'. He wiped his blade clean on the dead buck's shirt and slipped silently on, moving closer to the dancing flame of the small campfire that was placed close to a boulder. He could see another buck sitting close to the flames, roasting him a hunk of meat.

The smell of that meat cooking got Preacher's mouth to salivating. Bear, it was. He could tell that even from this distance. And it was just about ready for gnawin' on. He worked his way closer to the fire and stood quiet for a time, moving only his eyes. These two, the one lying dead in the timber and this one sitting by the fire, were supposed to be the forward lookouts, Preacher figured. He felt he was still a couple of miles from the main party of outlaws and renegades.

Damn, but he was hungry.

He judged the distance, hefted the war axe another time or two, and let it fly.

The head of the axe caught the buck lower than Preacher had intended—striking and embedding in the Injun's neck—but it was righteous throw. The head drove deep, severing jugular and destroying voice box, and the Injun fell over, kicking and jerking, but dying.

Preacher hoped he wouldn't kick too hard and cause the meat to fall into the fire. The brave tried to get up, but it was all for naught. His blood poured out, weakening him, and he finally jerked his last and lay still.

Preacher moved quickly. He scalped the buck and mutilated the body, just like he'd done with the renegade in the woods, then grabbed up the meat and slipped back into the timber. He'd left Hammer picketed deep in the timber, with good graze and a bit of water so's he wouldn't get restless.

Preacher squatted down about a mile from the now-still and bloody camp and ate the bear. Preacher silently apologized to the bear for its death, then complimented it for being right tasty.

"Ay-eee!" he heard the faint shout, and knew that the bodies had been discovered. He smiled. Now the fun was really going to get good.

They'd be coming at him hard, now, with vengeance on

their minds. He'd mutilated those two pretty bad, and to make matters worse, had killed them at night. That meant, to their tribe, that they'd forever wander the land, unable to attain the great beyond and rest in the land of plenty.

Preacher finished the bear meat and wiped his hands on his buckskins. He wanted to belch but was careful not to. He couldn't afford the noise. There were Injuns out yonder that were just as good in the timber as he was. And they'd be moving toward him at this very moment. He stood up slowly and carefully and listened for several heartbeats.

He now had two war axes, having taken another one from the careless buck by the fire. He carefully shifted locations, moving as silently as death's own hand through the brush and timber. He came to a little fast-moving crick and followed it for a time, working his way north, staying just at the edge of the timber, just inside the Wallowas.

Preacher froze by a huge old tree as his ears picked up a very slight sound on the other side of the crick. He moved his eyes left and right. One brave, and he was a big one, much larger than the average Injun. He made his silent way toward Preacher's location. Sensing the way the Injun moved, Preacher felt he hadn't been spotted. The buck would have tensed slightly if he'd spotted Preacher.

The Injun stopped and stood tall and silent for a time. Sniffing the air, probably, Preacher thought, for an Injun and a non-Injun smell different to those who have trained their blowers to tell the difference.

The brave would have to get a lot closer than he was before Preacher dared make even the slightest motion, for at this distance, the renegade would disappear before Preacher could use knife or axe. He sure didn't want to risk a shot and have the whole damn bunch of them down on him.

The renegade slowly turned his head, and in the very faint moonlight filtering through the trees, looked right at Preacher.

13

Preacher lowered his gaze to the brave's chest. He knew that looking directly at a person can sometimes bring to life a sense that ordinarily lies dormant. Preacher remained as still as the tree he stood by. He willed himself to be a part of the tree, to be as one with the earth. It worked for him most of the time.

This time it didn't.

With almost a silent cry of jubilation, the brave spotted him and jumped for the creek and Preacher.

Preacher stepped away from the tree and flung the war axe. The heavy head took the brave in the face, embedding in his skull. The renegade threw up his hands, dropping his own axe, and fell without a sound to the ground, landing on his back.

"Pretty good axe," Preacher muttered, as he went to work mutilating the body with his knife. He scalped the Indian and stuffed the hair behind the wide leather belt that for this night, replaced his bright sash. He worked the axe out of the Indians' skull and wiped the blood away on the dead man's leggings. Satisfied with his work, Preacher moved warily but quickly away from the death scene, working his way toward where he believed the main body of hostiles to be camped.

He had left his rifle in the boot, for he did not want to be hampered by a long gun this night. He had his pistols, but this was a night for knife and axe.

He moved through the brush and timber without a sound, walking a short distance and then stopping, to listen, let his eyes sweep the terrain, and to sniff the air.

A few hundred yards later, he smelled wood smoke. He stood silent for a moment, until he had pinpointed the location of the smoke. He turned to the west and moved toward the source of the smoke.

He stopped and sank slowly to the ground, on his belly, when he saw that there were too many men around the fires for him to take on. Preacher was a brave man, but he wasn't stupid.

He backed away from that camp and slipped around it, changing direction. He almost made a fatal mistake when he came to a clearing, then hesitated at the last second. Something just didn't seem right.

Then his eyes found what his sixth sense had warned him about. Two men, standing just inside the timber on the other side of the tiny meadow, thick with grass and heady night fragrance of summer's flowers.

White men, for an Indian would never have been so careless. Preacher waited, to see just how impatient the sentries might turn out to be. And it wasn't a long wait.

"This is stupid," he heard one say, the words carrying to Preacher plain. "I can't understand what in the hell we're on guard for?"

"Hell, don't ask me, 'cause I shore don't know," the other one replied, disgust in his voice. "Them movers shore ain't gonna try no attack, and Red Hand's done got the Cayuses offen us. I think it's plumb ignorant bein' out here when we could be warm in our blankets."

"I left me a squaw on the Payette to join this bunch. I want some pretty bangles to take back to her. We'll have our way with them mover women 'til we git tarred of 'em a-whinin' and complainin' and squallin' and then kill 'em and go through they possessions."

What nice folks, Preacher thought. Just lovely. While they talked, Preacher took that time to move. He slowly circled the meadow and entered the timber, working his way up to within a few yards of the so-called sentries.

"I be right back," one of the outlaws said.

"Where you goin'?"

He mumbled something in a low voice and stepped back into the timber, unbuttoning his trousers as he walked.

He walked right into Preacher's big knife. Preacher lowered the throat-cut body to the ground, and walked right up to the remaining sentry.

"Took you long enough," the man said. "Now stand here and keep your eyes open whilst I—"

"Die," Preacher finished the statement as he buried a war axe in the man's skull. He grabbed the man's shirt to prevent the body from thudding the ground, and lowered the dead outlaw to the earth. He scalped both men and mutilated the bodies.

Preacher figured he'd pushed his luck just about as far as he cared to push it this night. He began his walk back to Hammer. He was about halfway back to where he'd picketed his horse when he heard the first shout, coming from 'way behind him. Someone had found the bodies of the two sentries.

He immediately dropped down to the earth, in some scrub bushes, and waited for a few moments, curious to see what would come of this.

"Goddamn you, Red Hand," the shout came from not too far from where Preacher lay. The voice belonged to Bum. "I thought you told me you'd fixed it with the Cayuses?"

"This is not Cayuse work," Red Hand's voice was tight with anger but still controlled. "I have the assurances of the warriors in this area that we are to be left alone."

"Well, who else would be workin' this area?" Jack Harris asked.

"Preacher," Moses said quietly. "He's amongst us, boys."

"That ain't possible!" Bum shouted. "He's good, but he ain't that good."

"Aii-yee!" the call pierced the night, as the bodies of the Indians were found.

The men began running toward the sound and Preacher slipped out of the bushes and started toward his horse, circling wide of the timber where he'd left the dead Injuns. Heading deeper into the timber, Preacher stopped when he caught movement just ahead of him. Two Indians running almost noiselessly through the timber, both of them carrying rifles. They ran past Preacher, not more than twenty feet from where he stood. No sooner had they jogged past, Preacher stepped out and continued on toward Hammer.

A shot split the night far behind him. "I got him!" someone called.

Preacher smiled as he walked. You got one of your own, you fool, he thought. What a pack of ninnies.

He reached Hammer, swung into the saddle, and headed south, following an old game trail. When he felt he had put enough distance behind him, Preacher stopped and made a cold camp for the rest of the night. He went to sleep smiling, knowing there would be damn little sleeping in the camp of Bum and Red Hand for the remainder of this night.

Preacher met the wagon train a few miles south of where the trail crossed the Powder. Two of Red Hand's warriors had made the mistake of trailing Preacher out of the Wallowas. He now had their scalps tied to Hammer's mane, in addition to the other scalps he'd taken.

"Wagh!" Nighthawk said, spying the scalps. "You had an interesting night of it, did you not, Preacher?"

"Got right borin' there toward the last," Preacher replied. "Weren't no fun left to it foolin' with greenhorns, so's I pulled out. But I reckon I did leave them in some manner of disarray, I 'spect."

"What are those things?" Swift asked, riding up and pointing to Hammer's mane. A half a dozen others rode with him, including Edmond and Richard.

"Scalps, Swift. Human hair. The top-knot, mostly. When I make war, I like to leave the enemy a little sign that it ain't nice to fool with Preacher."

"That's disgusting!" a mover said.

"Actually," a mover said,"I have read where some historians believe the white man originated scalping, not the Indians. What say you about that, Preacher?"

Preacher shrugged his shoulders "Some tribes scalp, others don't. Most do. I 'spect scalpin's been goin' on ever since the knife was invented. That's what I think. Swift, they's a right nice place to circle about two mile ahead. Circle 'em tight, 'cause we close to the action now. Keep everyone inside and when folks got to leave the circle, have armed men with them at all times."

The wagonmaster gave the mountain man a curt nod of his head and turned his horse. The others followed, except for Richard and Edmond.

"I think them scalps of yourn done irritated the man, Preacher," Dupre opined. "They cut agin the grain of his Christian holdin's."

"It's a barbaric practice and I fail to see what you have accomplished by doing it," Edmond put his penny's worth in.

"Demoralization," Richard said.

"Do what?" Beartooth asked, looking at the missionary.

"It lowers the morale of the enemy."

"Oh. Do tell?" the big mountain man said. "Do that mean that Preacher done good?"

Richard noticed the twinkle in the man's eyes and sighed. He held a strong suspicion that these mountain men were not nearly so ignorant as they would like others to believe. On more than one occasion he had noticed lapses in their horrible grammar that led him to believe they were merely having a good time at the expense of others.

"I would have to say yes to that question."

"Wagh!" Beartooth hollered. "You a hero agin, Preacher."

Dupre put a hand to his heart and proclaimed, "My hero!"

"I think I am going to faint," Nighthawk lisped.

"I'm of good mind to just shoot all of you," Preacher said, and rode off.

When the wagons had been circled and the women were busying themselves with preparing supper, the mountain men gathered at their own camp, as always away from the main body of movers, and talked.

"I think we'll have at least one full day of safe crossin'," Dupre offered. "That'll put about half the wagons on each side of the Powder."

"That's the way I see it," Preacher concurred. "Then when the men is busy on the second day, Bum and Red Hand will hit us and they'll come a-foggin', boys. There ain't gonna be no feeler attacks. They'll try to make the first one do it."

"And they's a chance they could do 'er, too." Beartooth offered up the sobering thought. "We're gonna be spread pretty damn thin."

"Everybody that can shoot is gonna have to be well-armed," Preacher said. "We got weapons aplenty, so Jim, you check each wagon for powder and shot. Dupre, see that every boy of age and the girls, too, if they can handle a gun and they parents allow it, is armed. Beartooth, you and Hawk check out the crossin' at first light." He paused for a moment. "I shore hope God looks down and smiles on fools, 'cause we sure got a bunch gathered here. Includin' us," he added.

Red Hand and Bum were still livid over the dead that Preacher had left behind him. Some of Red Hand's renegades were very nervous about continuing with the planned fight that lay ahead of them. Preacher's medicine was too good, they warned Red Hand. There will be other wagon trains—plenty of them, so the talk goes—so why not wait? Let this one go on.

"Fools, cowards, old women, fops!" Red Hand yelled at them, shaming them. "Look around you. We are two hundred strong. Preacher is but one man. The others with him are nothing. The whites in the train are not skilled fighters. They are women and small children. No. We attack as planned."

He walked to Bum's side. "This better work, outlaw. If the first day does not find us in control of the wagons, we will have men leaving us. Both yours and mine."

"Your warriors thinkin' that Preacher's medicine is too strong, Red Hand?"

Red Hand stared hard at the man. His dark eyes were unreadable. "Yes," he finally said. "And maybe it is." He turned and walked away.

Jack Harris had stood quietly and listened to the exchange. Now he felt he had to speak his mind. "Bum, that took a hell of a man to do what Preacher done the other night, and an even better man to slip away oncest it was done. Some of the boys is right edgy, I got to say."

Bum nodded his head. "I think Preacher's even got Red Hand thinkin' 'bout quittin'. I don't think he will quit. His honor's at stake now. But he's thinkin' on it."

"So is some of our people."

"You?"

Jack shook his head. "No. Not me. I'm in this 'til it's over. One way or the other. Way I see it, Preacher and all them others has got to die. If they was to get through and tell what they know 'bout us, the Army would be shore to send men in after us, and all that'd be waitin' for us would be a rope. And that makes my neck hurt just thinkin' 'bout it."

Bum was sure in agreement with that. "This time tomorrow, Jack, they'll be plenty of women and girls for us to be usin'. And a few of us will have gold aplenty to spend back East. Me, I'm gonna take my share and retire from this business. I'm gonna change my name and buy me a little business of some sort back acrost the Muddy and settle down. Civilization is movin' this way, and it's comin' fast. Ten years from now, they'll be people all over this area."

Jack doubted that. In fact, he doubted everything that Bum had just said. The man was an outlaw, and that was all he would ever be. He watched as Bum walked over to the small fire and poured a cup of coffee.

Get out of this! His mind warned him. *Pack your kit and saddle up and ride.*

But he knew he wouldn't do that. Knew he had to finish the wagon train and actually look down on Preacher's dead, bloated body. And the bodies of everyone on that train. He had a good thing going, this leading wagon trains to ambush. If anyone lived to talk about it, he'd be finished.

"What you ponderin' so heavy, Jack?" Bum asked him.

Jack forced a smile. "Thinkin' about all them women on the train."

"We gonna have us a high ol' time for sure," the outlaw said with a grin. "I cain't hardly wait."

Ride out! the words again popped into Jack's brain. He shook his head to clear it.

He looked at his comrades, sitting and squatting and standing in small groups. They were filthy. Clothing hanging in rags. Stinking and unshaven and ignorant. They were working ten times harder being on the dodge side of the law than they would holding down regular jobs.

Too late for that, Jack mused.

He looked south. Tomorrow would tell the story. Tomorrow would either be feast or famine for them all. He touched the butt of a pistol.

Tomorrow.

14

Preacher sat Hammer just above the banks of the Powder, his eyes taking in everything around him. It was very peaceful, very serene, and very quiet. No birds sang or flew, and no other animal had been to the river for a drink in several hours, not that Preacher could tell. The silence was a dead giveaway.

"Well, Hammer," he spoke to his horse. "I reckon they just went and outsmarted themselves. I could figure maybe Bum bein' that stupid, but not an old firebrand like Red Hand. So I tell you what we're gonna do, ol' friend . . ."

He told his horse and then sat there for a time, chuckling. "Yes, siree, Hammer," he said as he lifted the reins. "They's gonna be some mighty mad outlaws and Injuns when they see what's happenin' over here."

"Are you out of your mind?" Swift yelled, jerking off his hat and throwing it on the ground. "That's the craziest thing I ever heard of."

"Not so crazy," Nighthawk said. "Not perfect, either. But it's a good plan."

"Why?" the wagonmaster demanded.

"Make them come to us," Richard said. "Yes. I see. We can have the river on two sides of us. We have access to water that way, and our main forces could be concentrated on the other two sides. Yes, we have ample supplies for an extended siege, and plenty of shot and powder. We can start gathering tall grass for the animals and keep them on short rations for a few days. I think it's a fine plan."

It was at this point that the river made a curve, much like an upside-down V, the river wide on both sides, and narrow at the tip of the inverted V, where the trail crossed.

Swift thought about Preacher's plan for a moment, then nodded his head. "It's better than us losing a lot of people." He lifted his bugle and tooted on it.

The wagons did not circle, but rather formed up into a long rectangular box-like fort, with the stock inside the box. Swift assigned young people to scoop up the mess the livestock would make. It was going to be close and odious, but all felt they could wait out the outlaws and Indians.

Men went to work immediately cutting down small trees and clearing them of branches. The logs would be used first as barricades from bullets and arrows, then, if need be, to use in the building of rafts to cross the river, although, at this point, Preacher did not think rafting would be necessary.

Across the river, Red Hand glared at Bum, his eyes hot with anger. "It is far too early in the day to stop for nightfall. Why don't they begin crossing? Why do they stop and build fortifications?"

"I don't know," Bum lied, for he knew perfectly well what the movers were doing. He had a sinking feeling in his guts that Preacher had won another round. The outlaws were slap out of supplies. They were out of coffee, beans, sugar, salt, flour—everything. They had planned on existing on the supplies taken from the wagon train. Now? He didn't know.

"We've got to attack, Bum!" Jack Harris said. "We've got to attack now, man."

"Yeah," Bull said. "We let them movers get all set over there, and we'll never pry 'em loose from there. We're out of grub, Bum. We ain't got nothin' to eat. And as soon as the shootin' starts, there won't be even a rabbit within five miles of this place."

Bum was thoughtful for a moment. "Preacher's countin' on that. He's countin' on us sendin' people out on a hunt. 'Cause come the night, him and them other ol' boys down yonder is gonna slip out and circle around on all sides of us, waitin' for a hunter to go out for game. And that hunter ain't never gonna come back. *Goddammit!*"

"To attack now would be folly," Red Hand said. "We would have to cross several hundred yards of open land, then ford the river. They would pick us off as easily as stepping on a bug. If we wait until night, many of the new warriors who have joined us will not take part. They will not fight at night."

He walked away, to join a brave who was motioning to him. They talked for several moments, then Red Hand returned. "We are out of food." He shrugged his muscular shoulders. "Of course, Indians are accustomed to that. So what do you say now, Bum Kelley?"

"I don't know," the outlaw admitted.

"Stalemate," Richard said, standing beside Preacher, Swift and several others, as they looked toward the seemingly deserted timber across the river.

"How long could we last?" Melody asked.

"Days," Preacher told her. "The last two or three wouldn't be easy to take, 'cause the stock'll be squallin' for feed. But it'd be a discomfort to them whilst doin' 'em no real harm."

"Won't those thugs across the river go hunting for food?" A mover's wife asked. It was mid-morning of the second day camped by the river. No hostile action had been initiated by the other side, but all could see the thin tentacles of smoke from their campfires.

Preacher smiled. "Take a look around you, ma'am. You see Beartooth and Nighthawk and Trapper Jim or Dupre?"

Everybody turned their heads and looked. "No," Edmond said. "Where are they?"

Preacher pointed to the other side of the river, as a horse came slowly walking up to the edge of the timber. A man was tied in the saddle. Using a spyglass, Swift could see the arrow still sticking out of the man's back.

"He's been scalped," the wagonmaster said. "And he's stiff in the saddle."

"Yeah," Preacher said. "And comin' from that direction, I 'spect that's Beartooth's work. It's like I been figurin'. Them folks over yonder is gettin' hongry. They slap out of supplies. I 'spect they was countin' on feedin' off the supplies carried in this train. We done spoiled their plans, turned everything topsy-turvy. Now they sendin' out hunters and them ol' friends of mine is sendin' the hunters back without their hair. Hee, hee, hee!" he chuckled. The others looked at him strangely as he chuckled in dark humor. "I do love it when a plan works out."

"Will they attack, do you think?" a woman asked him.

"They might. But if they do it'll be a hard one, in the hopes they can take us on the first run. But more than likely it'll just be a short attack to let us know they ain't forgot us and they'll be waitin' further on up the trail. If they had any sense, they'd go on and leave us be."

Preacher looked across the river. If he thought either one of the leaders would honor a flag of truce, he'd borrow a petticoat and wave it at them and palaver with them. But Bum had about as much honor as a stump and Red Hand was even worse when it come to dealing with whites. Anyway, Preacher mused, that was just a dream. Red Hand could always drift back into the wilderness, but Bum's situation was a different one. He had to keep trying until he succeeded in stopping the wagon train cold and killing everyone in it.

If the outlaw leader had had any foresight about him, he'd

have had hunters out killing game and smoking and jerking the meat. But 'if' don't put a scrap of food in nobody's mouth.

So what would I do if I was in Bum's place, Preacher thought. I'd pull out right now, get a lot of distance between this place and the next point of ambush, and I'd be huntin' all the time. That's what I'd do, Preacher wound it up.

Melody broke into his thoughts as he caught the last of her question ". . . what month is it?"

"July," a mover replied. "Near the last, I think. I'll ask my wife. She's keeping a diary of our adventure."

Adventure! Preacher thought sourly. Then he had to smile and shake his head and silently ask himself this: Why are you so sour about it? You're damn sure a part of it.

Swift awakened him. "They're crossing the river, Preacher. Left and right."

Preacher was fully awake and out of his blankets just about the time the words left his mouth. He looked up at the sky. It was cloudy with no moon.

Good night for it, he thought. "Get everybody up and ready. Buckets filled for flame arrows. The women can handle that. Have the men stand ready for a fight. Assign the younger kids to load weapons. Move."

Preacher took his position by a wheel and stared into the darkness. He found him a target—albeit a long way off—and pulled the Hawken to his shoulder and let 'er bang. The man, he couldn't tell if it was an outlaw or a renegade, screamed once and fell face first into the river.

A mover fired and another scream was heard in the night, followed by a lot of fancy cussing and floundering around in the water.

One Indian got close and Swift drilled him right through the brisket. The warrior hit the wet bank and lay still. "Damned red savages!" he shouted.

"Problem is," Preacher muttered under his breath, "they was here 'fore us." Then he saw a hat that he remembered seeing miles back, long before he'd reached Fort Hall. He lifted his Hawken, sighted just under the brim of the hat, and gently squeezed the trigger.

The big ball struck the outlaw smack between the eyes and tore out the back of his head. The man never knew what hit him.

"Adam's down and dead!" a man called. "My God, the whole back of his head is blowed off."

"Forward!" Bum shouted. "Charge, men! Charge!"

A mover's wife said a very ugly word and cut loose with a shotgun. An outlaw began screaming in pain, the birdshot taking him in the face and neck, peppering him and blinding him in one eye. He began running toward the wagons, screaming in rage and hate. The mover's wife gave him another charge, this time at much closer range. The shot tore into his throat and knocked him off his boots.

Hot bright flames began dancing in the timber on the outlaw's side of the river.

"Somebody's burnin' our possessions!" a man shouted. "Lookee yonder." He turned around and pointed.

Richard leveled his rifle and shot the man in the ass. "Wow-eee!" the outlaw squalled, and went running for the river. He jumped into the water and sat down, letting the cold river waters momentarily soothe his butt.

Preacher grinned. His friends across the river had slipped in as soon as the outlaws had slipped out and fired their camps.

"Goddamn you, Preacher!" Bum shouted. Then he began shouting out all the things he'd do once he got his hands on Preacher.

"You wanna fight me, Bum?" Preacher shouted back. "How about it, you yeller-bellied son of a bitch? Just you and me, winner take all."

Red Hand halted his men, flattening them out along the river's bank, safe from shot. "We will see what kind of a man we have joined with," he told his people.

The firing stopped. A half a dozen men, from Bum's bunch and Red Hand's, had left to return to their burning camps, to salvage what they could and to see what had become of the guards, both white and red. All pretty well suspected they would find them dead.

Bum didn't know what to say, but he knew he had better choose his words carefully, for to an Indian, even a renegade, a challenge was something not to be taken lightly. If he screwed this up, Red Hand would take his men and leave.

"I don't trust you, Preacher!" Bum shouted from the night. "'Sides, I ain't got nothin' to gain from whuppin' your butt."

"True," Red Hand muttered. "There is that to be considered."

"You kill me, Bum. You got one less mountain man on this train."

Red Hand smiled grimly. "And there is that to be considered, as well."

"You guarantee me when I kill you your buddies will pull off from the train?"

"I can't speak for them, Bum. Just for me. I tell you what. I'll make it a real sportin' event. I'll fight two of you at oncest. You and that sorry damn Jack Harris. Now, I can't see how you can refuse me that."

"Nor can I," Red Hand said.

"If they do not fight him, I do not wish to ride with them any longer," a Kiowa renegade said. "It is not good to be associated with cowards. Besides, I have thought for some time that there is a secret that Kelley is keeping from us."

"What could it be?"

"I don't know. But he lies."

"He has always lied. What is so different about this time?"

"The value of what is in the wagons."

Red Hand grew thoughtful. The Kiowa was right, of

course. Bum had turned evasive each time. Red Hand tried to question him about the wagon train. "We will see what happens this night," he finally said.

"It's some sort of trick, Bum," Jack Harris whispered hoarsely. "Don't you be believin' nothin' that damn Preacher has to say."

"Yeah, I know. But if we don't fight him, we could see Red Hand and his bunch pull away. You know that, don't you?"

"Come on, Bum!" Preacher yelled. "How 'bout it, Jack? Or are the both of you so damned yeller you got petticoats under your britches?"

The Kiowa chuckled and even Red Hand was forced to smile.

"It's a trick, Red Hand," Bum yelled. "It's nothin' but a damn trick. Don't fall for it."

"He is a coward," the Kiowa said. "I am taking my followers and leaving. Now."

"Wait! There is something in that wagon train that is of great value. The white man's money, perhaps. If that is the case, we could use it to buy more guns and powder and shot. Think about that."

"Bum Kelley is afraid of this man called Preacher."

"Perhaps that is true. But Preacher is a man that any warrior would respect. Perhaps we are confusing respect with fear." Red Hand knew he was telling a blatant lie; Bum Kelley was so afraid of Preacher he was probably pissing in his pants. But he wanted the Kiowa and his band to stay with the group. "Stay with us. When the time is right, we shall attack the wagon, seize the money, and kill Bum and his people."

The Kiowa nodded his head. "I like that. All right. I shall stay. But only if you give Bum to me. I have a thought that he will not die well."

Red Hand smiled in the night. "It is done. Preacher!" he shouted. "It is Red Hand."

"What do you want, you damn renegade?" Preacher returned the shout.

"Your ugliness is exceeded only by your ability to lie. We do not blame Bum for not taking your offer. Since you are not to be trusted, we can only believe that your offer is a trick. You are trying to split our forces and it will not work. Go to hell, Preacher!"

"I never said he wasn't smart," Preacher muttered.

"Do you hear my words, Preacher?"

"Yeah, I hear you. You best break away from Kelley, Red Hand. You stay with that buzzard puke and he'll get you killed. You best think about that"

"Buzzard puke!" Bum shouted. Then he began reiterating all the things he was going to do to Preacher once he got his hands on him.

Many of the women in the wagons held their hands to their ears.

"It's over now," Preacher said to Swift. "See 'em slipping acrost the river? Ain't no use in shootin'. They're out of range."

"So we've bought some time, is that it?"

"That's about it. But we didn't lose nobody this night, and we can start crossin' the river in the mornin' knowin' we won't be attacked."

"We should count our blessings for the small things," Edmond said, walking up.

Preacher glanced at him. "Way I look at it, stayin' alive ain't no small thing."

15

"Pulled out last night and headed north," Dupre said, swinging down from the saddle and heading straight for the coffee pot. "And they didn't even look back."

"They gonna be a raggedly-assed bunch," Beartooth added. "'Cause we shore made a mess outta they camps."

"Clothes needed burning," Nighthawk said, speaking perfect English. "Fleas and other crawling and jumping insects had infested the material."

Richard sighed as he listened to the man speak. Whenever he tried to engage the Crow in conversation, the Indian resorted to grunting and broken phrases.

"We left six more dead at the camps," Trapper Jim summed it up. "And they's several bodies floatin' in the river."

"So our adversaries, while still quite formidable, have been drastically reduced in numbers," Richard said.

Beartooth looked at Dupre. "What the hell did he say?"

"Take heap many scalps," Nighthawk grunted, hiding his smile. "Count plenty coup."

"Oh, for pity's sake!" Richard said, and stalked away.

The wagons began crossing the Powder that day and by late afternoon of the next day, all were across and the fording was accomplished with only one minor incident: Young Avery fell off his horse and very nearly drowned because no one in the party would offer to help him. The young man and his father were universally despised among the settlers. Edmond saw what was happening and tossed the youth the end of a rope and dragged him out.

"You didn't do nobody no favors," Preacher told him.

"I couldn't just sit there and let the young man drown!"

"I could." Preacher lifted the reins and rode off.

The wagons headed north by northwest, rolling through Thief Valley, then called Grand Ronde Valley, and that night camped close to the mountains. They found good water and plenty of good graze for the livestock.

"Any of you folks ever tasted salmon?" Preacher asked a group of settlers. None had. "Not all Cayuses is on the prod. We'll run into some friendly ones and I'll barter for fish. It's right tasty. I think you'll like it."

Although it was summer, the weather was unpredictable in that area. When the movers awakened the next morning, they found the sky gray and the temperature hovering around the freezing mark.

"My God!" Swift exclaimed. "It is going to *snow?*"

"It might," Preacher told him. "Anything's possible in this country."

On the fifth day after the failed attack by the Powder, Beartooth rode up to Preacher at the head of the column. "Gettin' plumb borin', Preacher."

"I hope it stays that way."

The huge mountain man grinned. "Tell the truth, so does I. Nighthawk ought to be back today or tomorrow. Be right interestin' to find out where Bum and Red Hand is plannin' on springin' their next surprise."

"They've crossed the Columbia and is waitin' for us up to the north." He smiled. "But they's in for a long wait, 'cause we ain't crossin' the Columbia and headin' north."

Beartooth looked hard at him. "What you got ramblin'

around in that noggin of yourn, Preacher? We got to cross the Columbia, man."

"No, we don't. And we ain't gonna. We gonna raft these pilgrims acrost the Fall and stay to the south side of the river."

"You've lost your mind, man! You can't take these damn wagons thataway."

"I know a way, Beartooth. I spent two year out here, 'member? I got a way all figured out in my mind. It's gonna be rough, but we can do it."

Dupre had ridden up and was listening with amazement on his face. He shook his head. "I know the way you're talkin' about, Preach. You gonna be crossin' the Sandy four times. You best think about that."

"The Sandy ain't nothin'. Bum and Red Hand's got scouts watchin' the crossin'. Bet on that. They got people lookin' and waitin' all over the north side of the river. So we'll stay to the south. By the time they figure out what's happened, we'll be so close to the fort they daren't attack."

"Have you told Swift?"

"No. Hell, don't none of these movers know nothin' 'bout this country. When you're lost as a goose you ain't got no choice in the matter; you got to follow the leader."

"But you said yourself they's gonna be scouts of Bum's and Red Hand's watching the fall," Beartooth protested.

"Sure they are. But we ain't crossin' the Deschutes there. We're gonna cross further south."

"There ain't no damn place further south!"

"Yes, there is." Dupre spoke the words softly. "You're a damn fool, Preacher. You plannin' on takin' these greenhorns through pure virgin country. It ain't never been done afore."

"That's what makes it so interestin'," Preacher told him with a wide smile.

"Do you realize that we're gonna have to *build* a damn road?" Beartooth asked. "The way you're talkin' about ain't nothin' but a game trail."

"Yep."

"These wagon's ain't never gonna stand the trip, Preacher."

"They'll stand it."

"You're a damn igit!"

"You wanna quit?"

"I didn't say nothin' about quittin'. Did you hear me say anything 'bout quittin', Dupre?"

"Nope."

"Fine," Preacher told him. "I'm glad all that's settled. Now you can quit your bitchin'. You know the way we're goin', so put your thinkin' cap on and close your mouth. Start thinkin' of ways to make it easier."

The mountain man shook his head in exasperation. "They *ain't* no easy way!"

"Then we'll do it the hard way." He smiled. "And we'll be the first to do it."

They crossed the Blues at its narrowest point and headed northwest. They camped at a spot that in the years to come would be called Emigrant Springs. Only a few miles north of the springs, Preacher turned the long line westward and headed for the Umatilla River.

"Normally," Preacher told Swift, "the Cayuse Injuns would be real friendly. I've stayed with 'em many times and et their food and slept in their tipis. Usually this country would be swarming with their horses. But as you can see, it's deserted. That means they've pulled 'em close to their villages and gettin' ready for war. That don't necessary mean that they'll attack us. I know the headman, and he likes me. So that's a plus. Howsomever, there are a few minuses."

Dupre smiled hugely and nodded his head. "Shore are. Like a bunch of young bucks lookin' to impress the gals with scalps, for one."

"I thought you men knew the chief?"

"Oh, we do. They probably wouldn't hurt *us*. But they might kill all of *you*."

"Comforting thought," Swift muttered. "But someday the Oregon Trail will be safe for all."

"Big Medicine Trail," Beartooth said. "That's what the Injuns call it. Kinda hard for me to get used to callin' it the Oregon Trail."

It turned cold and the winds began blowing. If the movers thought they'd seen winds on the empty prairies east of the mountains, this changed their minds. Anything that was not secured properly—"right and tight," Preacher called it—was blown off and scattered all to hell and gone. So much canvas was ripped and torn that Preacher ordered it all taken off the ribs and stored until they were out of the wind.

They lost half a day trying to round up the livestock that had drifted, trying to find comfort from the cold winds, and two very difficult days later, during which the wagon train managed to cover only a few miles each day, another birth was recorded on the trail.

It was a very long and hard birthing, and the woman's screaming was a nerve-wracking thing for all to hear. The mother had never been very strong, and shortly after the birthing, the woman died. The husband refused to accept the baby—a little girl—blaming the child for the mother's death. She was given to the Ellsworth woman to care for. The mover flatly refused to go any further. No amount of coaxing would change his mind. He flung himself across the mound of earth that covered his young wife and wailed out his grief.

"Rainin' too damn hard to move anyways," Preacher said. "We'll just stay here and wait it out. Maybe that feller will get over his grief come a new dawnin'."

Just before a cold and rainy dawn would break, a single pistol shot brought the sleepers out of their blankets.

"I bet I know what that was," Preacher said.

"Yeah," Dupre said. "I shore wouldn't bet agin you."

The young widower had stuck the barrel of a pistol in his mouth and pulled the trigger, blowing out the back of his head. He lay sprawled across his wife's grave.

"Git some shovels," Preacher said, disgust in his voice. "Be easier digging up this fresh grave and just layin' him beside his wife. I figure that's the way he'd want it."

"That's sacrilege, sir!" Edmond objected.

"Oh, shut up! Don't get up in my face, Edmond. Not now. I'll hurt you, boy," Preacher told him, then turned his back and stalked off. "Any man who'd shoot hisself over a damn woman is a fool! Anybody who'd shoot theyselves over just about anything's a damn fool. Life is for the livin', 'cause when you dead, you dead a long time."

"I have never known a man that hard," Richard said, rain water dripping off the wide brim of his hat.

"Hard country, Bible-shouter," Beartooth told him. "This country feeds on weaklin's. I 'spect the day will come when this trail is lined with graves, from beginnin' to end. Three months after they're planted, won't be no trace of them. You best get used to it."

He walked off to join Preacher.

"Dig up the grave and bury Jacob beside his wife," Swift ordered. He sighed, steam fogging his breath. "It probably won't be the last one we'll bury before we reach our destination."

"I'm beginning to wonder if it's all worth it." A mover spoke the words to no one in particular.

No one responded to his words, the men just picked up shovels and began digging in the rain-soaked mound of earth.

16

The wagon train moved on, leaving behind them a lonely grave and the box of a wagon. The young couple's meager possessions were given to those most in need, the wheels taken for spares, and the canvas given to a family who had lost theirs in the high winds. They averaged about eight miles a day, the men having to literally hack a road out of the narrow trail, using axes and pure sweat and muscle.

When they reached the Umatilla River, two families announced they were leaving the train and heading northeast, toward the Walla Walla, to make their homes near the new Whitman Mission. They simply could not, or would not, endure the trail any longer. No one tried to dissuade them; most of the movers were just too damn tired to care.

The wagon train rolled on, with not one hostile Indian being seen. Nighthawk had reported that Bum and Red Hand had spread their people out north of the Columbia, in the wilderness along the Klickitat River.

"Just like I figured," Preacher said. "Time they figure out that we didn't cross the Columbia at the Dalles, we'll be so far into the Southern Cascades they'll never find us."

And as Preacher had predicted, when the train did meet up with some Cayuses, they were friendly. Preacher bartered for enough fresh salmon to give everyone on the train a good meal and learned that only a few of the tribe had taken to the warpath. Those that had were operating—for the most part— north of the Columbia.

But the Cayuses shook their heads and made the sign of a crazy person when they learned that Preacher was going to take the wagons across the mountains south of the river.

"It cannot be done," a sub-chief told Swift. "That is impossible."

"It ain't never *been* done," Preacher corrected the wagon-master. "But that don't mean it can't be done." Preacher talked long with the sub-chief and the man inspected the gee-gaws in the trade wagon driven by Jim. After two hours of palavering, the men solemnly shook hands.

"What was all that about?" Richard asked.

"They're goin' to help us cross the Deschutes," Preacher told him. "I gave him everything in the wagon, and the wagon. That'll be one less we got to pull acrost the mountains, and it'll give us an extra team."

"But that river is miles and days away!" Swift objected. "How do you know these savages will be there?"

"'Cause they gave their word to me and we ain't never lied to one another, that's why. Move out, Swift." He pointed. "The promised land is thataway."

Jim was grateful to be shut of the wagon and back in the saddle. But like the other mountain men, he had his doubts about getting a wagon train through the Cascades.

"There ain't much feed in there for the livestock, Preacher," he reminded the man.

"That's true in spots."

"Mighty boggy in there, Ol' Hoss," Dupre added.

"Yep. In spots."

"Ropes is gettin' raggedy," Beartooth said. "And we gonna have to shore use them for snubbin' these wagons and lowerin' down them mighty steep passageways."

"Once we get them built," Preacher said.

Nighthawk shook his head at that. "Ummm," he said.

"Great God in Heaven!" Swift said, taking his first look at the Deschutes. "We'll never get the wagons across that."

"We'll get them across," Preacher told him. "Get your people buildin' rafts. This part's the easy part. Once we get 'crost is when the fun starts."

The crossing was made, but it was not done without loss. Several head of livestock were drowned in the river, and several wagons were lost when the ropes on a raft parted and the raft came apart. Since possessions were rafted across separately, the movers' goods were dispersed among other wagons and the pioneers could ride the mules. Preacher bartered with the Cayuses for saddles—he did not ask where they got them, although he had a pretty good idea—and one mover's wife shocked the entire train by putting on a pair of her husband's britches and riding the mule astride.

"Disgraceful," several of the women said. "How common can a person get?"

"Seems like a pretty good idea to me," was the opinion of most of the other women.

"No woman of mine would ever wear britches," a mover made the mistake of saying, and ten minutes later, his wife emerged from their wagon wearing a pair of his britches. "You got something to say about this?" she challenged him.

"No, dear," he said meekly.

Melody and Penelope looked at one another and smiled. Moments later they had changed from their now somewhat less than elegant riding habits into britches.

Dupre took a long look at the derrieres of the ladies, threw his hands up into the air, and proclaimed, "C'est bon! Magnifique!"

Preacher had spent weeks looking at their derrieres. He had nothing to say.

"Here, now!" Swift said, eyeballing the britches-clad ladies. "I'll have none of this on my train. You women get back into proper clothing."

"Make us," Melody threw down the challenge.

Swift muttered under his breath and walked away.

"I'm tellin' you for a fact," Preacher said, "I can see the day comin' when women is gonna have the vote."

"Never!" Beartooth said. "Of course," he added, scratching his woolly mane, "I ain't never voted so I reckon it wouldn't make no difference nohow."

On the morning the train was to pull out, Preacher told Swift, "We got to get over the mountains 'fore the snow flies, and she can fly early out here. This ain't gonna be easy, I'm warnin' you of that right now. But I said I'd get your through, and I'm gonna do just that. So toot on that bugle of yourn, Swift, and let's tackle the last leg."

Swift smiled at him. "Tell you the truth, Preacher, I'm getting just about as sick of that damn bugle as you are."

The two men laughed, clasped each other on the shoulder, and walked off together, toward their horses. And while they had no way of knowing it, both of them were destined for the pages of a few history books. They would be the first to lead a wagon train over the rugged Cascades Mountains. But since that claim would always be in dispute, it would be taken out of the history books. Taken out long before the mass migration of the late '40's and early '50's.

When Preacher was told of this, he wasn't surprised, since he wasn't aware it was even in any books. His reply was typical: "Hell, I don't read about history, pilgrim. I *make* it!"

Book Three

1

O beautiful for spacious skies,
For amber waves of grain,
For purple mountain majesties
Above the fruited plain!
America! America!
God shed His grace on thee
And crown thy good with brotherhood,
From sea to shining sea!
Katharine Lee Bates

"We're gonna have about two and a half days of fairly easy travel," Preacher told Swift and a few others, after they broke for lunch. "Then you got to lighten the wagons. And I mean discard everything that ain't absolutely necessary. The folks ain't gonna like it, I know that, but it has to be. You think goin' through the South Pass of the Rockies was bad, wait 'til you see Hood and what's all around it."

Swift nodded. "I'll tell them."

"Don't just tell them. Stand right there until they do it. We're a-fixin' to go straight up and then straight down, half the time right into a bog, and we'll be doin' it over and over and over agin. Most beautifulest and gawd-awfulest country you ever will see. Start shakin' down the movers, Swift."

On the second day after crossing the river, the train came to a series of hills, long steep hills. That night, the movers began throwing possessions away in earnest. There was a lot of crying and fussing over many things that were being dumped by the trail, but in the end, the wagons were lightened considerably.

Preacher told them to stay in camp the next day and dump some more out of the wagons. "You just don't know what you're a-fixin' to get into, folks. But I do. You'll kill them oxen tryin' to get all this crap over the trail. The mules will just not move once they figure out they can't pull it. Dump more, people. Get busy. Lighten them wagons."

"Is it really this bad, Preacher?" Richard asked. "The people are very upset."

"I can't make it sound as bad as it really is," Preacher told him. "It don't make me feel like no big man makin' folks throw away things I know they toted what must seem like halfway around the world. But it's either that, or they break down or their oxen dies in the middle of the Cascades and they walk out with nothin'. Think about that."

"All right, Preacher," the missionary said, reluctance in his voice.

"Richard, have the movers wash their wagons to get all the dried mud off. You'd be surprised how much weight is just ahangin' on them wagons."

"Yes. You're right. Of course."

Preacher found the lady who was keeping a journal of her adventures and asked her if she was still keepin' her notes up. She assured him that she certainly was. "Well, ma'am, I hope you got lots of paper and ink and quills," he told her. "'Cause you shore got a lot of scratchin' and scribblin' to do over the next month or so."

She smiled at him. "Would you like to see what I have written about you, Mister Preacher?"

"No, ma'am!" Preacher's reply was quick. "This trip's been de-pressin' enough without my doin' that."

The movers hit a dense forest of pine, fir, and redwood. Many of the redwood soared several hundred feet into the air. On the first day after entering the Cascades, the wagon train traveled only three miles. The movers fell into their blankets and went to sleep exhausted after a day of cutting and dragging trees out of the way. The trail they hacked out of the wilderness was a narrow one, just wide enough for a single wagon. Fallen trees had to be dragged out of the way, huge rocks and jutting roots had to be first hacked at and then dug out. The only graze for the livestock was swamp grass. Preacher warned them that only a few miles further they would encounter laurel, and that if the livestock ate it, they would die.

Lowering wagons down mountain sides by snubbing ropes to trees became commonplace for these pioneers, and they were all working harder than they ever had in their lives. They no longer asked themselves if it was worth it. They were afraid of what their answer might be.

Mothers put ropes around the waists of their children and led them single file, to prevent a small child from running into the thick tangle of vegetation that grew all around them. Any child lost in there would more than likely stay lost—forever.

They worked their way up hill more than a half a mile high, and then half a mile down the other side. That took a full day of brutally hard work, both for humans and animals. Slipping and sliding and cussing. Most went to their blankets without even eating the evening meal. They were too exhausted to eat.

"By now," Beartooth said, "I reckon Red Hand and Bum will know that we didn't come crost the Columbia and they'll be hard on followin' the trial we're blazin'."

Preacher nodded his head in agreement and accepted a cup of coffee from Nighthawk. "Won't do 'em no good." He smiled and winked at his old friend. "You know where we are, don't you, Bear?"

"Tell the truth, I ain't rightly sure."

"Five more days and we'll hit the valley."

Beartooth stared hard at his friend. Then the huge mountain man's face brightened under his beard and his eyes twinkled. "By the Lord, we've done the impossible, Preacher."

"Looks that way, ol' hoss."

"You goin' to tell the movers?" Jim asked.

"No. I do that, and they'll get all anxious and in a hurry and somebody will get hurt in haste. We've made better time than I figured we would. I got to hand it to these folks. They got grit, I'll give 'em that."

"I got me a hunch that when they cross the last ridge and stand lookin' down into the valley, they'll give up any plans of goin' north crost the Columbia and just settle right there," Dupre said. "I know a little somethin' 'bout farmin', and that's good land for it. Damn shore rains enough," he added.

"We'll be hittin' that in a couple of days, I figure," Preacher said. "But the worst is behind us."

"What you gonna do when we get these pilgrims to the promised land?" Beartooth asked him.

"Loaf for a couple of days, then head back East to the mountains. I got me a little task to do."

"And what might that be, Preacher?" Dupre asked.

Beartooth, Jim, and Nighthawk all grinned at one another.

"I got me a score to settle with a feller name Bum and an Injun named Red Hand. You boys can come along if you like."

"Well, my goodness gracious!" Beartooth said. "Thankee kindly for the in-vite. I allow as to how I might just do that. How 'bout you boys?"

"I wouldn't miss it for the world," Jim said.

"I'd feel left out by not goin' along. How 'bout you Night-hawk?"

"Ummm!"

Many of the rogue Indians that had joined Red Hand had now left him. It was obvious to all that Preacher had tricked them and taken the southern route across the Cascades. Even the most stupid among them knew that to attempt to follow would amount to naught. By the time they recrossed the river and picked up the trail of the wagon train, the movers would be across the mountains and into the valley. To attack a wagon train that close to the fort would be very foolhardy.

Even many of Red Hand's own band had given up in disgust and headed back to more familiar ground. Bum's band of trash and outlaws had shrunk to about twenty-five.

On a cool early autumn morning, Bum watched as Red Hand and his people saddled up and broke camp. He walked over to the renegade.

"Givin' up?" the outlaw asked.

"There will be another time," the Indian said. "To pursue now would be pointless. We ride back east."

"Mind if me and my boys ride with you?"

"Do as you wish." He swung into the saddle. "We will cross the river just north of where the Snake flows." He turned his pony's head and rode off.

Bum walked back to where his men lay on the ground. Leo tossed a stick into the fire and said, "No women, no gold, no nothin'."

"It ain't over yet," Bum said, then smiled.

"Whut you grinnin' 'bout?" one of his men asked him.

"Well, I'll just tell you," Bum said, sitting down and pouring a cup of coffee. "It come to me whilst I was talkin' with Red Hand. Seedy, didn't you tell me you'd been to Fort Vancouver recent?"

"Only about six months ago."

"And the brand new buildin' for the missionary's church was not in the fort?"

"Oh, no. It's a good three, four miles from there. They built it a-purpose there so's the Injuns would feel better 'bout comin' in to it."

Bum sipped his coffee and chuckled. "Bustin' our butts for nothin'. That's what we been doin'."

"Whut you mean?" Leo asked, scooting closer to Bum.

"Them folks in the wagon train don't know us. How could they? They ain't never seen us. Don't nobody at the fort know us. It stands to reason that them women missionaries and the gold is gonna be at the church. Seedy said the livin' quarters was in the rear of the buildin'. It's three, four miles from the fort. All alone, ain't it, Seedy?"

"You bet."

"Preacher and them sorry friends of hisn is sure to be hell-firin' back toward us to finish this fight," Bum said with a grin. "All we got to do is be a little careful and just head straight west from here and then cut south. You boys see what I'm gettin' at?"

"Kind of," Jack Harris said. "But ain't that sort of risky? If we're thinkin' along the same lines, that is."

"Not really. We can go in and grab the gold and the women and be gone hours 'fore anybody discovers the bodies. Far as that goes, we can kill some damn Injuns and chuck their bodies in there and burn the place down. Who'd know the difference?"

"I like that," Beckman said. "We could grab us a couple of young squaws, hump 'em 'til we're ready to go, and then kill 'em."

"Good idea," Bum said. "They's lots of fall berries now and the squaws'll be out pickin' 'em to make pemmican. Should be easy to grab a couple young ones. But we're gonna have to be real quiet about it and when the deed is done, we're gonna have to move fast and far. And we're gonna have to be careful about which tribe the squaws belong to."

"Amen to that," Slug said. "I damn shore don't want no Digger woman."

"That wasn't what I meant!" Bum admonished him.

"Oh," Slug said.

"When do we ride?" Waller asked.

"Let's give Red Hand and his boys a couple of hours to get clear away. We can be breakin' camp and packin' up now, just in case that damn renegade left someone behind to snoop and spy on us."

"What *did* you mean?" Slug asked.

"Oh, forget it, Slug!" Bum said.

"Which would you rather have on your trail, Slug?" Jack asked. "A peaceful Injun, or a Blackfoot?"

"Oh!" Slug said. "Right."

Preacher rode slowly back to the wagon train. He had not told any of them that on that day, they would be done with the mountains and looking out over the huge valley that lay south of the Columbia. They had reached the promised land.

Despite the fact that most of the movers considered him to be a sarcastic, heartless, and sour man—Preacher was none of those things—he was proud of this bunch of pilgrims. They had done what no one, to the best of his knowledge, had ever done. And he knew that all of them with the exception of Wade and his two-bit kid, Avery, would be bigger and better people for the trip. Preacher knew, too, that not all of them would survive out here.

Injuns would get a few, the fever would take a few more, accidents and other mishaps would claim still a few more. But those that would live could be proud of what they'd done.

And speaking of Avery and his pa . . .

The father had gotten all up in Preacher's face just the day before, after Preacher had raised his voice and fussed at the young man for being a laggard, which he certainly was. Lazy no-count pup. The father said when they crossed the mountains, he was gonna put a butt-whipping on Preacher that the mountain man would never forget. So Preacher knew that he was gonna have to stomp on Wade some.

Preacher was looking forward to it. He'd had a belly full of the man. No dancing this time around.

Preacher rode through the timber, figuring the movers had about five hundred more yards to go 'fore they broke free and could stand on the plateau that overlooked the valley. He carefully tucked his smile away.

Beartooth winked at him when he rode back to the train. "Gonna tell 'em?"

"Not just yet." He looked up at the sky. Not even noon yet. He looked at a man leaning on his axe and looking at him. Preacher was not well-liked and he was well aware of that fact. It bothered him not a whit. "You figure on that tree maybe fallin' down all on its own, Brewer?" he asked cheerfully.

The mover gave him a dirty look and went back to chopping.

Preacher rode up to Melody. "Come on," he told her. "I want to show you something. Richard, you and Edmond and Penelope come along."

Preacher stopped them just before timber's edge.

"This is it?" Penelope asked, looking around her. "This is the same thing we've been seeing for weeks."

"Y'all ride out there on that flat and take a good look. Go on. I'll wait here."

Preacher stepped out of the saddle, eased the cinch on Hammer, and squatted down, chewing on a blade of grass.

"Yeeee-haw!" he heard Richard shout.

"Waa-hoo!" Edmond momentarily forgot his churchly bearing.

A mover rode up, his long rifle at the ready. "My God, is it the red savages?"

"Nope," Preacher said, standing up. "You home, pilgrim."

2

The pioneers, many of them ragged and gaunt, stood on the plateau and gazed in disbelief at the lush and green valley that lay before their eyes. Many of them wept, still others dropped to their knees and prayed, giving thanks to God for getting them safely through the wilderness. Only a few of them included the mountain men in those prayers . . . at first. Then, as they realized they never would have made it without the help of Preacher and his friends, they all formed a huge circle and linked hands, offering quiet prayers for Preacher, Dupre, Nighthawk, Trapper Jim, and Beartooth.

"We ought to be fairly blessed, I reckon," Beartooth said to his friends, standing away from the circle of pioneers.

"That's good," Jim said, "for I 'spect that we're gonna need all the help we can get when Gabriel sounds the call."

Swift decided at that moment it was a good time to rally the movers and get them down from the plateau. He gave a mighty blast on his bugle and like to have scared the mountain men out of their britches.

"That does it," Dupre said, when he had settled his badly jangled nerves. "I'm a-gonna snatch that bugle away from him and stomp it so flat not even an angel could toot it."

Laughing, Preacher calmed his friend then turned to Jim.

"Jim, ride yonder to the river and get one of them Injuns that's always hangin' around to canoe you 'crost and tell the chief factor we got a whole passel of pilgrims waitin' on this side. You might as well spend the night and ride back in the mornin'."

"See you boys then," Jim said with a grin. "I'll be thinkin' 'bout you when I belly up to the bar."

"Don't you drink up all the whiskey now, you hear me," Dupre warned him.

Jim waved and rode off toward the river.

"Are we reasonably safe from Indian attack here?" a mover asked Preacher.

"No," the reply was flat and fast given. "But you are safer here than at any other time behind you. If some of you are thinkin' 'bout stayin' on this side of the river and farmin', best thing you can do is build your cabins close together for protection."

"We are thinking that, Preacher. It's so beautiful." He stuck out his hand and Preacher shook it. "Thank you, sir." He looked at the others. "Thank you all."

"I reckon," Dupre said, after the man had left them, "that we could take a few days time to see that these pilgrims know how to notch logs and the like."

"That would be the Christian thing to do, all right," Beartooth said.

"I think you're all plumb loco," Preacher said.

Nighthawk looked at him. "Ummm!"

That night the skies opened up and it started raining.

"Never fails out here," Preacher said. "Wettest damn place I ever been in all my en-tar life. I'd sooner build me a cabin under a waterfall."

"I long for the Rockies," Dupre said. "You figure on winterin' where, Preacher?"

"I ain't give it no thought. Damn shore ain't gonna be near here, I can tell you true on that."

"You might oughta wrap your robe around that blonde-haired filly and snuggle up clost to her when the snow flies," Beartooth suggested. "She'd keep a man warm, I'm thinkin'."

"Bes' thing for you to do is close that fly-trap of yourn," Preacher told him.

"I be's hongry around my mouth," Beartooth wisely took the suggestion to heart. "I'd like to have me a bear steak right about now, just a-fairly drippin' with fat."

"Dream on," Dupre said. "That mover's woman over yonder said she was a-cookin' up mush and we's welcome to eat with them."

"I *hate* mush."*

"It ain't bad if she'll let it harden some and then fry it in fat. Get it crispy and it's right tasty," Preacher said. "My momma use to fix it thataway for breakfast. But I ain't no friend to gruel." He took a sip of coffee. "Was you boys serious 'bout stayin' around for a time and lendin' a hand so's these poor helpless children can get set up for winter?"

"Why not?" Dupre said. "You got anywheres else you got to be in a hurry?"

"Can't say as I have."

"Then it's settled," Nighthawk said.

"Oh, all right," Preacher had to grouse about it a little. "If I didn't I'd never hear the last of it. Y'all'd rag me about it forever. Personal, I think you all got you eyes on some mover's woman. That's what I think. Come the spring y'all probably still be here, scratching in the ground and plantin' taters and the like."

They were still bitching, telling the most outrageous of lies and insulting one another when the last lantern in the wagon train was turned down.

---

*Boiled corn meal and water.

Melody and Penelope and Richard and Edmond arranged for passage across the Columbia and Preacher was out hunting when they left—deliberately gone. About half the wagon train elected to cross the river to settle on the north side, the remainder choosing to remain on the south side. Despite his grumblings and sour attitude—which by now everybody knew was all an act and not the real Preacher—the mountain man really liked the pilgrims and in a way, felt responsible for them. It was a strange feeling for the normally solitary man. So the time went by quickly in the building of corrals and stables, stockades and the homes that would stand inside them. One day Preacher looked up and found that he and the others had been in the valley almost three weeks.

"Time do fly when a body's a-havin' fun, don't it, Preacher?" Dupre said with a grin.

Preacher nodded, his eyes on Beartooth who was returning from the fort, and pushing his mount hard. Dupre followed Preacher's eyes and said, "Somethin's wrong, Preach."

"I gleaned that right off. Where's Jim and Hawk?"

"Out huntin' supper."

"It better not be fish. I'm gettin' mighty tired of fish."

"I didn't say they was spearin' it. I said they was huntin' it. Must be time for us to leave, you're gettin' crotchety and hard of hearin', too."

"I ain't neither."

"Is too."

Beartooth swung down. "Ol' John Billingly was at the fort, provisionin' up for the winter. He just come in from the East. Says Red Hand and his bunch was ridin' hard back to their own territory, but without Bum Kelley and his bunch. And they was two raggedy lookin' hardcases just a-hangin' around the fort. They pulled out quick when they spied me eyeballin' 'em."

"Have some coffee and tell us the rest of it," Preacher told him.

"How'd you know they's more?"

"'Cause you wouldn't have been forcin' that poor animal of yourn to tote you so fast if there weren't. I swear if you get any fatter, we gonna have to buy an elephant from some circus for you to ride."

"You're an unkind man, Preacher," Beartooth said, pouring a cup full of brew that looked strong enough to melt a horse-shoe, and probably was.

"What I am is truthful. What else is they?"

"That church that your sweetie is livin' at is located a good four mile from the fort. Plumb isolated, it is. Chief factor told me it was done deliberate so's the Injuns would come to it better."

"And Richard told me they would keep the gold at the church headquarters," Preacher said. "Do they have any fightin' men out at the church?"

"Nope. Couple of tame old Chinooks is all. They sweep and dust and the like, the factor said."

"I don't like it," Dupre said. "I don't like it at all."

"Neither do I," Preacher agreed. "I think what we'll do is this . . ."

It was an emotional farewell from those settlers who had stayed south of the river. The women and the kids squalled and the men stood brave and fought back tears. Preacher cut it short, waved farewell, and the mountain men turned their horses and rode away. The settlers watched them until they were out of sight and then with a sigh, turned and once more began preparing their cabins for the winter that was not far off.

Preacher and his friends rode east for a day, camped, and then come the morning, headed north, just in case Bum had men watching them.

"You know where they's a good crossin' on the Columbia, Hawk?" Preacher asked.

"No. But I know where we *can* cross . . . if the water's low and we're lucky."

Days later they were still looking for Bum and his gang.

The chief factor at the fort had been warned by Dupre about the large amount of gold carried by the missionaries, and the danger of an attack on the church by the Kelley gang. The factor had listened, and then informed the Frenchman that while he would do what he could to insure the safety of the missionaries, those who choose to settle far away from the fort were really not his concern.

His words sounded a lot colder than they really were. The factor just didn't have the manpower to look after everybody. No one had asked the missionaries to come out—they did that on their own. His primary concern was to protect the goods of the company who employed him.

The mountain men ran into a hunting party of friendly Cayuses and stopped to palaver with them.

"Southwest of the Lewis," the leader told them. "Just on the edge of the big timber. Many whites are camped. They are not friendly and we did not attempt to camp near them. They are not trappers. I don't know what they are . . . I think perhaps they are thieves. I do not trust them."

Preacher thanked him and they rode on.

"Five open hands of men," Nighthawk said. "That's a goodly number, but somewhat less than we faced a month ago."

"A lot of his followers have left him," Preacher said. "Maybe we'll get lucky and put an end to Bum Kelley."

Beartooth wasn't so sure about that. "That no-count's been around a long time, Preach. A lot of men has tried to put him in the ground."

"I'd settle for Jack Harris," Dupre said. "He's been givin' trappers and guides and the like a bad name for years."

"I'm greedy," Preacher replied. "I want 'em all."

* * *

Nighthawk touched the white ashes and smiled. "We're no more than half a day behind them."

"Twenty-five to thirty men," Preacher said, after walking around and carefully inspecting the campgrounds. "And a nasty bunch they is, too."

"No bloody bandages layin' around," Dupre said. "Looks like they're all in pretty good shape."

"They're headin' for the fort," Jim told them. "That sign's as clear as leaves on a tree."

"I know a shorter way," Beartooth said. "We can be there a couple of hours 'fore them."

Preacher swung into the saddle. "Let's ride."

"He didn't even say goodbye," Melody said, gazing out a window of the mission.

The afternoon was clear and bright and cool, with not a single cloud in the sky, a welcome relief from the rain that usually fell. Frost had colored the land that morning, laying a heavy mantle of white that was gone as soon as the sun touched it. Winter was not far away.

"Oh, Melody," Penelope said. "Why can't you see that he's entirely the wrong man for you? Yes, he's handsome and dashing and daring and all of that. But he's wild, Melody. He's like the wind. He doesn't belong in a house. He'd feel confined, like a chained animal. It wouldn't be fair to ask him to change his ways. He belongs to the mountains and the wild, high country."

Melody turned from the window. She smiled sadly. "I know all that, Penelope." Suddenly, she giggled. "Can you just imagine the looks on Mum's face if I should suddenly show up back East with Preacher in tow?"

The two young women burst out laughing at just the thought.

"Or better yet," Penelope said, "with all *five* of them!"

Richard and Edmond walked into the sitting room, curious to see what all the giggling was about.

"What in the world . . . ?" Edmond inquired.

"Girl talk," Melody told the young men. "You wouldn't understand."

Richard walked to the window that Melody had just left and stared out, silent for a moment. He turned to face the group. "It's odd that Preacher didn't stop to say goodbye. Swift told me they left very abruptly."

"What are you saying?" Penelope asked, walking across the room to stand by his side.

"I'm . . . not sure. But I became friends with Preacher toward the last. And I am sure that something is not right about their leaving. I just have a feeling that their sudden departure might be a ruse of some sort."

"A deception?" Edmond asked. "No. I don't believe that. What would be the reason?"

Richard spread his hands. "I don't know. It's just a feeling I have. I'm probably wrong."

"I'm sure you are," Edmond said smugly. "We shall never see those men again."

"That outlaw and the gold we have hidden here at the church," Melody said.

"What about it?" Edmond asked.

"Preacher may have received word that the gang had not given up and were coming this way. He and his friends may have gone to attack them, or head them off, or something like that."

"Pure romantic balderdash!" Edmond said with a laugh. "Melody, you became mildly infatuated with the man and had a mental fling. Put him out of your mind and settle both feet back on the ground. You'll not see that will-o'-the-wisp again." With a knowing and not a terribly kind laugh, he left the room.

Richard stared hard at Edmond's back. "Sometimes," the missionary said, "I believe that man is not far from being a fool!"

3

"They're about a mile ahead of us," Nighthawk said, slipping back into camp after making his silent reconnoiter on foot. "Twenty-eight of them. No guards out."

"No doubt in your mind it's Bum?" Jim asked.

"No doubt," Nighthawk said, pouring a cup of coffee from the pot set on the rocks beside a hat-sized fire.

"They's gonna be some of them no-counts out permanently 'fore the dawnin'," Preacher said, a grim tone to the words. His gaze touched the eyes of his friends. "Anybody don't want to do it this way, say so now."

The four other mountain men looked at him, their eyes hard. Dupre finally said, "I ain't got no use for murderin', child-rapin' scum. Let's do it."

The others nodded their heads in agreement, then set about gathering up their gear. They were grim-faced as they worked, for this was to be a bloody night.

There were only small pockets of law west of the Missouri River, and not a hell of a lot more law than that between the Missouri and the Mississippi. These mountain men ran wild and free, and they answered to few codes of conduct. But those they did subscribe to were the basic ones that decent men everywhere held to: Steal a man's horse in the wilderness and you set him afoot to face possible death. So stealing a man's horse called for a hanging or a shooting. On the spot. You did not lie except in jest, for here a man's word was held as tight a bond as a contract done up in some fancy law office. A man did not bother a good woman or child (or even a bad woman in most cases). Harm a woman, and the penalty was almost certainly death. Rape a woman or child and the penalty was certain death, often in very unpleasant ways.

The mountain men led a wild and rough existence, and the justice they dealt was just as wild and rough and unforgiving as the land which they lived in and fought in and, for most, eventually died in.

On this night, the five mountain men shoved pistols behind their sashes, added war axes to that, and picked up their Hawken rifles.

They began making their silent way toward the outlaw camp of Bum Kelley. They took their time, wanting to arrive just when most of the outlaws would be getting ready to roll up in their stinking blankets. With any kind of luck this night, the outlaws would sleep forever, and the missionaries and no telling how many countless others, blissfully unaware of the danger the outlaws presented, would live normal, happy lives—or as normal and happy as could be in the wilderness.

With any kind of luck.

The ambuscaders neared the camp, broke up, and silently moved forward, stopping their stealthy advance just at the edge of the clearing. The fires were dying down and men were grumbling about the cold as they prepared to roll up in their blankets.

Preacher spotted several thugs that he recognized, and assumed that Bum was already in his blankets. He lifted his Hawken and blew one standing man straight to Hell and into the hot embrace of Satan. The others opened fire a split second later.

The night roared with gunfire and the air became choking with gunsmoke from the muzzle loaders.

"Now!" Preacher screamed and charged the camp, a knife in one hand and a war axe in the other.

Moses reared up from the ground, his dirty face pale and his eyes wide in fear. Preacher smashed his skull with the axe and jumped over the dead man.

Beartooth, using both axe and knife ended the life of Jennings while Nighthawk finished Halsey with an axe. Jim ended Bobby's vicious life of crime as Dupre buried his war axe into the head of Keyes.

Preacher threw his axe with deadly accuracy, the head burying deep in Beckman's skull and bringing the outlaw down dead. He fell into the fire. Preacher worked his axe free and let the man burn. They needed a little more light to work by, anyway.

Slug made the terrible mistake of trying to best Beartooth strength to strength. The huge mountain man broke the outlaw's neck and let him fall bonelessly to the cold ground.

"Damn your eyes!" George screamed at Preacher as he jumped for the man. Preacher buried his knife in the man's stomach and ripped upward. He jerked his blade free and stood over the body.

The camp fell silent. The mountain men looked around as they stood in the middle of the carnage. There appeared to be no one left alive.

Bum, Jack Harris, Leo, and Bull had jumped for their horses when the first shot was fired. They rode bareback, holding on to the mane, the horses just as wall-eyed and trembling with fear as the men on their backs.

Dipper, Waller, and Burke had run wild-eyed into the night. They left their horses and all their possessions behind in their frantic dash to get clear of the bloody ambush. No matter, they could always kill again and steal more horses. They headed for Fort Vancouver.

"Bum ain't here," Dupre said.

"Neither is that damnable turncoat Jack Harris," Preacher said.

"I count twenty-one," Nighthawk said. "Seven got away. I will see very quickly in what direction."

Preacher did some fancy cussing as he stood in the clearing of death.

"We'll track them, ol' hoss," Dupre assured his friend. "We'll get them."

"Bet on it," Preacher said in a low menacing tone.

Beartooth dragged Beckman out of the flames and tossed some water on him, putting out the burning clothing. "He smelt bad enough alive," the mountain man said.

"Three on foot heading for the fort," Nighthawk said. "Four mounted men headed straight east."

"I'll take care of them on foot," Preacher said, reloading his weapons. "Let's get back to camp and saddle up. You boys track Bum—and you can bet it's Bum and Jack on horseback—and I'll catch up with you along the way. Hawk, leave rocks piled for me, will you?"

Nighthawk nodded and the men took off at a trot for their camp. An hour later they were hard on the trail of those who had survived the ambush.

"We got no food, no saddles, and we left most of our weapons back at the camp," Bum griped. "I ain't never been in no spot like this before."

They had stopped to get a drink of water at a little creek and to rest their horses.

"I wonder how many got away?" Leo questioned. "I seen a half a dozen shot to bloody rags in they blankets."

"I never figured Preacher would pull something like this," Bum said. "If it was Preacher and them."

"It was," Jack Harris said sourly. "And Preacher will do anything. He don't play by no rules. I tried to warn y'all 'bout Preacher. That's the most meanest man that ever walked these mountains."

"I think I seen Dipper and Burke get free," Leo said. "Maybe one more. I don't know for sure. It all happened so damn fast all I could think of was gettin' free and safe." He looked at his hands in the faint moonlight. They were trembling. He wasn't sure his legs would support his weight if he tried to stand up.

"I'm just wonderin' if and for how long Preacher and them others will track us," Bum said.

"They'll track us," Jack replied bitterly. "And they'll track us 'til Hell freezes over."

Preacher rode directly for the fort, taking trails those on foot would avoid. The three outlaws had to head for the fort; they had nowhere else to go. Once there, he told no one what had happened. The factor might frown on folks ambushing other folks. His presence was reported to Richard, who told none of the others the news. He immediately saddled up and rode in to see the mountain man. Preacher was camped outside the walls.

"Melody was rather upset when you left without saying goodbye, Preacher," he told him.

"She'll get over it."

"Oh, my," Richard said.

"Oh, my, what?"

"Here comes that Wade fellow."

Preacher looked up and grunted. "He best keep on goin'. I ain't got the patience right now to mess with that fool."

"You there!" Wade called, his good-for-nothing son with him. "You! Mountain man. I came to call you out."

"You best go on, Wade, and leave me alone. Mess with me now and I'm gonna wind your clock."

Without another word, Wade hit him, the blow unexpected. Preacher hit the ground, flat on his back.

"Fight! Fight!" someone from the fort yelled.

Preacher slowly got to his moccasins and spat out blood from a busted lip. "All right, mover," he said, low menace in his voice. "You got this comin' to you." He faked a blow, Wade flicked a hand to deflect it, and Preacher tossed a hard right fist to Wade's mouth. The blow snapped his head back and brought blood to his mouth.

Preacher busted him with a hard left fist that landed on the side of the man's jaw and Preacher followed that with a right to Wade's gut.

Wade backed up, shaking his head and trying to catch his wind. Preacher pressed him, landing blows to the man's shoulders and face and stomach. Preacher back-heeled the man and sent him tumbling to the ground. Avery screamed curses at Preacher and jumped at him, both fists flailing the air. Preacher timed a punch perfectly and it landed smack on his nose, flattening it and sending blood squirting. Avery squalled and sat down on the ground.

"Goddamn you!" Wade yelled, getting to his boots. "That's my son you struck."

"And a piss-poor kid he is, too," Preacher told him. "He must take after his pa."

Wade swung and Preacher turned, the blow catching him on the shoulder. The blow hurt, for Wade was a big and powerful man. A bully. Like father, like son.

Preacher popped a fast left that smacked Wade on the mouth, bringing new blood to the man's lips.

"'En 'is 'ow, Pa," Avery blubbered, both hands covering his busted and bloody beak.

"What'd you say?" Wade cut his eyes to his son.

"He wants you to clean my plow, Wade," Preacher interpreted. "But I allow as to how I got something to say about that." Preacher jumped up into the air and kicked Wade in the face, the kick knocking the man back to the earth. He landed heavily on his butt and his teeth clicked together from the sudden impact with the ground.

"Are you gonna rest or fight?" Preacher taunted the man.

Wade slowly got to his feet. His face was bloody and swelling and he was mad clear through. So far he had not been able to land an effective blow on the mountain man.

Preacher cut his eyes. The smart-aleck kid was crawling behind him, so his pa could shove him tumbling. Preacher side-stepped and gave Avery the toe of his moccasin right in the gut. The young man howled in pain and fell sprawled out on the ground, gasping for breath.

Wade came at Preacher like a wild bull, his face filled with hate, and his mouth spewing out cuss words, all of them directed at Preacher and his ancestors. None of it was in the least complimentary.

Preacher stuck out a foot and tripped the man, sending him to the ground, face first. Wade kissed the grass and came up sputtering and spitting out dirt. Preacher stepped in close and hit the bigger man twice, a left and a right to the jaw. Wade staggered back, regaining his footing just at the last moment. He lifted his fists.

"Aw, give it up, man," Preacher said. "You're done."

Wade lumbered forward and took a wild swing at Preacher. Preacher sighed and popped him again, a left and a right, to belly and jaw.

Still the big man would not go down. "Come on, mountain man!" Wade sneered. "Fight! I got you whipped now."

"You 'bout a fool, Wade," Preacher told the man. "This fight is stupid. Give it up and I'll buy you a drink."

"'Ick 'is ass, Pa!" Avery screamed, mush-mouthed, getting to his big feet.

"I 'bout had enough of you, too, boy," Preacher told the young man.

Avery told Preacher where to go and what to stick up a certain part of his anatomy when he got there.

Preacher narrowed his eyes and gave the young man the back of his hand right across the mouth. The force of the blow knocked Avery to the ground.

When Preacher turned around to face Wade, the big man was standing, grinning a bloody smirk at Preacher.

With a knife in his hand.

4

"I really don't think you know what you're doin', Wade," Preacher told him, his voice cold and low. "But if you don't put that knife up, I'm gonna kill you, man. And I ain't gonna tell you that but one time."

The chief factor stepped through the crowd, a cocked pistol in one hand. "Withdraw, sir!" he ordered Wade. "Or stand and die."

With a snarl, Wade sheathed his blade and stood staring at Preacher. Wade's chest heaved and blood dripped from his busted nose and mouth. "There will be another day, Preacher," he warned. "And you may wager on that."

"Why?" Preacher asked him. "Are you that anxious to die, Wade?"

With a snort of derision, Wade shoved and elbowed his way through the crowd. He helped the light of his life to his feet and together they walked off.

"Preacher did not start this trouble," Richard informed the chief factor. "We were standing here chatting when Wade bulled his way up to us and demanded that Preacher fight him. The man is a troublemaker, sir."

"Yes," the man said, uncocking and securing his pistol. "Unfortunately, I know that only too well. The family has been in this area just about a month and already that Wade fellow has been involved in three altercations. That son of his is no more than a common hooligan and vandal. I fear neither of them will come to a good end. The father does not seem to realize that I can bar him from this fort. And I might just do that. Good day, gentlemen."

"Richard," Preacher said, after several trappers he knew had congratulated him on a good fight and the crowd had broken up, "go on back to the church and charge your pistols and rifles. They's three bad ones headin' this way. I believe I can stop them. But if I don't, it's gonna be up to you."

"Bum Kelley and his gang?"

"Bum Kelley ain't got no gang no more. Not none to speak of, that is. The buzzards and the varmits is a-eatin' on most of his gang up south and east of Soda Peak."

Richard swallowed hard. "You and your friends did them in?"

"That we did."

Richard decided he really did not want to know the how of that statement. "The Indian renegade and his bunch?"

"Broke up and long gone."

Richard looked around him to make sure they were alone. "Bum and his people were coming after the gold?"

"That they were—and the women. I don't think you'll have to worry with Bum no more. Just as soon as I deal with them three no-counts comin' for your place, I'll hook up with my friends and we'll chase Bum down and dispose of him."

He held out his hand and Richard shook it.

"Likely as not you won't see no more of me, Richard," Preacher told the man. "You tell Melody and the others good-bye for me." He smiled. "You're a good man, Richard. I watched you grow over the weeks. You toughened up, both in mind and body." He clasped him on the shoulder with a hard hand. "You'll do to ride the river with, man."

It was only after Preacher had ridden off, that Richard realized he had just been paid the highest compliment a mountain man could offer.

"Goodbye to you, friend," the missionary whispered to the afternoon. "And may God bless and keep you and your friends as you ride the mountain passes."

Preacher didn't ride far that day. He rode north of the mission and picketed Hammer on good graze and a small pool of water and waited. Maybe he was wrong. Maybe the three survivors of the ambush were not going to attack the mission, maybe they were just heading for the closest point of civilization. Maybe the thugs were coming here to steal or beg or buy supplies and horses and then leave. But Preacher doubted that.

Although he'd never seen a tiger, he doubted one could change its stripes, and he felt the same about those who chose to ride the outlaw trail. Preacher knew that to a large degree, each man shaped his own destiny. People were not forced into a life of crime—they chose it willingly. Preacher had not one ounce of sympathy in his being for thugs and hoodlums and the like.

Preacher also knew that what he was about to do—depending on whether the trio showed up—cut across the grain of those who knuckled down and cowered under the watchful eye of any constable or sheriff's department. Man steals your horse, you hang him. Man threatened to do a body harm, you go after that person and put the harm on him 'fore he can do it to you.

He waited in the timber behind the mission.

Just after dark, he saw the three men slip to the edge of the timber and crouch down. He could hear the murmur of their voices but could not make out any of the words. He watched them point to the lamp-lighted windows of the church and living quarters.

Preacher stood and moved silently, making a wide circle and coming up by the side of the buildings, then working his way to the rear of the main building. He crouched down, his war-axe in his hand.

He smelled the man before he saw him. The man stank of filth and days-old sweat. The hoodlum came closer, so close Preacher could have reached out and touched him. He was going to do just that—sort of—in a few seconds. The man peered in through the precious glass of a back window, into a darkened room. He saw the man take a long-bladed knife from a beaded sheath.

Preacher rose like a wraith and buried the head of his axe into the man's skull. He rolled the man under the building.

"What was that?" came the hoarse whisper.

"Stubbed my toe," Preacher gruffly called.

"You're a clumsy igit, Waller. Did you find us a way in?"

"Right here."

"You see them women?"

"Yes. They's nekkid."

"Hot damn! I get first dibs."

What he got was the sharp head of a tomahawk right between the eyes.

"Dipper?" came the whisper.

"Right here."

"Waller with you?"

"Yeah."

"I seen some fine-lookin' horses in the stable."

"Good."

"Did you say them fillies was nekkid?"

"Yep."

"I'm on my way to glory, Dipper!"

"You shore is," Preacher said, as he lowered the cooling body to the earth.

One by one he dragged the bodies to a ditch far behind the church buildings and dumped them. He collapsed part of the bank over them and then threw small logs and branches over that. Sooner or later the men might possibly be discovered—

or an arm or leg of them would—but by that time the bodies would be so badly decomposed no one would be able to tell who or even what they had been.

Preacher looked toward the rear of the buildings, a thousand yards or more away. "You good folks rest easy now," he said. "Live a long life and be happy—compliments of Preacher."

Preacher rode away from the fort and made a cold camp. By noon of the next day, he was in the Cascades. By midafternoon, he had found the tracks of both his friends and Bum and his crud. By nightfall, he found the first small mound of stones left him by Nighthawk. To someone unfamiliar with his style of living, the stones would have been meaningless; to Preacher they spoke volumes. He made his camp and slept as soundly as he ever did.

Four days later, he caught up with his friends. They were standing over three mounds of earth.

"They kilt 'em whilst they slept," Beartooth said. "I didn't know none of these boys, but they appeared to be trappers. I reckon they had 'em a jug and drank theyselves silly 'fore they went to bed. They heads was all beat in. The rocks and clubs is over yonder, all bloody. So Bum and Jack and them others now got guns and the like. These bodies was stripped nekkid, so them no-good's now got skins on, I reckon. They taken everything so's they'll pass for trappers. How'd you do?"

"I took care of them three that went to the west and whupped Wade's butt good over at the fort."

"I'd like to have seen that," Dupre said. "What brought all that on?"

"I don't know. I reckon he was just feelin' lucky."

"You shoulda kilt him," Trapper Jim said.

"I would have but the chief factor butted in just at the last minute."

"Too bad," Beartooth said. "Let's ride."

* * *

Bum and his small party crossed over into Washington Territory, into what is now Idaho, and for the first time since the ambush, began to feel like they just might have eluded their pursuers. They could not have been more wrong.

None of them had even the faintest inkling of what manner of men rode after them. Bum and his men were thieves, murderers, cutthroats, and almost anything else that was evil and dishonest. Like so many others, they made the oftentimes fatal mistake of judging others by comparing them to self.

While no one who is even an amateur student of the West would ever write—or even think—that mountain men were paragons of virtue, most of the mountain men did operate under a loose code of conduct. They were wild and woolly and, as the Western saying goes "Born with the bark on," yet curiously drawn to alliances and bonding with like kind. A good woman was as revered as their own mothers, so even to think of doing harm to a good woman was enough to bring their wrath down on a person.

Bum and his bunch did not realize that Preacher and his friends, if it had to be, would pursue them all the way to New York City and drive them into the Atlantic Ocean.

"I believe we can rest easy now, boys," Jack Harris said. "Preacher and them friends of hisn has played out their string."

"Yep," Leo said, stretching out on his stolen and blood-stained blankets and sucking on a cup of coffee. "I think we can relax and start pondering on another job."

Miles to the west, five hard-eyed mountain men rode their ponies, their Hawken rifles across their saddle horns.

"I think we ought to lay low for a time," Bull said. "Let the news of this wagon train gettin' through to the blue waters git back East. Then they's people who'll come a-foggin' to the promised land. They'll have cash money and fancy wimmen and the like. Pickin's'll be fine, boys, fine."

"I agree, Bull," Bum said. "But we got to start lookin' hard for a cabin to winter in. The snow's done cappin' the low mountains. It'll be hard cold soon."

"We'll find some trapper's cabin and kill him," Leo said. "Lay in a stock of meat and jerk it. Preacher and them silly friends of hisn will think we've done left the country."

"I know a spot up on the Clark," Jack said. "Snug little cabin that'd do just fine. Trapper lives there with one of the prettiest little Injun gals you ever seen. She could keep us all happy durin' the winter and then we could kill her come springtime 'fore we pulled out. We'll catch her man out runnin' his traps and do him in quiet like."

"Sounds good to me," Bum said. "We'll head that way come the mornin'. Pretty little thing, you say, Jack?"

"Purty as a pitcher, she is. Shapely."

Preacher and the others stood over the ripped and torn body of the man. "Anybody know him?" Preacher asked.

"I thinks it's Parley," Jim said. "But the buzzards and the varmits been hard at work here. Kinda hard to tell."

Preacher rolled the man over on his stomach and grunted. A bullet hole in the dead man's flesh was obvious.

"Shot him in the back while he sat before his fire," Nighthawk observed.

"Four men," Dupre called from outside the small clearing. "It's Bum and them others for sure. Tracks are plain." He rejoined the group.

"We're gonna take 'em alive, boys," Preacher spoke the words grimly. "And we's gonna have us a court of law, all proper and legal like. Then when we find 'em guilty, we'll hang 'em."

"That sounds good," Jim said.

"Nighthawk, you be the judge," Preacher said. "I'll speak agin the bunch, Dupre, you defend 'em."

"Wagh!" the Frenchman recoiled. "I ain't got nothin' good to say about this pack of mad dog heathens."

"No, we got to do this right and proper now," Preacher insisted. "You just let them have they say and such as that. Then, after they's done, if you can find anything good to say about them, say it. Hell, it don't make no difference. We gonna find them guilty anyways. Jim and Beartooth's gonna be the jury."

"When the time comes, I shall don my proper robes to sit in judgement," Nighthawk said. "I have a fine buffalo robe in my pack."

"That'll be good," Preacher said. "Make you look plumb respectable." He glanced at the Crow. "Providin' you do something with them goddamn pigtails."

5

"They's noonin' by a crick," Dupre reported back. "So careless you'd think they was havin' a picnic." The day was cold, the approaching winter already opening its hand and closing chilly fingers over the high country. The men had awakened to a hard freeze that morning. The night before they knew they were close upon the outlaws and had elected to keep a cold camp, so the smell of wood smoke would not give them away. "They got a fire big enough to roast a bear. So's I reckon we could build us a small one for coffee."

"Bum and them's got a-plenty," Preacher said. "And it's already fixed. No point in usin' up any of our supplies when come the sundown, them down yonder ain't gonna have no further need for vittles."

"You make a good point," Nighthawk said. "Perhaps it is you who should be the judge."

"You be better. You can look sterner than me."

"Of course. You are correct. I also am much more handsome and certainly I present a much more regal appearance."

"Wagh!" Beartooth said. "He's got you on that, Preacher."

"English judges wear wigs," Jim said. "I seen a drawin' of 'em in a book one time. Them pigtails of Hawk's fit right in, seems to me."

"You be right," Beartooth agreed. "When do we move agin them murderers?"

"Right now," Preacher said, and stood up.

Leo decided the coffee was just about ready and dumped in cold water to settle the grounds. Suddenly he had the feeling of eyes on him. He looked around. He could see nothing.

"What's the matter with you?" Bull asked.

Leo shook his head. "Nothin'. Just had a shiverin' sort of feelin', that's all."

"That meat do smell good," Jack said. "I be hongry for a fact."

Bum was all stretched out comfortable on his stolen blankets, half asleep. He opened his eyes to the warbling of a songbird. Sure was pretty. He cut his eyes and saw something that was a lot less pretty. Beartooth, standing grinning at him from the bushes. The man had a Hawken rifle in his big hands, the muzzle pointed straight at Bum. Bum cut his eyes to Jack Harris. The man was squatting motionless, the muzzle of a pistol placed at the back of his head. Bum could see Leo staring up at Preacher, the mountain man holding him in check with a pistol. Bull was looking into the muzzle of a rifle held by Dupre.

"Well now," Preacher said. "That meat do smell good. So let's eat it up and then we'll settle down to business."

The outlaws were trussed up and dumped on the ground. They offered no resistance, and up to this point, no argument.

Preacher and his friends ate the meat and drank the coffee. Bum and what remained of his band lay on the ground and watched in silence.

Bum finally broke the silence. "Go ahead and shoot us, you sons of bitches! What the hell are you waitin' on?"

"Speak for yourself!" Leo said. "I'd a-soon delay the grave, if possible."

"The three that made it to the fort and the missionaries' church I tooken out," Preacher informed the outlaws. "They was a scabby bunch, they was."

"You recall their names?" Bum asked.

"Waller and Dipper was the only names I heard. Don't know who the other one was. Don't make no difference. He's just as dead as the others."

"You never gonna get us to no court of law," Bull boasted. "And since you ain't lawmen, what you're doin' is agin the law. You ain't got no right to hold us agin our will."

"You're wrong on all counts," Dupre told him. "We fixin' to have us a court of law. Right here." He pointed at Nighthawk. "And yonder sits the judge."

"A goddamn Injun?" Leo hollered.

"You best watch your mouth," Preacher told him. "It don't pay to make the judge mad."

Nighthawk rose and went to his pack horse, taking out a buffalo robe and slipping it on. He sat down on a large rock and said, "Court's in session. Commence the proceedin's."

"Who goes first?" Dupre asked. "Me or you, Preacher?"

"Me." Preacher wiped his mouth and rubbed his greasy hands on his buckskins. He looked at the trussed-up outlaws. "I'm the perser-q-tor."

"Prosecutor!" Nighthawk corrected.

"That, too," Preacher said. "Your honor, these here men a-fore you is scum. They's murderers and rapers and torturers. They ain't fit human bein's."

"Objection!" Dupre said.

"Hell, I ain't even got goin' good yet!" Preacher yelled.

"This is an outrage!" Jack Harris hollered. "I demand a real lawyer and a real judge. Not no goddamn Injun!"

"Objection overruled," Nighthawk said. "Proceed, Preacher."

"Where was I?"

"Not fit human beings."

"Oh. Yeah. Right. Your honor, these here four snakeheads is about as low as a human person can get. Buzzard puke is easier to look upon than these four . . ."

"I object!" Dupre hollered.

"Hell, I do too!" Bull squalled.

"All of you be quiet," Nighthawk said. "What is your objection, counselor?"

"Say what?"

"Counselor. That's what you are at this moment. A counselor. Now what is your objection?"

"I ain't really got one. Hell, I agree with everything Preacher said. But ain't I s'posed to object ever'time he says something? I seen a trial back . . . oh, twenty-five year ago, I reckon it was. Judge had him a wooden hammer and was beatin' on the table and hollerin' 'bout half the time. And one or the other of them lawyers was always objectin' 'bout somethin'."

"You are supposed to object when the prosecution brings up some point that you disagree with," Nighthawk told him.

"Oh. Well, hell. I might as well lay down and take a nap, if that's the case."

"No, you don't!" Bum yelled.

"I got to pee!" Leo bellered.

"Order in the court!" Nighthawk thundered. "Does the prosecution have anything else to say?"

"I say we hang the bastards," Preacher said.

"Yeah, me, too," Dupre said.

"You can't say that!" Nighthawk told him. "You're supposed to be defending these no-good, sorry, good-for-nothin's." He caught himself. "Strike that from the record and the jury will disregard my comments."

Jim nudged Beartooth. "That's us."

"Why disregard it?" Beartooth asked. "It's all true."

"What record?" Jim asked.

"Somebody's s'posed to be writin' all this down," Leo yelled.

"Well, don't look at me," Jim protested. "I can't write."

"Stand the accused up before me," Nighthawk said.

The four were jerked to their feet. Jack yelled, "This ain't no legal court of law. I demand a judge. I got rights."

"I sentence the four of you to be hanged by the neck until

you are dead, dead, dead, dead," Nighthawk said. "And may God have mercy on your souls."

"Halp!" Bull bellered.

"Get the ropes," Preacher said.

"I have to dismiss the court," Nighthawk told him.

"Well, dismiss it," Preacher replied.

"Let's get on with the hangin'," Jim said.

"Don't be in such a rush!" Bum squalled.

"I thought a court of law was supposed to show mercy and compassion?" Jack asked.

"We have the right to an appeal," Bull said.

"Now, that is true," Nighthawk said.

"How do we go about that?" Dupre asked. "This is gettin' right complicated."

"I think the prisoners got to go before another judge," Beartooth said.

"We ain't got no other judge," Preacher said.

Jim looked at the four. "I reckon that means that you boys is outta luck."

"Halp!" Jack bellered.

"Now what do we do?" Dupre asked.

"Hawk's got to dismiss the pro-ceedin's," Jim said. "Soon as he does that, I'll go fetch the ropes."

"I hate ever' damn one of you people!" Bull yelled.

"Vengeance is mine, sayeth the Lord," Jack reminded the group.

"But He ain't here," Preacher said. "So we're actin' in His place."

"Court is adjourned," Nighthawk said, then frowned. "I think that's the correct term."

"Halp!" Leo hollered.

"They funnin' with us," Jack said, sweat dripping off his face. "They ain't really gonna hang us."

"That ain't no collar for a tie he's a-fixin' over yonder," Bull said.

Jim was tossing four ropes over a limb. The open nooses dangled and swayed ominously.

The four outlaws were hoisted up into their saddles—rather, saddles they had killed the trappers for—and the nooses placed around their necks.

"You boys wanna pray?" Preacher asked, meeting their scared eyes and lingering for a moment at each man. His own eyes were hard as flint.

"Swing wide the gates to Heaven!" Leo shrieked.

"That'll be the day," Dupre muttered.

"Lord, I'm a-comin' home!" Bull shouted.

"No, you goin' in the other direction," Beartooth corrected.

"Forgive me of all my sins!" Jack Harris moaned. "All the men and women and children I've kilt and robbed and raped and done all them other bad things to."

"Disgusting," Nighthawk said.

"Goddamn you to the fiery pits of Hell, Preacher!" Bum Kelley said.

"Odd thing for a man in your position to say," Preacher told him, then whapped the horse on the butt. Bum Kelley and his bunch dangled and kicked and twisted and swung.

The men waited until the outlaws had kicked their last, then lowered them down and dumped them in a shallow ravine, collapsing rocks over the bodies.

"You wanna say something over the tomb?" Dupre asked Preacher.

Preacher thought about that. "Yeah. I do." He took off his hat and the others did the same, none of them not knowing quite what to expect from their friend. Preacher was famous for a lot of things, including his sometimes profane and always odd eulogies.

Preacher took a breath and said, "Here lies Jack and Leo and Bull and Bum. They run their race and now it's done. They was sorry crap without no class. So bend over, Satan, and let 'em kiss your ass!"

6

Theirs was a solitary breed, and a breed that regrettably did not last long in American history. Progress pushed them aside. But on this late fall day in the year of 1837, the four mountain men lingered long over coffee that morning. No one had put it into words, but all knew that here was where the trail forked.

"Where you gonna winter, Jim?" Dupre asked.

"I got me a little cabin over on the Flathead. It was right snug last time I seen it. I reckon it's still there. I'll soon know. You?"

"I get on right good with the Nez Perce. They was a fine-lookin' squaw lost her man last time I was through there. I told her I'd be back 'fore the snow flew. I reckon it's about time to head that way. Nighthawk?"

"My grandfather is old. I will go to his lodge and we will talk of things past. He will die this winter, I am thinking. I want to see that he is buried properly. Bear?"

"I'm gonna look up Lobo and see if he's still livin' with them buffalo wolves. If he ain't, I might winter with him and let him put me to sleep each night listenin' to his damn lies. Preacher?"

"I don't know," Preacher tossed out the dregs from his cup.

"I got the restless flung on me. I might head south. Then again, I might head east. I just don't know."

"You best be makin' up your mind, ol' hoss," Beartooth told him. "The snow's fixin' to fly soon."

"Yeah. I know it." He began rolling his blankets and gathering up his kit.

Within minutes, the mountain men had packed up and were in the saddle.

"I wish I could say all this has been fun," Preacher said, "but I'd be lyin' and that's something I never do."

"Wagh!" Dupre said. "It'll be a relief not to have to smell your stinkin' feet."

"What will be a greater relief," Nighthawk said, "is not having to listen to Beartooth's stomach grumble when he does not eat eight times a day."

"Or listen to Dupre try to sing those awful French songs," Jim said.

The men smiled at each other for a moment, and then rode their separate ways without another word.

That afternoon, Preacher topped a rise. Careful not to skyline himself to unfriendly eyes, he paused and looked westward, his thoughts of Melody.

"Mayhaps I should have partook of them charms of hern, Hammer. I might have the re-grets about not doin' that some cold winter's night. But I 'spect we'll be back that way 'fore too long. I don't know why I say that, I just feel it." He settled his hat on his head and lifted the reins. "Well, good horse, you wanna go see some country we ain't seen afore?"

Hammer snorted and shook his head.

"Well, let's us go then."

And the mountain man called Preacher began another ride into the pages of history.

THE FIRST
MOUNTAIN MAN:
PREACHER

1

1813, Ohio

Leaving his brother sleeping in the bed behind him, the boy
stepped out of the bedroom and into the upstairs hallway. He
moved down to the end of the hall to his parents' bedroom,
where he stood just outside their door for a moment listening
to his pa's heavy snoring.

His pa's snores were loud because he slept hard. He worked
hard too, eking out a living for his family by laboring from
dawn to dusk on a farm that was more rock than dirt, and took
more than it gave.

His ma was in there too, though her rhythmic breathing
could scarcely be heard over her husband's snores. She was
always the last to go to bed and the first to get up. It was
nearly two hours before dawn now, but Art knew that his
mother would be rolling out of bed in less than an hour, starting another of the endless procession of backbreaking days
that were the borders of her life.

"Ma, Pa, I want you both to know that I ain't leavin' 'cause
of nothin' either of you have done," the boy said quietly. "You
been good to me and there ain't no way I can ever pay you
back for all that you done for me, or let you know how much

I love you. But the truth is, I got me a hankerin' to get on with my life and I reckon twelve years is long enough to wait."

From there the boy, who had been christened Arthur, but was called Art, moved down to his sisters' room. He went into their room and saw them sleeping together in the bed his father had made for them. A silver splash of moonlight fell through the window, illuminating their faces. One was sucking her thumb, a habit she practiced even in her sleep; the other was clutching a corncob doll. The sheet had slipped down, so Art pulled it back up, covering their shoulders. The two girls, eight and nine, snuggled down into the sheet, but didn't awaken.

"I reckon I'm going to miss seeing you two girls grow Art said. "But I'll always keep you in my mind, along with Ma and Pa and my brother."

His good-byes having been said, Art picked up the pillowcase in which he had put a second shirt, another pair of pants, three biscuits, and an apple, and started toward the head of the stairs.

Although he had been planning this adventure for a couple of months, he didn't make the decision to actually leave until three days ago. On that day he stood on a bluff and watched a flatboat drift down the Ohio River, which flowed passed the family farm. There was a family on the flatboat, holding on tightly to the little pile of canvas-covered goods that represented all their worldly possessions. One of the boat's passengers, a boy about Art's age, waved. Other than the wave, there had been nothing unusual about that particular boat. It was one of many similar vessels that passed by the farm every week.

To anyone else, seeing an entire family uprooted and looking for a new place to live, traveling the river with only those possessions they could carry on the boat with them, might have been a pitiful sight. But to Art, it was an adventure that stirred his soul, and he wished more than anything that he could be with them.

Art was nearly to the bottom of the stairs when the sudden chiming of the Eli Terry clock startled him. Gasping, he nearly dropped his sack, but recovered in time. He smiled sheepishly at his reaction. The beautifully decorated clock, which sat on the mantel over the fireplace, was the family's most prized possession. His mother had once told him, with great pride, that someday the clock would be his. Art reckoned, now, that it would go to his brother. His brother always put more store to the clock than he did anyway.

Recovering his poise, Art took a piece of paper from his pocket, and put it on the mantel beside the clock. It was addressed to "Ma and Pa."

At first he hadn't planned to tell anyone in his family that he was leaving. He was just going to go, and when his folks woke up for the next day's chores, they would find him gone. But at the last minute he thought his parents might rest a little easier if they knew he had left on his own, and had not been stolen in the middle of the night.

Art had enough schooling to enable him to read and write a little. He wasn't that good at it, but he was good enough to leave a note.

Ma and Pa
Don't look for me for I have went away. I am near a man now and I want to be on my own. Love, your son, Arthur.

With the note in place, Art opened the front door quietly and stepped out onto the porch. It was still dark outside, and the farm was a cacophony of sound; frogs on the pond, singing insects clinging to the tall grass, and the whisper of the night wind through a nearby stand of elm trees.

Once he was out of the house and off the porch, Art moved quickly down the path that led to the river. When he reached the bluff, he turned and looked back. The house loomed large in the moonlight, a huge dark slab against the dull gray of the night. The window to his parents' bedroom was gleaming softly in the moonlight. It looked like a tear-glistened eye, a symbol that wasn't lost on Art. A lump came to his throat, his eyes stung, and for a moment, he actually considered abandoning his departure plans. But then he squared his shoulders.

"No," he said aloud. "I ain't goin' to stand here and cry like a baby. I said I'm a'goin', and by damn I'm goin'."

He turned away from the house.

"Sorry about sayin' 'damn,' Ma, but I reckon if I'm goin' to be a man, I'm goin' to have to start talkin' like a man."

Art left the beaten path, then picked his way through the brush down the side of the bluff to the river's edge. To the casual observer, there was nothing there, but when Art started pulling branches aside, he uncovered a small skiff.

He had found the boat earlier in the year during the spring runoff. No doubt it had broken from its moorings somewhere when the river was at freshet stage, though it was impossible to ascertain where it had come from. Art didn't exactly steal the boat, but he did hide it, even from his father. And he assured himself that if someone had come looking for the boat, he would have disclosed its location. But, as no search materialized—at least none of which he was aware—he got to keep the boat.

The boat provided him with a golden opportunity, and it wasn't until it came into his possession that he seriously began considering running away from home. He was leaving, not because of any abuse, but because of pure wanderlust.

If he put into the current now, some two hours before dawn, he would be six miles downriver by sunrise. By sundown he would be forty miles away. Throwing his sack into the bottom of the boat, he pulled it out of its hiding place, pushed it into the water at the river's edge, got into it, then paddled out to midstream and pointed downriver.

Under way now, he looked back toward the bank and saw that he was moving at a fairly good clip. It wasn't until that moment that he realized this might well be the last time he would ever set eyes on the land of his birth. That realization did not weaken his resolve.

Art had an oar, but as the current was swift and steady, no

rowing was required to establish locomotion. Rather, he used the oar as a tiller to keep the boat centered in the river.

The boat moved downstream much more swiftly than he would have thought. By mid-afternoon he was already farther from home than he had ever been in his life.

He ate a biscuit.

He watched the sun set from the middle of the river. The sun flamed a wide, fan-shaped bank of clouds, turning them into a brilliant orange-gold. The river itself took on a light, translucent blue, as pretty as he had ever seen it. He began looking for a good place to put in, and saw a fallen tree lying half in and half out at the water's edge. He rowed over to the tree, tied his boat to it, and used its branches to hide the boat from view. Only then did he allow himself to eat the second of his three biscuits. His meal consumed . . . what there was of it . . . he stretched out in the bottom of the boat and went to sleep.

Two days later, his biscuits and apple gone, he was feeling pretty hungry when he saw several boats gathered beneath a high bluff. Halfway up the bluff was a large cave, and a hand-lettered sign explained that this was "Eby's River Trading Post." Even from the boat, he could hear loud conversation, laughter, and the music of fiddles and a jug. He could also smell the enticing aroma of roasting meat.

Art had no money, but he was mighty hungry, so he paddled ashore, hoping to be able to trade a little work for food. He tied the boat up to an exposed tree root, then walked up the path toward the mouth of the cave.

A few wide boards, supported by upright wooden barrels, formed a counter that stretched across the front of the cave. Behind it, in the cave itself, were several shelves and boxes and barrels of goods, from whiskey, to clothing, to flour, bacon, beans, and 'taters. A red-faced, rather plump man was manning the counter and when Art walked up, the man came toward him.

"What can I do for you, sonny?"

"You have food here?"

The man laughed, then pointed back into the cave. Two women were cooking over an open fire.

"What's the matter with you, boy, that you can't smell it?" the man asked.

"I can smell it," Art replied. On his empty stomach, the smell of cooking food was about to drive him mad.

"Sonny, you ask anybody up and down the whole Ohio, an' they'll tell you that Eby's got near 'bout anything you could want," the man went on. "We got roast pork, chicken, rabbit, squirrel, and possum. We got fried dove, catfish, and carp. We got biscuits, cornbread, beans, 'taters, and gravy. You go back down and tell your ma she don't have to cook no supper tonight 'cause we got anything she might want right here. Yes, sir, for ten cents you can feast like a king."

"Are you Mr. Eby?"

"Mr. Eby?" The man chuckled. "Don't many folks call me mister," he said. "But yeah, I'm Eby. Now, you goin' to run down and tell your ma what I said?"

"My ma's not here.

"Well, who is here? Your pa?"

Art shook his head. "Ain't nobody here but me."

"You mean a boy like you is out here, travelin' on his own, with no family?"

Art pulled himself up to full height. He was tall for a twelve-year-old, and strong from at least three years of doing a man's work.

"By damn, I'm near to full-growed," Art announced resolutely. "I reckon I can travel without a family if I want to." He thought the use of the phrase "by damn," was particularly effective.

Eby held up his hand. "Whoa, boy, don't be takin' no

offense to my palaverin'. Your dime's as good as the next fella's, I reckon. What'll you have?"

"I'd love some pork and beans," Art said.

"Why, sure, boy, just show me your dime and I'll serve it right up to you."

Art cleared his throat and ran his hand through his hair. "Uh, well, that's just it, mister. I ain't got no dime. I ain't got no money a'tall."

"You ain't got no money?"

"No, sir."

"Well, now, if you ain't got no money, would you mind tellin' me just how the Sam Hill you was a' plannin' on eatin'?"

"I thought maybe I could work some for it," Art said.

Eby shook his head. "Boy, I got no need for someone to work for me. I got me two women back there, as you can see. They all the workers I need, and they don' cost me nothin', one of 'em bein' my wife and the other'n bein' her sister."

"Do you know of anyone who needs any work done?" Art asked. "I'm a good worker, I'm strong, I been carryin' my own load for the better part of three years now."

"This here ain't no hirin' hall," Eby said gruffly. "If you got a dime, I'll give you some supper. If you ain't got no money, then get the hell out of here and don't be takin' up space."

"Give the boy somethin' to eat," a tall, bearded man said.

"I ain't givin' him nothin' iffen he don't pay for it."

The tall man produced a dime, slapping it down on the counter with a loud snap. "Here's your goddamn dime. Now give the boy some vittles!" he ordered.

"No, sir," Art said, shaking his head, holding his hand out toward the tall, bearded man, and walking away. "I thank you kindly, sir. But I don't aim to take no charity."

"Who said anything about charity?" the man replied. "I've got a flatboat down here, loaded with goods that I'm takin' to the Louisiana Territory. If you're willin' to work for your keep, I'll take you on."

Art smiled broadly. "Yes, sir!" he said. He turned back

toward the counter. "I'll have me that pork and some beans now," he said. "And maybe some 'taters."

Scowling, Eby went back to the cooking fire, spooned up some beans and potatoes, cut off some pork, and put it on a tin plate. He brought the plate and a spoon back to the counter.

"Thanks," Art said.

"Seems to me like there ought to be a biscuit go with that," the man who had bought the supper said.

Eby reached under a cloth and pulled out a biscuit, then set it beside the plate.

"The name's Harding," Art's benefactor said. "Pete Harding. What's yours?"

"Art."

"Art? That's all?"

Art thought for a moment. Harding seemed to be a nice man; certainly he had bought a meal and was promising employment. But Art was planning on making a clean break from his past, and he didn't want anything that would make that connection, including a last name.

"Art's all the name I use," he said.

Harding laughed. "If that's good enough for you, then I reckon it's good enough for me. How'd you get here anyway? Did you walk?"

"No, sir. I come by boat," Art said.

"Well, after you eat your supper, come on down and help me get loaded up. Then, if you're a mind to go with me, why, I reckon you can tie your boat on behind. Or else, leave it here."

"You got a boat you want to leave here, I'll keep it for you till you get back," Eby said. "Won't charge you but a dollar to keep it for a whole month."

Harding laughed. "Yeah, in a pig's eye you will," he said. He stroked his beard and looked at Art. "Boy, you don't have any money at all?"

"No, sir."

"Well, if that boat don't mean nothin' personal to you, why

don't you just sell it? That way you can go on downriver with me, and have a little money besides."

"Sell the boat? Why, yes, I reckon I could," Art said. The boat had served its purpose, getting him away from home. Now he truly was on his own, and any money the boat brought would have to be good.

"All right, Eby. What'll you give the boy for the boat?"

"Fifty cents."

"It's worth five dollars," Harding said.

"Not to me, it ain't."

"As many people as you got comin' through here, you could give the boy five dollars for the boat, then turn right around and sell it within a week to someone else for seven dollars."

"I'll give the boy three dollars."

"Four," Harding said.

"All right, four dollars."

Harding looked at Art. "What do you think, son? It's your boat, and your decision."

"Four dollars?" Art said. "I've never had that much money in my life. Yes, I'll sell it."

"Give the boy four dollars," Harding said.

"Where's the boat?"

"I'll take you to it," Art said.

"We'll take you to it," Harding corrected. Then he looked at Art. "After you make the transaction, we've got work to do."

"Yes, sir!" Art said.

Harding had unloaded his goods there, in order to do some business with the folks who had tied up at the trading post. It took no more than half an hour to get them loaded back onto his boat. It was a flatboat, nearly as wide as it was long, with a small cabin at mid-deck. A long tiller, which could also be used to propel the boat, stuck out from behind the boat. Every available square inch of the boat was covered with cargo; bales of cloth, pots, pans, various kinds of tools, barrel staves, hoops, and three cases of Bibles.

When the boat was loaded, Harding invited Art to step aboard.

"It's time for us to get a'goin'," he said.

"We're going to run the river at night?" Art asked.

Harding shook his head. "No, we'll put in a couple miles downstream," he said. "It'll be safer than staying here with the river pirates."

"River pirates?"

Harding's searching look covered both sides of the river, into the rocks and behind the trees.

"They like to hang around river stops, like trading posts and the like," he said. "That way they can get a good look at what the boats are carrying, and if they see anything they like, they'll go cross-country till they can find a place to set up an ambush. What with the river meanderin' back and forth, it's easy enough for them to get ahead of a boat."

"You mean there might be pirates here right now?"

"Truth to tell, boy, I wouldn't put it past Eby himself. I've always suspected him, but I've never been able to prove it. If I ever got proof, I'd get some of the other boatmen together and we'd clean this place out."

Harding cast off the line, then using the tiller, worked the boat out into the center of the river. He pointed it downstream and, as had been the case with Art's skiff, the current provided all the propulsion they needed. The only difference was that the flatboat didn't travel quite as fast as the skiff.

"Come here," Harding said once they were under way.

Art stepped to the rear of the boat.

"Take the tiller," Harding said. "You may as well start learning right off."

"Yes, sir," Art said, taking the tiller in his own hands. He could feel the surge of the water, and the control he had over the boat. It was similar to what he experienced with the skiff, though as the flatboat was bigger, the tiller longer and with more surface area, he felt a much greater pull.

"You're doing a good job," Harding said, sitting down on a bale of cloth. Reaching down into his pocket, he pulled out a pipe, filled it with tobacco, then using a flintlock and steel mechanism, managed to get his pipe lit. A few minutes later, he was puffing contentedly.

"How far do we go before we put in?" Art asked.

Harding laughed. "You tired already?"

"No, sir!" Art replied, his face stinging in embarrassment. "I just meant, well, I just wondered, that's all."

"Not much longer," Harding said easily. He took a few more puffs while he studied Art. "Run away from home, did you?"

"No, I . . ." Art started; then he decided that it was time to be honest with the man who had helped him. "Yes, sir," he said sheepishly. "I ran away."

"Trouble at home?"

"No. I just wanted to . . ." He let the sentence trail off, and Harding laughed.

"You wanted to see the creature, didn't you?"

"See the creature?"

"That's just a saying, son. It's a saying for folks like us."

"Like us?"

"You and me. There are some folks who are born, live, and die and never get more'n ten miles away from home in any direction. Then there's folks that's always wondering what's on the other side of the next hill. And when they get over that hill, why, damn me if they don't feel like they got to go on to the next one and the next one, and the next one after that. They're always hopin' they'll find somethin' out there, some sort of creature they ain't never seen before. I know it's that way with me."

Art smiled. "Yes, sir," he said. "I'd say it's that way with me too."

"Pull in over there," Harding said. "We'll camp here, tonight."

2

"Get up, boy!" a gruff voice ordered.

Art was jerked awake when someone grabbed him and pulled him up from the bale of cloth he was using for a bed.

It was still dark, but in the ambient light of the moon, Art could see that two men were holding Harding. One of the men had the point of his knife sticking into Harding's neck, far enough that a little trickle of blood was streaming down. One flick of the hand, Art knew, and Harding would bleed his life away in seconds.

The third man, the one who had so abruptly awakened Art, was now holding Art's arm twisted behind him. He put pressure on the arm and Art winced in pain, but he didn't cry out.

"What'll we do with the kid?" the one who held Art asked.

"Knock him in the head and throw him overboard," the man with the knife replied.

Art's captor was holding a club, and he raised it over Art's head in order to accomplish the task.

"No, wait! Eby told me he give the boy four dollars for that boat. Check his pockets, he ain't had no chance to spend it yet."

"That right, boy?" his captor asked, smiling at Art. Two of his teeth were missing and his breath was foul. "You got four dollars on you?"

The man started to put his hand in Art's pocket, but in order to do so, he had to loosen his grip. That was all that was needed, for as soon as the grip was relaxed, Art twisted away and jumped into the river beside the boat.

"Goddamnit, Percy, you let him get away!"

"Couldn't help it, Deekus. The little sumbitch was slick as a greased hog."

This close to the bank, the river was only about chest-deep, but it was dark, and Art moved up under the curve of the boat keel so he couldn't be seen by those on board. His heart was racing. These men must be some of the river pirates Harding had told him about. And the fact that they had mentioned Eby's name seemed to prove Harding's theory about Eby's involvement with the pirates.

"What'll we do with Harding?" Percy asked.

"Well, we know he's got some money, 'cause Eby seen 'im doin' a lot of business back at the trading post," Deekus replied.

"That right, Harding? You got yourself a poke hid some'ers on this here boat?"

"If I did, I wouldn't tell you, you sorry sack of shit."

"Oh, I think you'll tell us," Deekus said. "Break one of his fingers, Clyde."

Even from his place of hiding, down in the water, Art could hear the bone pop as Clyde broke one of Harding's fingers. Harding gasped in pain, but he didn't cry out.

"Harding, we know you got the money hid on the boat, and you know that we're a' goin' to find it. All we're askin' is that you make it easier on us, and we'll make it easier on you."

"Yeah," Percy added with a demonic giggle. "We'll be real nice to you. We'll kill you fast, instead of slow."

"Go to hell," Harding said. His refusal was followed by the sound of another snapping bone, and another gasp of pain.

"You got ten fingers and ten toes," Deekus said. "And ole'

Clyde there, he's the kind of fella that likes to make other folks hurt. So, you can tell us now, or you can just let Clyde bust you up, one bone at a time, until you do."

Carefully, and quietly, Art pulled himself back onto the boat, boarding it at the bow. Harding and the three men who were working him over were back at the stern.

Art had no idea why he was doing this. Every impulse and nerve in his body was screaming at him to run. The night was dark enough, and the woods by the riverbank were thick enough that he could easily get away from them. And yet, here he was, crawling back onto the boat.

Keeping low, and staying behind the bales of cargo, Art slipped into the mid-deck cabin from the front end. He knew exactly what he was looking for, because he had seen them early that afternoon.

It was considerably darker inside the cabin than it was on the deck of the boat. Art couldn't see six inches in front of his face, so he had to do everything by feel. On the other hand, there was some advantage to that, because even if the pirates were looking right at him, they wouldn't be able to see him.

Art's fingers closed over what he was looking for—two fully charged, primed, and loaded fifty-caliber pistols. Picking them up, he eased both hammers back quietly, then moved to the stern door of the little cabin. He was less than ten feet away from the pirates, but they couldn't see him.

"He ain't goin' tell us nothin', Deekus," Percy complained.

"I reckon you're right," Deekus said. "We may as well kill 'im now, and get it over with."

Deekus drew back his knife, ready to plunge it into Harding's chest. It was at that exact moment that Art fired. The gun roared and bucked in his hand, while the muzzle flash lit up the deck like a bolt of lightning. For one instant in time, all action was frozen and Art could almost believe he was looking at a drawing. In a harsh white-and-black tableau, he could see Deekus's expression of shock and pain as he looked down at the gaping hole in his chest, the surprise on Clyde's face, and the fear in Percy's eyes.

"What the hell?" Percy shouted.

Only Harding was jolted into action. Dropping to one knee, he grabbed Deekus's knife, then, with a quick underhand flip of the wrist, threw the knife at Clyde. The knife buried itself in the pirate's neck and, with a gurgling sound, Clyde reached up to pull it out, too late, for it had already severed his jugular.

Only seconds before, Percy had been one of three armed river men, easily in command of the situation. Now he was the only one left, and he realized that his position had suddenly become very perilous. With a roar of anger and desperation, he raised his own knife and started toward Harding.

Because Harding had thrown the knife at Clyde, he was unarmed. Still on one knee on the deck, Harding rolled to his right, just barely managing to avoid Percy's lunge.

"Mr. Harding!" Art shouted. "Here!" He thrust the other pistol toward Harding. Harding grabbed it, then spun toward Percy, who was just now recovering from his failed lunge.

Percy turned back toward Harding, then realized too late that Harding was no longer unarmed. Harding pulled the trigger, and Art watched as the impact of the heavy ball knocked Percy backward, over the boat rail. He hit the water with a splash, then floated away, leaving a thick, black stream of blood in the water behind him.

Harding checked the two men who were still on board. He leaned down over Deekus.

"Is he . . . is he dead?" Art asked from the shadows of the cabin.

"Dead as a doornail," Harding replied. "You did a job on him, boy."

"Oh," Art said rather pensively.

Harding dragged both Percy and Clyde to the edge of his boat. "Get the hell off my boat, you bastards!" he said angrily as he pushed them over. They fell into the water with a little splash.

Harding stood there for a long moment, looking down at the three floating bodies. He spat down at them.

It was not until then that Art came out of the cabin. He too looked down at the dead pirates.

"Are we just going to leave them here?" Art finally asked.

"Hell, yes, we're going to leave them here," Harding responded. "You don't think I'm going to take the time to dig graves for those sons of bitches, do you?"

"No, sir, I guess not."

"Let the alligator-garfish feed on their sorry carcasses. I just wish they weren't quite dead yet, so they could feel it."

"Yes, sir," Art said.

Harding looked up at the sky. "It'll be getting light soon," he said. "We may as well get under way. Untie the forward line."

Art picked his way to the bow, then untied the line that held them secure to an overhanging branch. Harding poled them away from the bank, then out into the river. After they reached midstream, the current took over and, once more, they moved rapidly down the river.

"Take the tiller, boy," Harding said. "I've got to tend to this hand."

Art watched as Harding pulled on both his fingers, grimacing. in pain as he straightened them out. After that he rummaged through the little pile of firewood until he found a stick just the right size. He put the stick alongside his two fingers, then called Art over.

"Take some of that rawhide cord there and bind these fingers to this here splint."

Art started to do what Harding said, but as soon as he began wrapping the rawhide around the badly swollen fingers, Harding winced in pain. Art stopped.

"Don't stop, boy, else I'll have a couple of useless hooks

here, instead of fingers," Harding said. "And do it pretty tight. It's goin' to hurt a mite, but I'll be the one hurtin', not you."

"Yes, sir," Art said. He wrapped the cord around the two fingers.

"Not so tight that it cuts off the blood," Harding cautioned.

Art nodded, then finished the task, cutting off the rawhide and tying it secure. Harding held his hand out and looked at it.

"Doubt there's a doctor this close to St. Louis who could've done a better job," he said. "I'm proud of you, boy."

"Glad I could help."

Art went back to the tiller. By now the sky had turned a dove-gray, and streaks of pink slashed through the eastern sky. Harding got a fire going, then disappeared into the cabin. He came out a moment later with a pot, which he placed over the fire. After a few minutes, the rich aroma of brewing coffee permeated the boat.

"Coffee comes so dear that I don't generally drink it, 'cept on Sundays," Harding said. "But I reckon this occasion is special enough for us to have some this mornin'."

"What's the occasion?" Art asked.

"Well, you saved my life," Harding said. "Now, that might not be all that much of an occasion to some folks, but it sure is to me."

"I didn't do much."

"The hell you say," Harding said. "Once you went over the side of the boat and into the water, you could've kept on going and they would've never found you. But you came back. And you saved my life."

"I . . . I wish I hadn't had to . . ." Art let the sentence hang.

"Kill a man?" Harding asked.

Art nodded.

"First time you ever had to do it?"

Art nodded again.

"Well, of course it is, you bein' no older'n you are. How old are you, Art?"

"I'm, uh, sixteen," Art said.

Harding just looked at him.

"All right, I'm thirteen. Well, nearly so anyway," Art insisted.

"Nearly thirteen. So that means what? That you're twelve?"

"Yes, sir," Art admitted sheepishly.

Harding poured two cups of coffee, and handed one to Art. Art took a swallow, then frowned a little at its bitter taste.

"You're used to having milk and sugar in your coffee?"

"Milk, sometimes a little syrup or honey," Art said.

"Well, you'd best get used to having it black. You see, you can purt' near always have coffee with you. You can't always have milk or sugar."

Art took another swallow. "It's good," he said.

Harding laughed. "You're going to do fine, boy. And don't worry none 'bout that no-count son of a bitch you killed. His kind always die young. If you hadn't killed him, someone else would have."

"I just wish it hadn't been me."

"Listen to me, boy," Harding insisted. "He may have been the first one you've killed, but he won't be the last one you're going to have to kill. Not by a long shot. Not if you are going to survive out here. You've got to realize that, and not dwell none on it. Maybe you are only twelve years old by the calendar, but today, you showed me you're a man."

"Because I killed someone?"

"No. Any fool can kill. But you came back to help me, when you could've easy gotten away. There's lots more things that go into making a man than the number of years someone has lived. Live long enough, and the years will come to ever'one. The other things—honor, duty, and knowin' how to do what's right—don't come to ever'one, but they done come to you. Let nobody tell you different, Art. You're a man now. And I'm glad to call you my friend."

Harding stuck out his hand. Art started to shake it, remembered the broken fingers, pulled back, then realized that the

broken fingers were on Harding's left hand. Smiling, he gave
Harding a good, strong, grip.

Harding explained to Art that they were no longer on the
Ohio River, but were now on the Mississippi. The Mississippi
was broader, and the current stronger than it was on the Ohio,
and the boat moved a lot faster. One of the first things Art
noticed was the number of felled trees. During his trip down
the Ohio he had seen maybe as many as a hundred downed
trees, but here, there were literally thousands of trees on the
ground.

"I've never seen such a thing," Art said in awe.

Harding chuckled. "Well, boy, you left home to see the
wonders of the world. This is one of them."

"But how can this be? Was there such a wind that it could
blow this many down?"

"It wasn't the wind that did it. It was the trembling earth."

"Trembling earth?"

"Shakers. Some folks call 'em earthquakes. What happens
is, the ground just starts to shaking something awful, shaking
so bad a fella can't even stand up."

"You seen such a thing?"

"Yep, it happened a couple of years ago," Harding said.
"Trees was fallin', and the earth was opening up, sulphur
commenced spewing into the air. All the shakin' and trem-
blin' made the Mississippi River flow backwards. And it
pushed it right out of its channel for a bit, to form a new lake."

"I would sure like to see somethin' like that."

Harding laughed out loud. "Well, when we get to New
Madrid, don't tell any of them folks that. I reckon they've
seen enough of it over the last couple of years."

"Is that where we're goin'? New Madrid?"

"Yep. It's in the Missouri Territory."

"What's there?"

"New Madrid is a good marketplace," Harding said. "Folks buy there, then take it up to St. Louis, or on down to New Orleans. I plan to sell everything I got on this here boat. Then I'm going to sell the boat. Then, after a couple of days of raisin' hell and havin' a good time, I'll buy myself a horse, ride back to Ohio, get me another boatload of goods, come down here to do the same thing all over again."

"You're going back to Ohio?"

"Sure am. That's where I can get goods the cheapest. The trick in this or any business is to buy cheap and sell high," Harding said with a laugh. "What about you? You're sure welcome to come along with me. You can be my partner if you want to."

"I . . ." Art started, but with a wave of his hand, Harding interrupted him.

"I know, you don't have to say it. You're anxious to see the creature."

Smiling, Art nodded. "I reckon I am," he said.

"Well, I can't say as I blame you. And as long as you're plannin' on seein' the creature, why, I figure New Madrid is as good a location as any to start."

New Madrid was a booming town of nearly three thousand people, spread out along the west bank of the Mississippi River. There were nearly one hundred flatboats and scores of skiffs tied up along the riverbank, and less than one hundred feet from the river's edge on a street called Waters Street, nearly as many wagons, carts, horses, and mules.

The wooden structures of the town were built right up against each other; leather-goods, stores, trading posts, cafes, and taverns. Art realized that, like the trees, the earthquake must have also destroyed New Madrid. That was the only way he could explain the fresh-lumber appearance of all the buildings. Even now, half-a-dozen new buildings were going up, but whether they were a sign of the town's growth and progress, or merely the reconstruction of destroyed buildings, he didn't know.

In addition to the sound of hammering and sawing coming from those buildings under construction, the air also rang with the clanging of steel on steel, emanating from the blacksmith shop. These sounds of commerce were clear evidence of the vibrant new community. Waters and Mill Streets, the two streets that ran parallel with the river, were crowded with people, visitors as well as permanent residents.

It didn't take Harding long to sell his goods. Once his task was accomplished, he came back to Art, holding a handful of money. He counted out ten dollars in silver, and handed it Art.

"What's this for?" Art asked.

"Your wages," Harding said. "You earned them."

"But I was only with you for a couple of weeks," Art said. "You fed me, and gave me transportation. You don't need to pay me as well."

Harding laughed. "Son, you're going to have to learn your own value. Anytime you sell your services to someone, sell them for as much as you can get. If you are going to argue, argue for more, not less."

"Yes, sir."

"Besides, whether you did ten dollars worth of labor isn't the question. You saved my life, and that's certainly worth ten dollars to me. Now, do you want the money or not?"

"I want the money," Art said.

"I thought you might come around," Harding said. "Now, since you will soon be going to go your way and I'm going mine, what do you say we go to a dram shop and have a beer?"

"A beer? Well, I . . ."

"Hell's bells, boy! Are you going to tell me you don't like beer?"

"I don't know," Art admitted. "I've never had a beer."

Harding laughed. "You've never had a beer?"

"No, sir. My mom didn't hold with drinkin'. Not even beer."

"What do you think about it?"

"I've never give it much thought, one way or the other."

"Then it's time you did give it some thought," Harding said. "You've got some catchin' up to do. Come on, it'll be a pleasure for me to buy you your first beer."

The sign in front of the building read WATSON'S DRAM SHOP. Inside the saloon was a potbellied stove that, though cold now, still had the smell of smoke about it from its winter use. A rough-hewn bar ran across one end of the single room, while half-a-dozen tables completed the furnishings. The room was illuminated by bars of sunlight, shining in through the windows and open door. Flies buzzed about the room, especially drawn to those places where there was evidence of spilt beer.

"Mr. Harding, good to see you back in New Madrid again," a man behind the bar said. He was wearing a stained apron over his clothes, and a green top hat over a shock of red hair.

"Hello, Mr. Watson. I hope you haven't sold all of your beer."

"I just got a new shipment down from St. Louis," Watson answered, taking a glass down from the shelf, then holding it under the spigot of a barrel of beer. "What about the boy?" he asked.

"Don't let his looks and age fool you," Harding replied. "Art's as good a man as I've ever come across. I reckon he'll have beer too." He looked over at Art. "That right?"

"Yes, sir. I'll have a beer," Art replied, watching as the mug filled with a golden fluid, topped by a large head of white foam.

"Here you go, boy," Watson said, sliding the first mug over to him.

Art raised the glass to his lips and took a swallow. He had never tasted beer before and had no idea what to expect. It was unusual, but not unpleasant.

"Here's to you, Art," Harding said, holding his own beer

out toward Art. For a moment, Art didn't understand what he was doing, but when Harding tapped his mug against Art's, he realized it was some sort of ritual, so he followed along.

Art had that beer, then another.

"Let's go," Harding said, suddenly getting up from the table.

"Where are we going?"

"There's a certain etiquette to spendin' money in a town like New Mardrid, and part of it is that you spread your money around. This is my favorite place. I spend all my money with Watson, then he's liable to start takin' me for granted, while all the other places will be resentful. Do you see what I mean?"

"I guess so," Art replied.

"Besides, we all have our own way of looking for the creature," Harding added with a twinkle in his eye. "I've always been of the opinion that it might be in the next dram shop."

Art followed Harding out the door, then up the boardwalk toward the next drinking establishment.

A wagon rolled by on the street. Driving the wagon was a tall, rawboned man, dressed in black. He had beady eyes, high cheekbones, a hooked nose, and a prominent chin. A short, stout, very plain-looking woman was sitting on the bench beside him. The wagon had bows and canvas, but the canvas was rolled back at least two bows. As a result, Art could see the third occupant of the wagon, a girl about his own age. She was sitting on the floor with her back leaning against the wagon side opposite from Art. As a result, when he glanced toward her, he saw that she was looking directly at him. For a moment their gazes held; then, embarrassed at being the recipient of such scrutiny, Art looked away.

"Ah, here we go," Harding said. "Let's pay a visit to Mr. Cooper."

Cooper's saloon was almost an exact copy of Watson's, with a bar and a few tables and chairs. However, there was a card game in progress here, and Harding joined it.

Cardplaying was another of the vices his mother had warned him against. But as beer drinking was proving to be a rather pleasant experience, Art decided he would investigate cardplaying as well. So, drinking yet another beer, he leaned against the wall and watched the card game.

As he stood leaning against the wall, Art happened to see a "pick and switch" operation lift a man's wallet. The victim was a middle-aged man who was standing at the bar, drinking his beer while carrying on a conversation with another man. A nimble-fingered pickpocket deftly slipped the victim's billfold from his back pocket. At that moment, a big, black-bearded man came in through the door, and Art watched as the pickpocket passed the pilfered wallet off to the man who had just come in.

The entire operation was so quick and smooth that the victim never felt a thing. No one else in the saloon saw it happen, and if Art had not been in the exact spot at the exact time he was there, he wouldn't have seen it either. The accomplice walked directly to the table where Harding and three others were playing cards.

"May I join you, gentlemen?" Blackbeard asked.

"Sure, have a seat," Harding offered congenially. "Your money is as good as anyone else's. What do you say about that, Art? Isn't his money as good as anyone else's?" Harding asked, teasing his young partner.

"It would be, I suppose, if it really was his money. Trouble is, it isn't," Art said easily. "He stole it."

3

Art's matter-of-fact comment brought to a halt all conversation in the saloon.

"What did you just say, boy?" Blackbeard asked with an angry growl.

"I said it isn't your money."

"What the hell do you mean by that?" Blackbeard sputtered.

"Yes, Art, what do you mean?" Harding asked.

Art looked over toward the bar. Nearly everyone in the place had heard his remark, and now all were looking toward him with intense interest.

"This man," Art said, pointing to Blackbeard, "has this man's poke." He pointed to the middle-aged man who was standing at the bar. It wasn't until that moment that the man standing at the bar checked his pocket.

"What the hell? My poke *is* missing!" he said.

"I don't know what this boy is talking about!" Blackbeard said. "Hell, I just this minute come in here. I haven't even been close to the bar."

"He's right," another man said. "I seen him come in."

"If somebody took that man's money, it wasn't me," Blackbeard said.

"Oh, you didn't take it," Art said.

"Boy, you ain't makin' a hell of a lot of sense," Cooper said. Cooper was the man who owned the place. He was also working the bar. "First you accuse Riley there of takin' McPherson's poke; now you say he didn't take it."

"I said he *has* the poke," Art said. "I didn't say he took it." Art pointed to the original pickpocket, who was now at the far end of the bar, trying to stay out of sight. "That's the man who took it. He picked the man's pocket, then gave it to Mr. Riley when he came in."

"By God! I don't care if you are just a pup," Riley said. "A fella doesn't go around accusin' another fella of somethin' lessen he can prove it."

"I can describe my purse," the man at the bar said. "It's made of pigskin and it's sewed together with red yarn. My wife made it for me."

"Well, this seems like a simple enough problem to solve," Harding said. He looked at Riley. "Why don't you just empty your pockets on the table? If you don't have it, then we'll just go on about our business."

"That sounds reasonable," one of the others in the saloon said.

"Yeah, if you didn't take it, just empty your pockets and be done with it."

"To hell with that. I ain't goin' to empty my pockets just 'cause of some snot-nosed boy's lie."

Harding looked over at Art. "You're sure about this, are you, Art?"

"I'm sure," Art said.

"Empty your pockets," Harding said. This time his tone was less congenial.

"Wait a minute! You are going to take this boy's word over mine?"

Harding scratched his cheek. "Yeah, I reckon I am," he answered easily. "See, here's the thing, Riley. I don't know you from Adam's off-mule. But I do know this boy and he's already proved himself to me. So if truth be known, I reckon I'd take his word over that of my own mama. Now, either empty your pockets on the table, or by God I'm going to grab you by the ankles, turn you upside down, and empty them for you."

"The only thing you are going to empty is your guts," Riley said, suddenly pulling a knife.

"Look out!" someone shouted.

"He's got a knife!" another yelled.

"Yeah, I sort of figured that out," Harding said.

There was a scrape of chairs and a scuffling of feet as everyone else backed away to give the two belligerents room. Riley held his knife out in front of him, moving it back and forth slowly, like the head of a threatening snake.

Harding pulled his own knife; then the two men stepped away from the table to do battle. They raised up onto the balls of their feet, then crouched forward slightly at the waist. Each man had his right arm extended, holding his knife in an up-turned palm. Slowly, they moved around each other, as if engaged in some macabre dance. The points of the knives moved back and forth, slowly, hypnotically.

Art watched them. The fight with the river pirates had been deadly, but it had also been quick and spontaneous. This was the first time he had ever seen two men fight face-to-face, each with the grim determination to kill the other. Although he had a vested interest in the outcome—for surely if Riley killed Harding, he would then turn on Art—yet he was able to watch it without fear. He was certain that the day would come when he would find himself in this same situation. Some inborn sense of survival told him to watch closely, and to learn, not only from the victor, but also from the vanquished.

"You ever seen one of them big catfish they pull out of the river?" Riley asked. "You see the way they flop around when they're gutted? That's how it's going to be with you. I'm going to gut you, then I'm goin' to watch you flop around."

Riley made a quick, slashing motion with his knife, but

Harding jumped out of the way. Mistaking Harding's reflexive action as a sign of fear, Riley gave a bellow of defiance, and moved in for the kill, lunging forward.

It was a fatal mistake.

Harding easily sidestepped the lunge, then taking advantage of Riley's awkward and unbalanced position, counter-thrust with his own knife. Because Riley was off balance, he was unable to respond quickly enough to cover his exposed side. He grunted once as Harding's knife plunged into his flesh.

The blade slipped in easily between the fourth and fifth ribs. Harding held it there for a moment, then stepped up to Riley and twisted the blade, cutting-edge up. As Riley fell, the knife ripped him open. Harding stepped back from his adversary as Riley hit the floor, belly-down. Almost instantly, a pool of blood began spreading beneath him.

"Boy," Cooper said to Art. It wasn't until that moment that Art and the others in the saloon realized that Cooper was holding a double-barreled shotgun, and had been throughout the fight. "You look through Riley's pockets there. For your sake, and for the sake of your friend there, you had better come up with McPherson's purse. 'Cause if you don't, I reckon we might have to hang the both of you for murder."

"Wait a minute!" Harding complained. "How can you call this murder?" He pointed to Riley's body. "You saw that he drew the knife first. Hell, everyone saw it."

"Seems to me like he didn't have much of a choice," Cooper said. "You all but called him a thief. If he wasn't the thief, then he had every right to defend his honor."

Art looked at Harding.

"Go ahead, Art," Harding said easily. "If you say Riley has McPherson's wallet, then I've got no doubt but that he does."

At that moment Riley's accomplice, the man who originally made the pick, started to leave the saloon.

"Hold it right there, Carter," Cooper called out to him. "If the boy's right, if he finds the wallet, then you're goin' to be the one we'll be askin' questions."

"Wait a minute!" Carter said. "What if he does find McPherson's purse on Riley? That don't prove I had anything to do with it. It just means that Riley took it."

"Huh-uh," Cooper said. "Everyone agreed that Riley had just come in through the door and didn't come nowhere near the bar. That means if he has McPherson's wallet, the only way he could have it is if you give it to him."

Art knelt beside Riley's body. He hesitated for a moment.

"Go ahead, boy. Look for it," Cooper said.

Nodding, Art took a deep breath, then stuck his hand in one of the back pockets.

Nothing.

The other back pocket produced the same result. Art tried to turn Riley over, but Riley was a big man and his inert weight made turning him difficult. Harding started to help him.

"No!" Cooper shouted, and he pulled back the hammer on one of the two barrels. "Let the boy do it alone. If he finds that purse, I don't want nobody claimin' that, somehow, you sneaked it to him."

"All right," Harding said, backing away.

Straining with all his might, Art finally got the body turned over onto its back. Riley's eyes were still open, and they gave the appearance of staring right at Art. Gasping, Art pulled back slightly.

"He ain't goin' to hurt you none, boy. He's dead," Cooper said. "Get on with it."

Art searched Riley's front pants pockets without success, then reached into one of the man's jacket pockets. He came away empty-handed. Now, there was only one pocket left.

"This is it, boy," Cooper said. "If it ain't in that pocket, then you done got a man killed for nothin'. And don't think it'll go easy on you just 'cause you're young."

"It's in there," Art said resolutely.

But it wasn't. He stuck his hand all the way down and felt the entire pocket. When he pulled his hand out, it was empty.

"Haw!" Carter said. "I reckon this proves the boy was lyin'."

Art's stomach tumbled in fear. Almost in desperation, he put his hand back in Riley's jacket pocket, and this time, he felt something. Grabbing it, he realized that whatever he was feeling wasn't actually in the pocket, but was behind a layer of cloth. Something was sewn into the lining of the jacket.

"I think I've found it!" Art said.

"Pull it out. Let us see it," Cooper said.

"It's behind . . ." Art started to say, then seeing Riley's knife, he picked it up and used it to rend the fabric. After that, it was easy to wrap his hands around the wallet.

"Glory be!" McPherson said. "That's my purse!"

"Damn your hide, boy!" Carter shouted from the edge of the bar. As Art looked toward the one who had let out the bellow, he saw that Carter was pointing a pistol at him.

Carter fired, just as Art leaped to one side. The huge-caliber ball dug a big, splintered hole in the wide-plank floor. Though the bullet itself didn't strike Art, he was sprayed in the face by the splinters that were ejected when the bullet passed through the floor.

On top of the roar of Carter's pistol, came a second, even louder blast. This was from Cooper's shotgun, and Art saw Carter's chest and face turn into instant ground sausage. Carter pitched backward, dead before he even hit the floor.

"Free beer to anyone who helps drag that trash out of here," Cooper said as he stood there holding the still-smoking gun.

The offer of free beer was all the inducement necessary. Instantly, it seemed, half-a-dozen men sprang forward. It took them but a moment to drag the two bodies out into the alley behind the dram shop. Leaving them there, they hurried back inside for their reward.

Although neither Art nor Harding joined the detail in dragging the bodies out, they didn't lack for beer. McPherson, whose poke Art had saved, bought a round for each of them.

After the round furnished by McPherson, Harding suggested that it might be better if they moved on. As a result, Art, who by now had drunk five beers, was a little unsteady on his feet as he followed him outside.

"Does this sort of thing happen often?" Art asked.

"What sort of thing?"

"What sort of thing?" Art repeated, surprised by the question. He nodded toward the bar they had just left. "The knife fight. I mean, that man was trying to kill you."

"Yeah, he was," Harding answered easily. "That's why I killed him."

"I've never seen anything like that before."

"The hell you say. What about the business down on the river?"

"That wasn't the same thing," Art said. "The fight on the river happened real quick. This . . . I don't know . . . this sort of unfolded real slow. One minute everyone was having a nice time, and the next minute you and that man Riley were fighting."

"Have you thought about what caused us to fight?"

"You said he wanted to kill you."

Harding chuckled. "I mean, have you thought about why he wanted to kill me?"

"I guess because . . ." Art paused.

"Because I asked him to empty his pockets," Harding said. "And the reason I asked him to do that was because you had just accused him of stealing."

"Oh!" Art said. "Then *I* was the cause."

Harding chuckled again. "No, not really. Riley and Carter brought it on themselves. Stealing is not the safest way to make a living out here. If someone plans to make his livelihood that way, then he damn well better be prepared to face the consequences. And in this case, the consequences were pretty severe."

"Yeah, I guess they were," Art said rather pensively.

Harding reached over and rubbed his hand through Art's hair. "Look, Art, it's like I told you back on the boat when you killed that son of a bitch who was trying to kill me. Life is hard out here. Look around you, and you'll see an eagle killing a mouse, a snake killing a frog, and a fox killing a rabbit. If you aren't ready to face up to that, then you may as well go on back home to your mama and papa. Do you understand?"

"Yes, sir, I reckon I do," Art said.

"Good."

"But I don't reckon it's ever goin' to be somethin' I will enjoy doin'. Killin' someone, I mean."

"Son, I pray to God that you never do get to where you enjoy it. There's a difference between doin' somethin' that you have to do to survive, and doin' it for the pure, evil pleasure of it. And when you stop to think about it, it's those who do take pleasure from it who are going to wind up giving you the most trouble."

"Yes, sir," Art said.

"Well, that's enough teaching for now. I've saved the best for last. Come on, I want you to see the Blue Star."

The Blue Star dram shop was decidedly more attractive than the other saloons had been. Where the others had been thrown together with unpainted, ripsawed, raw lumber, the Blue Star was a carefully finished building. The outside was painted white, and trimmed in red. It was also a two-story building with a false front that made it look even taller from the street.

"Doesn't look like this building suffered any from the earthquake," Art said.

"Oh, but it did. It went down, just like the others did. But whereas everyone else has only halfway built their buildings, Mr. Bellefontaine decided he would return the Blue Star to its original state, complete with paint and all the furnishings. The other bar owners were a little put out with him, and if truth be known, I think most of them are sort of privately hoping that the earthquakes come again to sort of even things out for them. Come on, let's go in. If you think it looks nice from out here, wait until you see the inside."

The inside lived up to Harding's promise. Instead of rough-hewn lumber, the bar was finished mahogany, and behind the bar was a large, gilt-edged mirror. Scores and scores of elaborately shaped and colored bottles stood on the counter in front of the mirror, their number doubled by the reflection. At the back of the room, a finished staircase climbed up to a balcony that overlooked the ground floor. Though he couldn't see it all, he knew that the balcony went as deep as the saloon itself, so there had to be rooms upstairs as well. The interior of the bar was lit, not by unfiltered sunlight, as had been the case with the others, but by a brightly shining chandelier. As a result the windows were closed, and no flies were crawling around on the customers' tables. Even these tables, Art noticed, were made of finished wood.

"Oh, my," Art said, looking around.

"Impressive, huh?" Harding asked. "My friend, there is not another dram shop like this on the Mississippi, not from St. Louis to New Orleans. And I ought to know, for I have been in just about every one of them."

"It is beautiful," Art said. "I don't think I've ever seen anything like it."

"You can see now why I saved this for last."

As soon as they chose a table, a woman came over to join them.

"And, as an added attraction, the Blue Star has something that none of the other dram shops have," Harding added, smiling at the approaching woman. "It has women. Art, meet Lily."

"Well, Harding, I hear you've had a busy night," Lily said by way of greeting.

"You mean you've already heard?"

"Word of a killing gets around fast. Even if it is some no-count like Moe Riley, who needed killing."

"You knew him?"

"All the girls knew him," Lily said. "And there won't be any of us shedding any tears over the likes of him."

Art had never seen a woman who looked like Lily. There were dark markings around her eyes, her lips were as red as ripe cherries, and her cheeks nearly so. The top of her dress was cut very low, and it gapped open so that Art could actually see the swell of the tops of her breasts. He couldn't stop staring at her.

Bellefontaine brought three beers to the table. Art didn't remember ordering, but he picked up the beer and began drinking it. Whereas the taste had been somewhat foreign to him when he began the evening's drinking spree, he now found that he liked it. He drank nearly half the mug before he set it down. As he looked at Lily's breasts again, they seemed to be floating in front of him. His head was spinning, and he felt very peculiar.

"Do you like what you see, Art?" Lily asked, looking directly at Art.

"Yesh, ma'am," Art said. His tongue was thick and he found that he couldn't make it work as easily as he normally could. He pulled his tongue out of his mouth, felt it with his thumb and forefinger, then looked down at it, trying to see it.

Lily laughed. "I'll say this for your boy, Harding. He's a polite one, calling me ma'am."

"He's not my boy. He is my friend and business partner."

"Business partner, is he? He's a fine-looking young boy, I'll give you that. But isn't he a little young to be a business partner?"

"Well, he *was* my partner," Harding said. "And he still could be if he wanted to, but he wants to see the creature."

"Yesh, shee the creasure," Art repeated.

"Uh-huh," Lily said. "Well, it ain't 'the creature' he's been lookin' at since he come in here." She stared right at Art and grinned broadly. He was still trying to see his tongue. "Ain't that right, sonny?"

"Whash right?" Art asked, his speech still slurred.

"I just told your friend here that I don't believe you been lookin' at the creature tonight. I think you've been lookin' somewhere else." She grabbed Art by the back of his head, then pulled his face down onto her breasts. He could feel the warm smooth skin against his face, and he reacted quickly, pulling away.

All the other patrons in the tavern had a good laugh at Art's expense.

"I . . . I'm shorry," Art said, blushing in embarrassment.

"Hell, sonny, don't be sorry," Lily said with a whooping laugh. "If I didn't want men to see my titties, I wouldn't wear clothes like this."

Art had not only never seen a woman who looked like this, he had never heard one talk like this.

"You're embarrassing him, Lily," Harding said.

"I'm not embarrassing him. I'm giving him an education," Lily said. "Here, Art, as long as we are at it, have yourself a good look." She unbuttoned two more buttons, then opened her bodice, exposing her breasts all the way to the nipples. "Do you like what you see?"

Again, there was reaction from the others in the tavern. Lily didn't stop at exposing herself to Art. She opened her blouse wide, then turned toward the others in the tavern, curtsying formally as they whistled, cheered, and beat their hands on the tops of the tables.

She turned back toward Art. "Well, we know what they think about them, but what about you? Do you like my titties?"

"I think your titties are very nice," he finally said.

Lily whooped again. "Nice," she said. "I have to tell you, sonny, nice is not a word folks use much around Lily Howard. I do appreciate it, though."

"Are you a painted woman?" Art asked.

"A painted woman? Well, yes, I reckon I am."

"Come on," Harding said, taking Lily by the arm. "You've got a room upstairs, don't you?"

"Right at the head of the stairs, honey," Lily replied. "As if you didn't know that. You've been there enough times."

This time the laughter was at Harding's expense.

"Well, so I have," Harding admitted. "But what do you say we go again? I think Art has seen as much of 'the creature' as he needs to see."

"I could get Sally to join us. We could teach the boy a thing or two, we could," Lily offered.

"The boy has grown a lot since he came to me," Harding said. "But I don't think he's ready to be that grown just yet."

"Okay, honey, whatever you say," Lily replied. She put her hands on his shoulders, leaned against him so that the spill of her breasts mashed against his chest, then looked up at him.

"Here, watch that. Else we'll be startin' right here."

Smiling, Lily took Harding by the hand and led him to the foot of the stairs.

Harding looked back toward his young friend. "Art, I'll be back in a little while," he said. "In the meantime, why don't you get something to eat? I think it might do you good."

As Art watched them climb the stairs, it was almost as if he was watching himself watch them leave. He had never felt such a peculiar sense of detachment from his own body.

"Another beer, sonny?" Bellefontaine asked.

"What? Oh, uh, no, thank you," Art replied. "I think I'd rather have something to eat, if you've got it."

"I got bacon, eggs, taters right here, if that's to your likin'."

"That'll be fine," Art said. He stood up, almost too quickly, and had to grab the edge of the table to steady himself.

"You all right, boy? You look a little unsteady on your get-along there," Bellefontaine said.

"I'm all right. I think I'll jush step out back to the privy," he slurred. "I'll be right back."

"Take your time, sonny. Wouldn't want you to wet your pants," Bellefontaine said, laughing loud at his own joke.

"I told the boy I wouldn't want him to wet his pants," Art heard Bellefontaine telling someone as he stepped out into the alley.

It was quite dark outside, and Art wondered how long he and Harding had been drinking the beer. He wasn't surprised by the dark. He had watched it get progressively darker after each beer, because he'd found it necessary to visit the privy after each one. He had never peed as often as he had been peeing since he arrived in New Madrid. He wondered if something was wrong with him. Using the privy, then feeling much better, he turned to go back into the tavern to have his supper.

Suddenly he felt a blow to the back of his head! He saw stars, his ears rang, then he felt himself falling. After that, everything went black.

4

Harding awakened to the aroma of coffee. When he opened his eyes, he saw Lily sitting on the edge of the bed, holding a cup of coffee.

"Uhmm," he said. "Is that for me?"

Smiling, Lily handed it to him. "I'll just bet you don't get service like this from all your other women."

"What other women?" Harding asked, receiving the cup from her, then taking a welcome swallow of the brew. "You're the only woman for me, Lily. Hell, you know that."

Lily laughed out loud. "You are full of it, Mr. Pete Harding," she said. "I know at least three other women right here in New Madrid you have bedded."

"Well, yes, but I had to pay them for it."

"Here, now, what are you trying to do? Cheat a poor working girl out of her money? Of course you had to pay them for it . . . just like you are going to pay me."

"Oh, Lily, now I am really hurt," Harding said. "And here I thought you invited me to your place out of love."

"Compassion, maybe, but not love," Lily teased. "Besides, this is what I do. I'm a . . . what did the boy call me? A painted lady?"

"Oh, shit!" Harding said, sitting up quickly. "Art."

"What about him?"

"I just left him sitting there last night."

"I'm sure he'll be all right. He looked like a pretty resourceful young man to me."

"He's very resourceful," Harding said. "And about the finest person I've ever run into, regardless of his age. But he was also drunk."

Lily laughed again. "He damn sure was. Cute too."

"The thing is, he's never been drunk before. I think I'd better go down and try to find him."

Harding swung his legs over the edge of the bed. As soon as he did so, Lily hiked up her nightgown and straddled him.

"Wherever he is, he has waited this long," she said. "Don't you think he could wait just a little longer? This one is free."

Feeling himself reacting quickly to her, Harding lay back down. "He could wait just a little longer," he said.

Art felt the sun warming his face, but that was the only thing about him that felt good. He had a tremendous headache, and he was very nauseous. He was lying down, and even though he had not yet opened his eyes, he knew he was lying on sun-dried wood, because he could smell it. He was also in motion. He could feel that, as well as hear the creak and groan of turning wagon wheels, and the steady clopping sound of hooves.

The last thing he remembered was leaving the tavern to go to the privy. What was he doing *here?* For that matter, where exactly *was* here?

Art opened his eyes. It was a mistake. The sun was glaring and the moment he opened his eyes, two bolts of pain shot through him.

"He's awake," a girl's voice said.

Putting his hand over his eyes, Art opened them again. Now that he was shielding his eyes from the intense sunlight,

it wasn't as painful to open them. Peering through the sepa-
rations between his fingers, he looked at the girl who had
spoken. She appeared to be about his age, with long, dark
curls hanging down and with vivid amber eyes staring intently at him. There was something familiar about her and for
a moment, he couldn't figure out what it was. Then he remembered. She was the girl he had seen in the passing wagon
yesterday afternoon.

Was it yesterday afternoon? Somehow it seemed much
longer ago than that.

"Who are you?" Art asked.

"My name is Jennie."

"Whoa, team," a man's voice said. The wagon stopped.
"Boy?" the same voice called. "You all right, boy?"

Art sat up and as he did so, his head spun and nausea swept
over him.

"I've got to throw up," he said, leaning over the edge of the
wagon. He threw up until he had nothing left, which didn't
take long as his stomach was nearly empty.

When he was finished, he looked back into the wagon. Besides the girl who had introduced herself as Jennie, there was
a man and a woman in the wagon. Both of them were staring
at him as if had just turned green.

"I'm sorry about that," he said.

"Had a bit too much to drink last night, did you?" the man
asked.

"Yes, sir," Art said. He felt the back of his head. There was
a bump there that was very tender to the touch. "At least, I
reckon I did." He felt another wave of nausea, and once more
he leaned over the edge of the wagon. Although he didn't
think he had anything left to throw up, he managed a little.
Mostly, though, it was a painful retching.

"I'm sorry," he said again.

"That's all right; anytime you got to throw up, you just do
it," the man driving the wagon said. "My name is Younger.

Lucas Younger. I own this here wagon. This is my wife, Bess. What's your name?"

"Art."

"Art what?"

"Just Art. I ain't got no last name."

"Why, Art, honey, that can't be right," Bess Younger complained. "Ever'one has to have a last name."

"I ain't got one," Art said resolutely.

"Don't bother the boy none, Bess," Younger said. "If he don't want to give us his last name, he don't have ta'."

Art looked around outside the wagon. They were on a road of some sort, now passing through swampland. On either side of the road he could see stands of cypress trees, their knees sticking up from standing pools of water. "Where are we?" he asked. "What am I doing here?"

"You sure ask a lot of questions," Younger replied.

"Last thing I remember is orderin' my supper. But I don't remember eating it."

"From the way you looked when we found you, you didn't eat your supper. You drank it," Younger said.

"Oh . . ." Art groaned. He put his hand to his head. "I did. I drank beer. I drank a lot of beer." He looked up again sharply. "What do you mean, when you found me?"

"Just what I said, sonny. Me, the wife, and the girl there found you. You was lying out in the road leavin' New Madrid. The wife thought you was dead, but soon as I got down and looked at you, I know'd you wasn't dead."

"You say you found me on the road leaving New Madrid?"

"Sure did."

"My money!" Art said. He stuck his hands in his pockets, but they came out empty.

"Boy, if you had any money on you, somebody took it offen you a'fore we come along," Younger said. "I hope you don't think we took it."

"No," Art said. "No, I don't think you would take my money, then take care of me like this."

"Glad you know that."

"Where are we now?" Art asked.

"Oh, we're some north of New Madrid, headin' on up to St. Louie. This here road we're on is called the El Camino Real. That means The King's Road."

"We saved back a biscuit for your breakfast if you're hungry," Bess said.

At first thought, the idea of eating something made Art feel even more queasy. But he was hungry, and he reasoned that, maybe if he ate, he would feel better.

"Thank you," he said. "I'd like that."

"Jennie, get him that biscuit."

"Yes, ma'am," Jennie said. She fumbled around in some cloth, then unwrapped a biscuit and handed it to Art. He thanked her, then ate it, hoping it would stay down.

It did stay down, and before long he was feeling considerably better.

"Right after you left, the boy went out the back door to the privy," Bellefontaine replied to Harding's question. "He never come back in. When you find him, tell him he owes me for the supper he ordered."

"How much?"

"Fifteen cents ought to do it."

Harding put fifteen cents on the counter, then pointed toward the back door. "You say he went through there?"

"Yep. Ain't no use in lookin' back there, though. I got to worryin' some about him, seein' as how he didn't come back, so I went out there to have a look around myself. He wasn't nowhere to be found."

Despite Bellefontaine's assurance that there was nothing to

be seen out back, Harding went outside to have a look around. Art was nowhere to be seen.

After satisfying himself that Art wasn't behind the Blue Star, Harding checked all the boarding houses in town. Art hadn't stayed in any of them. Then he checked the other taverns, and even checked with all the whores on the possibility that Art might have decided to give one of them a try. Nobody had seen him. He decided it was time to talk to the sheriff.

The sheriff was in his office, feet propped up on a table, hands laced behind his head. A visitor to the office was sitting on a stool near the cold stove, paring an apple. One long peel dangled from the apple, and from the careful way he was working it, it was obvious he was going to try and do it in one, continuous peel.

"Sheriff Tate, I'm Pete Harding."

"Hell, Harding, I know who you are," the sheriff answered. "After the show you put on last night, I reckon ever'one in town knows who you are.

"Damn!" the apple peeler suddenly said. Looking toward him, Harding saw that the peel had broken.

"Ha!" Sheriff Tate said. "That's a nickel you owe me."

"I could'a done it if he hadn't come in," the apple peeler said. "Him walkin' on the floor like he done jarred it so's that it broke."

"You're full of shit, Sanders," the sheriff said. "It would'a broke whether Harding come in here or not. Pay your nickel."

Sanders took a nickel from his pocket and slapped it down on the sheriff's desk. Then, looking at Harding with obvious disapproval, he left the office.

"Now," Sheriff Tate said, putting the nickel away. "What do you need, Harding? If it's about last night, don't worry about it. Enough folks have given statements about what happened that there ain't even goin' to be an inquiry."

"It's not about last night," Harding said. "Well, yes, I guess it is, in a way. I come in here with a boy named Art. He was working on the boat with me. The thing is, I've lost him."

"What do you mean, you lost him?"

"I left him at the Blue Star for a while when I left to, uh, conduct some business."

Sheriff Tate laughed. "Conduct business? You mean going off with one of the whores, don't you?"

"Yes," Harding admitted. "And when I came back . . . this morning . . . the boy was gone."

"Well, hell, Harding, you didn't expect him to sit there the whole night, did you?"

"No. But I've checked with every place he could possibly be. I've checked all the boardinghouses, taverns, even the other whores. Nobody has seen him."

"You think something happened to him?"

"I'm a little worried about him, yes. He drank quite a bit of beer last night. I'm pretty sure he had never had one before. Nobody's reported anything to you, have they?"

"You mean like a body?"

"Yeah," Harding said with a sigh. "That's exactly what I mean."

"Far as I know, we only got two bodies in this town right now," Sheriff Tate. "Riley and Carter. And I reckon you know about them."

"What about the river? What if someone threw a body in the river?"

"Unless they went to the trouble of weighing the body down, it'll come back up within an hour," Sheriff Tate said. "And what with the bend in the river, it pretty near always stays right here. You think maybe, him bein' drunk and all, he might'a fallen in the river?"

"I don't know," Harding replied. "I hope not."

"Well, I'll keep my eyes open and if I see anything, I'll let you know."

"That's just it, I won't be around after today. I've bought

myself a horse and I'm ridin' back up to Ohio to put together another load of goods. I just thought I'd see what I could find out before I left."

"You got 'ny reason to suspect foul play?"

"No."

"Was he plannin' on goin' back to Ohio with you?"

"No," Harding said again. "He said he would be going on from here."

"Well, there you go then. Most likely, that's what happened to him. We had a couple of wagons pull out of here early this morning, bound for St. Louis. Could be he went out with one of them."

"That's probably what happened," Harding said. "Sorry to have been a bother to you."

"Ah, don't worry about it. I'm sure he's all right, but like I said, I'll keep my eyes open."

"Thanks," Harding said.

It was midafternoon by the time Harding rode out of town. He headed north, intending to cross the river just above the juncture of the Ohio and Mississippi. That way, he would only have to cross once.

"Art, I don't know where you got off to, but I'd feel better if I knew for sure that you were all right," he said, speaking aloud to himself.

There were nearly three dozen other wagons parked where they made camp that night. Although few of the wagons were traveling together, and some in fact were even going in opposite directions, it was quite common for wagons traveling alone on the frontier to join with other travelers at night in a temporary wagon park. And not only wagons, but travelers on horseback as well, for at least a dozen single men had staked out their horses and thrown their bedrolls down within the confines of the wagon camp.

Such an arrangement not only granted company and the opportunity for some trade, it also provided the safety of numbers against attack from hostile Indians or marauding highwaymen. Younger asked Art if he would mind doing a few chores.

"I'll be more than glad to. It's little enough to pay you back for your kindness."

"I was just doin' my Christian duty," Lucas replied. "But if you're up to workin' for your keep, first thing I want you to do is help me get this tarp up." Younger began untying the canvas on one side of the wagon, and indicated that Art should do the same thing on the other.

Art untied his side, then he and Younger unrolled the canvas, stretching it across the wagon bows so that the wagon was covered. After that, Lucas did something that Art thought was rather strange. He tied a red streamer to the back of the wagon.

"There, that'll do just fine," Tryeen said.

"What's the red flag for?" Art asked.

"Never you mind about that," Lucas replied. "You just take the team down to water. Then, when you come back, check with the Missus. I 'spect she'll have some chores she'll be a'wantin' you to do for her."

"Yes, sir, I'll be glad to do anything she wants," Art said.

Art took the team down to water. When he returned, Bess gave him a bucket and had him get some water for cooking. Then she had him gather wood for the fire.

Looking around the camp, Art saw Younger going over to the area occupied by the men who were traveling alone, mostly those who had ridden in on horseback. He had no idea what he was saying to them, but some of them were visibly animated by the conversation, for they began moving around in a rather lively fashion, while looking back toward the

Younger wagon. After visiting with them for a few minutes, Younger returned to the wagon. "Jennie," he called. "You've got some business to take care of, girl. Get on up here."

It wasn't until then that Art realized he hadn't seen Jennie since they made camp.

"Jennie, get up here now," Younger called, a little more forcefully than before. "You know what you have to do."

Jennie crawled out from under the little tent that had been made by dropping canvas down around the edge of the wagon. Art gasped in surprise when he saw her. Jennie no longer looked like a little girl. She looked much more like a woman, and not just any woman, but like a painted woman, the way Lily had looked at the tavern back in New Madrid.

Younger spoke directly to Art. "Boy, I'll thank you to stay out of the wagon now until after Jennie is finished with her business."

"Finished with her business? What business?" Art asked.

"Business that ain't none of your business," Lucas replied with a hoarse laugh. "Now, just you mind what I say. Stay out of the back of the wagon. The missus will keep you busy enough."

"Yes, sir," Art replied.

"Jennie, you ready in there?"

"I'm ready," Jennie's muffled voice replied.

Suddenly, and unexpectedly, Younger let out a yell.

"Yee haw! Yee haw! Yee haw! Sporting gentlemen!" he shouted at the top of his voice. *"Now is your time! If you are after a little fun, you can get it here! Yee haw! Yee haw! Yee haw!"*

Nearly a dozen men of all ages and sizes began moving toward the wagon, most from the area where the riders were encamped, but a few from some of the other wagons as well. Art watched them approach, wondering what this was all about.

The men stood in a line behind the wagon. The first in line handed some money to Younger, then climbed up into the wagon. Because of the canvas sheet that was covering the wagon, Art couldn't see what was going on inside.

After a few minutes, the first man came out, adjusting his trousers. Some of the other men said something to him and he answered, then several of them laughed. Because Art was standing near the fire that had been built several feet in front the wagon, he was too far away to hear what was being said.

"Mrs. Younger, what's going on back there?" Art asked. "What's Jennie doing in the wagon with all those men?"

Bess Younger looked uneasy. "I got no part with that business," she said in a clearly agitated voice. "And neither do you."

"But Jennie's in there," Art said.

"I told you, you got no business worryin' about that. So you just don't pay it no never mind," Bess said.

"I know I ain't got no business. I was just curious, that's all."

"Don't be curious," Bess said. "Sometimes, what you don't know don't hurt you. You'll be wantin' to sleep with us tonight?"

"I aim to, yes. That is, if you and Mr. Younger don't mind."

"We don't mind. We figured you'd be goin' on to St. Louis with us. I just thought you ought to know that we ain't got no extra blankets for you to make your bedroll. But I reckon if you want to, you can sleep up on the wagon seat. There's a buffalo robe up there that you can wrap up in if it gets too cool."

"Yes, ma'am, thank you, ma'am," Art said.

Art ran errands for Bess Younger until long after dark, gathering wood for the breakfast fire the next morning, and even rolling out dough for tomorrow's bread. All the while men from all over the camp continued to make their way to stand in line at the back of the wagon. When Art finally finished all his chores and climbed up onto the seat to go to sleep, there were still men waiting in line at the back of the wagon. But because a tarpaulin drop separated the wagon seat from the bed of the wagon, he was still unable to see what was going on.

He was asleep when he heard Jennie and Lucas Younger

talking. By the position of the stars and moon, he figured it to be after midnight.

"We done pretty good tonight," Lucas was saying. "Near 'bout ten dollars we took in."

"Please," Jennie said. "Please don't make me do this no more. I don't like it."

"We all got to do things we don't like," Younger said. "Besides, you got nothin' to complain about, girl. You could be workin' in the fields, pickin' cotton with the niggers. Would you rather be doing that?"

"Yes, sir. I'd rather be doing that."

"That's just 'cause you're crazy," he said gruffly. "Now crawl into your little nest under the wagon and get to bed. I don't want to hear no more 'bout this."

The little canvas-enclosed area where Jennie had pitched her bedroll was beneath the forward part of the wagon, just under Art. As a result, she was no more than two feet from him, separated only by the bottom of the wagon. Art could hear her rustling about as she got ready for bed. He started to call out to her, but something held him back. Instead, he just lay as quietly as he could.

Then, later, when all the rustling around had stopped and everything was still, he heard Jennie crying. She was being quiet about it, stifling her sobs as best she could, but there was no mistaking what he heard. Jennie was crying.

Why was she crying? Art wondered. What was it Younger was making her do in the back of that wagon?

"Ten dollars, Bess," Art had heard Younger telling his wife just before they went to sleep. "We made us ten dollars here tonight."

"I can't help but think that it is Satan's money," Bess replied in a troubled voice.

"The hell it is," Younger said. "It's *my* money." He laughed at his own joke.

5

They had been on the trail for the better part of four hours the next morning. Jennie was sitting in the back of the wagon, dozing sometimes, other times just looking off into the woods alongside the road. Bess was driving the team; Younger and Art were walking alongside the wagon to make it easier on the mules.

A couple of times Art tried to do something to cheer Jennie up, popping up suddenly beside her, or throwing little dirt clods at her. The only time he managed to get through to her was when he turned upside down and walked on his hands for a few yards. When he was upright again, he thought he saw her smile.

But the smile, as hard-won as it was, was short-lived. It was no time at all before Jennie was morose again. Art didn't think he had ever seen anyone looking as sad as Jennie did, and he wished he could do something to make her feel better.

That opportunity presented itself about mid-afternoon. Looking over into a little clump of grass, Art happened to see a tiny bunny. Reaching down, he picked it up and held it. The rabbit was so small that it barely filled the palm of his hand. It was furry and soft, and he could feel it trembling in fear as he held it.

Jennie! he thought. This was bound to cheer her up.

He trotted back to the wagon, holding the rabbit in such a way that it was obvious to Jennie, even as he approached, that he had something.

"Look what I found," he said, though he still hadn't showed her what he was holding.

"What is it? What do you have?" Jennie asked.

"Huh-uh, you'll have to guess."

"Oh, now, I'm not good at guessing. Please tell me what it is.

"I'll do better than that," Art said. "I'll give it you. It's yours to keep." He held the little rabbit out toward her.

"Oohhh!!" Jennie squealed in delight as she held the wriggling little piece of fur in her hands. "Oh, thank you! He is so pretty."

Jennie's face lit up brighter than it had been at any time since Art first saw her. She held the little rabbit to her cheek. "What's his name?" she asked.

"Oh, that's not for me to say. He belongs to you now. You'll have to name him," Art said.

"I think I'll call him . . ."

That was as far as she got. Unnoticed by either one of them, Younger had walked quickly up to the wagon. Reaching over the edge of the wagon, he grabbed the little rabbit, then turned and threw it as far as he could.

"Mr. Younger no!" Jennie screamed, while Art watched the little bunny flying through the air, kicking ineffectively. It fell hard, several feet away, bounced once, then remained perfectly still.

"I told you, I don't hold with that kind of business," Younger said. "Keepin' rabbits 'n such as pets is for babies and chil'run. You're a woman, full-grown now, and it's time you started actin' like one."

"Yes, sir," Jennie said contritely.

"And you," Younger continued, turning toward Art. "Next time you bring in a rabbit, it better be big enough to make into a stew."

"Yes, sir," Art said, mimicking Jennie's response.

Younger moved on up toward the head of the team. He reached out to grab the harness of the off-mule, using it to help pull him along.

Art looked up at Jennie and saw that tears were sliding down her cheeks. He had hoped to cheer her up, but wound up making things worse. He felt very bad about it.

"I'm sorry about the rabbit," he said quietly.

"It's all right. You couldn't do nothin' about it," she answered with a sniff.

"Why do you call your pa Mr. Younger?"

Jennie looked at Art in shock. "He ain't my pa," she said.

"Oh, I see. He's your step-pa then? He married your ma, is that it?"

Jennie shook her head. "Mrs. Younger ain't my ma."

"They ain't your ma and pa?"

"No. They're my owners."

"Owners? What do you mean, owners?"

"I'm their slave girl. I thought you knowed that."

"No, I didn't know that," Art said. "Fact is, I don't know as I've ever knowed a white slave girl."

"I ain't exactly white," Jennie said quietly.

"You're not?"

"I'm Creole. My grandma was black."

"But how can you be their slave? You don't do no work for 'em," Art said. "I mean . . . no offense meant, but I ain't never seen you do nothin' like get water or firewood, or help out Mrs. Younger with the cookin'."

"No," Jennie said quietly. "But gathering firewood, or helping in the kitchen, ain't the only way of workin'. There's other ways . . . ways that"—she stopped talking for a moment—"ways that I won't trouble you with."

"You mean, like what you was doin' with all them men last night?"

Jennie cut a quick glance toward him. The expression on

her face was one of total mortification. "You . . . you seen what I was doin'?"

"No, I didn't really see nothin' more'n a bunch of men linin' up at the back of the wagon. Even when I went to bed, I couldn't see what was goin' on on the other side of the tarp."

"Do you . . . do you know what I was doing in there?"

Art shook his head. "Not really," he said. "I got me an idea that you was doin' what painted ladies do. Onliest thing is, I don't rightly know what that is."

Jennie looked at him in surprise for a moment; then her face changed and she laughed.

"What is it? What's so funny?" Art asked.

"You are," she said. "You are still just a boy after all."

"I ain't no boy," Art said resolutely. "I done killed me a man. I reckon that's made me man enough."

The smile left Jennie's face and she put her hand on his shoulder. "I reckon it does at that," she said.

"You don't like doin' what Younger is makin' you do, do you?"

"No. I hate it," Jennie said resolutely. "It's—it's the worst thing you can imagine."

"Then why don't you leave?"

"I can't. I belong to 'em. Besides, iffen I left, where would I go? What would I do? I'd starve to death if I didn't have someone lookin' out for me."

"I don't know," Art said. "But seems to me like anything would be better than this."

"What about you? Are you going to stay with the Youngers?"

"Only as long as it takes to get to St. Louis," Art replied. "Then I'll go out on my own."

"Have you ever been to St. Louis?" Jennie asked.

"No, have you?"

Jennie shook her head. "No, I haven't. Mr. Younger says it's a big and fearsome place, though."

"I'll bet you could find a way to get on there," Art said. "I'll bet you could find work, the kind of work that wouldn't make you have to paint yourself up and be with men."

"I'd be afraid. If I try to get away, Mr. Younger will send the slave catchers after me."

"Slave catchers? What are slave catchers?"

"They are fearsome men who hunt down runaway slaves. They are paid to find the runaways, and bring 'em back to their masters. They say that the slave hunters always find who they are lookin' for. And most of the time they give 'em a whippin' before they bring 'em back. I ain't never been whipped."

"I can see where a colored runaway might be easy to find. But you don't look colored. How would they find you? Don't be afraid. I'll help you get away."

"How would you do that?"

"Easy," Art said with more confidence than he felt. "I aim to leave the Youngers soon's we get to St. Louis. When I go, I'll just take you with me, that's all. You bein' white and all, you could pass for my sister. No one's goin' to take you for a runaway. Why, I'll bet you could find a job real easy."

"Maybe I could get on with someone looking after their children," Jennie suggested. "I'm real good at looking after children. You really will help me?"

"Yes," Art replied. He spat in the palm of his hand, then held it out toward Jennie.

"What . . . what is that?" Jennie asked, recoiling from his proffered hand.

"It's a spit promise," Art said. "That's about the most solemn promise there is.

Smiling, Jennie spat in her hand as well, then reached out to take Art's hand in hers. They shook on the deal.

Half an hour later they stopped to give the team a rest. Younger peed right by the side of the road, making no effort to conceal himself from the women. Buttoning up his trousers, he came back up to the wagon.

"Art, they's a cow down there," he said. He reached down into the wagon and pulled out a piece of rope. "I want you to go down there and get her, and bring her back up here. Tie her off to the back of the wagon."

"You mean just go get her?" Art asked in surprise. "How can I do that? Doesn't she belong to anyone?"

"Yes. She belongs to me," Younger said.

"But how can that be? I thought you said you hadn't been up this way before."

"The cow belongs to me because I say she does," Younger said irritably. "Now, go get her like I said."

"I'd rather not," Art said. "I'm afraid that would be stealing and I don't want to steal from anyone."

"It's not stealing," Younger insisted. "Look, the cow is just standing out there. If she belonged to someone, don't you think she would be in a barn somewhere? Or at least in a pen. Now, go get her like I said."

Art thought about it. On the one hand, he felt a sense of obligation to Younger for taking him in. On the other, he was sure that the cow didn't belong to Younger, so taking it would be stealing. It was clear, however, that if he didn't go get the cow, Younger would, so the end result would be the same. And if Art was being ordered to take the cow, then he didn't think it would be the same thing as him stealing.

"All right," he said, taking the rope. "I'll get her."

"Good lad," Younger said. "You're going to work out just fine."

They hadn't gone more than a mile beyond that when two horsemen overtook them. Both riders were carrying rifles and they rode up alongside the wagon, demanding that it stop. One of the riders was about Younger's age; the other looked to be little older than Art. Art was sure they were father and son.

"Something I can do for you gentlemen?" Younger asked.

"Hell, yes, there's something you can do, mister," the older of the two riders said. He pointed to the cow. "You can untie our cow from the back of your wagon."

"This is your cow?"

"You're damn right this is our cow."

"Art, untie that cow right now," Younger ordered. "Give it back to the rightful owners."

"Yes, sir," Art said, walking back toward the cow.

"I'm sorry about that," Younger said to the two men.

"What I'd like to know is, what are you doing with our cow in the first place?"

"I can see how it might look a little suspicious," Younger said. He pointed to Art. "But the boy there had the cow with him when we picked him up on the road."

"You say the boy had the cow?"

"He did. He said he had a hankerin' to go to St. Louis, and he offered me the cow in exchange for my wife and me to take him there."

Art heard Younger's lie, but he made no attempt to dispute it.

"If you was a mite older, boy, you'd be hanging from yonder tree," the older rider said as Art passed the end of the cow's lead rope up to him.

"He's near as old as I am, Pa," the younger rider said. "Seems to me like that's old enough to hang."

The older man shook his head. "No. I don't take to hangin' boys." He pointed his rifle at Art. "But hear this, boy. If I ever see you in these parts again, I'll like as not shoot you. I figure the earlier you can stop a thief, the less grief other folks will be getting from him."

"I don't think the boy meant to steal the cow, mister," Younger said. "He told us he found it walkin' down the road. I think he thought the cow had just wandered off."

"Uh-huh. You say you just picked him up, did you?"

"Yes, sir, my wife and I did. Figured it would be a Christian kindness to take him in."

"Well, you'd better watch that he don't steal ever'thing you got and leave you in the middle of the night," the older of the two riders said gruffly. "Come on, son. Let's get Nellie back into the barn."

The riders left then, at as fast a trot as the cow would allow. Art waited until they were well out of earshot before he spoke.

"Mr. Younger, it wasn't right, you telling those men I stole that cow."

"I didn't tell them you stole it, I told them you found it," Younger said. "Besides, you saw how they were. If they had thought I took it, they would've hung me. Would you have wanted that on your conscience?"

"No, I reckon not," Art replied. It didn't occur to him to tell Younger that his conscience would have been clear since he had opposed taking the cow in the first place.

"I guess we'll just have to be more careful next time, won't we?"

Art didn't answer.

"Let's step up the pace a little," Younger said, running his finger around his neck collar. "This place don't sit well with me.

6

When they stopped that night to make camp, there were no other wagons around. Younger griped a bit about the fact that nobody else was there.

"You'd think for sure there'd be some travelers here," he complained. "They's a goodly supply of wood, grass, and water. The land is flat, makin' for easy campin'. Seems to me like it's the perfect place to stop, only ain't nary a traveler in sight."

Jennie didn't say a word, but Art knew that she was happy they were alone. That meant she didn't have to entertain any men.

After supper, Younger asked Art to come with him to look for some dewberries. "I seen me some back a ways, so there's likely to be more around here some'ers. Iffen we can gather us up a mess of berries, I'll have the missus make a dewberry pie. I reckon both of you young'uns would like that."

Art thought of the blackberry pies and cobblers his mother used to make, and his stomach growled. It had been quite a while now since he had anything like that.

"Yes, sir, I'd like it a lot," he said.

"Well, then let's get to lookin'," Younger ordered.

The two left the campsite, Younger carrying a shovel with him, while Art had two empty buckets. Younger indicated that they should go out into the woods, so they left the wagon trail. To Art fell the job of breaking through the brush, while Younger had the somewhat easier task of following along behind.

They were nearly half a mile deep into the woods when Art saw several of the fruit-laden bushes. "There are some over there," Art said, pointing, already tasting the dewberry pie.

"No, them's too little to make a good pie," Younger said. "Let's walk on down a little farther and see what we can find. The bigger and fatter the berry, the sweeter it is. And the sweeter the berry, the better the pie."

"Little? If you think those berries are little, they must grow awful big here. Those are about as big as any I've ever seen," Art said.

"Don't be smart-mouthin' your elders, boy," Younger said.

Art was surprised by Younger's vitriolic response.

"Sorry, didn't mean nothin' by it," he said.

"Uh-huh. And I suppose you didn't mean nothin' by tryin' to talk Jennie into runnin' away with you when you got to St. Louis either."

Art didn't answer.

"You prob'ly thought I didn't hear what you was sayin' to her. But I got ears like an old hound dog and I heard ever' word."

"It ain't right, what you're makin' her do," Art said. "She don't like it, and I don't think it's right."

"You don't think it's right, do you?"

"No, sir. Not even a little bit," Art said resolutely.

"Well, let me tell you somethin', boy. It ain't none of your business what I do with her. That girl belongs to me, bought and paid for."

"I don't hold with no kind of slavery either. Black or white," Art said.

"Yeah, well, what you think don't matter. And you already showed me that you ain't goin' to be worth a damn when it comes to takin' advantage of the lay of the land, so to speak. Iffen you had acted quicker when I told you to take that cow, like as not we would've been long gone before them folks discovered what happened. What you almost done was get me hung."

"That ain't right, Mr. Younger, and you know it," Art said. "In the first place, even if I had gotten that cow the first time you told me, they would have still caught up with us. And in the second place, what you done wasn't right. I don't hold with stealing, and those men were right to be mad."

"So what you are telling me is, you're planning on traveling with us, but you don't plan to help out along the way. Is that right?"

"Not if helping out means stealing."

"Uh-huh. I sort of thought that," Younger said. "That's why I aim to leave you here for the buzzards to pick over your bones."

During the entire conversation, Younger had been walking just behind Art. Now these words, coming from behind him as they were, had a chilling effect, and Art turned.

"What do you mean, leaving me here for the buzzards to pick over my bones?" he asked.

Younger answered Art by swinging his shovel at him. Art threw up his arm at the last minute, but it did little to ward off the blow. He felt a sharp pain in his arm, then a smashing blow to the side of his head.

Younger looked down on Art's still form.

"I should'a left you lyin' alongside the privy back there in New Madrid. But you had near fourteen dollars on you and I figured anybody as young as you, with that much money, must be a pretty enterprisin' fella. Too bad you turned out like you done. A young boy like you would'a been pretty good at stealin' and such. We could'a made out pretty well along the trail, if you'd'a had enough sense to listen to me. But some folks are just too hardheaded to listen."

Younger began digging a grave then. He started it with every intention of making the grave six feet deep, but after a few minutes he got tired of digging. He looked at the hole he had dug, then at Art's still form. Figuring it was deep enough, he rolled Art's body over into the hole, and started covering him with dirt.

It began to rain . . . just a few drops at first, then the rain came harder, and harder still.

"Shit!" Younger swore loudly. He looked down at Art's body. It was only half covered with dirt from the waist down. "Shit, shit, shit!" He sighed. "Well, don't blame me for leavin' you for the wolves and sech," he said. "I was goin' to bury you proper, but I ain't goin' to stay out in no downpour to do it."

Picking up the two empty buckets and throwing the shovel over his shoulder, Younger started back toward the wagon. He didn't look back at the melancholy sight behind him.

The rain continued to fall, drumming into the trees, sifting down through the limbs, and causing little rivulets to run and form pools on the ground below.

When he felt the rain on his face, Art reached for a blanket to pull over his head. He thought he and Pa had fixed the leak in the roof, but it must've come back. Reaching for the blanket, he got nothing but a handful of leaves.

Leaves?

What were leaves doing in his bed?

When Art opened his eyes, he saw, not the roof over his bedroom, but the low-bending limb of a nearby tree. Because of the darkness, that was all he could see. He felt a weight on the bottom half of his body and, sitting up, saw that he was covered with dirt.

Suddenly it all came back to him. Younger had tried to kill him . . . in fact, Younger thought he *had* killed him, and left him half-buried in the woods. He didn't know why Younger had only half-buried him, but he was grateful that he had, for if Younger had finished the job, he would surely be dead by now.

Pulling himself out of the grave, Art fought the dizziness for a few minutes until he felt good enough to walk. Then he started back toward the wagon. He wasn't entirely sure what he was going to do when he got there Younger did have a rifle, after all, while Art had no weapon of any kind. But he would do something, even if it was no more than stealing Jennie away from him and setting her free.

But Art learned rather quickly that it wasn't going to be as easy getting back to the wagon as he thought it would be. In the first place, he could still feel the pain of the blow from the shovel. And that pain, coupled with the dizziness it caused, compounded by the pitch-black darkness, made it difficult for him to retrace their path. In addition, it was raining, and dark, and he was in totally unfamiliar territory.

Somewhere along the way he became completely disoriented. He walked for two or three miles before he realized that if he had been going in the right direction, he would have been to the wagon long before now.

Frustrated, and now nauseous, both from the blow on the head and the physical exertion, he saw a large, flat rock protruding from the side of a little hill. Crawling under the rock, he lifted his knees to his chin, wrapping his arms around his legs in an unsuccessful attempt to stay warm and dry. He was cold, wet, tired, and miserable.

He thought of his home, back in Ohio. The entire family would be asleep now, warm, snug, and dry in bed, under cover, while rain beat down upon the roof and against the windows. He had always liked the sound of rain at night; he liked the idea of being inside, in a warm, dry bed, while it was cold and wet outside.

Outside.

Where he was right now.

Art felt a choking in his throat, a stinging of the eyes, and warm drops of water joining the cold rain, sliding down his cheeks. They were tears, and he was crying.

Damn it, he was crying!

"No!" he shouted, shaking his fist at the heavens. "No! I am not going to cry like a two-year-old baby! I put myself here, and whatever it takes to survive, I'll do. If I have to steal, then as God is my witness, I will steal! And if I have to kill again, I'll kill again, but by all that's holy, I will survive!"

"Where's Art?" Jennie asked when Younger returned to the wagon alone.

"It ain't none of your concern where he is."

"Where is he?" Bess Younger asked, looking over Younger's shoulder back into the woods.

"If you must know, the sonofabitch ran away," Younger said. "That's the thanks you get for trying to help someone."

"Why would he do that?" Bess asked. "I thought he was anxious to go to St. Louis."

"You tell me why he would do that," Younger replied. "We've been providing him with three good meals a day, a place to sleep at night, and a safe way of travel. So how does he repay us? By running off like a thief in the night." Younger put the two buckets and the shovel into the wagon. "Well, let's get goin'. What with the rain and all, I'd like to find us a better place to stay."

"What?" Bess asked in surprise. "I thought we were going to stay the night here. The team has already been unhitched and I've started rolling out the dough for tomorrow. Besides, you said yourself this was a good place to stay."

"Yeah, well, I must've been wrong," Younger said. "There ain't nobody else here; they must know somethin' we don't know. If you ask me, this may be a floodplain. Could be that with a good rain, there could come a flood and we'd find ourselves under water come mornin'. You wouldn't want that, would you?"

"No," Bess agreed.

"Then do what you got to do to get ready to go. I'll hitch the team up."

Jennie helped Bess tidy up the wagon as Younger hitched up the team. When she moved the buckets and shovel, she noticed something on the end of the shovel blade. She examined it closer, then she gasped.

"What is it?" Bess asked.

"Miz Younger, they's blood on the shovel," Jennie said. "Oh, Lord, it's Art's blood, ain't it? Mr. Younger done killed Art."

"Hush you mouth, girl," Bess said sharply. "He didn't do no such thing."

"Then whose blood is that?"

Bess picked up a rag and wiped off the stain, then held up the rag for a closer examination. "Hmmph," she said. "It's not blood at all. It's nothing more than the stain of a few berries."

"Are you sure?"

"You're not questioning me, are you, girl?"

"No, ma'am, I reckon not."

"You just finish tidying up and don't worry your mind anymore about that boy. Truth to tell, he's prob'ly better off on his own. Looked to me like him 'n Mr. Younger was goin' to get cross-wise with each other one of these days."

"Yes, ma'am," Jennie said.

As the wagon rolled through the night and the rain, Jennie sat in the right, rear corner, trying to stay dry and warm. If Art really did run away, it would be the best thing for him. But was that really what had happened? And was worry about a flood the real reason for pulling out in the dark? As long as she had been with the Youngers, they had never moved on in the dark.

She was also concerned about the stain on the shovel. Mrs. Younger had insisted that it was nothing but a berry stain, but it looked too red for that. On the other hand, Mrs. Younger wasn't an evil woman. She was actually kind to Jennie, and it was obvious that she didn't approve of what Younger made her do. From time to time Jennie had overheard them arguing, with Mrs. Younger begging him to stop forcing Jennie to be with men. Her entreaties had always fallen on deaf ears, but the very fact that she had championed Jennie's case improved her standing in Jennie's eyes.

Maybe Mrs. Younger was right. Maybe it was just berry stain. Jennie didn't know if God would listen to prayers from a sinner like her, but she prayed, fervently, that Art hadn't been killed.

7

Finding Younger was easy. The rain had left the trail soft, and Younger's wagon wheels cut ruts that were easy to follow. Nevertheless, it was nightfall of the following day before Art came upon a small encampment area filled with travelers. Nearly ten wagons and as many riders were gathered together for the night.

Moving up closer to the campground, Art used the light of a dozen fires to study the wagons. Then he saw what he was looking for: a canvas-covered wagon marked by a red streamer. Though it was sitting aside from the others, it wasn't isolated, for several men were queued up behind the wagon, just as before. Younger was standing at the back, collecting money from the men who were just arriving, then directing them to the end of the line. Mrs. Younger was in front of the wagon, sitting on the tongue, staring into the fire. Art knew she didn't approve of all this, but he also didn't believe she tried hard enough to prevent it.

Lying on his belly under a bush, Art fought mosquitoes and insects while he watched long into the night. Finally the last man who had entered the wagon came crawling out. After exchanging a few words with Younger, the man drifted away, disappearing into a night that was now lit only by the moon, since most of the fires had burned down to a few glowing coals.

"All right, Jennie, girl, that there was the last 'un," Art heard Younger call. "You can come on down now. Bess? Bess, come on out now."

It wasn't until then that Art realized that Mrs. Younger had gone to bed in Jennie's little nest beneath the wagon. He watched as Mrs. Younger and Jennie traded places, Mrs. Younger climbing up into the wagon, while Jennie crawled into the little canvas-drop area underneath. Younger climbed into the wagon behind his wife; then all movement stopped.

Art stayed where he was, waiting at least another hour, until he was absolutely certain everyone in the camp was asleep. Then he made his move, starting toward the wagon. The moon was so bright that he decided not to cross the opening upright, but to crawl on all fours until he reached the right front wheel. There he stopped and waited a few minutes longer, just to make sure no one had seen him. Not until he knew with absolute certainty that he was alone did he call out.

"Jennie," he whispered.

No answer.

"Jennie. It's me, Art!"

A small stirring came from behind the canvas. "Art?" Jennie replied.

Above him, inside the wagon, Art heard Younger groan and move.

"Shh!" Art cautioned.

The canvas parted and Jennie stuck her head out. "I saw blood on the shovel and I was afraid you were dead!" she said. "But Mr. Younger said you ran away, and I guess he was right."

"He was only partly right," Art said. "And you were almost right." He put his hand to the back of his head. "The blood on his shovel was mine. He tried to kill me with it, and must've thought that he had."

"What are you doing here?" Jennie asked.

"I came to get you."

"No, I can't go. I told you, I belong to Younger. I'm his slave."

"Even if you are his slave, he doesn't have the right to treat you like this. Especially with what he makes you do. Come on, I'm going to take you out of here."

"Where will we go? What will we do?" Jennie asked.

"I don't rightly know," Art admitted. "I haven't figured that part out yet, but anything has to be better than this."

Jennie crawled out from under the little shelter. "Wait," she said. "What about my things?"

"You're wearing your clothes. What else do you need?"

Jennie looked back toward the little tent. Art was right. She didn't need anything else.

"Let's go," she said.

Holding his finger up to his lips as a caution to be quiet, Art led her down into the woods.

"Hey! Come back here!"

Younger's sudden and unexpected call startled them.

"Run!" Art shouted, and the two of them ran into the woods. They ran for several minutes before Art said they could stop running. They stood there then, leaning against a tree, gasping for breath.

Jennie started to say something, but Art held up his hand, signaling her to be quiet. He listened for a long moment before he was satisfied that Younger wasn't coming after them.

"All right, you don't have to be so quiet now," he said. "He's not coming."

"Oh!" Jennie squealed happily. She threw her arms around Art in a spontaneous embrace. "Oh, you are wonderful!"

"Yeah, well, no call for you to do all that," Art said uneasily, backing away from her embrace.

"I know, it's just that I'm free," she said. "I'm free!"

* * *

Younger wasn't sure what woke him up. It wasn't anything he heard as much as it was something he felt. He sat up quickly.

"What is it?" Bess asked.

"Nothin'," he said gruffly. "Go back to sleep."

He started to lie down again, then decided that as long as he was awake, he might as well get out of the wagon and take a leak. He had just reached the ground when he saw, by the light of the moon, two people moving toward the edge of the woods. He didn't have to look twice to identify them. They were Jennie and Art.

How could it be Art? He was certain he had killed him.

"What is it?" Bess called down from the wagon. "What's going on?"

"Give me my rifle."

"What?"

"My rifle, goddamnit! Give it to me!" Younger shouted.

By now the commotion had awakened some people in adjacent wagons.

"What is it, Indians?" someone asked.

"Indians?" another repeated.

"Indians!" a third shouted, giving the alarm.

Younger took the rifle from Bess and aimed it toward the woods. He didn't even have a real target now, for they had disappeared in the trees. He was so angry that all he wanted to do was shoot and hope he hit one of them. And he didn't care which one it was.

He pulled the trigger, but heard only the snap of the hammer striking the pan. When he reached up to pull the hammer back, his thumb felt the powder in the pan and he realized that it was still damp from last night's rain. He hadn't bothered to clean his gun and replace the powder.

"Damn you, boy!" he shouted. "Damn you!"

By now, half-a-dozen other armed men had raced to the scene.

"Where are the Indians?" one of them asked.

"Indians?" Younger replied, confused by the question. "What Indians are you talking about?"

"The Indians you saw!"

"I didn't see no Indians."

"Then what the hell were you just trying to shoot at?"

"My slave girl got stole from me," Younger said. "I was trying to shoot the son of a bitch what stole her."

"You talking about the little girl you was whoring?" one of the others asked.

"Yes."

"By God, if I'd'a known that, I'd'a never got out of bed. I'll be damned if I'll help you get back a slave girl you ain't doin' nothin' with but whoring."

Grumbling, the others started back toward their wagons. The self-appointed spokesman of the group turned back toward Younger.

"Mister, I don't think decent folks want your company anymore. It might be better if you would leave camp before breakfast in the morning."

"Why would I want to do that?" Younger asked.

"Because if you don't, we may just tie you to a tree and give you a good whipping."

Like New Madrid, Tywappiti was a river town, consisting of two streets that ran parallel with the river, intersected by three streets than ran perpendicular. All the buildings were of brick construction, a residual benefit of the fact that Tywappiti's main industry was brick-making.

Younger was still griping about losing Jennie when he pulled into town.

"If you ask me, I'm just as glad she's gone," Bess said. "What you was makin' that girl do wasn't Christian."

"She's a colored girl. It ain't the same with colored girls,"

Younger insisted. "Why, they's some farms that breeds 'em like breedin' animals. Leastwise, I wasn't doin' that."

"She isn't colored."

"Her grandma is pure-blood African, and that means she's a fourth colored. Even someone who is one-eighth is the same as colored," Younger said. He stopped the wagon in front of a general store. "Anyhow, you been a'wantin' to get into a town so's you could buy a few things, ain't you? Well, here we are. And we got money for you to buy because of what I was doin' with that girl. So don't you go puttin' me down because of it."

While Bess was in the general store, Younger went into the saloon. As it happened, a couple of men who had been his customers a week or so earlier were in there as well.

"Younger!" one of them called. "Come, have a drink with us!"

Nodding, Younger joined them. "Whiskey," he told the barkeep.

"Hey, I'm glad to see you've made it as far as Tywappiti. You goin' to be settin' up business here? 'Cause if you are, I plan to pay that little ole' girl of your'n a visit."

"What girl is that?" one of the others in the saloon asked.

"He's got him a Creole girl, prettiest little thing you ever seed," the first man explained.

"She's gone," Younger said.

"Gone? You mean you sold her?"

Younger shook his head. "No, she got stole from me."

"Well, hell, that ain't no problem. We got us some slave chasers in this town can find anyone."

"Problem is, she don't look colored. She could pass for white, folks would never find her."

"Ain't that many places around here she could go. Believe me, if she can be found, Boyd Jensen can find her."

"How much will it cost me?"

"Sometimes it don't cost nothin'. Sometimes he just buys the slaves before he goes lookin' for 'em. Course, he gets 'em at a bargain rate. Then, once he finds 'em, he makes his money when he sells 'em.

When Younger drove his wagon north out of Tywappiti later that day, he was much less agitated about the loss of Jennie. Bess commented on it.

"I'm glad to see you ain't mad anymore."

"Yeah," he said. "Well, you can't stay mad forever."

Younger reached his hand around and felt the fat purse in his pocket. He was 250 dollars richer than he had been when they rode into town, the result of a deal he made with Boyd Jensen. He planned to keep that little transaction secret from his wife. No sense in letting her know of his windfall. And no sense in letting her know how he had handled the situation with Art. He had come up with a brilliant solution. It was not only satisfying, it was profitable.

Art and Jennie were exhausted and starving. In the six days since they left, they had eaten nothing but berries. They had found a patch of mushrooms, but Art knew that some mushrooms were poison, and he didn't want to take a chance on getting the wrong kind. Thus it was that when the three riders came upon them, Art would have been unable to resist them, even if he had known their purpose.

Though he had no idea of the immediate danger they posed to him, their very appearance was somewhat alarming. All three were rough-looking men, bearded and dirty with ragged looking clothes. But it wasn't the state of their clothes that caught Art's attention. It was the pistols stuck in their belts and rifles protruding from saddle sheaths.

The leader of the group had narrow, gray eyes, a three-corner puff of a scar on his forehead, and terrible-looking, twisted, yellow teeth.

"Well, now, lookie here," he said. "You folks must be Art and Jennie."

Art was about to deny it, thinking it couldn't be a good sign that these men knew who they were. But before he could deny it, Jennie gave them away.

"How do you know our names?" she asked.

Art groaned inwardly.

The leader of the group chuckled. "Well, missy, we know your names because you are both slaves, and we are slave hunters by profession. Anytime we go after runaway slaves, we purt' near always know their names."

"I'm no slave!" Art said sharply.

"You got papers to prove that you ain't?"

"Papers? No, I'm white! Why would I have to have papers provin' I'm not a slave?"

"'Cause I got papers provin' that you are," the leader of the group said. He pulled a paper from his pocket, then opened it up and began to read. "Bill of sale from Lucas Younger to Boyd Jensen." He looked up and smiled,."Boyd Jensen, that's me."

He continued reading. "Two white-skinned slaves, a Creole girl, Jennie, age fourteen, and a high-yella boy named Art, age thirteen." He folded the paper and put it back in his pocket. "Jennie and Art," he said, pointing to the two. "A Creole girl and a high-yella boy. White-skinned slaves, that's you. You did belong to Lucas Younger, but I bought you, so now you both belong to me."

Pulling his pistol, Jensen pointed it directly at Art. "Now, you ain't goin' to give your new owner any trouble, are you, boy?"

"No," Art said.

Jensen cocked his pistol, and the metallic click of the hammer coming back made a chilling sound. "Didn't think you was. Boys, put 'em in shackles."

The other two riders climbed down from their horses, each

of them carrying a length of chain and shackles. One of them went over to Jennie, who stuck her hands out without question. Obviously, she had been through this before. Art left his hands by his side.

"Stick your hands out here, boy," one of the two men said gruffly. He grabbed Art's wrist, clamped one of the shackles on it, then brought the other one up to secure it as well.

With Art and Jennie secured, one of the men passed a chain around the shackles, connecting them to each other, and ultimately to the saddle of one of the horses.

"You chil'run keep up now," Jensen said as his two cohorts mounted their horses. "Don't give me no trouble and I'll be good to you. I won't go too fast." With everyone mounted, they started down the road. Although Jensen kept his promise not to go too fast, it still required a very brisk walk for Art and Jennie to maintain the pace. By nightfall, Art was exhausted, and he couldn't help but wonder how Jennie could possibly keep up.

8

As Jensen and the others rode into town pulling Art and Jennie along behind them, several of the town's citizens turned out to look them over in curiosity. By now both Art and Jennie were so tired and dispirited that they were barely aware of the fact that they were the center of attention of just about everyone in town.

They stopped in front of one of the larger buildings. A sign on front of the building read:

Tywappiti Traders' Market
Buyers and Sellers Welcome
Auctions Every Saturday
Tools, Machinery, Slaves

"Keep an eye on 'em," Jensen said as he dismounted.

Jennie shuffled over to sit down on the edge of the wooden porch.

"Get up, you," one of the men said, jerking hard on the chain. As the chain was looped around in a way to be attached to both of them, Art tried to spare Jennie by taking up the energy of the jerk, but he couldn't. Jennie was pulled off the porch, and landed, facedown, in the dirt in front of the trade market.

"Haw!" the one who jerked the chain said. "D'you see that, Pauley?"

"Leave 'er be, Dolan," Pauley said. "Let 'er sit down."

"You gone soft on her, have you?" Dolan asked. "You ain't a'thinkin' ole' Boyd's gonna let you sample this girl, are you? 'Cause I tell you true, he ain't goin' to do it. He aims to get as much as he can out of her, and he figures if any of us mess with her, she won't bring as much."

"Let 'er sit down," Pauley said again. "Let both of 'em sit down."

"Sit," Dolan said, making a motion with his hand.

Art helped Jennie up; then they both sat on the edge of the porch. A moment later Jensen came back out of the building with another man.

"See what I told you, Sheriff? They both as white as you or me," Jensen said. "But I got papers says they're slaves, the both of them."

"Sheriff?" Art said, perking up. "Are you the sheriff?"

"I am."

Art held up his hands. "Turn us loose, Sheriff. We aren't slaves."

"You got any papers says you aren't?" the sheriff asked.

"No, I don't have any papers," Art answered. "Why should I? People don't go around carrying papers saying they aren't slaves."

"Them that was slaves at one time do," the sheriff replied. He looked at Jennie. "What's your name, girl?"

"Jennie."

"Jennie what?"

"I don't know as I got a last name," Jennie replied.

"And you?"

"Art."

Jensen handed the sheriff a piece of paper and the sheriff looked at it, then nodded. "According to this, a Creole female named Jennie and a young, male high-yella named Art were

the property of one Lucas Younger. That property was transferred by a bill of sale to Boyd Jensen. I'm Boyd Jensen."

"Wait a minute! I never belonged to Younger," Art said.
"I've never belonged to anyone! In fact, Younger tried to kill
me. Look at the back of my head. That's where he hit me with
a shovel."

"True enough, Sheriff," Jensen said. "Mr. Younger explained how this young buck went after his wife and he had
to hit him with a shovel to stop him. He said he knocked him
out, then went to get some water to throw on him to bring him
to, but by the time he got back, the boy was gone. Then that
night, the girl was gone too, so he figured the boy come back
for her. He sold 'em to me at a bargain, seein' as how I was
goin' to have to run 'em down."

The sheriff stroked his chin as he studied the two. Finally,
he nodded. "Take 'em inside. Tell Ancel I said if he wants to
buy 'em, it's up to him."

"Sheriff, you're making a big mistake!" Art insisted. "I'm
not a slave!"

"You ain't, huh? Then how come you ain't got a last name?"

"I'll tell you my last name. It's . . ."

The sheriff held up his hand, interrupting Art. "Never
mind, boy. You could make up a last name, wouldn't mean
anything now."

"Come on inside, you two," Jensen said. "I want you to
meet Ancel. He's a slave trader. If you think I was unfriendly,
you ain't seen nothin' till you see Ancel. Best you do every
thing he tells you to do."

Ancel was a very overweight man with a round face, bul-
bous nose, heavily lidded eyes, and a thin mouth. He handed
over a sum of money to Boyd Jensen.

Jensen counted the money, then put it in his pocket. He

smiled at Art and Jennie. "I want to thank you two for runnin' off like you done. It made me a handsome profit."

Ancel turned to a man who was standing nearby. "Take their shackles off, Frank, then take 'em on into the back and get 'em cleaned up," he said. "I'll be along directly."

Frank, who was a large, muscular man, put the club he was carrying under one arm. Then, getting the key from Jensen, he removed the shackles and gave the devices, plus the key, back to Jensen.

Art began rubbing his wrists, gratified that, after several days of wearing the restraints, he was finally free of them.

"Back there," Frank growled, pointing to a door.

There were two barred cells on the other side of the door. One of the cells was filled with black men, the other with black women. All were naked.

"Take your clothes off," Frank said. "Both of you."

Jennie began complying without question, but Art hesitated.

"I'm not going to take off my clothes," he said defiantly.

The muscular man hit him with the club at the juncture of the neck and shoulder. He inflicted the blow with an easy snap of the wrist, seemingly putting no power at all in it, yet the effect was devastating. Art felt a numbing pain run up his neck, then out his shoulder to his arm, and finally into his stomach, causing a nausea so severe that he thought, for a moment, that he was going to throw up.

"Take off your clothes," Frank said again. He did not increase the tone of his voice, but repeated it in the same cold, dispassionate way he had used earlier. Oddly, it was much more frightening than it would have been had he shouted the words.

Art looked over at Jennie, who by now was naked. It was the first time he had ever seen a naked woman and, though Jennie was still quite young, her small, but well-formed breasts and the little patch of pubic hair showed that she was indeed a woman. He had long been curious about seeing a woman nude, but his current state of despair and humiliation robbed him of any sense of satisfying that curiosity.

Jennie made no effort to cover her nakedness, but stood there as if totally detached from herself. Art decided that the best way to survive this was to be as much like Jennie as he could be. Making his mind a complete blank, he took off all his clothes.

"You two get over here," Buck said, pointing to a wooden platform. When they complied, two men came in carrying buckets of water. One man threw a bucket of water onto Art; the other threw a bucket onto Jennie. Each was given a piece of soap.

"Scrub yourselves down," Buck ordered.

Following Jennie's lead, Art did as he was instructed. Then, when they were both covered with soap, the second bucket of water was thrown onto them. Not until then were they taken to their respective cells. The door slammed behind Art with a loud clang. Though he wasn't the only one naked, he was the only one white. The others in the cell stared at him with as much curiosity as had been displayed earlier by those on the street.

A young boy, no older than Art, came up to him, then ran his finger along Art's skin. After that, he stared into Art's eyes.

"Your eyes be blue," he finally said.

"Yes."

"Ain't never seen no colored boy with blue eyes before."

"I'm not colored, I'm white," Art said.

"What you doin' in here then?"

"I don't know," Art said.

"I tell you why he's here," one of the others said. "He been passin', that's why he's here. He's a high-yella that's been passin' hisself off as white, but he got caught."

"I am white," Art said.

"Not as long as you in here, you ain't," one of the men said. "Don't make no difference what color skin you wearin'. When you in here, you as black as the blackest one of us."

Half an hour later a basket of cornbread and a bucket of molasses were shoved through the bars. The others swarmed around the food, but Art hung back. The boy who had commented on his blue eyes brought him a piece of cornbread with a dab of molasses.

"You better eat," the boy said. "This here be the only food we get today."

It wasn't until that moment that Art realized he was hungry. He took the piece of cornbread. "Thanks," he said.

The young black boy smiled broadly. "I be Toby," he said. "Who you be?"

"Art."

"Me'n you be tight," Toby said.

It took Art a moment to figure out what Toby meant; then he realized that Toby was offering to be his friend. Despite the misery of his condition, this unreserved offer of friendship warmed him, and he smiled at his new friend.

"Yes," Art said. "We're tight."

Bruce Eby had been doing very well in Ohio, until he was forced to flee to save his neck. For nearly three years he had run Eby's River Trading Post in a cave alongside the Ohio River. It was a place where he sold to travelers goods he had stolen from other travelers.

He was successful for as long as his operation was secret, and the operation was secret as long as the river pirates who worked for him left no witnesses. Normally they were pretty good about that. They would swoop down on the flatboats, be they commercial or immigrant, kill everyone on board, then steal everything of value and bring it back to Eby.

But his men got careless. They attacked a family that was traveling in two boats. They didn't realize this when they attacked the first boat, and before they knew what was happening, the second boat was upon them. There were six men in the family, all armed, and for the first time, the river pirates found themselves outnumbered. Two were killed, and two got away.

They thought their getaway was complete, certain that the immigrants, grateful for their escape, would continue their journey. But they thought wrong, for one of the immigrants remembered seeing the pirates at Eby's Trading Post. Tying their boats to the bank, they came back down river to the cave, where they found Eby and the two surviving pirates engaged in a serious conversation. That was all the evidence they needed, and that night they attacked.

Eby managed to escape, but his remaining two men were killed, as were his wife and sister-in-law. He didn't mourn his wife, a half-Indian that he had bought, and her half sister was full-bloodied Indian. But he did regret losing what had been a lucrative business.

He was in Missouri Territory now, trying to decide what to do next, when he happened upon the slave auction in Tywappiti. He had no real need of slaves, but he thought he would hang around and watch the auction anyway, because the sight of human beings being traded like cattle intrigued him. He actually got a perverse sort of pleasure from watching a wrenching family separation.

When they brought the female slaves out for auction, he was stunned to see that one of them was white. When he inquired about her, he learned that she was a Creole. And as she had never done much physical labor, no one expected her to bring very much money.

"I heard tell that the last man who owned her sold her services as a whore," one of the spectators commented.

"That's a hell of a thing," another said. "It's one thing to own slaves to do labor. That's in the Bible. But a man ought to treat his slaves decent, and turnin' a young woman into a whore, be she black or white, is a sin."

As it turned out, most of the men at the slave auction shared that same opinion, for when the bidding began, the girl known only as Jennie received only a few, halfhearted bids. Eby was able to buy her at a very cheap price.

Even as the male slaves were being brought out for their own auction, Eby had the girl tied to his horse. She was walking alongside him as he headed north to Cape Girardeau.

Jennie looked back, hoping to see Art, but Eby gave a jerk on the rope, and she had to turn back quickly to avoid falling down.

"Keep up, girl," Eby ordered. "Or by God I'll drag you all the way to Cape Girardeau."

By the time they led Art and the other men out of their cell and up to the sale block where they stood, nude, the women's sale had already taken place. The sales of the men and women were purposely separate because there were some family members who were being separated and the officials didn't want any difficulty.

It was a lively auction, with spirited bidding being done on several of the slaves, especially some of the bigger, more muscular ones. The auction was brought to a premature end, however, when a man named Matthews made a bid on all the remaining slaves. Art and Toby were in that lot, and as soon as the bidding was over, Matthews came up to auction block to pay for and claim his property.

"You boys go over there to the wagon and find you something to put on," Matthews said to the group of slaves he had just bought.

Art looked hard at Matthews, hoping to be able to get his attention, to explain to him that he wasn't supposed to be here.

"Art, don' do that. Don' never be caught lookin' into a white man's eyes," Toby warned. "They don' like that."

"I was trying to get him to look at me so I could say something to him."

Toby shook his head vigorously. "That be a good way to get yourself a whuppin'." Toby studied his new friend for a long moment. "You tellin' the truth, ain't you?" he finally said. "You ain't no high-yella pass in'. You really be white."

"Yes, I'm really white. That's why I want to talk to Mr. Matthews."

"That ain't goin' do you no good," Toby said. "I believe you, but the white folks ain' goin' to. They done sell you for a slave, so that mean you be a slave, no matter what."

"Damn it, can't they look at me and tell?" Art asked, exasperated by the situation.

"Boy, they look at you, all they think is maybe a white man crawled in your mama's bed one night. You look white, but it don't matter what your skin say. All that matters is what The Man say, and right now, The Man say you ain't white."

Matthews owned a brick kiln, and for the next six weeks Art, Toby, and the other slaves who were purchased, made bricks, watched over at all times by an armed guard. They were given a biscuit and coffee for breakfast, cornbread and greens for their supper. On Sunday they were given meat, generally fried salt pork.

Art did whatever it took to survive, learning from Toby how to avoid any direct contact with the guards, and how to be "not there."

"What does that mean, to be not there?" Art asked when Toby first suggested it as a means of survival. "How can you not be there?"

"It mean don't be there to The Man," Toby said.

"I don't understand."

"They's a horse tied to the pole that turn the mud grinder," Toby said. "What color he be?"

"He's, uh . . ." Art stopped to consider the question, then he smiled. "I don't know what color he is," he admitted.

Toby laughed. "That 'cause he ain't no horse, he a mule. And you didn't even know that, 'cause you ain't never see him."

"Sure I have, I see him every day," Art replied. "We walk right by him when we come to work."

"You walk by him, but you don't see him," Toby insisted. "That ole' mule, he be in his world, you be in your world, and the white man? He be in his world. What you do is, you just stay in your world and that way you not be there in his world. You not be in his world, he don' give you no trouble."

Over the next several days Art thought about what Toby had told him about "not being there," and was amazed at how accurate Toby's observations had been. Even the guards whose duty it was to watch them would often look right by them as if they weren't there.

It wasn't only Toby who understood this peculiar tactic. The other slaves knew it as well, and they could carry on a conversation among themselves, talking about white men in general or one in particular, right in front of them, and not be overheard. Or if they were, not be understood, simply because the whites felt that nothing the blacks could say or do would have any impact upon their own lives.

They did this by giving nicknames to all the guards and overseers. Matthews was "Ole Mistah Moon," because he had a very round, almost pasty-white face. One of the guards, who had a constant swarm of flies buzzing around a beard matted with expectorated tobacco juice, was called "Blowfly." Others were "Rabbit,"."Snake," and "Weasel."

Often one of the slaves would break into song, using a familiar tune but substituting their own lines and using the nicknames of the guards. One slave would do one verse, another would follow with a second verse, a third with a third verse, and so on for several verses. By the end of the song nearly every guard, overseer, or white man of any importance would have been the subject of the most degrading comments, right under their noses.

> *Ole Mistah Moon go chasin' him a coon,*
> *Oh yay, oh yay,*
> *But the coon so fast Mistah*
> *Moon fall on his ass,*
> *Oh, de oh-yah-yay.*

The trick, Art learned, was to enjoy the song without laughing. Laughter was not expected under the conditions in which the slaves worked, and if one laughed, it would break through the wall that separated the slaves' world from the masters'.

Then, one hot day when the work was particularly hard, the two water buckets were emptied faster than normal. Blowfly pointed to them. "Pick those up and come with me," he ordered Art.

Blowfly started toward the river with Art following along behind. When they got to the river's edge, Art filled one of the buckets with water, then set it aside. As he started to fill the other bucket, he saw Blowfly peeing in the first one.

"What are you doing?" Art asked. "That's our drinking water."

"Hell, white man's piss will just make it taste better," Blowfly said, buttoning his pants up again.

Art felt a rage bubbling up inside him like boiling water. He was holding the second bucket in his hand, and before he realized what he was doing, he swung the bucket at Blowfly, smashing it down hard on the guard's head. Blowfly's eyes rolled back in their sockets and he went down. Art kicked over the remaining bucket, then started running. He had run half a mile without stopping before he realized he should have picked up Blowfly's rifle.

But it was too late now. It was too late for anything but to keep running. If they caught him now he would, at best, be tied to the whipping post for striking a guard and running away. At worst, he could be hanged. He didn't know if Blowfly was alive or dead, but he had hit him as hard as he could.

He was at least a mile away before he heard the dogs. They had found Blowfly, and now they were coming after him.

Looking out into the river, Art saw a log floating down with the current. Without giving it a second thought, he dived into the water and started swimming toward the middle. He knew from his experience on the flatboat with Harding that the river was full of rip currents and whirlpools. It was an exceptionally dangerous river to swim in, but he had no choice.

The log was coming downriver faster than he realized, and he saw it go by before he reached the center of the stream. He was forced to swim hard downstream in order to catch up to it. Finally he reached it, then grabbed hold and hung there, panting from the exertion.

He could hear the dogs quite clearly now, and when he looked back he saw them gathered at the riverbank where he had gone in. A couple of the dogs jumped into the water, paddled out a short way, then with a few high-pitched barks of fright, swam back to shore and clambered back onto the bank.

"Where'd he go?"

The voice sounded clear, carried to him by the flat surface of the river.

"I hope the son of a bitch drowned," another said.

Art drew a deep breath and, while still hanging onto the log, ducked his head underwater. He stayed underwater for as long as he could, and when he raised up again, he saw that a fallen tree was blocking his view of the men, which meant that it was also blocking their view of him.

He was free. That was a condition he had taken for granted all his life, but never would he take it for granted again.

9

He had no idea where he was. He thought he might still be in Missouri Territory, at least, because he was still on the western side of the Mississippi River, but exactly where in Missouri, he couldn't say. It had been nearly a week since he had escaped. Since then he had survived on nuts, berries, and honey.

During his wanderings he had seen a lot of game: rabbits, squirrels, birds, even deer. But as he had no weapon of any kind, not even a knife, he had to watch in frustration as a veritable feast showed itself while remaining agonizingly out of reach.

Then he was awakened one morning by the unmistakable aroma of cooking meat. When he opened his eyes he saw a rabbit, cooking on a spit, over an open fire.

How had this gotten here? He certainly wasn't responsible. He hadn't even managed to make a fire yet, let alone kill, clean, and cook a rabbit. And yet, here it was. Was he dreaming?

Art went over to look more closely at the rabbit. The aromas of its cooking made him salivate and caused his stomach to growl in hunger. The smell was real and when he touched it, he knew he wasn't dreaming.

Moving quickly, as if frightened that it might go away, Art pulled the rabbit off the skewer, then began eating ravenously, pulling the animal apart with his hands and teeth, not even waiting for it to cool. When all the meat was gone, he broke open the bones and sucked out the marrow.

Not until he was finished eating, with a satisfying fullness in his stomach, did he begin to wonder once more where it could have come from. That question was answered when he heard a sound behind him. Turning quickly, he saw four Indians standing there.

One of the Indians made a motion toward his mouth with his hands, then pointed at the rabbit bones. Then moved his jaws, as if eating.

"Oh, damn! I ate your breakfast, didn't I? I'm sorry," Art said. "I was so hungry, I didn't know."

The Indian pointed to the bones, then to himself, then to Art. The meaning of the sign was unambiguous. He was indicating that he had given the rabbit to Art.

"You gave this to me?" Art asked. He repeated the Indian's sign, but in reverse.

"Uhnn," the Indian grunted, though he nodded yes.

"I, uh, have nothing to give to you," Art said. He made a motion toward himself and his ragged clothing, intuitively signaling that he was nearly destitute.

The Indian indicated that Art should go with them. They turned and started to walk away, but Art remained behind, not sure if he should go or not.

The Indian turned toward him once more, again indicating that Art should accompany them.

"Well, it was a good rabbit," Art said. "And I sure don't seem to be doing that well feeding myself. Besides, if you wanted to kill me, I reckon you would have done so by now. And I don't think you would have fed me first."

It was clear that the Indians had no idea what Art was saying. In fact, Art knew they wouldn't understand; it was just a way of talking out loud without actually talking to himself.

"All right, I'll go," Art said, following them.

With a grunt, the Indian turned and they began walking.

Although he had been somewhat re-energized by his meal, Art was still unable to keep up with the Indians. As a result, the Indians had to stop several times to wait for him. Finally, they came over a low ridge and Art saw, on the banks of a small river, an Indian village consisting of several wigwams, domed structures made of saplings, twigs, and woven grass. Men and women of the village looked up curiously; then the children and several dogs ran out to meet them. The dogs barked, while the children laughed and shouted back and forth to each other in excitement. One young boy, braver than the others, picked up a stick and ran up to Art. Art thought the boy was going to hit him. Instead, he just touched him, then, with a loud whoop, ran back to boast of his accomplishment to the others.

The four Indians led Art to the center of the little village, where an old man was standing in front of one of the lodges. The Indians who brought Art into the village spoke to the old man, who nodded, then turned to Art.

"You are English?" the old man asked.

"Yes," Art replied, though he wasn't sure he understood the question. Was he being asked if he was English, or if he spoke English?

"It is good that you are English," the old man said. "I am Keytano of the Shawnee. The Shawnee are allies with the English in their war with the white men who have come to take our land."

Art knew there a war was going on between the United States and England, but he hadn't paid much attention to it. Now he understood Keytano's question, and he was glad that he had answered as he had. If he had answered that he was American, they might have considered him an enemy.

"I'm glad you speak English," Art said.

"Yes, I speak English very good. I am friend to the English people. How are you called?"

"My name is Arthur," Art said. He wasn't sure why he used

the more formal version of his name. Somehow, he just believed that was the right response.

"Where is your home, Arthur?" Keytano's pronunciation made the name sound like Artoor.

Art didn't want to say he was from Ohio. He remembered a big battle with the Shawnee at Tippecanoe a few years earlier. The chief of the Shawnee, Tecumseh, was not at Tippecanoe, but he did fight at the Battle of Thames, and there he was killed. Some of Art's family's Ohio neighbors had been a part of the force that fought against Tecumseh.

"I have no home," he said. At the moment, it was a statement he could make truthfully.

"You are lost, Artoor?"

"Yes." This answer was even more truthful.

Keytano smiled broadly. "Now you are not lost. Now you have a home. You will become Shawnee."

Art thought of his present situation. He had the distinct impression he wasn't being invited to become Shawnee, he was being told to do so. If he refused the invitation now, he would in all likelihood insult them.

"I will be happy to stay with you," Art said.

And why not? he thought. At least with the Indians, he wasn't going to starve to death. And he might even learn a thing or two that he could put to good use.

"It is good," Keytano said. He shouted something, and a younger man appeared. "This is Techanka. Techanka is my son," Keytano said. "You will be the son of my son."

Techanka said something to Art.

"Do you speak English?" Art asked.

Keytano said something, and Techanka hit Art with an open-palm slap.

Surprised by the sudden show of hostility, Art jumped back and put his hand to his face.

"Artoor, from this day forth, you will speak in our tongue."

"But I don't know your tongue," Art said.

Techanka hit Art again.

"If you do not learn quickly, Artoor, you will be hit many times," Keytano said.

Art started to say something else, then realized that every time he spoke in English he was going to be hit. He caught the words before they left his tongue. It was obvious, however, that they were waiting for him to say something . . . anything . . . in their language. Then he smiled, and pointed at Techanka.

"Techanka," Art said.

Techanka smiled broadly and pointed to himself, nodding yes. "Techanka," he said.

Art pointed toward the old man. "Keytano."

Again, Techanka smiled and nodded his head. "Keytano," he repeated.

Art pointed to himself. "Ar . . ." He paused for a moment, then decided to use Keytano's pronunciation. "Artoor," he said.

This time Techanka raised his hands to the others, signaling them to speak as well. "Artoor!" they said in unison. Then, each in turn came up to Art, pointed to him, called him Artoor, then pointed to themselves and spoke their own name. One of those who introduced himself was a boy about his same age and size. He was Tolian, and Art learned that same day that Tolian was Techanka's son, and now his stepbrother.

The river was placid, though with a powerful enough current to keep him moving at a good clip. It was nearly dusk and the sun, low in the west, caused the river to shimmer in a pale blue, with highlights of reflected gold. If Pete Harding could find some way to save time in a leather pouch and call it up again, this would be one of the moments he would save.

Harding worked the tiller to keep the boat in midstream, thus taking maximum advantage of the current. This boat wasn't quite as large as the one he had brought down when

Art was with him. That was good, though, because then he'd had Art to help him. He was alone for this trip.

Harding missed Art, and he found himself thinking about the boy often, wondering where he was and hoping he was getting along well. A lot about Art reminded him of himself when he was younger. He too had left home at an early age, though in his case it was not by choice.

Harding was only fourteen years old when both his parents and his younger sister contracted pneumonia and died during a New York blizzard. Harding had been snowed in and unable to go for help. The ground was too hard to bury them, so Harding moved them to the barn and wrapped them in a tarpaulin. While the frozen bodies of his parents waited in the barn for the spring thaw, Harding spent the time just trying to survive.

When neighbors came to call that spring, they were shocked to find the fourteen-year-old boy living alone. He had had to cut his own firewood, had hunted and cooked his own food, and had even fought off an attack by a starving, frenzied pack of wolves.

Well-meaning people put Harding in an orphanage, but within six months he ran away and went to Ohio, where he hired on as a deckhand on an Ohio River keelboat. In that position he learned the rivers—the Ohio, the Tennessee, and later the Mississippi. When he felt he was ready, he went out on his own, buying his own flatboat and cargo, taking it downriver where he would sell his goods, then buy a horse for the ride back. Once back, he would sell the horse, buy a new flatboat and more cargo, and start all over again.

He had been on the rivers for ten years now, both as a hand and as his own man, and he knew not only the rivers, but the other men who plied them. There were several places along the rivers where the boats would tie up for the night, often in groups of five or six boats. Those were good times too, for at the "tie-ups" the boatman would play cards, tell stories, and share their food.

One such tie-up was at a place called Fox Point. Here, where the river had carved a natural basin at the river's edge, the bank was a wide, flat beach. Seeing it ahead, Harding noticed that three other boats had already put in for the night, and he began working his tiller, angling toward the landing.

A couple of boatmen saw him coming and, waving, they walked down to the edge of the water.

"Pete! You old river rat. You got 'ny whiskey? We done purt' nigh drunk all our'n," one of the men yelled, waving at Pete. He held out his hand, signaling for Harding to throw him a line, and when Harding did, he pulled the boat ashore, making the landing a lot easier.

"Hell, Caleb, I've never seen you when you hadn't drunk all your whiskey," Harding said as he stepped ashore. Not until his boat was made secure did he shake hands with Caleb and the others. Counting Harding, there were now seven boatmen ashore. A fire was already burning, and over the fire hung a black kettle.

Seeing that the men had opted for a community stew, Harding dug through his provisions, came up with a potato, an onion, a couple of carrots, and some salt pork.

"Better let me handle that," one of the others said, taking the viands from Harding. "I've got a good stew going here and I ain't goin' to let you ruin it."

"Ole Hank there thinks he's the only one can cook," one of the other men said.

"Well, now, he is a mighty fine cook," Caleb said. "Fact is, if he was a mite prettier, I'd marry him."

The others laughed.

The food was good, the tobacco mellow, and the whiskey smooth. The men were enjoying the long, lingering twilight when suddenly an arrow plunged deep into Caleb's chest.

Caleb looked down at the arrow as if he couldn't believe it was there; then, with an expression that was a combination of shock and pain, he looked up at the others.

"Fellas, I . . ." he began, then fell forward.

"To your guns, men!" Harding shouted, running toward his boat where he had two pistols and a rifle.

By now arrows were whistling all around them, sticking in the ground alongside, and plunking into the boats and splashing in the water. Two other men were hit; one went down with an arrow in his back, while Hank took one in the leg.

Harding reached his weapons first. Turning back toward the woods, he saw half-a-dozen Indians charging toward them, all with raised tomahawks. He shot the first one with his rifle, then raised one pistol and held it until the next Indian came into range. He fired again and that Indian went down as well.

By now some of the other boatmen had reached their weapons and they too began returning fire. One more boatman was killed, but at least four more Indians went down. Realizing they had lost the advantage of surprise, the remaining Indians turned and scurried back into the woods.

"Hurrah, boys! We've turned them away!" Hank shouted.

"Yeah, but they'll be back, and there are only four of us left," one of the others said.

"We had better reload quickly," Harding suggested. "Get the guns from the fellas who were killed. We'll be needing every one of them."

Scurrying around quickly, the remaining four men gathered up all the other weapons, loaded them, and waited for the Indians to return.

Instead of Indians, however, there came a thunderous boom. Immediately thereafter, a cannonball burst in their midst. A second cannonball smashed into one of the boats.

"Cannons?" Harding said in surprise. "The Indians are using cannons?"

"Indians my eye!" Hank said, pointing. "Lessen they've taken to wearin' them fancy red coats, it ain't Indians that's attackin' us."

Looking in the direction Hank pointed, Harding saw that

two field artillery pieces had been rolled out of the woods. Manning the artillery pieces were soldiers in uniform. The most prominent feature of each uniform was its red jacket.

The cannons fired a second time. Hurling toward the boatmen out of the twilight came a cloud of chain shot. Hank and the other two boatmen were cut down in the terrible carnage the chain shot created. Harding was the only one left.

By now, mercifully, the twilight had faded to the point of near-darkness. Staying on his belly, but always keeping a wary eye on the wood line from which the Indians had emerged, Harding abandoned his weapons and wriggled backward, down to the water's edge. He slipped down into the water quietly, and dog-paddled away from the shore, swimming all the way out to the middle of the stream. Once there, he took advantage of the current to swim downriver as hard and as fast as he could.

Behind him, he heard the whoops and shouts of the Indians. When he was far enough away, he crossed the river and came out on the other side. There, wet, cold, and exhausted, he looked back. The Indians were unloading the boats; then, as each boat was emptied, it was set to the torch. By the light of the burning boats he could see the Indians dancing in glee while a group of uniformed British soldiers stood by, looking on.

Harding knew that America was at war with the British, but as far as he was concerned, the war was the business of politicians and soldiers.

"Damn you British bastards," Harding said. "You've just made this war my business."

10

Running hard down the path, Art skidded to a stop, then looked toward the center circle of the village. There he saw his goal—a vest, decorated with red-dyed porcupine quills, hanging from an arm at the top of a thirty-foot pole. He had only to reach that pole, climb it, and grab the vest to claim his prize. However, seven other contestants had the same objective in mind.

It was six months now since Art had joined the Shawnee, and he was participating in a week-long festival that gave thanks for the warmth of the sun, the nourishment of the rain, and the supply of fish and game by which the village fed itself. The most significant part of the festival, however, was the Counting Out ceremony, a rite of passage in which boys became men.

Part of the passage to manhood was the young men's participation in the games. The winner of the games won a handsome vest. The desirability of the vest was not just due to its attractiveness, though the village's most skilled weaver and decorator was always chosen to make it. The real value of the vest was based upon its symbolism, for whoever won it would be an honored member of the community from that point forward. For the rest of his life, he would bring the vest out and display it proudly at special events, and would be treated with great deference by the others in the village.

There were eight candidates for manhood today, each one beginning at individually assigned starting points outside the village. From there, they had to successfully negotiate numerous obstacles before reaching the outskirts of the village itself. The preliminary obstacles consisted of temporary constructions such as moats to be crossed, tunnels to be crawled through, walls to be scaled, and ropes to be climbed. With the completion of the first part of the circuit, the difficulty increased dramatically; for from that moment on, the contestants would not only face the course obstacles, they would have to compete against each other as well. And anything that prevented one's opponent from reaching his goal, short of inflicting serious bodily injury, was considered fair.

From the onset the men, women, and younger children of the village had gathered to shout encouragement to the eight participants. The last leg of the circuit was shared by all the contestants, so nearly everyone from the village had gathered to cheer their favorites on.

Art was warmed to hear his own name called as he started toward the pole, where hung the prize.

"Artoor! Artoor! Artoor!" several shouted in excitement as Art, who was now in the lead, prepared to cover the final one hundred yards.

Art was nearly exhausted by the ordeal, but he smiled and waved to acknowledge the cheers of the crowd.

"Tolian! Tolian! Tolian!" the crowd began to chant.

Art looked back over his shoulder and saw that Tolian had just completed the first part of the contest and he too was on the final leg. Though Art would have preferred to be far in front of everyone, he was glad that the one closest to him was Tolian, for he and his stepbrother had become best of friends over the last six months. It didn't surprise him to see Tolian so close, however, for the two had been competitors from the very beginning. Their rivalry was good-natured, though, and each would go to the aid of the other in a moment, should that ever be required.

By now three other contestants were in view, so that five of the eight who had started were still in the hunt. One of the remaining participants was Metacoma, a young man who had long been Tolian's rival and enemy. Art had tried to befriend everyone, but because he was Tolian's brother, a position accorded as much validity as if they had actually been born brothers, Metacoma now considered Art his enemy as well.

Suddenly a wall of fire flared up in front of Art, igniting so quickly and with such ferocity that he could feel the blast of heat. It was a planned obstacle, ignited by one of the village elders, but Art had been paying such close attention to those running up behind him that he was not looking ahead, and he nearly ran headlong into the flames.

Gasps and squeals of surprise and excitement erupted from the spectators, and they drew closer to see how the contestants were going to overcome this spectacular of all the hurdles.

The fire served the purpose of stopping Art long enough for the others to catch up. For a few seconds the five young men stood there, contemplating the latest in the long series of challenges they had encountered.

"Ho!" one of the other young men shouted to his rivals. "Would you have a small fire stop you? Cower, if you wish. I will claim the prize."

The young man backed up a few feet, then ran toward the fire. He leapt through it, but even before he disappeared, Art saw his clothes catch on fire. He could hear the young man screaming in pain from the other side, where someone quickly threw him to the ground, rolling him over to extinguish the flames. The young man's approach had clearly failed.

"Artoor! Come!" Tolian shouted.

"What is it?" Art asked.

"We can help each other, if you will trust me," Tolian said.

"You want me to trust you?"

"My brother, have I given you cause not to trust me?" Tolian asked.

Art laughed. "Only every time we have competed," he replied.

"Well, that is true," Tolian agreed. But you must trust me now. Either we work together, or the prize will go to another."

"What would you have me do?" Art asked.

"See that tree," Tolian said, pointing to one near the wall of fire. "Neither of us can reach the bottom limb without help. But if you give me a lift up, once I am there I will reach a hand down to you. We can then climb above the fire and leap over it. When we are on the other side, it will again be each for himself."

Art hesitated. He was probably setting himself up for one of Tolian's tricks, but there seemed to be no other choice.

"All right," he agreed. "I will do as you ask."

Quickly, they ran to the tree and, as promised, Art gave Tolian a boost to reach the lowest limb. Once in the tree, however, Tolian started to climb immediately, showing that he had no intention of helping Art.

"Tolian, you would do that to me?"

Tolian laughed. "I cannot believe that you let me trick you again. When will you learn, my brother?"

"Tolian, look!" Art shouted. He pointed across to another tree where the two remaining contestants had come to the same agreement. And, like Tolian, the one who had been helped into the tree betrayed the one who had helped him and was climbing quickly.

"That's Metacoma. Would you betray me, my brother, as Metacoma has betrayed his friend? Are you just like him?"

Art knew that Tolian would not want such a comparison made.

"I am *not* like Metacoma!" Tolian insisted with a shout of

frustrated rage. Trapped by circumstances, he started back down the tree to help his brother.

Art smiled. Tolian had a degree of self-respect, and he had just played upon it, shaming Tolian into seeing that if he abandoned him, he was no better than the hated Metacoma.

"Hurry!" Tolian shouted, holding his hand down. "He is getting ahead of us!"

With Tolian's help, Art reached the bottom limb of the tree. As soon as he had a good grip, Tolian let go and scampered up quickly. He climbed above the flames, then jumped over to the other side, hitting the ground at about the same time as Metacoma. He rolled as he hit the ground to break his fall. Art, though several seconds behind the other two, got over the flames as well.

The wall of fire had been the last physical barrier the contestants had to conquer, and now nothing remained but a dash of seventy-five yards to the center of the circle and the pole from which hung the prize.

Metacoma had a slight lead on Tolian and Art, and was almost to the pole when Tolian suddenly launched his body at Metacoma's legs, bringing him down in a heap. The unsuspecting Metacoma slammed into the ground, while Tolian, who had been prepared for the impact, regained his feet as easily as if he were a cat. Now Tolian had the lead and he reached the pole first.

Tolian started up the pole. He was halfway to the top when Metacoma, having recovered quickly, shinnied up the pole, reached up, grabbed Tolian's foot, then yanked him back down. With a shout of anger and surprise, Tolian was pulled from the pole, falling nearly fifteen feet to the ground.

"I have won!" Metacoma shouted in exultation. He looked over his shoulder at Tolian, who, momentarily stunned by the fall, was struggling to his feet and shaking his head to clear it. "Stay there, Tolian!" Metacoma called down to him. "Watch me claim my prize!"

Metacoma laughed, then climbed the remaining fifteen feet. When he reached the top and stretched his hand out to snatch the prize, however, he discovered that a final obstacle had been put in the way of the contestants. Every time he reached for the vest, it began to bounce around, jerking just out of his grasp. That was because a long cord was attached to it, and standing below at the other end of the cord was a man whose job it was to make this, the final task, as difficult as all the rest.

Metacoma reached for the vest again, but managed to snatch nothing but thin air. He kept lunging for it, and once he made such a desperate grab that had he not urgently wrapped both his arms around the pole, he would have plunged to the ground. The crowd gasped with anticipation, then sighed with relief that Metacoma had regained his hold, for a fall from that high up the pole would surely have inflicted serious injury.

By now Tolian had regained his wits enough to begin climbing the pole as well. All around the circle people who had already counted him out now cheered his efforts.

For the moment Art was convinced that he was entirely out of it, for even if he attempted to climb the pole now, he would be the third one on the pole, and the farthest away from the prize. He looked over at the man who was manipulating the vest by pulling on the long cord, and saw that he had just managed to pull it out of the way of Metacoma's grasp.

Suddenly Art got an idea. Grabbing a knife from the belt of someone who was standing nearby, he ran over to the man who was manipulating the vest.

Holding on to the pole with both legs and one arm, Metacoma reached for the vest. He felt his fingers touch it.

"I've got it!" he shouted in triumph.

At that precise moment, Art made a quick slice at the cord. The cord severed and the vest dropped.

Metacoma's scream of frustrated rage was joined by Tolian's

shout of surprise; then both calls were drowned out by the shouts of the villagers as they realized what had just happened.

Art was some twenty yards from where the vest fell, and he started toward it. Tolian recovered quickly, slid down the pole, then dived for the vest just as Art did. The hands of both young men wrapped around the vest simultaneously, and neither would let go.

The cheers died in the throats of the villagers. They wanted to cheer for the winner, but which one was it? Both young men had apparently reached the prize at the same time. The rules, though very lax as to what impediments the contestants could put in each other's way during the quest, were quite specific about the conclusion. Once the vest was clearly in the grasp of a contestant, the game was over and the contestant was the winner. But in whose grasp was the it?

Art and Tolian lay on their stomachs, breathing hard from exertion. Though neither would let go, they did not fight each other for possession. Instead, they just lay there to await the decision of those who would judge the contest.

Art saw that Tolian was bleeding from wounds in his forehead and lip.

"Are you hurt, Tolian?" he asked.

"No," Tolian replied. "How can I be hurt? I have won!"

Though Art did not try to take the vest from Tolian, he shook it once to emphasize that his claim of victory was every bit as strong as his stepbrother's. "Don't be so quick to declare victory," he cautioned.

Tolian looked back toward the pole where the vest had been hanging, and he saw Metacoma leaning against it, his head lowered in a posture of defeat.

"Yes, well, at least Metacoma did not win," Tolian said.

By now some of the other contestants were beginning to drag into the circle, some limping with injuries, others holding their arms or heads painfully.

"Aiyee, aiyee . . . hear me now!" Keytano shouted.

The villagers grew quiet to listen to the decision.

"There is not one winner, there are two winners," Keytano said. "Tolian and Artoor will share the prize!"

"But how can they share the prize?" one of the villagers asked. "There is only one prize."

"We will cut the vest into two pieces," Keytano said.

Suddenly Art remember a Bible story his mother had once read to him. In a dispute over who was the real mother of a baby, King Solomon offered to solve the dilemma by offering to cut the child into two pieces, giving half of the child to each mother. One mother agreed to the solution, but the other withdrew her claim, rather than see the child harmed. Solomon then awarded her the child.

Art let go of the vest and stood up.

"No," he said. "The vest should not be cut. There should be only one winner. I relinquish to my bother, Tolian."

"Aiyee! I have won!" Tolian shouted in excitement. Clutching the vest tightly, he jumped up, then began dancing and whooping with joy.

"You have done a good thing," Keytano said. "It is good that Tolian has won."

"I see you've never heard of Solomon," Art said, smiling wanly and speaking in English.

"The King in the Jesus-God book," Keytano said, also speaking in English. "Yes, I have heard of Solomon. But the woman with the child was not his daughter. Tolian is the son of my son."

"And I am the son of your son."

"You are the English son of my son. Tolian is the Shawnee son of my son. But because I am of good heart today, I will not punish you for speaking English."

Art realized then that this was the first sentence he had spoken in English in over six months. Though he missed hearing his own language, he had to admit that the total immersion in Shawnee had helped him learn the language rather quickly.

Language wasn't the only thing Art had learned while living with the Shawnee. He knew how to make traps to capture game, he knew how to find deer by becoming a deer, he knew how to watch the birds as they went to water at night so that he could find water. He knew which plants made medicine to heal wounds and which plants would treat pain. If, ever again, he found himself alone in the woods, he would not starve.

Jennie's situation had improved. It wasn't that Eby was a kinder owner than Younger—Eby was every bit as despicable as her former owner had been—but Jennie rarely saw Eby because he had borrowed money and, on his note, pledged all the income she could generate until his debt was repaid. As a result Jennie was no longer relegated to doing business from the back of a wagon, but was working in Etta Claire's Visitation Salon, a first-class house of prostitution.

Etta Claire, was Etta Claire Dozier, a former prostitute who, for fifteen percent of the take, provided room, food, and a convivial atmosphere for the girls.

For the first time in her life Jennie had a room of her own, complete with a vanity and mirror. She had clothes to wear and regular meals, and a real bed. If it weren't for the fact that she still had to entertain men, she would believe that life couldn't be better.

Before, Jennie had been on her own, servicing one man after another under all conditions. Here, at least, she was able to use a bed. Also there were other girls working in the house, so she wasn't expected to take care of everyone all by herself. Having other girls around helped in other ways as well. The girls taught her things she needed to know, telling her about various oils and lubricants that would make the process less painful, as well as showing her tricks that would give her more control over a man's endurance. That way if she was with someone who was extremely unpleasant, she could shorten the time he spent with her. On the other hand, if she was with someone who was gentle and she wanted to stay longer with him, she could prolong the session.

Although Saturday night was always the busiest night, Jennie was able to tolerate it because the next day was Sunday. All visitors would have to leave by six o'clock Sunday morning. Then the house would be closed for the rest of the day. That was a day of much-needed rest for all the girls, and they generally had a late breakfast, then slept, sewed, or visited. All of the girls were friendly with each other, and these times together were the closest thing to a family life Jennie had ever experienced.

Jennie's best friend was a girl named Carol. At eighteen, Carol was closest to Jennie's age, and the two had exchanged their life stories. Like Jennie, Carol had been a prostitute from a very early age. Carol had been born to a prostitute. She didn't know her father, but had gone through a succession of "uncles" until one of them raped her when she was twelve. She ran away from home when her mother didn't believe her. Since she had been raised by a prostitute, going into the business didn't seem that unusual for her.

Carol poured a cup of coffee for herself and for Jennie, then added generous amounts of cream and sugar. She brought the cup over to Jennie, who was sitting on a cushion in the window seat, looking out at the river.

"Tell me more about Art," Carol said, settling down on the window seat alongside her friend.

"I don't know no more to tell," she said. "I only know'd him for a short time."

"Is he handsome?"

"He ain't but a boy."

"And you are just a girl. Is he handsome?" Carol asked again.

Jennie laughed. "I reckon he is. Leastwise, he's goin' to make a fine-lookin' man someday."

"Maybe, when he's a fine-lookin' man, he'll come for you. He'll come for you and take you out of the life."

"He can't never come for me. You forget, I ain't just in the life. I'm a slave. I got no choice."

"Maybe he'll buy you. If he loves you, he'll buy you."

"Oh, I don't reckon he loves me none. I mean, he can't hardly do that, seein' as he's white and I'm Creole."

"But you said yourself that he stole you away from Mr. Younger."

"He done that, all right. But then we got catched, the both of us. Now, even though he's white, he's a slave, same as me."

"Have you ever been with him?" Carol asked.

"What? You mean lie with him?"

"Yes."

Jennie shook her head. "Ain't never," she said. "Been with a heap of men, but never with Art."

"How many men you reckon you've been with?" Carol asked.

"Lots of 'em. How about you?"

"Lots of 'em," Carol replied.

"Why do you reckon men like to do it so?"

"I don't know, but they surely do. And it don't seem to make no difference to them who they are with; one woman seems to be 'bout as good as another to them," Carol said.

"That's true."

"They say that if you lie with the right man, it can be good for a woman too," Carol said.

"Really? Has it ever been good for you?" Jennie asked.

Carol shook her head. "No. It ain't never been good."

"It ain't never been good for me neither."

"Maybe it would be good for you if you were with Art."

"Maybe," Jennie agreed.

Carol laughed. "See there. You are in love with him."

"Am not," Jennie said, joining in the laughter.

"Are too," Carol insisted.

"Maybe," Jennie said.

"You know what you ought to do? You ought to think of Art when you are with the other men," Carol suggested. "If you would think of Art, it might not be so bad."

It was two days later, and Jennie and Carol were sitting in the parlor waiting for the evening's business to begin, when Jennie shared something with Carol.

"It worked," she said.

"What worked?"

"What you told me to do. Whenever I'm with a man now, I think of Art."

"Oh! And do you like it now?" Carol asked.

"No, I still don't like it. But it's better."

"I wish I had someone I could think of," Carol said. "I know. I'll think of Art too."

"No, you can't," Jennie said. "He belongs to me."

Both girls laughed.

11

It was the perfect place from which to launch an ambush. The river was only navigable on the east side of the island, so the flatboats would have to maneuver very carefully in order to negotiate the island.

There were two other advantages to the island. One was that it was heavily infested with old-growth timber, thus making concealment easy. The other advantage was that the island was south of the confluence of the Ohio and Mississippi, so that downstream traffic from both rivers would be passing by. That doubled the targets of opportunity.

Unlike his days on the Ohio, when Eby was primarily a front for the pirates working the river, he was now taking an active role in the venture. He no longer had an easy outlet for the goods that were stolen. That meant that the operation was much less profitable than it had been because he had to make deep discounts on the stolen goods in order to sell them. It was that lack of profitability that had forced him to get personally involved.

He had seven men with him, and two swift skiffs. Having so many people further decreased the profit from the stolen merchandise, but it also made the operation less dangerous.

Most of the flatboats would have a crew of no more than

three or four men, and often, the hands were mere boys. There were always guns aboard, but rarely were the boat crews prepared for a swift attack, especially from a force of eight men. On several previous occasions the crew had abandoned the boat at the first sign of attack, thus leaving Eby and his men with nothing to do but pull the flatboat ashore and begin unloading.

At the moment, Eby was high in a tree, using a spyglass to search upriver. Below him, a few of his men were playing cards, while a couple others were throwing their knives at a tree. One was sound asleep.

"Damn you, Philbin! I know damn well you didn't have that card!" one of the cardplayers exclaimed.

"You men shut up down there! You want to queer the whole deal for us?" Eby shouted.

Eby had no sooner finished his scolding than he heard laughter. The laughter had not come from any of his men, so he opened the telescope and began the search.

In addition to the laughter, he heard someone speaking. Then he saw the boat coming around the bend, some one thousand yards upriver.

Eby snapped the telescope shut, then slid down the tree and joined the others. He wore a smile that spread all across his face.

"Here comes one, boys, and from the way she's ridin' in the water I'd say she's a fat one."

"How many men?" Philbin asked.

"Only three."

"We got us easy pickin's, boys," Philbin said. "Easy pickin's."

Each of Eby's men was armed with two pistols and one rifle. For the next couple of minutes, they busied themselves priming, charging, and loading their weapons. Then, when all was in readiness, they moved down to the skiffs, climbed into the boats, and waited.

Eby watched as the awkward flatboat maneuvered into the mainstream. It began to drift to one side.

"Earl, get her back in the middle and keep her there," the

flatboat master said. "Else we'll ground on a sandbar, then I'll have you three boys out, standin' in cold water up to your ass, pushing us off. And with the weight we're a'carryin', that ain't goin' to be no easy task."

"Yes, sir, Mr. Varner," the boy on the tiller said.

"Shoot the boy on the tiller first," Eby whispered to the others. "With him dead, they'll start driftin', and like as not they'll wind up on one of the sand shoals."

Two of Eby's men, the better marksmen, aimed at the tiller. They waited until Eby gave them the word.

"Now!" Eby said.

Both rifles boomed as if one, and the heavy impact of two large-caliber balls knocked the helmsman overboard. He floated away from the boat.

"Earl!" one of the other boys shouted.

"Never mind him, boys. Get your guns!" Varner shouted.

"Go!" Eby commanded, and the two skiffs pulled out into the river, then paddled hard toward the flatboat. True to Eby's prediction, the flatboat hung up on a sandbar.

Guns boomed and smoke billowed across the water as the pirates and the flatboat crew exchanged fire. The master of the flatboat went down almost immediately, and the two remaining boys were killed soon after that. By the time to two skiffs reached the boat, there was nothing left of the fight but the sight and smell of gunsmoke, now hanging in a great cloud over the river.

"Careful, boys," Eby cautioned as they climbed aboard. "Could be someone's left alive, just hidin' out."

With guns and knives drawn, the pirates climbed onto the flatboat. The master lay on his back at the stern of the boat, eyes open and looking sightlessly into the bright, blue sky. The other two crewmen, boys of no more than thirteen or fourteen, lay dead as well, one amidship, the other near the bow. The third boy, the one who had been the helmsmen, was in the water, facedown. He had drifted ashore into a growth of cypress trees, and was now hung up on one of the gnarled roots.

"All right, boys," Eby said, putting his gun away. "Looks like we're in the clear. Let's start unloading."

Eby jerked the canvas cover off the stack in the middle, then bellowed out loud.

"Bibles!" he growled angrily. "This entire boat is loaded with Bibles! What the hell are we going to do with them?"

"Maybe we can sell 'em," Philbin suggested. "I know lots of folks with Bibles."

"Look what's printed on the cover," Eby said disgustedly. "How are we going to sell them?"

"I can't read," Philbin said. "What's it say?"

Eby picked up one of the Bibles and read from the cover. "This Bible printed especially for St. Mary Catholic Church, New Orleans," he said. With a roar of frustrated anger, he threw the Bible out into the river.

"But stealing is wrong," Art told Tolian.

"When you were white, you did honor to the things that were white," Tolian said. "But now you are Shawnee, and you must do honor to the things which are Shawnee. There is great honor for the Shawnee to steal from his enemy. If you wish to become accepted as a warrior, you must steal a horse from the camp of the Osage."

"Very well," Art said. "I will go with you tonight."

Since coming to Keytano's village nearly a year ago, Art had learned a great deal about the Shawnee, including their history. He knew about their God, Moneto, a supreme being who ruled the entire universe, dispensing blessings on those who earned his favor and sorrow upon those who displeased him. He had already known about the great Shawnee leader, Tecumseh.

But he learned also that it wasn't just the whites who did battle with the Shawnee. They had been displaced from their ancestral lands by other Indian nations, forced out of Pennsylvania and Ohio into Kentucky, Indiana, and Illinois. Now the Shawnee were scattered over a wide area, and Keytano and his band had crossed into Missouri. But here, they encountered Osage and Missouri Indians.

Keytano's group had built a village on the Castor River, in an area of the Missouri Territory that was unoccupied, either by the whites or any other Indian tribes. But even though they'd tried to find an uninhabited area, the Osage, their nearest Indian neighbors, didn't appreciate the encroachment, and often sent hunting parties to take game from areas close to the Shawnee. They did this, not due to a lack of game near their own villages, but rather as a show of possession.

Because there were many more Osage than Shawnee in Missouri now, Keytano was very careful not to provoke them into war. But from time to time, young Shawnee warriors would prove their courage by individual acts of bravery. Tolian had planned an act of bravery, and invited Art to go with him. He was going to sneak into the Osage hunting camp, steal a horse, then return.

It was much easier said than done. The nearest Osage village was three hours ride away. If Art and Tolian left just after sundown and rode hard, they would reach the Osage village in the middle of the night. They could take the horses and be back just before sunup . . . provided they weren't caught.

As planned, they reached the village at about midnight. The Osage encampment was pitched on the banks of a small stream, and Art could see, by the light of the moon dancing on the water, about a dozen lodges. He also saw a remuda of horses. The remuda was right in the center of the village, so that he and Tolian would have to pass by the lodges in order to reach it.

They tied their horses to a bush, then got down on their hands and knees and began crawling toward the village. They had both practiced crawling great distances for several nights, and two nights ago, Art had crawled from a long distance outside their village into the wigwam of Metacoma. There, he had stolen one of Metacoma's most prized feathers, then worn it proudly the next morning for all to see.

"I took it from you as you slept last night," Art said, returning the feather to the angry Metacoma.

Now, the stealth Art and Tolian had practiced would be put to the maximum test, for if one of the sleeping Osage villagers woke up to see them, they would be killed.

A dog barked, but both Art and Tolian had come prepared. Each was wearing a sack full of bones around his neck. They opened the sacks and scattered the bones. The dogs converged on the bones, and in a moment's time, were completely absorbed in their eating.

Art and Tolian were right outside one of the lodges when a warrior came out. Art felt a quick stab of fear shoot through him, and he dropped to his stomach and lay very quietly, looking up at the warrior. Art held a knife in his hand, watching warily as the warrior relieved himself, then walked over toward the remuda for a look at the horses.

Finally, after what seemed like an eternity, the warrior went back inside. Art and Tolian lay quiet for a few moments longer, then cautiously slipped over to the remuda.

As they tried to grab a couple of the horses, the animals whinnied and stamped and snorted, and Art was afraid that someone would come out to see what was going on.

"Easy, horses," he said in English. He could speak Shawnee now, but still, in moments of stress and tension, he slipped naturally into English. "Easy, horses. We are just going to take a little trip together. Now, wouldn't you like that?"

Finally Art's soothing talk calmed the horses, and he and Tolian threw halters around two beautifully spotted ponies and began leading them out of the village.

They had nearly made it back to their own horses when

they were jumped by an Osage sentry! The attack caught Art completely by surprise, and he was knocked flat. He looked up in terror to see the sentry, who was grinning from ear to ear, about to come down on him with a raised tomahawk.

But the sentry, who was much older than Art, grew careless. Intent only upon claiming coup on the would-be horse thief, he didn't notice Tolian come upon him. With a furious shout, Tolian drove his knife deep into the Osage's stomach. The Osage tried to twist away, but that was the worst thing he could do, for it caused Tolian's knife to make a fatal tear across his abdomen. The Osage fell to the ground with a death rattle in his throat.

Tolian pulled the knife out, cleaned it, then slipped it back into his scabbard. He looked at the man he had just killed, then immediately turned away and threw up.

Art remembered his own feelings when he had killed the river pirate, and he knew exactly what his friend was going through.

"Come, my brother," Art said, getting up from the ground. "We must go quickly."

Tolian stood there for a moment longer, looking down at the dead Osage sentry.

"Come," Art said again, putting his hand on Tolian's shoulder.

"Wait," Tolian said. Tolian dropped to one knee beside the Osage, grabbed the dead man's hair, put his knife to the sentry's scalp, then turned his face away as he completed the scalping.

"Now we can go," he said, holding the bloody scalp in his hand.

When they returned, they showed the horses they had stolen, and Tolian displayed the Osage's scalp. As a result of their adventure, both Tolian and Art were made warriors. That entitled them to sit in, and participate in all, future war councils. This action raised the young men's status in the eyes of the other villagers, but it created so much jealousy in Metacoma that it just widened the gulf that was already there.

"I am in your debt," Tolian told Art when the two were talking later that day.

"How are you in my debt?"

"You did not tell the others that I was weak like a woman, and that I became sick, when I killed the Osage."

Art started to tell Tolian that he too had become sick after killing for the first time, but he stopped short of saying the words. To tell Tolian that he had already killed might be construed as bragging.

"You saved my life, my brother," Art said. "You are the bravest warrior I know."

"Yes, and now your life belongs to me," Tolian replied. "I must watch out for you for all time. You will become my burden. Perhaps it would have been better to let the Osage have your scalp." Tolian laughed, and ran his hand through Art's hair.

It was being on the war council that brought to an end Art's idyllic sojourn with the Indians. Keytano called all the warriors together to hear a redcoat warrior chief.

Since Art and Tolian were very new warriors, as well as the youngest, their seats on the council were on the very last circle. This was good, because Art was far enough from the center of the circle that their visitor, a major in His Majesty's Army, did not realize that Art was white.

"To Keytano, Chief of the mighty Shawnee, I, Major Sir John Loxley, bring greetings from General Sir Edward Parkenham, on behalf of His Royal Britannic Majesty," the red-coated officer said.

Keytano translated the words for his warriors.

"As you may know," Major Loxley continued, "His Royal Highness is presently at war with the United States. The Shawnee nation, aware of His Majesty's high regard for your people, and equally aware of the mistreatment you have received at the hands of the Americans, have been wise enough to form an alliance with England.

"I am here to call upon that alliance now, and ask that you make war against all Americans who are west of the Mississippi River. If we are successful in inflicting serious damage to this distant frontier of the United States, we shall, when we sue for peace, inherit all of the Louisiana Territory. Such territory, to be called British Louisiana, will then be closed to any further colonization, and will be preserved as a permanent sanctuary for our Shawnee friends."

As Keytano translated the last paragraph, the Indians whooped their appreciation.

"Ask the English officer what he would have us do," Techanka said.

"New Madrid, Cape Girardeau, Sainte Genevieve, and St. Louis are important towns along the river," the major replied after the question was translated for him.

"But, of those towns, St. Louis is too large, and Sainte Genevieve is nearly as large and is also quite far. That leaves Cape Girardeau or New Madrid as possible targets, and after some consideration, we have decided that you can be most effective by striking at Cape Girardeau. It is a river town of no more than five hundred, though it is becoming a river port of increasing importance."

"Are there soldiers at Cape Girardeau?" someone asked.

"Only two or three," Loxley answered. "And that makes it an even more attractive target, for New Madrid has been well fortified. Now, in return for your attacking the Americans at Cape Girardeau, we are prepared to furnish you with one hundred rifles and ten thousand rounds of ammunition."

In the entire village there were only two rifles. One of the rifles belonged to Keytano, the other to Techanka. At the British officer's offer of one hundred rifles and ten thousand rounds of ammunition, the Indians began to shout and whoop in excitement. No longer able to stay quiet in the camp, they leaped up and began dancing around, making signs as if they were already holding a rifle.

"Eeeeeyaaaa!" Tolian shouted, his excitement as great as that of anyone else.

"Understand, I cannot give you those weapons until after you have proven your loyalty to the Crown. You must make your first attack with whatever weapons you now possess. But after you have proven yourselves, I will return with the promised weapons," Loxley said. "My friends, I wish you success in your battle against our common enemy, the Americans."

After Loxley left, the Shawnee conducted war dances and sang their war chants. Then they broke up to apply their own medicine to the weapons at hand, and to invoke the blessing of Moneto on their endeavor.

Art participated as fully as any of the others in all of the war preparations, to include dancing, whooping, singing, and painting his face and body with the special symbols that gave him his personal medicine. After the ceremonies, it was time to feast. Everyone ate well, for though Loxley had held back the rifles, he had brought two pigs and three goats. When all went to bed that night, the air was redolent with the aroma of the evening's banquet.

Art lay in his blankets inside the wigwam, listening to the measured breathing and quiet snores of Tolian and his sister, Sasheen, as well as Techanka and his wife. The wigwam was warm and comfortable because of the heat that radiated from the stones that encircled the still-glowing coals. A burning ember popped, sending up a brief shower of sparks.

Art was troubled. Although he had participated in the war dance, and had painted his body with the symbols of his own personal medicine, he did not want to go to war against the men, women, and children of Cape Girardeau. That would be like going to war against his relatives, friends, and neighbors back in Ohio, for they were not only white, as he was, they were also American.

He could refuse to join the war party when they left the next morning, but to do so would open him up to the charge of cowardice. Metacoma especially would point out to the others that Art had no stomach for war. And though Tolian would be more generous in his treatment, his private assessment of the situation wouldn't be that different.

Another popping ember from the burning wood caused Art to look back at the fire.

He gasped.

"Grandfather!" he said. "How did you . . . ?"

Keytano held up his hand, as if cautioning Art to be quiet. Keytano's deerskin breeches and shirt were bleached nearly white. The shirt was decorated with an eagle, made from colored beads. He was wearing a vest, like the one that had been the prize in the coming-of-age games. Art knew Keytano had won the vest nearly fifty years ago. Keytano was carrying a feathered staff, also a personal totem from his past.

Art had never seen Keytano dressed in such a fashion, and he wondered why he was wearing such clothes now. These weren't the clothes of someone about to go to war. This was ceremonial dress of the highest order.

"You are troubled," Keytano said. "You do not want to go to war against the Americans because you are American."

"I am . . . Shawnee," Art replied.

"Yes, you are Shawnee," Keytano agreed. "And though you told us you were English, I know that you are American. Now you are a warrior with two hearts. Both hearts are strong and both hearts should be obeyed. Your American heart tells you not to go to war against Americans and so you should not."

"But my Shawnee heart?"

"Someday you will leave the Shawnee and return to your own people," Keytano said. "Even though you will be with your own people, you will still have a Shawnee heart. If the

Americans go to war against the Shawnee, then you must listen to your Shawnee heart."

"I could never make war against the Shawnee," Art said. He looked down at his hands, then held them up to examine them, as if contemplating the white skin. "Just as I cannot make war against Americans. I am pleased that you are wise and can under . . ." Art looked up, then gasped again. Keytano was gone.

"Keytano?"

"Aiiiieeeee! Aiiieeeee! Techanka! Techanka!" a woman's voice cried from outside the wigwam. Her voice was loud and piercing and it awakened everyone inside. They were just sitting up as the woman stuck her head in through the opening. It was Techanka's mother, Keytano's wife.

"Mother, what is it?" Techanka asked. "Why are you crying so?"

"It is Keytano," she said. "He is dead."

Art jumped up from his blankets. Keytano must have fallen dead just outside. He hurried outside, but there was no Keytano to be seen.

"Where is he?" Art asked, looking around.

"He is here," Keytano's wife said, pointing to her wigwam.

By now several of the others had gathered, attracted by the wailing and the commotion. Art followed Techanka into the wigwam.

Keytano was lying on a bed of fur and blankets. His eyes were open but unseeing. Techanka dropped to his knees beside his father, then reached down to close his eyes. While still touching him, Techanka began to chant the Shawnee funeral song. The funeral song expressed grief over the loss, confidence in Keytano's entering the Spirit World, and thanks to Moneto for allowing others to share in Keytano's life.

As Techanka sang, his wife and Keytano's widow began making preparations for the purification. Part of the purification called for the dressing of Keytano in his funereal clothes.

Techanka's mother unwrapped a parcel, made of deer hide. This was Keytano's personal totem bundle, and inside were his clothes, clothes that were as secret and private to the individual as the contents of a medicine bag. Although the feathered staff and the vest had been seen by others, until this moment, nobody but Keytano and his wife had ever seen the breeches and shirt.

Except Art.

Art had seen it all, just a few minutes earlier, when Keytano came to visit him.

Art sneaked out of the village before light the next morning, a few hours before the attack was to take place. He'd planned to take one of the horses from the village, but changed his mind at the last minute, deciding that if he took one he would be branded a thief. He didn't know if he would ever return to the Shawnee, but if he did decide to come back, he wanted to be welcomed. He had arrived at the Shawnee village without a horse, and he would leave without one. Except for the clothes he was wearing, and the knife at his waist, Art took nothing away that he hadn't brought to the village.

His had gone about five miles when he saw a campfire. Curious as to who it might be, he approached it cautiously, until he saw that it was Major Loxley and two other British soldiers. Sneaking up as close to them as he could, he listened in on their conversation.

"Sir John, you aren't really going to give those Indians firearms, are you?" one of the men asked.

"Heavens, no," Loxley replied. "Once our victory is complete, I am to be governor of this wretched area. Do you actually think I would want a bunch of armed savages to contend with?"

"But without guns, their attack against Cape Girardeau will surely fail," one of the soldiers said. "True, there are no American soldiers there to defend the town, but nearly all of the citizens of the town are armed, and they have blockhouses to retreat to in the event of an attack."

"It doesn't matter. The attack on Cape Girardeau is but a ruse. I fully expect the Indians to fail, and no doubt with a substantial loss of life."

"Loss of whose life?"

Loxley laughed. "Indian, American, it's all the same to us. The more of the blighters who are killed, the easier it will be for us to control the situation after we take over." Using a burning ember, Loxley lit his pipe. "Now, you two get back to Leftenant Whitman. Tell him to move the men into the boats so that we may proceed to Commerce. But make certain that he understands he is not to launch the attack until I am there to take command. With the Indians providing a diversion at Cape Girardeau, Commerce will fall into our hands like a ripe plum."

Both men saluted, then mounted their horses and rode off. Loxley moved over to a tree where, undoing his pants, he began to urinate. Taking advantage of Loxley's distraction, Art sneaked into the camp. The skills he had learned with the Shawnee were particularly helpful now, for he was able to pick up Loxley's rifle and pull back the hammer before Loxley even knew he was there.

When he heard the hammer being cocked, Loxley froze. "My dear sir," he said calmly, and without turning around. "You seem to have caught me in a most awkward position."

"I reckon I have," Art said.

"May I turn, sir?"

"You can turn."

Slowly, Loxley turned to face Art. "Blimey, you're but a boy," he said.

"I'm a boy that's holding a gun on you," Art replied.

"Wait a minute, I've seen you before," Loxley said, staring closely at Art. He raised his hand and pointed. "Yes, now I know. You were at the Shawnee War Council yesterday, weren't you? But you're not Shawnee, are you?"

"I'm an American," Art said.

"An American, you say? Well, it would appear, then, that we have a rather taxing situation here, don't we?"

Art didn't answer.

"Yes, indeed," Loxley said. He took a couple of puffs from his pipe and studied Art through the cloud of smoke that his action generated. "So, what are you going to do now?"

"I don't know," Art said. "I'm not sure."

"Are you familiar with the game of chess, young man?"

"No."

"Ah, it's too bad. You really should take up the game sometime. It's a wonderful game. But there is a saying we have in chess. The saying is, it is your move."

"My move?"

"Yes, dear boy. That means that whatever happens now is up to you. So, what now?"

Art hadn't really given the situation any thought beyond this moment. He wasn't sure what he should do, but somehow he knew that he had to stop the attacks on Cape Girardeau by the Indians, and on Commerce by the British.

"We're going back to the Indian village," he said. "You're going to tell them that you lied to them about the guns and ammunition you said you would give them."

"And why, pray tell, would I do that?"

"Because I'm holding a gun on you," Art said.

"Indeed you are," Loxley said. He smiled. "Fortunately for me, but unfortunately for you, the pan in the rifle you are holding isn't primed. Whereas, the pan in this pistol is." He pulled a pistol from his belt and pointed it at Art.

Art pulled the trigger and the hammer snapped forward. There was a spark from the flintlock mechanism, but no flash in the pan and no discharge. Loxley was telling the truth.

Art looked down at the inert rifle, then out of the corner of his eye, saw that Loxley was about to pull the trigger on his pistol. Art jumped to one side just as Loxley fired. The pistol ball missed, though it came so close that he could feel the wind of its passing.

Tossing his pistol aside, Loxley pulled his sword, then smiling confidently, advanced slowly toward Art.

"It is almost heresy to put you to sword," he said as he made tiny circles with the sword point. "Only those whose names are recognized by the peerage are entitled to the blade. And you, sir, have no name." He laughed. "I know, I shall give you a name of the peerage. I will give you the name of an old arch-enemy of mine. I dub thee Sir Gregory of Windom Shire."

With three quick slashes of his sword, Loxley brought blood from Art's left shoulder, his forehead, then his right shoulder. When he stepped back, Art could see his own blood on the blade of the sword, and he could feel the sting of the cuts the blade had inflicted. He put his hand his forehead, touched the wound, then brought it back down to see the blood on the tips of his fingers.

"Sting a little, did it, Sir Gregory?" Now Loxley was standing sideways with his left hand on his hip, his right side and the extended sword toward Art.

"You say this fella Gregory is an enemy of yours?"

"Oh, yes, an enemy of quite long standing," Loxley said. He did a sudden thrust, which almost caught Art. Only his lightning-quick reflexes enabled him to avoid being skewered.

"Well, if Gregory is your enemy, then that's a good enough name for me," Art said.

Loxley danced toward Art, still presenting only his right side as a target. Art had drawn his knife, but it was totally inadequate against the sword. But though he couldn't counterattack, he was quick enough and dexterous enough to avoid every thrust.

Then disaster struck. While avoiding one of Loxley's increasingly closer thrusts, Art tripped and fell flat on his back.

In a heartbeat Loxley was on him, with the point of his sword just over Art's chest.

"It's over, lad," Loxley said, panting from the effort of chasing Art about. "You've been quite a pest. My only regret is that you are going to die too quickly."

Loxley was just about to make the final death lunge when an arrow whistled over Art and buried itself in Loxley's chest. Loxley dropped his sword and reached up to grab the arrow. Even as he wrapped his fingers around it, however, the light faded from his eyes and he collapsed across Art's legs.

Quickly, Art scrambled out from under Loxley's body, then stood up to see Techanka and Tolian coming toward him. Behind them were at least three dozen others from the village.

"So, my brother," Tolian said. "Again I have killed another to save your life."

"Yes," Art replied.

"You left early," Techanka said. "Did you plan to attack the Americans without us?"

Art drew a deep breath, then shook his head. "No," he said. "I did not plan to attack the Americans at all."

"This I knew," Techanka said. "It came to me in a dream last night. It is good that you did not lie."

"This too is not a lie," Art said. "The red soldiers will not give you guns and ammunition. I heard them talking. They want you to attack the town of Cape Girardeau so that they may attack another town, Commerce."

"Yes, that is a good plan. We attack one place while the red soldiers attack another," Techanka said.

"Wait a minute, you aren't still planning to attack Cape Girardeau, are you?"

"Yes."

"But why? Don't you understand what I told you? The British want your attack to fail. They want many Indians and many Americans to be killed."

"We must attack. Keytano gave his word," Techanka said. "It is not for me to break the word of Keytano."

"But many of you will be killed."

"We are not like you," Metacoma said. "We are not cowards who fear death."

Techanka held up his hand to still Metacoma. Then he looked at Art. "Go, now," he said. "You are no longer my son. You are no longer the brother of Tolian. You are no longer Shawnee."

"I am not the enemy of the Shawnee," Art said.

"Today, you are not the enemy of the Shawnee. But if we meet again, and if my people are at war with your people, we will be enemies."

Art looked toward Loxley's horse. If he had the horse, he might be able to reach Cape Girardeau before the Shawnee. Then he could at least warn them of the impending attack. But the thought came too late. By rights the horse belonged to Tolian, who had killed the major, and Tolian was already holding the animal, talking to it in soft, comforting tones. Whatever was going to happen at Cape Girardeau and Commerce was going to happen. With a sigh of frustration, Art turned and walked away.

12

There was no getting around it. St. Louis just had too many people. Everywhere Art looked he saw people, moving up and down the boardwalks, crowding into the stores and overflowing the dram shops. The streets were filled too, with men on horseback as well as carriages, carts, and wagons, drawn by horses, mules, and oxen. It had rained recently, and the street was a quagmire of manure and mud.

But it was the smells that Art was having the hardest time with. Having spent just over a year living in the great outdoors with the Indians, he found the pungency of manure and rotting garbage, as well as several other unidentifiable odors, nearly overpowering. Some St. Louis citizens countered the odor by holding perfumed handkerchiefs to their nose, but most seemed adjusted to it.

The clothes Art had left home with had worn out long ago and he was now wearing buckskins; both shirt and trousers. Although most of the people he saw were wearing more traditional clothing, there were enough dressed in buckskins to keep him from being totally out of place. Only his hair was a little different from the others, as it was long and braided into pigtails. He did see several men with long hair, but no one else was wearing pigtails, so he undid his own, then shook his head, letting his hair fall freely to his shoulders.

Art had managed quite well in the woods, easily finding his way to St. Louis. He had learned from the Indians how to trap rabbit and squirrel for his meals, as well as what roots and plants he could eat. Also, as he followed the river north, he'd had an abundance supply of fish. But survival in St. Louis required a different set of skills. Here, money was more important than hunting or trapping, and Art didn't have one cent to his name.

Even as he was contemplating his lack of money, he happened across a possible remedy when he walked past a freight warehouse. Here, one wagon was being unloaded and two more were waiting to be moved up to the warehouse dock.

"I don't know where he is, Mr. Gordon," he heard one of the men say to another. "This is the third day this month he ain't showed up when he was supposed to."

Mr. Gordon, who was apparently the foreman of the warehouse, walked over to the edge of the loading dock and spat a stream of tobacco juice. He wiped his mouth with the back of his hand, then reached down into a pouch for a fresh supply.

"I'd fire James right now if I could find someone else to work in his place."

"They ain't that many people want to work unloadin' wagons," the first man said. "It's hard work."

Art turned and walked back to the dock. "Mr. Gordon?" he said.

Gordon was obviously surprised to be addressed by name by someone he had never seen before. "Who are you?" Gordon asked, pausing before he stuffed a handful of the tobacco into his mouth. "And how do you know my name?" He poked in a few of the loose ends.

"I heard this man address you by name," Art explained. "I

also heard you say you would hire someone if you could find them. Well, I need a job, and I'm not afraid of hard work."

"I appreciate the offer, son, but you ain't nothin' but a boy," Gordon said. "This here is man's work."

Putting his hand on the side of the wagon and his foot on a wheel spoke, Art vaulted up into the back of the wagon. The wagon was loaded with barrels of flour. Art picked up a barrel, lifted it easily to his shoulder, then carried it over to a pile of similar barrels on the dock. He put his load down, then turned around and looked at Gordon.

"Is there anything to do any harder than what I just did?" he asked.

Gordon laughed, spitting a few pieces of tobacco as he did. "No, not that I know of," he said. "You willin' to do that all day long for a dollar?"

"Yes, sir."

"Then you got yourself a job, boy. I'm Gordon, that fella there is Tony. You do what Tony tells you to do, and you'll be all right. What's your name?"

"I'm Art."

"Art what? What's your last name?"

Art paused for a moment. His unwillingness to use his last name had caused difficulty for him back in Commerce. Many slaves did not have last names, and when he didn't give his, the sheriff was ready to believe that he was a slave. He still didn't want to use his family name, not so much to avoid being found now, for he was certain his parents had long since given up the search, but because he didn't want to take a chance on bringing any dishonor to the name. Then he remembered the name of Major Loxley's enemy. "Gregory," he said. "My name is Art Gregory. But please, call me Art."

"Art, is it?" Gordon looked over at Tony. "Tony, here's your new helper. His name is Art."

"Well, Art, grab yourself another barrel," Tony said, picking up one of his own. "We got two more wagons to do after this one."

"Yes, sir," Art said, going right to work.

Gordon stood by, watching Art and Tony at their labor for a moment or two. Then satisfied that Art was going to work out, he went on his way.

It was after dark before all the wagons were unloaded. Tony, Art's coworker, was a heavy-limbed man with broad shoulders but a prominent belly. He was bald on top of his head, but wore a full beard. A scar ran from the bottom of his left eye, down across his cheek, and into a misshapen lip. His two top front teeth were missing. Although it was relatively cool, both Tony and Art had worked up a sweat, and Tony wiped his face with a towel, then tossed the towel to Art.

"Thanks," Art said.

"You're all right, boy," Tony said. "I thought I might have to carry your load too, but you matched me lift for lift. I'm glad Mr. Gordon put you on."

"I am too," Art said.

"Come on, let's go to the Irish Tavern and get us a beer," Tony suggested.

"I'll have to get paid first," Art said. "Where do we go to get paid?"

"Paid? We don't get paid till Saturday. That's payday."

"We don't get paid today?"

"No, sir. Like I said, no pay till Saturday."

"Oh," Art said, disappointment obvious in his voice. "What day is this?"

"Tuesday, the eighteenth."

"What month?"

"What month?" Tony replied. He laughed. "Where you been, boy? It's October eighteenth, 1814."

"I sort of figured it was getting on toward fall."

Tony studied Art for a long moment. "Where you been, boy, that you don't even know what month this is?"

"I've been sort of drifting around," Art replied, not wanting to be too specific with his answer. "Here and there."

"Uh-huh. And you ain't got no money. I mean, you ain't got one dime, have you?"

"No, sir, I reckon not."

"What the hell, boy? How was you plannin' on eatin' between now and Saturday?"

"I'll get by. I can always go down to the river and catch a fish. Or I can go out into the woods. A body can never starve in the woods."

"The hell you say. You must know the woods pretty good to say that. I mean, if I suddenly found myself in the woods like that, I'd probably starve."

Art remembered his first experience in the woods. If he had not been found by Techanka and the other Shawnee that day, he would have starved.

"It is something you have to learn," Art admitted. "You can't just go out into the woods and start living off the land."

"So, you're what? Plannin' on goin' into the woods tonight, then comin' back in tomorrow to work?"

"Yes, sir, I reckon I've got to do that. I don't know any other way to get anything to eat, other than to catch it and kill it myself."

"Wait a minute," Tony said, holding up his finger. "If you really need money all that bad, let me go talk to Mr. Gordon. Perhaps we can talk him into paying you ahead of time."

"You don't have to do that," Art said.

"Yeah, I do. You're a good worker and I don't want you to up and quit. Else, I might wind up with James again."

Tony turned out to be an effective advocate for Art's cause, for two minutes later he returned with a silver dollar, which he ceremoniously presented to Art.

"Now, what do you say we get us that beer?" Tony asked.

"Do you mind if I get somethin' to eat first?"

"You can eat at the same place we get the beer," Tony said.

The Irish Tavern was run by Seamus O'Conner, a large, round-faced Irishman who wasn't opposed to delivering a homily with the whiskey, beer, and food he served in his establishment. He kept order in the place by the judicious use of a sawed-off piece of a hoe handle, and more than one drunk who began making trouble would wake up in the alley behind the Irish Tavern with a headache that wasn't entirely brought on by drink.

Art had a meal of corned beef, cabbage, and potatoes fried with onions. Tony, who had three beers while Art was eating, sat across the table from him, marveling at the young man's prodigious appetite.

"How long's it been since you et, boy?" Tony asked.

"I had me a squirrel a couple of days ago," Art said.

"A squirrel?"

Art nodded.

"You ain't been livin' in the city, have you?"

Art shook his head no.

"Where you been?"

"Like I said, I've been sort of wanderin' around the last year or so." Art wasn't ashamed of the time he spent with the Shawnee, but if they had carried through with their plans to attack Cape Girardeau, it might not be a good idea to be associated with them.

"Where is he now?" a loud voice suddenly asked. "Would someone be for tellin' me where I can find the whore's son who took the job o' James O'Leary?"

"Oh-oh," Tony said, looking toward the door.

Art, who had his back to the door, looked around. A large man, one of the biggest men Art had ever seen, was standing just inside the door, his face set in an angry scowl.

"Who is that?" Art asked.

"That would be James O'Leary," Tony replied.

At about that same moment James plowed into the room, heading for the table where the two were having their supper. James was focused entirely on the task at hand and he rushed forward, bent forward at the waist. He made no effort to go around the furnishings, but pushed through them, leaving tables and chairs overturned in his wake. Others in the saloon, not wanting to incur James's anger, jumped up and moved out of the way, giving the big man plenty of room.

"You?" he said, pointing to Art when he got closer to him. "Would it be you who took my job now?"

"I took *a* job," Art said. "It wasn't your job, because you weren't there."

"Now, he's got you there, James, m'boy," Tony said, trying to ease the situation. "You know yourself, you been absent from work more than you been there. And I don't mind tellin' you, that's made it a lot harder on me."

"I'll be hearin' no blarney from the likes of a black-heart like you," James said to Tony. "Sure'n this is between me and . . ." When James looked directly at Art, he stopped in mid-sentence and the expression on his face changed. It wasn't until then that he noticed just how young Art was. "Faith 'n begorrah, how old would you be now?" he asked.

"I'm old enough to do the work I was hired for," Art replied.

"Aye, lad, but the question is, would you be man enough to hold on to the job?"

"He more than held his own, James. Which is more than I can say for you when you show up drunk," Tony said.

"'Tis not the work I'm inquirin' about now. 'Tis the lad's will to hold on to what he's got. How about it, boy? Are you man enough to fight for your job?" James asked, smiling evilly at Art. He put up his fists. "What say you we have a bit of a brawl? Just the two of us, right here, right now. Whoever wins the fight keeps the job."

"Come on, James, you got near a hundred pounds on the boy," one of the others said.

"Yeah, if you're going to fight, make it a fair fight," another added.

"Well, now, you tell me how to make it fair and I'll be glad to be doin' that. But would you be for tellin' me how the I can make it fair for a little pissant that ain't no bigger'n a pup?" James asked.

"Give him the first punch," someone said.

"Yeah, that's it. Give him the first punch," another added.

"I'll give him the first punch. He can hit me anyway he likes," James said. He stuck his chin out.

"Wait," Seamus called from behind the bar.

"And for what would I be waitin'? Pray tell me that now, Seamus O'Conner."

"Let the lad take his first punch with this," Seamus said, holding up the sawed-off length of a hoe handle.

James looked at the hoe handle, then at Art. "All right lad, I'm game. I'll give you the first blow, and you can use the club. I wouldn't want anyone to be sayin' that James O'Leary took unfair advantage of a wee lad like you. But you better make it a good one, boy, 'cause afterward I intend to mop the floor with your sorry carcass."

"Here, lad," Seamus said, putting his club in Art's hand. "It has put more than one thickheaded Irishman on the floor."

Art took the club. It was about eighteen inches long and an inch in diameter.

"I don't want to fight," Art said, handing the club back to Seamus.

"See there, Seamus?" James replied. "The lad has no stomach to fight. He wants to just walk away and let me have my job back."

"No," Art said. "I didn't say that. I plan to keep the job. I just said I don't want to fight you."

"Well, laddie, sure'n you can't have it both ways now,"

James said. He took the club from the bartender and gave it back to Art. "You'll be for givin' up the job, or for fightin' me. Now, which is it to be?"

"I . . . I reckon I'm going to have to fight you," Art said.

A wide smile spread across James's face. "Tell me, lad, would you have any family in these parts?"

"Family?" Art asked, surprised by the question.

"Aye. I'm goin' to hurt you, boy. I'm goin' to hurt you real bad, and we're going to need to know who to notify after I break you in two."

Some of the others laughed, and James turned his head toward them to acknowledge their laughter. That was the opening Art was looking for, and he did something that was totally unexpected.

Using the section of hoe handle, Art jammed the end of it hard, just below the center of James's rib cage. That well-aimed blow to the solar plexus knocked all the wind out of James. He doubled over in pain, trying, without success, to gasp for breath.

Doubled over as he was, James's head was about even with Art's waist. This gave Art the perfect leverage for a smashing blow, and raising up on his toes, he used both hands to bring the club down hard. Everyone in the tavern heard the pop of the club as it hit the back of James's head. James fell face-down, then lay on the floor, not unconscious, but still gasping for breath and now totally disoriented.

Calmly, Art went back to his supper while several others bent down to check on James. Finally, they got James over on his back, and gradually he recovered his breath. Then, groggily, he got up and staggered over to a chair, where he sat for a while, leaning forward as if trying to recover his senses.

During this time the tavern was strangely quiet, as everyone looked toward James to see what he would do, then toward Art to see how he would react. To the abject shock of everyone present, Art showed no reaction at all. He continued to eat as calmly as if absolutely nothing had happened.

After several minutes, James got up, ran his hand over the bump on the back of his head, and looked over at the table toward Art.

"Hell," James said. "Sure'n I never wanted the goddamned job in the first place." He turned and left the tavern.

"Let's hear it for the boy!" someone shouted, and the room rang with "Huzzah!"

Over the next several weeks, Art worked hard and saved his money, using only what was necessary to buy food and some clothes. He even got a haircut so that he bore little resemblance to the half-wild boy who had wandered in to St. Louis fresh from the Shawnee village.

From newspaper stories he read, Art learned that the Shawnee had attacked Cape Girardeau. Though frightening, the attack had actually had little effect, because the entire population of Cape Girardeau was able to take shelter in a blockhouse that had been constructed down by the riverfront just for that purpose. In frustration, the Indians had burned some of the buildings of the town.

The newspaper article said that it was believed that the attack was due to the result of an alliance between the Shawnee and the British. It was pointed out, however, that since Tecumseh's death, there had been little activity from the Shawnee.

It appeared that Commerce was not attacked, and for a moment Art wondered why. Then he remembered that Major Loxley had given specific instructions not to launch the attack until he was present. And since he was killed, he'd never shown up to lead it.

As Art caught up with the news that had occurred since he left home, he learned that the war with England was not going very well for America. The invasion of Canada had failed, Washington, had been captured, the White House burned, and President Madison forced to flee for his life. It was said that he even spent one night in a chicken coop.

Art didn't know much about presidents and such. His father had told him that a president was sort of like a king, except he was elected by the people. Art didn't really know anything about kings either, but he was pretty sure that no king had ever spent a night in a chicken coop.

Much of the problem, according to the newspaper, was in the government's inability to recruit soldiers. Unless their own homes were directly threatened, nobody wanted to fight. It was difficult to get men from Ohio to fight in a battle that threatened only New York, and equally difficult to get New Yorkers to defend Virginia. As a result, the British could mass their troops in any one location and, despite the fact that they were fighting on America's soil, nearly always have the numerical advantage.

One evening, after Art got off work, he was contemplating his situation as he walked toward the room he had rented. His back hurt, his hands were calloused, and every muscle in his body ached. He was growing weary of the work. It wasn't that the work was too hard, or that he thought himself too good to do that kind of labor. It was just that he had left home to seek adventure, and he could hardly call loading and unloading freight wagons a fulfillment of that quest.

Then, as he passed the high-board fence that surrounded an empty lot, he noticed that a new bill of advertising had been posted with the other flyers that cluttered the wall. He paused to read it:

> *MEN OF COURAGE*
> *Gen'l Andrew Jackson of*
> *Tennessee seeks an army of patriots.*
> *MEN OF ADVENTURE*

You are called upon to
turn back the British despots
who have invaded our country.
Enlistments will take place at
LaClede's Landing
on Tuesday, the fifteenth Instant
whereupon a fifteen dollar signing
bonus will be paid.
You will receive a private's pay of
fifteen dollars per month,
plus all food and lodging.
JOIN NOW!
MEN OF COURAGE

The more Art thought about that offer, the better it sounded. The fifteen-dollar bonus would just about double the amount of money he had. And if his food and lodging were to be furnished, then there would be little need to spend any of his salary.

That was the practical side of Art's consideration, but it was not what finally tipped the scales in favor of enlisting. That decision came about because Art was ready to move on. Joining the army to fight in a war seemed like a natural next step in his search for adventure.

Art didn't give notice of his intent to quit his job until the night before he did so. He felt guilty about leaving Tony without an assistant, but James had come around several times over the last few weeks, sober and contrite, and anxious to help. Indeed, James had even done some part-time work, and Mr. Gordon had told him that he would consider rehiring him if another opportunity presented itself.

Art's leaving provided that opportunity. As a result, James and Tony invited Art to have a beer with them that night, as a means of saying good-bye. Tony lifted his mug of beer in a toast.

"You were a good coworker Art. I will miss you."

"Thank you," Art said.

"And if anyone would be for askin', I will tell them I learned a good lesson from you," James said, lifting his own mug.

"Oh?" Art replied. "And what lesson would that be?"

"Just because someone is a wee little shit, that don't mean he can't pack a punch like the kick of a mule. You can bet that James O'Leary will never again give the other man a chance to take a first punch," he said. He rubbed the back of his head.

Art and the others laughed and drank, far into the night.

13

The next morning dawned cold and threatening. Art gathered the few belongings he had and threw them in a rucksack. For just a moment he looked around at the little room where he had been living, saying good-bye to it for one last time.

On his belt Art wore the knife that he had brought to St. Louis, the one that given him by Keytano. In his pocket he had fourteen dollars and thirty-five cents. On his feet were a pair of real leather boots. He put on a recently purchased wool-lined coat as a guard against the weather, then stepped out into the cold, dreary day.

A little over eighteen months ago, a young, naïve, practically helpless young boy had slipped out of his parents' home with nothing to his name but three biscuits and an apple. Since that fateful morning he had been forced to kill a man, had been robbed, beaten, and left for dead, and had nearly starved in the woods. He had lived with a band of Indians who were the sworn enemies of Americans, then arrived empty-handed in a large and hostile city.

Despite all that, he now had clothes on his back, boots on his feet, and money in his pocket, all the result of his own enterprise. He was only fourteen years old, but in any way of measuring, he would be considered a man of means.

There were nearly forty people gathered at LaClede's Landing when Art arrived. A little surprised at the number, Art looked around at the other men who had gathered in response to the recruitment poster. This gathering appeared to represent men from all stations of St. Louis life. There were businessmen in suits, and laborers in rags. There were frontiersmen, backwoodsmen, farmers, and men of color, both Indian and black. There were people of all ages, from very old to quite young. Some of those gathered here were even younger than Art.

A table and a chair were set up at the head of the group. Someone was sitting in the chair, but from this angle, Art couldn't see him very well. He could see a second man, though, for he was standing. This man was wearing a military uniform of blue and buff.

"All right, you men, gather round," the man in uniform called out. There was a shuffling of feet as those who had gathered hastened to do his bidding.

"I am Sergeant Delacroix," the man in uniform explained. "But as far as you are concerned, I am God. You will, at all times, obey me and anyone else who is put in authority over you. Is that clear?"

"Yes, sir," the men said as one.

"Now I want you all to form a line right in front of this table, then come sign your name on the paper. As soon as you sign, you will be soldiers in the United States Army."

"When do we get our fifteen dollars?" one of the men asked.

"What's your name?" Delacroix asked.

"Mitchell. Lou Mitchell."

"Well, Mitchell, you'll receive your money soon as you get on the boat."

"I got me a wife'll be needin' that money, mister. It ain't gonna do her no good, that money bein' on the boat with me."

"It's sergeant, not mister," Delacroix corrected. "And as far as your wife is concerned, she can come down to the boat to see you off 'n you can give her the money then."

Mitchell seemed satisfied with the answer and he nodded affirmatively. Delacroix looked out over the others. "Any more questions?"

There were none.

"Then line up here at the table and commence signing, those of you who are going to sign. Anybody who ain't goin' to sign may as well leave now."

A few men left, but most of them formed a line. As they waited, they laughed and spoke excitedly to each other. Not wanting to push his way in front of anyone else, Art moved patiently to the end of the line along with several of the very young boys.

"You boys," Sergeant Delacroix called to them, making a shooing motion toward the younger bunch. "There ain't no need in you boys a'hangin' aroun' here. The U.S. Army ain't about to waste no time with babies."

Grumbling, the young boys left, but Art stayed. He no longer considered himself a young boy. Besides, he was fairly sure that the sergeant wasn't referring to him, and even if he was, he believed that if he pressed the issue, he might get away with it.

Evidently, the sergeant had other ideas.

"That means you too, boy," Sergeant Delacroix said to Art. "I got no time to be givin' you sugar titties to suck on. Get on, now, like I said. This here is for full-growed men only."

"Hold it there, Sergeant Delacroix," someone called. There was a haunting familiarity to the voice. "If this lad wants to join up with us, I'll be glad to have him."

"But, Cap'n, he's just a pup."

"He's more than a pup. How are you doing, Art? I haven't seen you in a while."

Art had begun smiling from the moment he heard the voice. The man who had been sitting at the table now stood. This was the captain, and Art was surprised to see that it was none other than Pete Harding, the boatman Art had come down the Ohio with.

"Mr. Harding," Art said happily, sticking his hand out. "It's good to see you again."

"That's *Captain* Harding to you, boy," Sergeant Delacroix corrected, putting emphasis on the word "Captain."

"Captain Harding," Art said.

"So you want to join up with us, do you?" Harding asked.

"Yes, sir, I sure do."

"Well, we'll be happy to have you," Harding said. "Sergeant, I want you to sign this young fella up. And don't be fooled by his age. I know him to be a good man."

"Very well, Cap'n, if you say so," Sergeant Delacroix replied begrudgingly. "What's your name, boy?"

"Gregory," Art said. "Art Gregory."

"Say, Mr. Delacroix," one of the others said, speaking to the sergeant.

"It's *Sergeant* Delacroix," Delacroix explained again. "If you recruits don't learn the ways of the Army, I'll make you wish you had."

"All right, Sergeant, then," the recruit said. "Oncet we sign up with you, where at is it we're a'goin'?"

"You'll be given two hours to get your affairs in order. Then you'll report back to the riverfront, where you'll be issued your equipment."

"And be give our money?" Mitchell asked, repeating his earlier concern.

Sergeant Delacroix sighed. "Yes, Mitchell, and be given your money. After that, we'll load you all onto a boat. Once we are loaded, we'll start downriver, putting in at all the ports until we find the English," Harding said.

"What do we do whenever we find them English?" someone asked.

"We fight 'em," Sergeant Delacroix answered resolutely.

"Fight 'em? You mean, with guns and sech?"

"The United States is at war with England," Sergeant Delacroix explained patiently. "We ain't goin' to be askin' 'em to no fancy dress balls."

"What about fightin' the heathens?" another asked. "I got me a brother lives down in Cape Girardeau. The Indians attacked them last month. I'd kind'a like to get back at 'em."

"I can answer that question, Sergeant," Captain Harding said. Then, addressing the others, he began to speak.

"Men, our country, our very way of life, is in danger. If we lose to the British, we are going to have to cede most of our country back to them. Right here, where you are standing, will more'n likely become British. They've come right out and said so. In addition, the British are making all kinds of promises to the Indians, telling them they will be able to get all their land back if they turn against us. And the Indians that are Britain's biggest allies are the Shawnee. So, to answer your question, if we encounter the Shawnee, we will fight them as well."

"We're going to fight the Shawnee?" Art asked.

"Yes, we are. That is, if we run across them," Harding said. "But we aren't going to go looking for them. Our primary concern is the British."

"Your primary concern might be the British, Cap'n, but like I said, I aim to kill me a couple of them Shawnees if I can," the man who had posed the first question replied. "Fact is, if I see any of 'em while we're a floatin' down the river, I aim to shoot 'em outright."

"And you would be?" Harding asked.

"Edward David Monroe."

"Listen to me, Private Monroe," Harding said resolutely. "There will be no shooting of Indians, or anyone else, unless and until Sergeant Delacroix or I give the word. Is that clearly understood?"

"What about . . ."

"I said, is that clearly understood?" Harding repeated more forcefully than before.

"Well, yes, I reckon it is."

"That is yes, *sir,* Private," Sergeant Delacroix said. "Any time you speak to an officer, you will say 'sir.'"

"Yes, sir," Monroe said sullenly. It was clear that he didn't particularly approve of the policy of not shooting Indians, nor did he appreciate being chastised. It was equally clear that he knew there was nothing he could do about it.

It was even colder later that afternoon when twenty-two men, the total number who actually signed the recruitment papers, returned to the riverfront. Some of the men had family members with them, including Private Mitchell, the one who had been so concerned about the fifteen-dollar bonus. Once the money was passed out, Mitchell took it over to his wife, a rather mousy-looking woman, and handed it to her. He embraced her, then turned and walked quickly toward the gangplank that led onto the boat. Art noticed the tears coming down Mrs. Mitchell's face, and he looked away, not wanting to intrude on the privacy of her sadness.

Art and the other men followed Captain Harding and Sergeant Delacroix onto the boat. Longer and wider than the average flatboat, it was more like a barge, but like a flatboat, depended upon the river current for its propulsion and long steering oars for its direction.

Although there was a small cabin amidships, it was only large enough for Captain Harding and Sergeant Delacroix. Both Harding and Delacroix had their blankets thrown down inside, away from the elements. Art and the other men would be out on the deck, exposed to the weather for the entire river passage.

Upon reporting for debarkation, each man had been issued a blanket. Except for Sergeant Delacroix and Captain Harding, the men wore clothes of homespun cotton or wool. Art continued to wear buckskins, believing that the leather did a better job of blocking out the wind than the cotton, or even the wool from which the homespun clothing was made.

Wrapping up in the issued blanket, Art found a place on the deck where he could sit with his back against the rail. That kept the wind off, and with the blanket and his wool-lined jerkin, did a passable job of keeping him warm.

The men had also been issued rifles, and as they drifted south, Sergeant Delacroix gave them their orientation on the weapon. Hefting one in his hand, he began a speech that sounded as if he had given it many times before.

"Men, this here is a government-issue, U.S. Military 1803 half-stocked, short-barreled, flintlock rifle. It fires a fifty-two-caliber lead ball weighing just over one ounce. That ball is propelled by black powder, which you will keep dry at all times. For that purpose, you have also been given a powder horn." Delacroix held up one of the powder horns to show what he was talking about. "Attached to the powder horn is a small measuring cup. One level cup of powder supplies the charge for the ball. The rifle is fired in the following manner."

Sergeant Delacroix poured a measuring cup of powder down the barrel of the rifle he was holding, then used a ramrod to drive down a wad of paper to hold the powder in place. Once the powder was in place, he dropped a ball into the end of the barrel and, again using the ramrod, drove the ball down.

"Once the ball is loaded, a small amount of powder is placed in the firing pan. Make certain that the flint is in position to cause a spark"—he checked the flint—"then draw back the hammer, raise the rifle to your shoulder, and . . ."

He completed his sentence by pulling the trigger. There was a flash, pop, and puff of smoke at the base of the barrel, followed immediately by the booming report of the charge itself. A flash of fire and a large cloud of smoke billowed out from the end of the barrel. The rifle's recoil caused Sergeant Delacroix to rock back. As a result of the burnt powder, a dark smudge now garnished his cheek. He smiled at his men as he continued his lesson.

"At a range of one hundred yards, this rifle has enough power to drive the ball one inch deep into a white oak plank. I can assure you, speaking from my own experience, it is quite powerful enough to stop any enemy."

The U.S. Military 1803 was Art's very first rifle, and though technically it belonged to the Army, it was in his hands, and that was the same thing as his owning it.

After his discourse on the rifle, Sergeant Delacroix began holding drills on board the boat as they drifted south on the current. He taught them how to stand at attention, come to present arms, right shoulder arms, port arms, and order arms.

The verbal instructions and arms drill given, Sergeant Delacroix then allowed the men to load and fire their weapons, choosing as targets trees along the bank as the boat continued its passage south.

Art learned very quickly that he was a natural at shooting. At first, Sergeant Delacroix picked only the larger trees as targets for the men, but he kept picking smaller trees and smaller still until, finally, he was pointing at saplings that were little bigger around than the thickness of a man's wrist. And yet, with every shot Art took, bits of exploding bark would mark the strike of the ball.

"You are a pretty good shot, Private," Sergeant Delacroix said begrudgingly. "Nearly as good as I am." Delacroix made no offer to demonstrate his own prowess.

"Well, I can see now that your saving my life that night was no mere accident," Captain Harding said that evening. "Sergeant Delacroix informs me that you are the best marksman in our company."

"Thank you," Art said.

"Have you ever used a rifle?"

"My father had a Kentucky long rifle," Art said. "I used to hunt squirrels with it."

"No doubt your family never went without meat when you were on the trail. By the way, your last name isn't really Gregory, is it?"

"No, sir."

"I didn't think so. Do you want to tell me what it really is?"

Art didn't answer.

"The reason I ask is, someone should know. You're about to go into battle, Art. I'm sure you know that means that you could be wounded, or even killed. Don't you think your family would like to know what happened to you?"

"I think they'd rather believe I'm alive somewhere," Art replied. "See, as long as they think that, then I am alive, leastwise in their mind."

"I suppose," Harding agreed.

"Besides which, if I ever do something to disgrace the name, I'd just as soon it be somebody else's name."

"Have you been in contact with your family since you left?"

Art didn't answer. Instead, he looked out over the edge of the boat at the riverbank, now slipping ever deeper into its shroud of evening shadows. From time to time, when he thought of his family, he realized that he did miss them. He wondered how they were getting along, and when he did remember to say his prayers, he would always include a prayer for their well-being. He tried to avoid thinking about them, though, because at this late date, he didn't want to start having second thoughts about what he had done.

"You don't want to talk about your family, do you?" Harding asked.

"No, sir, I'd as soon not."

"Well, then we will talk about something else. For example, what happened to you that night back in New Madrid? When I came back, you were gone."

"I'm not sure what happened," Art admitted. "I went outside to pee, and the next thing I knew I woke up in a wagon headed north."

"With your money gone, no doubt," Harding said.

"Yes, sir."

"I have been feeling guilty about that night ever since I left you. I don't know what got into me to cause me to just leave like that."

Art smiled. "As I recall, you wanted to go somewhere with that painted woman."

Harding laughed. "Ah, yes, Lily, her name was. A lovely young woman who is often misunderstood."

"Misunderstood?"

"There are those who would find fault with the profession she has chosen to follow, but I say she does a great service for men who sometimes find themselves in need."

"Like you were that night?"

"Yes, like I was that night," Harding said. "So, while I was satisfying my need, someone hit you over the head and robbed you. But at least you got a wagon ride all the way to St. Louis, so some good came from the evil."

Art started to tell Harding how the wagon owner had also left him for dead, but decided that Harding already felt bad enough, so he held his tongue. Then he thought to tell him of his year with the Indians, but decided this would not be the best time to do so. If they encountered Shawnee during their trip down, it would no doubt be the same village he had been staying with.

What if they did encounter Shawnee? What if a battle broke out between them? Would he have it in him to fire on his Shawnee brothers? Keytano had suggested that his white heart could not make war against his Shawnee heart. But Techanka had let him know, in no uncertain terms, that if they met again, they would meet as enemies.

Three days after leaving St. Louis, the boat put in at Cape Girardeau. They were met by a few of the merchants of Cape, anxious to sell goods and services to the Army. They were met also by a lieutenant and four soldiers, recently stationed at Cape Girardeau to defend against any repeat of the Shawnee attack.

"Any more sign of the Shawnee?" Captain Harding asked the lieutenant in charge.

"No, sir."

The lieutenant's name was William Garrison. He was a member of the regular Army and had fought against the British since the war began. He was bitter about being assigned to the wilderness of the Far West where his only adversaries were Indians.

"I doubt that those heathen cowards will attack, now that we have defenses in place," he went on. "The blockhouse is now equipped with a cannon and a swivel gun, sufficient to turn back any Indian endeavor."

"Do you have any idea where their village is?" Harding asked. "I've heard they might be on the Castor River."

"I've no idea where they are."

"You haven't sent out a scouting party to try and find them?"

"With all due respect, Captain, I have made no effort to engage the heathens. Prior to my assignment here I was fighting against the British. They are real soldiers. That is why I am happy to tell you that I have orders attaching myself to your command. I'll be going to New Orleans with you."

"General Jackson seems to think that the British troops are massing around New Orleans, getting ready to launch an attack. We are assembling whatever troops we can muster, but I'm sure that the British are going to have us outnumbered and outgunned. It will be good to have someone of your experience with me."

"Well, sir, I've been to New Orleans," one of the citizens of Cape Girardeau said. "And there ain't nothin' there but a bunch of Frenchmen, Creoles, and half-breed nigras. There ain't a damn thing there worth fightin' for, and if you ask me, they ain't nothin' going to happen there. If you want to know where all the action is, why, it's goin' to be right here, either with the heathen Indians or the swinish British. The redskins and the redcoats," he added, laughing in such a way as to suggest it wasn't the first time he had ever told the joke.

Harding laughed politely. "Redskins and redcoats," he said, turning the phrase over in his mind. "Sounds to me like they were meant for each other. It is a marriage. But the question is, was it made in heaven? Or was it made in hell?"

"A marriage?" the man asked, confused by the analogy.

"A figure of speech, sir," Captain Harding said. "Merely a figure of speech. Now, if you and the good citizens will excuse me, I must get my men rounded up. We are continuing on to New Orleans.

14

Lieutenant Garrison took over Sergeant Delacroix's duties as chief of training, and as they proceeded downriver, he continued with the instruction. His instructions included incessant drilling, which began each evening when the boat put ashore for the night.

"You know what I'm beginning to think?" Monroe mused as he was cleaning his rifle.

"No, what are you beginning to think?" Finley asked.

"I'm beginning to think we ain't never goin' to see no fightin'. All we're goin' to do is drill, sleep outside, stay wet, cold, and hungry with nothin' good to eat."

"Now, hold on there," Mitchell said. "What do you mean you ain't getting anything good to eat? Is that the thanks I get for cooking for you?" Even as Mitchell spoke, he was making corn dodgers by wrapping a paste of cornmeal, lard, and water around his ramrod, then holding the ramrod over an open fire, baking the mixture into bread. He leaned over to examine his work and, noticing that it was not quite ready, put it back into the fire.

"How much longer before they are done?" Monroe asked.

"Soon," Mitchell replied.

"Is that all we're havin' for our supper? A few corn dodgers?"

"Not a few, one," Mitchell said, holding up his finger. "One apiece."

"Damn, wouldn't some meat be good about now? Ham, or chicken, or just about anything," Monroe said. He looked around the camp. "Now where do you think Art's got off to?"

"I'll be damned," Sergeant Delacroix said. "Captain Harding, look what's coming."

Delacroix's exclamation caused Harding to look up. He saw Art coming out of the woods, a broad smile on his face, and a string of game, specifically six rabbits and three squirrels, hanging around his shoulders.

"My word," Lieutenant Garrison said. "How do you suppose Private Gregory came by those? I didn't hear any shooting, did either of you?"

"Private Gregory is a resourceful young man," Harding said.

"I wondered where he had gotten off to," Delacroix said.

"I thought perhaps the boy had deserted us," Lieutenant Garrison said.

"Oh, I knew he hadn't deserted," Delacroix said. "I was against signing him up at the beginning, but the boy has certainly proved himself to me. And now, I'm sure he has just proven himself to the men as well."

"Do you think he will share his good fortune with them?"

"Oh, I have no doubt of that," Harding said.

"Then perhaps I will go see him and make certain that we get our share," Garrison said.

"You'll do no such thing," Harding said, stopping Garrison in his tracks.

"What do you mean?" Garrison replied, surprised at Harding's comment.

"He's the one who trapped the game. Whatever disposition he makes is up to him."

"Captain, I realize that you are not a regular officer," Garrison said. "Perhaps, therefore, it is incumbent upon me to widen the instruction I have been giving to the men, to include you as well. We are officers, sir, you and I. And as officers, we are entitled to respect, authority, and certain, shall we say, benefits? One of those benefits is a disproportionate share of any legal booty gained by the command. In this case, the game that Private Gregory has taken."

"That might be the way of things back East," Harding said. "But it's not how it is out here. Whatever Private Gregory does with his game is up to him."

With a sullen expression on his face, Lieutenant Garrison resumed his seat on a fallen log.

Settling down by the fire, Art began skinning and cleaning the animals. Then he cut skewers and, in less than an hour, had all the meat roasting over the fires. When it was done, he took three choice pieces of the flame-broiled meat over to Captain Harding, Lieutenant Garrison, and Sergeant Delacroix.

"I thought you might like this," he said, holding out the meat.

Gratefully, they took the food.

"Won't you eat with me, Art?" Harding asked.

"Captain Harding, I'm just a private," Art said. "Lieutenant Garrison and Sergeant Delacroix already told me. Privates and officers don't socialize."

"This isn't socializing. This is business," Harding said.

"Very well, sir."

Harding smacked his lips appreciatively. "Mmm, this is very good," he said. "You've come a long way, Art. You're a woodsman, hunter, cook. And you have certainly made a believer of Delacroix. He tells me you are the best man in his company. In fact, he wants me to make you a corporal."

"I don't think I would want to be a corporal, sir," Art said. "I have enough trouble just taking care of myself."

"Taking care of yourself, huh? Like feeding the entire company?"

"Wasn't all that much," Art demurred.

"I don't agree with you," Harding said. "But I do agree with Delacroix. I've just promoted you to corporal."

Art smiled. "I don't see as I deserve it any more'n anyone else, but I appreciate it," he said.

"Cap'n Harding! Cap'n Harding!" someone shouted. "Come quick!"

"What is it?" Harding asked.

"It's Bedford and Nunlee, sir."

"Bedford and Nunlee? I put them out as sentries," Delacroix said. "What about them?"

"They're dead."

Upon hearing that, the others in the bivouac started toward the woods where Bedford and Nunlee had been last seen.

"Stay where you are!" Harding ordered. "There's no need in everyone going out to see. Corporal Gregory, take six men and investigate. The rest of you, stay alert."

"Corporal Gregory?" Monroe asked. "Did he say Corporal Gregory?"

"Good for him," Mitchell said. "He's the best of the lot, he should be a corporal."

Mitchell and Gregory were among the six men Art took with him. When they got closer, they could see two bodies lying on the ground. Several arrows were protruding from the bodies and both had been scalped.

"Shawnee," Art said.

"What?" Monroe asked.

"These arrows," Art said. "They are Techanka Shawnee."

"You can tell that just by looking at them?"

"Yes."

Suddenly there was a whir, then the thumping sound of

arrows striking flesh. One of the six men went down. The remaining arrows buried themselves in the ground close by.

"Form up into two ranks!" Art shouted. Without question, the men followed his orders. "First rank, fire!"

The three men in the first rank fired. Immediately, Art began pouring powder into the barrel of his gun, readying it for a second discharge. Even as he did so, he gave orders to the second rank to fire.

Again, the sound of guns echoed back from the woods.

"Second rank, reload!" Art shouted. "First rank, fire as you are loaded!"

"Art, here come some of our men!" Mitchell shouted happily, and Art turned around to see several others coming, led by Sergeant Delacroix.

One hundred yards away, protected by a tree, Tolian drew back his bow and took a careful bead on one of the Americans. He was aiming at the one who seemed to be giving orders to the others. The American was looking back toward another group of men who were running from the camp to join them. When he looked back around, Tolian recognized him.

"Artoor!" he said under his breath. He released the tension on the bowstring. He couldn't shoot his brother, could he? Then he remembered that Techanka had said that Artoor was no longer his brother, that if they met again as enemies, they would be enemies.

"Tolian, many more have come," Techanka said. "We must go!"

"Wait," Tolian said. He drew back the bow again. It was a long shot and the arrow would need to travel far, so he pulled the bow back further. Suddenly there was a cracking sound as his bow snapped under the pressure.

"Come!" Techanka said. "We must go now!"

Disgusted with the broken bow, Tolian tossed it aside and looked again across the distance to Art.

"The Great Spirit has spared you this time," he said under his breath. "Perhaps that is as it should be. Perhaps you were not meant to die today." Tolian turned to follow the others, who ran quickly back into the woods.

"Fire!" Sergeant Delacroix shouted, and fire and smoke billowed from the ends of the barrels as several men discharged their weapons. The balls whizzed into the trees, clipping limbs and poking holes through leaves. As soon as that line fired, the second line raised their rifles to their shoulders, awaiting the order to shoot.

"Sergeant Delacroix, they're gone!" Art shouted.

"Wait!" Delacroix ordered. "Lower your weapons!"

Reluctantly, the men did so.

"Save your powder, boys, we're just shooting into empty trees."

"Two dead and one wounded," Lieutenant Garrison said angrily. "Two dead and one wounded while we still sit idly here in camp."

"And what would you propose that we do, Lieutenant Garrison?" Harding asked.

"I propose that we take the fight to the enemy," Garrison said. "Let me take ten men in pursuit of the devils."

"No," Harding said. "Our first priority is to proceed to New Orleans with as many men as we can muster. We will be extra vigilant, and if they return, we will be ready for them. But I will not take the time, nor risk the men, to hunt them down."

"If not an attack against them, then at least let me take a few men out to find them, the better to be forewarned should they attempt another adventure against us," Garrison said.

"You may take four men," Harding said. He held up a cautionary finger. "But remember, this is only to find them. You are not to engage them."

"Yes, sir," Garrison said.

"I would recommend that you take Corporal Gregory as your second in command," Harding said. "He seems to be uncommonly at home in the woods."

"Very good, sir," Garrison replied. But as he walked away, he spoke in words that were too quiet to be overheard by anyone. "I'll be damned if I will take a snot-nosed boy as my second in command."

Acting upon his own, Garrison ordered six men to go with him. He was convinced that six men he had trained, obedient to orders, would be the equal to several times that many Indians. And he wouldn't need Corporal Gregory. Especially as Gregory seemed to exhibit total and unqualified loyalty toward Harding.

Tolian was sitting on a log eating a strip of dried horse meat when a scout reported to Techanka.

"Are they coming after us?" Techanka asked.

"Yes. Seven men."

Techanka looked surprised. "Seven? Are you certain there are only seven?"

"Yes. They walk like this," the scout said, and he held up his fingers to demonstrate that the Americans were now approaching in a drill-field order.

"That is no way to go to battle," one of the Indians said. "Perhaps they are coming to talk."

"Is Artoor with them?"

"No," the scout replied.

"Then I do not believe they are coming to talk, for if they were, they would have Artoor speak for them."

"What shall we do?"

"We shall wait for them," Techanka said. "And when they are close enough, we will kill them all and take their weapons."

"Yip, yip, yip!" Metacoma barked in excitement. "After this, we will have many stories to tell around the council fires!"

"Quiet!" Techanka cautioned. "Do you want the Americans to be frightened away by your shouts?"

Chastised, Metacoma grew quiet.

"Come," Techanka said. "We will take our positions and wait for the Americans."

The scout showed Techanka the route the approaching Americans were taking, so it was easy for Techanka to put his warriors in hiding for them. He put three behind some rocks, three more lay down on top of a little hill, and the remaining six hid in the woods. When all were in position, Techanka went up the trail for a short distance to determine if any of his warriors could be seen. He could see no one, even though he knew exactly where to look. Then, satisfied that all was in readiness, he hurried back to his own position.

He could hear the Americans before he could see them. Their steps were striking in rhythm, like the beating of a drum, and they were making a lot of noise as they came up the trail. Techanka took one last look around to make certain no one was exposed; then he crouched again and waited.

The warriors had been told not to attack until Techanka gave them the word, so he waited until the Americans were well within range. He didn't want any of the Americans to escape, and because he had more warriors and the advantage of surprise, he was sure that none would. He watched as they came into view, and he studied the faces of each of them because he wanted to know the men he killed.

The one who appeared to be the leader was a rather small man with a dark, drooping mustache. He was the one Techanka wanted for himself, so he drew back the bow and aimed carefully.

"Aiiiyeee!" he shouted as he loosed the arrow.

His arrow buried into the chest of the leader, and his shout caused the others to shoot as well.

Only two of the other Americans were hit with the opening fusillade, leaving four who could return fire. But without leadership, all four remaining Americans fired at once, and they fired without taking aim. Afterward, they threw down their guns and turned to run.

They didn't get very far.

15

Six boats of American volunteers, one of them carrying as many as one hundred men, put ashore just south of Natchez. There, the officers of the various units met and organized themselves into a regiment, electing from among their own number the regimental, battalion, and company commanders.

Captain Harding had left St. Louis with twenty-eight men. He'd picked up five men in Cape Girardeau, including Lieutenant Garrison. At the Birds Point bivouac ten days ago, he'd lost nine men to the Indians, including Lieutenant Garrison. He arrived at Natchez with only twenty-one. His was the smallest individual unit present, but despite that, he was elected to the rank of major, and given command of a battalion of one hundred. Additional officers were elected from within the ranks of the battalion to become company commanders. Sergeant Delacroix was one who was elected, becoming a captain and assuming command of Harding's original group. Art was promoted to sergeant, while Cooper and Monroe were both promoted to the rank of corporal.

After the election, Major Harding called for a meeting of all his officers and sergeants in order to organize. Once the organization was complete, he dismissed them, though he asked Art to stay behind for a moment.

"I want to thank you for agreeing to be a sergeant," he said.

"I must confess, Major, I feel a little foolish ordering men around who are much older than I am," Art said.

"Art, you are a boy in years, that's true. But you are the equal to any man I've ever met in worth," Harding said.

"Thank you, sir," Art said. "It's gratifying to have your approval."

"Not only my approval. You have earned the respect of every man in your company."

They were silent for a moment. Then Art asked, "What's it like? Being in a battle? I mean a real battle, against soldiers and such. Not the little fight we had with the Shawnee."

"Don't know as I can answer that for you," Harding replied. "Seein' as I've never been in that kind of battle myself. But I reckon you'll do just fine."

"I hear everyone talking and bragging. Some of 'em can't wait to kill an Englishman."

"And what about you?"

"I don't feel that way," Art said. "I mean, I'll do what I have to do, but I can't say as I'm lookin' forward to killing anyone."

"That's because you've already had to do it," Harding said. "And you know it's something you do only when it absolutely has to be done. It's for sure not somethin' a body takes pleasure from doin'."

"I guess that's it," Art said. "When it comes to it, I reckon I'll do my share of killin' along with everyone else. But I don't aim to brag about it, before or after."

As they talked, Art looked around the camp. Earlier in the day the bivouac area had been alive with movement and sound, as necessary camp activities were performed and drilling and instruction continued. But it was completely dark now. More than five hundred men had crawled into their shelters, or gone to ground, and those who were still active could be seen only in silhouette against the orange, flickering glows of the many campfires. It was quiet also, except for the hushed whisper of the flowing river and a few subdued conversations.

"How is it that you were able to change so, Art?" he asked.

"I beg your pardon?"

"How'd you go from bein' a boy, not even able to take care of himself, to what you are now?"

"I had no choice, Major. I've been on my own all this time, so it was a matter of survive or die."

"I can see how that would make a man of you," Harding said. "But I am curious about one thing. Why did you enlist?"

Art chuckled. "I was loading and unloading freight wagons," he said. "I figured it was time to move on, and this seemed as good a way as any. If you don't mind my asking, why are you here? What made you give up your boat for this?"

Harding reached down into his own knapsack, then pulled out a pipe. He began filling the bowl with tobacco.

"You been following this war any?"

"No, sir, I have not."

"Not a lot of folks have," Harding said. "You would be amazed at how many people there are in this country who don't even know that we are at war with England."

"Why are we at war with them?"

"To be honest with you, I'm not sure I know why the country is at war. I know why I am."

Harding told about the fight on the Ohio River where Indians, aided by British artillery, had killed all his friends.

"I made a vow then and there to fight against them," he said. "So when I ran across Ole' Hickory, I joined up."

"Ole' Hickory?"

Harding chuckled. "That's what a lot of folks call General Andy Jackson."

"You think we'll win this war?"

"We've got to," Harding said resolutely. "If the English win, they'll be takin' over all the land west of the Mississippi River.

There's a lot of land out there, and I plan to see it someday. And when I do see it, I want it to be American land I'm seein'."

"How much land do you reckon there is out there?" Art asked.

"You heard of Lewis and Clark, haven't you?"

"Aren't they the fellas that traveled all the way out to the western sea?"

Harding nodded. "The Pacific Ocean," he said. "Lewis and Clark followed the Missouri as far as they could, then struck out on foot. And according to them, there's a whole lot more land that hasn't even been looked at than we've already got. Land that goes on as far as a body can see, and then, when you get there, it goes on again, for day after day after day."

"And there is nobody out there?" Art asked.

"Nobody out there but Indians," Harding answered. "And not that many of them, I'm told. Nothing but bears and beaver, game and fish, trees and mountains."

Art's eyes sparkled in excitement. "Oh, now, wouldn't that be something to behold?"

Harding chuckled. "You've got that 'see the creature' look about you."

"If 'the creature' is out there in all that land you're talking about, then I reckon I do want to see it," Art admitted. "In fact, soon as this little fracas is over down in New Orleans, I reckon I'll just go on out there and take me a look."

"There's more to it than just going out there to take a look, son," Harding said. "There's mountains that touch the sky, deserts as big as seas, and who knows what else. It's going to be more than just a mite dangerous."

"The more you talk about it, the more interesting it sounds," Art said.

Harding laughed. "I thought you'd probably say something like that. What would you say if I told you I had the exact same idea in mind? How would you like for the two of us to go out there together?"

"You want to go too?"

"Sure. I told you a long time ago, I'm as eager to see the creature as you are." He waved his hand in the general direction of the river. "I've been up and down Old Strong near on to forty or fifty times I figure. There are no creatures hereabout that I haven't seen. I'd love to go west, at least as far as the mountains, maybe even all the way to the Pacific Ocean. What do you say? Shall we go take a look?"

"Yes!" Art replied. "Yes, I'd love that!"

The regiment to which Art now belonged was assigned to Brigadier General Humbolt's Louisiana Volunteers.

"Hey, who is this Humbolt fella?" Private Monroe asked. "I come down here to fight with General Andy Jackson . . . Ole' Hickory hisself."

"You will be fighting for General Jackson," Delacroix told him.

"That ain't what the major just told us. He said we was now a part of General Humbolt's Division."

"And Humbolt's Division is a part of General Jackson's Army," Delacroix explained patiently. He looked at the others. "Men, do yourselves and your country proud. We've been assigned to the middle of the line."

"What's that mean?" someone asked.

"It means we're a'goin' to be right in the thick of all the fightin'," another explained.

With that comment, Harding's Legion came to the realization that the drill and practice and bragging and anticipation were all over. There was no more talk of what they were going to do, it was now a matter of *doing* it.

General Jackson put his Army into position along the banks of the Rodriguez Canal. There, he built a fortified mud rampart, just over half a mile long, anchored on the right by the Mississippi River and on the left by an impassable cypress swamp.

That meant there was no way the British troops could reach New Orleans without coming right through Jackson's Army.

Jackson's Army was a polyglot force consisting of units of the regular army as well as New Orleans militia, free blacks, frontiersmen such as Harding's Legion, and even a band of outlaws and pirates led by Jean Lafitte.

The British Army they were facing was one of the finest military assemblages in the world. It was led by General Sir Edward Parkenham, the thirty-seven-year-old brother-in-law of the Duke of Wellington. Parkenham, a much-decorated officer, was commanding a force of tough, proven British Regulars: the 4th, 21st, 44th, and 93rd Highlanders. These were the same regiments that had defeated Napoleon at Waterloo, and more recently burned the Capitol in Washington. This magnificent Army was augmented by the 95th and 5th West India Regiments.

On the 28th of December, Parkenham launched a strong advance against the Americans, but was repulsed. On New Year's Day Parkenham moved his artillery into position, then started a day-long artillery barrage. As the British guns opened fire, the sound of thunder rolled across the open field. Immediately thereafter, the shells came crashing in, exploding in rosy plumes of fire, smoke, and whistling death.

Although some of the regulars in Jackson's Army had undergone an artillery barrage before, this was a new and terrifying experience for most of the men. They shuddered in fear as heavy balls crashed into the cotton bale barricades behind which the American soldiers were taking shelter. Explosive shells burst inside their ranks, sending out singing pieces of shrapnel.

It was in this bombardment that Harding's Legion suffered its first casualty. Corporal Mitchell, the man who had worried so about making sure his wife got his enlistment bonus, was decapitated by one of the cannonballs. The sight of one of their own, alive and vibrant one moment and headless the next, unnerved many of the men, and some would have fled had their officers not stopped them.

Art remembered the touching scene on the riverbank between Cooper and his wife, just before they left St. Louis. He thought of Mrs. Mitchell and felt an overwhelming sense of sorrow for her loss.

16

In the chilled, predawn January darkness, American sentries and listening posts realized that something was afoot. After several days of relative quiet, they picked up a great deal of movement over on the British side. Art and the others were rousted from their bedrolls and moved quickly to the barricades. There, Harding's Legion took up its assigned position, right in the center of the line. Looking down along each side of him, Art could see the other defenders, holding their rifles and shivering in the cold, though he suspected perhaps many were shivering from fear as well.

Surprisingly, he felt no particular fear, and this allowed him to be a dispassionate observer. And what he saw was four thousand Americans, facing a British force that was nearly twice their number.

Gradually, the sky grew lighter, but an exceptionally thick fog rolled in so that, even with the coming of dawn, the Americans still couldn't see the British troops. They could hear them, though, and they listened with quickened souls as the English officers called out their commands.

"Fix bayonets!"

The order, repeated many times, was followed by the unmistakable clicking sound of bayonets being attached to the ends of the long British "Brown Bess" rifles. The rifles were so long that when the bayonets were affixed they were almost like pikes, and in the hands of trained soldiers, they made quite a formidable weapon.

Shortly after that, the Americans faced a new terror. The British began their attack with a broadside of rockets. Art had never seen anything like it before. He watched with as much fascination as fear: seeing first the flare of their launch, gleaming even through the morning mist, then the glare of their transit, and finally the projectiles themselves as they emerged, spitting fire, from the fog to explode over the heads of the Americans.

After the barrage, there followed several moments of silence. In its own way, the silence was as frightening as the whoosh and explosions of the rockets had been. Then, quietly at first, but gradually increasing in volume, they heard from the fog the muffled-jangle of equipment and the rhythmic drumming of feet. The sound grew louder, and louder still, until it was a drumming that resonated in the pounding of each waiting American's pulse.

Thump, thump, thump, thump, thump.

Suddenly there came a sound that, to some, was like the wailing of demons from hell. It was the high-pitched, haunting squeal of the bagpipes. As the noises grew louder and louder from the fog, a nervousness began to ripple up and down the American lines, and some of the soldiers began shift about anxiously. They looked back over their shoulders several times, as if searching out the most desirable escape route. Harding noticed the unease among his troops.

"Easy, men. Easy," he said, speaking calmly. "Stand your ground now."

By now the noise of drumming feet and wailing bagpipes was nearly deafening.

"Come on!" one of the soldiers suddenly shouted. "What are you waiting for? Don't stay out there in the fog making noises!" He climbed to the top of the barricade, and would have run toward the unseen enemy if a couple of his friends hadn't grabbed him and pulled him back down.

Thump, thump, thump, thump.

Art stared into the thick mist, straining to see. For several long moments there was nothing. Then, as if apparitions were suddenly and mysteriously forming in the mist, the British Army materialized. Art saw the magnificent but intimidating sight of beautifully uniformed and well-trained soldiers in a disciplined battle-line-front formation. Their bayonets were fixed and the rifles were thrust forward.

Not until this very moment could the Americans do anything more than wait. Relieved that the opportunity for some action was here at last, Harding shouted out his orders at the top of his voice.

"Count off," Harding instructed, and the men responded.

"One!"

"Two!"

"One!"

"Two!"

They shouted throaty responses until the entire battalion was counted off.

Those who were number one would kneel and fire the first volley. Then number two would fire while number one reloaded.

"Major, we got to get outta here!" Private Monroe said. "They's more'n twice as many of them as they is of us. And with this dampness and all, it ain't all that certain our powder will explode!"

"Stay where you are," Harding said calmly. "Their powder is going to be just as wet."

"Yes, but they's a lot more of them than they is of us, and they got bayonets. We're crazy to stay here like this," Monroe insisted.

"Take it easy, Monroe," Art said.

"I don't need no wet-behind-the-ear, snot-nosed boy to tell me to take it easy," Monroe said derisively, glowering at Art.

"At least Sergeant Gregory ain't cryin' and peein' in his pants," one of the other soldiers said. "Now shut up and keep watchin' out for the British, or keep on a'yappin' and start watchin' out for me."

The last comment had the desired effect, and though Monroe was still twitching nervously, he was no longer talking about it.

"Hold your fire, men, hold your fire," Harding instructed. "Don't fire until you can clearly see their belt buckles."

The British advanced to a distance of about forty yards. At that point they halted. Then their officers' commands, loud, clear, and confident, floated across the misty distance between the two forces so that the Americans could hear the orders as well as the British soldiers for whom the orders were intended.

"Extend front!"

As if on parade, the British line extend out, fingertip to fingertip, eyeing up and down the rank in order to be properly aligned.

The officers stepped in and out of the rank, checking the alignment, here ordering one soldier to move up a step, there ordering another one to back up a bit. Only when the line was perfectly formed did the officers return to their position forward of the troops. The officers drew their sabers and held them up.

General Parkenham gave his order in a loud, clear voice.

"Forward at a double!"

The entire British line began running toward the ramparts, their bayonet-tipped rifles thrust forward. The officers ran before them, brandishing their swords.

This was a bayonet charge being made by battle-hardened and well-disciplined soldiers. Harding's Legion, as indeed most of the others of Jackson's Army, consisted of militia-

men, many seeing battle for the first time. They fought back
the bile of fear that rose in their throats, and they waited.

Art aimed at one of the soldiers. He held the aim for a long
moment, awaiting the order to fire. Then, capriciously, he
shifted his aim to another soldier, sparing, for no particular
reason, the first soldier.

Not until the British were at point-blank range did Harding
give the command to his battalion.

"Fire!"

Winks of light rippled up and down the American line as first
the firing pans, and then the muzzle blasts, flashed brightly.
Smoke billowed out in one large, rolling cloud as the sound of
gunfire rolled across the plain. Art saw his man go down.

The effect of the opening volley was devastating. In addition to the soldier Art shot, almost half of the British front rank
went down under the torrent of lead. The second volley did
as much damage as the first, so that when the huge cloud of
gun smoke cleared away, there was nothing before the Americans but a field strewn with dead or dying British soldiers.

The British Army was stopped in its tracks, almost as if
they had run into a stone wall. A few of the British soldiers
fired their weapons toward the Americans, but the volume
of their fire was pitifully small.

"Lord, Major, did you see that?" Delacroix asked excitedly.
Delacroix was from the regular Army, and one of the few American defenders who had actually been in battle before. "We cut
them down like so much wheat. They never had a ch . . ."

Delacroix stopped in midsentence when he saw that Major
Harding couldn't hear him. Although the firing coming from
the British lines had been weak and, for the most part, inef-
fective, at least one bullet had found its mark. Harding was
lying on his back, dead, from a wound in his forehead.

Art saw him at the same time, and he dropped to one knee
beside him.

"Major Harding!" Art said.

Delacroix, looking down at the boy and the major, shook his head sadly.

"There's nothing you can do for him now, son," Delacroix said.

Reaching down, Art closed Harding's eyes.

"Are you going to be all right?" Delacroix asked.

"Yes, sir," Art answered.

"Good man. Better get back in line, looks like they're comin' again."

Once more the English came across the field, though this time without benefit of pipe or drum, for fully ninety percent of the Highlanders, to include every piper and drummer, had been killed in the previous charges.

No longer an impressive front of redcoats and extended rifles, this was a ragged line of the desperate, brave, and foolish. The mighty yell of defiance that had issued from the throats of the attackers in the first wave was now a weak and disjointed cry from a few scattered men.

Again, the Americans fired, the volley as intense with this barrage as it had been the first time. British soldiers clutched breasts, stomachs, arms, and legs as blood seeped through their spread fingers.

Again, the line stopped, staggered, then turned and retreated back across the field.

All save one.

A single British lieutenant, screaming in rage and slashing at the air with his sword, continued toward the American ramparts even though every other man of the British Army was in retreat.

"Follow me, men, follow me!" the lieutenant shouted. Though he was now the sole target and could have easily been killed, the American defenders withheld fire, watching in morbid fascination as he used the bodies of his own dead to give him a foothold to the top of the rampart wall.

"Put them to the bayonet!" the lieutenant shouted, leaping down into the Americans, slashing out with his sword.

The Americans backed away from the sword, but not one made an effort to harm the lieutenant. Instead, everyone looked at him in awe.

Noticing his strange reception among the enemy, the British officer stopped screaming and lowered his sword. He looked behind him and, only then, realized that he and he alone had breached the rampart wall. He lowered his sword.

"Let's hear it for the lad!" someone shouted.

"Hip, hip!"

"Hooray!"

"Hip, hip!"

"Hooray!"

Half-a-dozen Americans moved toward the lieutenant. One of them took his sword, and to the young officer's surprise, they lifted him to their shoulders.

"Here's the bravest lad on the field today!" one of the Americans yelled, and once again, the Englishman was honored with cheers as he was borne on the shoulders of the men who, but moments earlier, had been his mortal enemy.

The British were unable to launch another attack because their commander, General Sir Edward Parkenham, had been killed by a bursting cannon shell. With his dying breath, Parkenham had ordered his successor to continue to press the attack. Wisely, however, the new commander had disobeyed, pulling the survivors off the bloodied field and leaving behind over two thousand of his men dead or wounded.

Only eight Americans were killed in the battle, and while most celebrated their great victory, Art could feel only sorrow over the loss of his friend, Major Harding. Harding and the other Americans who were killed were taken back to New Orleans, where they were given a military burial.

General Jackson attended the funeral, then sent word that he would like to talk to Art.

"Me?" Art asked when Delacroix took him the message. "Are you sure the general said he wanted to talk to me?"

"That's what he said."

"Why on earth would he want to talk to me?"

Delacroix shook his head. "I can't answer that question," he said. "But then, I learned a long time ago that you can't never figure out what a general has on his mind. Whatever it is, I expect you had better go see him. Generals ain't the kind of folks you want to keep waiting."

"Yes, sir," Art said.

"Here. Before you go, you ought to have this," Delacroix said, reaching out his hand. He was holding something.

"What is that?"

"It's a shoulder epaulet. Put this on your left shoulder."

"Only officers wear those."

"You are an officer," Delacroix said. "You was just made a second lieutenant."

Art held up his hand in refusal. "Captain, I expect you should give that to someone else, someone who earned it. Now that the battle is done and the danger over, I hear General Jackson is going to let everyone out who wants out. And I want out."

Delacroix snorted a half laugh. "Hell, boy, it probably ain't official. I'm not sure anyone as young as you can even be an officer. But far as I'm concerned, you earned this rank, and even if you take your discharge tomorrow, I figure you got the right to wear it for as long as you got left. I don't mind admittin' that I was wrong about you. When I first seen you back in St. Louis, I thought you was just some worrisome kid. But you sure changed my mind."

Hesitantly, Art took the epaulet. "I hope this doesn't cause any trouble with the other men."

"How do you think you got that?" he asked. "The other men elected you. Every one of them. Including, even, Corporal Monroe. Of course, part of it might be because as soon as you agree to take it, Monroe becomes a sergeant," Delacroix said, laughing.

"I'm real honored," Art said, pinning the epaulet onto his left shoulder. As he turned away from Delacroix, he was surprised to see the remaining men from the original twenty-eight who had left St. Louis together.

"Attention!" one of the men shouted, and all stood, then saluted, as Art walked by.

Awkwardly, Art returned the salute, then pulling himself up, walked by the standing men, heading for the house that had been put into service as General Jackson's headquarters.

"Thank you for coming to see me, Lieutenant," General Jackson said. He stared at Art for a long moment, a frown crossing his face.

"Damn, boy, how old are you?"

"I'm fifteen, General."

"You are fifteen and a lieutenant? That's not even . . ." He'd started to say legal, then stopped. "To hell with the regulations. I'm told that your men elected you to that position, and if they want you there, who am I to deny it? Besides, I know for a fact that Major Harding set quite a store by you. That's why he named you in his will."

"His will?" Art asked, surprised by the general's comment.

"I had all the officers make out a will and submit it to me before the battle," General Jackson said. "Were you related to Harding?"

"No, sir."

"But you knew him?"

"Yes, sir. We were friends from long before."

Was it long before? Art wondered. In terms of time, it had been only a year and a half ago since Harding had come to his rescue at Eby's cave. Only eighteen months, yet it seemed half a lifetime ago.

"Then maybe you will understand the rather strange wording of his will," General Jackson said. "He talks about something he calls the creature."

Art laughed. "Yes, sir, I know about the creature."

General Jackson stroked his chin, then looked over at one of the nearby staff officers.

"Colonel May, would you stand by, please, for the reading of the will?" General Jackson asked one of his staff officers. "Then I'll want you to witness it."

"Yes, sir," the colonel replied.

Taking a pair of spectacles from a box, then putting them on, carefully hooking them around each ear, General Jackson unfolded a document and began reading.

"To all who sees these presents, greetings. I, Peter Hamilton Harding, currently a major in General Jackson's Army of Tennessee Volunteers, and being of sound mind and body, but ever cognizant of the possibility of a premature appointment with my maker as the result of battle, do hereby make this last will and testament.

"First, I decree that any just debt owed by me shall be paid by any monies in my possession or due me."

General Jackson lifted his eyes from the reading and glanced up toward Art. "That has been taken care of," he said.

"Yes, sir."

Jackson continued reading.

"Second, all monies as may remain after the settlement of all just debt should be given to any church of the Protestant faith, said church to be selected by the regimental chaplain."

Again, Jackson looked up. "That too has been accomplished."

Reading again, Jackson continued. "And finally, I give profound regrets to my friend, Art, that I will be unable to see the creature with him. But to aid him in his own quest, I leave and bequeath my Hawken rifle and my pistol.

"Signed by Peter Hamilton Harding and witnessed by Pierre Mouchette Delacroix."

Jackson looked over at Colonel May. "Would you witness this, please, Colonel?"

Colonel May leaned over the table and affixed his signature to the place indicated by General Jackson.

"Lieutenant, you will find the rifle and pistol on a table in that room," Jackson said, pointing toward a door. "Take them and do honor to them, for they belonged to an honorable man."

"Yes, sir," Art said, feeling nearly as much pride now as sorrow.

If Art had wanted to go west to see the creature before, that desire was redoubled now. He felt a strong determination to carry out the plans he and Major Harding had made. It was no longer a drift without purpose. He felt as if he were on a mission.

17

It was March 22, 1815. For the first time in several days it was warm enough, and dry enough, for Art to strip out of his coat and slicker. The sun was out and he was enjoying its warmth, not only the rays as they fell on him, but also the convection heat that radiated back from the horse.

Art had spent twenty dollars for the horse, ten for the saddle, and five for his sack of possibles. He had about ten dollars remaining, and he planned to use the last of his money in St. Louis, buying everything he might need for the trip west.

He had considered going west from New Orleans, but that would have taken him through Mexico. He had fought for the United States, so like Harding, he wanted the land he saw to be American land. The best way to do that would be to follow the trail west, as established by Lewis and Clark. That meant following the Missouri River, and to do that, he would have to leave from St. Louis.

Suddenly, and with no warning, the ground gave way beneath his horse's hooves. The horse whinnied in surprise and pain, then fell to its right front knee. Art leaped from the saddle, both to avoid being thrown, and to keep from inflicting any further injury to his mount.

It wasn't until Art hit the ground himself that he saw the

problem. Recent rains had cut a channel between streams. Because the grass was high, the channel couldn't be seen, and when the horse had put its hoof down on the edge of the channel, the dirt wall had given way.

The horse stood up, but when it tried to put its weight on its right foreleg, it balked, pulling it up again sharply. Kneeling by the horse, Art picked up the leg for a closer examination.

He didn't have to search for the injury. It was a compound fracture, and the bloody stump of a bone was sticking through the skin.

"Oh," Art said, shaking his head and rubbing the wound gently. Even the softest caress brought pain, and the horse tried to pull its leg away. "Oh, Lord, I know that hurts."

Art had only owned the horse for a few months, but it had been both his beast of burden and his sole companion for the long ride. Feeling a lump in his throat and a stinging in his eyes, Art wrapped his arms around the horse's neck, embracing him. The horse looked at him with huge, brown eyes, begging the one who fed him, rubbed him down, talked to him, and cared for him, to do something to take away the hurt.

Art knew there was only one thing he could do. The stinging in his eyes gave way to tears as he loaded his pistol.

"I'm sorry, horse," he said. "There's no other way."

The horse continued to stare at him, not even looking away when Art raised his pistol and put the end of the barrel less than two inches away from the white blaze that shot down between the horse's eyes.

Art pulled the trigger. He felt something wet hit his face as the short, flat boom echoed back from the trees. The horse fell over on his side, bounced slightly, then was still.

Art ran his hand across his face, then held it out to look at it. He saw blood and brain-matter. Shutting his eyes, he turned away from the horse and walked several paces before he stopped, his gun down by his side, a small plume of smoke drifting up from the end of the barrel.

Art took several deep breaths, then turned back to the job at hand. There was no way to salvage the saddle. Right now, it was as worthless to him as the dead horse. But he took the saddle blanket and pouches, then snaked the rifle out of its sheath. Stuffing his possibles bag down into one of the pouches, he hitched up his trousers and started walking north.

He reached New Madrid four days after his horse went down. Coming into a town that soon after losing his horse was a pleasant surprise to him. It was even better that the town was New Madrid, because that gave him a sense of where he was. There was another surprise waiting for him at New Madrid. Tied up to the bank was the steamboat *Delta Maid.*

The *Delta Maid* was one of a growing number of steamboats on the Mississippi. The *New Orleans* had inaugurated steamboat traffic on the river, commencing operation in 1811. The *Delta Maid* was one of the more recent additions to the Mississippi steamboat fleet, entering service early in 1814.

Art knew the boat, because when he was in St. Louis, loading and unloading freight wagons, he sometimes took a load to, or brought a load from, the *Delta Maid.* As a result, he knew several of the deckhands, and even the captain of the boat. He wandered down to the river's edge, then began looking out at the boat to see if he could recognize anyone. He was seen first.

"Art, how are you, boy? What are you doing in New Madrid? Last time I seen you, you was in St. Louis."

The man who hailed him was the boat's engineer, John Dewey. Dewey was near the stern of the boat, standing in the shadows of one of the huge boilers.

"Hello, Mr. Dewey," Art replied. "Yes, sir, I was in St. Louis, but I went down to New Orleans to join up with General Jackson."

"Was you there when the battle was fought?" Dewey

asked. He stepped up to the boat railing and dumped the ashes from the bowl of his pipe.

"Yes, sir, I was."

"Well, good for you, boy. That was a heroic thing our soldier boys done down there. Taught them Brits a lesson they ain't likely to forget for a while."

"Mr. Dewey, you think there might be a job on the boat for me?"

"Well, now, you aimin' to be a river man, are you?" Dewey asked.

"Well, sir, I'd like to be a river man for a while anyway. My horse went down on me some way back, and I'm looking for a way to go to St. Louis."

"I could use a good man in the engine room," Dewey said. "Come on aboard, I'll talk to the captain for you."

"Thanks," Art said.

Captain Timmons was nearly a head shorter than Art. He was bald, but with a full, gray beard that reached all the way down to the beginning of a prominent belly. He wore a dark blue jacket with brass buttons and more trim across the front than Art had seen on any of the generals in the recent battle.

"Yes, I remember you, lad," Timmons said. "From what I observed of you, you were a good worker. A good worker indeed. So, 'tis a river man you want to be, eh? Well, I can't blame you. 'Tis quite a thing, being in command of this much power."

"Yes, sir," Art said.

"If you've a mind to, I'll take you on as an apprentice. A smart boy like you could be a riverboat pilot in no time."

"I appreciate the offer, Captain," Art said. "But if it's all the same, I'd rather work in the engine room."

"Here, now," Timmons said with a scowl on his face. "The engine room, is it? You'd rather break your back and cover your face with soot than be captain of the boat? What kind of ambition is that?"

"Perhaps the lad is looking to learn the business from the bottom up, Cap'n," Dewey suggested, with a glance that told Art to go along with him. "Sure'n there's nothin' wrong with knowing the boat from stem to stern."

Captain Timmon's scowl changed to a smile. "Aye, a good point, Mr. Dewey. A good point indeed. Very well, lad, if it's a fireman's job you seek, 'tis a fireman's job you'll have. Report aboard first thing in the morning."

"Thank you," Art said.

Art stood on the boardwalk in front of the Blue Star, recalling the last time he had been here. That was nearly three years ago. He smiled. What a babe in the woods he had been then.

Hitching up his trousers, he went inside. It hadn't changed. It was still well appointed with finished furniture and gilt-edged mirrors, but somehow, it didn't make quite as big an impression on him now as it had before.

"Come in, mister, come in," the man behind the bar called. "Pick yourself out a seat. Just come in on the *Delta Maid*, did you?"

"No, sir, but I'll be leaving on the *Delta Maid*," Art said. "How have things been with you, Mr. Bellefontaine?"

Bellefontaine looked surprised at being addressed by name. "Have we ever met, boy?"

"Yes, sir, we have. But I'm a bit older and a mite taller now than I was then. I was in here sometime back with Major . . ." The rank came automatically and he stopped in mid-sentence, then corrected himself. "With Mr. Harding. Pete Harding."

"Glory be, yes, I do remember you, boy. Just a minute. Lily!" he shouted. "Lily, get down here."

A woman appeared on the upstairs landing. She walked up

to the railing and leaned over to look down. "What is it?" she asked.

"Look who has showed up," Bellefontaine said.

Lily looked at Art, but it was obvious she didn't recognize him.

"Who is it?"

"You remember the boy who come in here with Harding that time? The boy that disappeared?"

Lily smiled broadly. "Oh, Lord, honey, was that you?" she asked, coming quickly down the stairs.

"Yes, ma'am, I reckon it was," Art replied.

Lily opened her arms wide, then pulled him to her. He could feel the softness of her full breasts under her embrace.

"Well, for crying out loud," she said. "Sit you down and tell me all about yourself. What happened to you that night? And where have you been since then. Lord, honey, you are growing into a handsome man, did you know that?"

Art blushed, and Lily laughed. "Now, ain't that cute. You're still innocent enough to blush. Damn if I'm not about half inclined to take that innocence away from you."

Art cleared his throat nervously, and Lily laughed again.

"Don't worry about it, honey. I don't do it for free, no matter how handsome the fella is. And I figure that, at this point in your life, you got better things to do. Now tell me about Pete. Where is that scoundrel, and when is he going to come see me again?"

The smile left Art's face. "I'm sorry to have to tell you this," he said. "But Pete's dead."

"Dead?" Lily gasped. Art was surprised to see her eyes fill with tears. "But when? How?"

Art told her the story of the Battle of New Orleans, playing down any role he'd had in it, telling it only from the perspective of having been an eyewitness.

Others, seeing Lily crying, came over to find out what was going on, so Art's telling was broadened to include them. He was surprised to see how many people knew and genuinely liked Pate Harding. But then, he didn't know why he should have been surprised. Harding was a very good man who had made a positive impression upon nearly everyone he'd ever met.

"Oh, uh, Mr. Bellefontaine, I owe you for a supper," he said.

"What?"

"That night I was here, I recall ordering my supper. I don't remember anything else until I woke up in a wagon, headed north. I figure you went ahead and fixed my supper anyway, and when I didn't come back, that meant you lost it. So, by rights, I should be paying for it."

Bellefontaine chuckled. "Truth to tell, I wound up getting paid twice for that supper," he said. "When you didn't show up for it, someone else bought it. Then, the next day, Harding paid for it. That was when he was out looking for you."

"Oh, honey, he turned this town upside down looking for you," Lily said. "I never saw anyone set so much store in another so fast. He was some worried about you, I'll tell you that."

"I wish there had been some way I could have let him know what happened to me," Art said. He laughed. "But to this day, I don't know myself."

"It's pretty obvious what happened to you," Bellefontaine said. "It's happened before. Someone knocked you in the head, then took your money."

"Yes, that's true. When I woke up in the wagon the next morning, I had a knot on my head and no money in my pocket."

"Uh-huh," Bellefontaine said. "And if truth be known, the fella that picked you up is more'n likely the one who hit you in the first place."

Art thought about Younger. Until this moment he hadn't considered the fact that Younger might have been responsible. As it turned out, Younger was so evil in every other way that the possibility had never dawned on Art. Now, as he considered it, he was almost positive that Younger was to blame.

"I'll be damned," Art said. "I do believe you are right."

"Well, it's not good to dwell on such things," Bellefontaine said. "Answer me this, boy. When's the last time you had a really good meal? I mean fried chicken, 'taters, beans, biscuits, maybe even a piece of pie."

Art smiled. "It's been a long time," he said. "It's been a really long time."

"Well, it ain't goin't be a very long wait till you do, 'cause I aim to whip you up just such a meal."

"I thank you, Mr. Bellefontaine, but I . . . ," Art started to tell Bellefontaine that he needed to save the money he had left in order to outfit himself for his trek west, but before he could speak, Bellefontaine interrupted him.

"I ain't goin' to be takin' no for an answer, boy," he said. "You see, this here ain't goin' to cost you one penny. It's all on the house."

"That's very nice of you," Art said. "But why would you do that?"

"Well, we could say it's because you was a friend of Pete Harding. And any friend of Pete Harding is a friend of mine," Bellefontaine said. "And that would be true. But we could also say it's because you fought down at New Orleans and I reckon that, because of what you done, this here territory is still part of America. I figure all you boys that fought down there is owed somethin'."

"Thank you," Art said.

Lily, who was still wiping the tears from her eyes, smiled through her tears and put her hand on Art's shoulder.

"Honey, I feel that way too, really I do," she said. "And I'm willin' to do somethin' I ain't never done before. I'll let you lie with me for free. Only, don't make me do it tonight. I don't intend to lie with anyone tonight. I need tonight to cry over poor, dear Pete."

"That's all right," Art said. "I understand."

Art didn't tell Lily that he wasn't going to be there tomorrow night. He was just as glad of it too. He still connected her to Harding and he felt as if it would be wrong for him to be with her. He knew that was dumb. After all, Lily was a whore and others were with her all the time. Harding also knew she was a whore and it hadn't bothered him. But somehow, Art's being with her wouldn't be the same thing.

"Lily, the boy . . ." Bellefontaine began, but Art got his attention, and with a small shake of his head, interrupted the revelation. Bellefontaine nodded his understanding.

18

Early the next morning, Art reported for work. Once on board, he walked out onto the hurricane deck of the *Delta Maid* and stood against the stern railing, then faced forward to look along the length of the boat. He could see the neat stacks of cargo and the long ricks of firewood.

Dewey told Art that his job would be to keep the boiler stoked with firewood and, when the time came, to join the other members of the crew in replenishing the supply of firewood every time they stopped.

Some distance forward of where Art was standing was the bow of the *Delta Maid*. Already, there was talk of outfitting special boats to go up and down the river, dredging a channel to facilitate faster travel by the steamboats. But that had not yet been done, so for now the bow of those boats already plying the river were shaped like a spoon, thus allowing them to slip easily over shoals and sandbars.

The *Delta Maid* was 160 feet long, with a beam of thirty-two feet. From her lower deck to the top of the wheelhouse, she rose forty feet. It was nearly sixty feet to the running lights at the very top of the twin fluted smokestacks.

The *Delta Maid* could carry 220 tons of freight and thirty-six cabin passengers. The large paddle wheel at the stern was eighteen feet in diameter and twenty-six feet wide. The wheel was rotated by a steam engine at a rate of twenty revolutions per minute.

The wheel was motionless now, and Art turned to look down where the paddle blades met the water. A twig hung up on one of the blades for a moment, then broke loose and floated on by the keel. He had never been on a steamboat before, and he couldn't help but be a little excited over the prospect.

"Cast off the lines, fore and aft!" Captain Timmons shouted from the pilot deck, using his megaphone to amply his orders.

"Aye, Cap'n, fore and aft!" his mate, who was down on the main deck, replied.

Captain Timmons pulled on the chain that blew the boat whistle, and its deep-throated tones could be heard on both sides of the river. Timmons put the engine in reverse, and the steam boomed out of the steam-relief pipe like the firing of a cannon. The wheel began spinning backward, and the boat pulled away from the bank, then turned with the wheel pointing downriver and the bow pointing upstream. The engine lever was slipped to full forward, and the wheel began spinning in the other direction until finally it caught hold, overcame the force of the current, and started moving the boat upstream.

They beat their way against the current, around a wide, sweeping bend, with the engine steam pipe booming as loudly as if the town of New Madrid was under a cannonading.

For the rest of the day the *Delta Maid* beat its way up river, with the engine clattering and the paddle wheel slapping and the boat itself being enveloped in the thick smoke that belched out from the high twin stacks.

Already the boiler furnace required restoking, and Art had gone through several ricks of wood, marveling at how fast their supply of fuel was being consumed. He was told their next fu-

eling stop would be Cape Girardeau. He couldn't help but
wonder if the fuel they had on board would last even that long.

"I tole' you I heered the boat a'comin'," Eby said to the
others. "Lookie there, over the top o' them trees. You can see the
smoke."

Eby had eight armed men with him, nine counting himself,
divided into three men each in three skiffs. They were waiting just north of a wide, sweeping bend.

"How much you reckon we're going to get offen this here
boat?" Poke asked.

"I'd say more than you could get off ten flatboats," Eby
replied.

"Lord, how we goin' to get all that out of here?"

"We'll scuttle the boat ag'in the sandbar," Eby explained.
Kill ever'one on board, then just take our time unloadin' it.
After we get ever'thing off it, we'll burn it."

The steam pipe boomed, and Poke jumped. "What the
hell? They got a cannon on that boat?"

Eby laughed. "That ain't no cannon," he said. "That's just
the steam engine. It does that sometimes, makes a noise so
loud you'd think it was a cannon."

"I just got a glimpse of it through the trees," one of the
others said. He pointed. "There, you see it?"

"Yeah," Eby answered. "I see it. All right, boys, get in your
boats and make sure your guns is primed and loaded. We'uns
is about to get rich."

Art saw them when he was out on the deck, picking up another bundle of wood. Glancing toward the riverbank, he saw
three boats waiting behind a fallen tree trunk. At first, he
thought it was just curious; then, when he realized that there
were three men in each boat, and that they were just sitting

there, he got suspicious. His suspicions were confirmed when he recognized one of them as Eby, the man who had run the cave trading post back on the Ohio. He remembered that when the river pirates had attacked Harding's flatboat, one of them had mentioned Eby's name. If Eby was here with eight other men, trying not to be seen, it had to be for some foul purpose.

Putting the bundle of wood down, he went back into the engine room.

"Where's the wood?" Dewey asked.

Without a word, Art picked up his rifle, and began loading it.

"What is it, boy? What's wrong?" Dewey asked.

"I think we're about to have company," Art answered.

"River pirates?"

"Looks that way to me," Art said. His rifle loaded, he started on his pistol.

"Mule!" Dewey shouted.

"Yes, sir?" Mule answered. Mule was a free black man who worked on the boat in the same capacity as Art.

"Spread the word around, we're about to get jumped by pirates," Art said. "Tell everyone to get to their guns."

"Yes, sir!" Mule replied, springing into action.

Dewey brought the engine to all stop. As soon as he did, the speaker tube whistled. Dewey knew that it would be the captain, wondering why the engine had stopped, so he walked over to the speaker tube and yelled into it.

"Pirates ahead, Captain!" he shouted.

"There they are!" one of the crewman yelled, and Art stepped out onto the deck to see the three boats suddenly dart out. They were paddling fast, using the momentum of the current of the river to bring them to mid-channel.

One of the men in one of the skiffs fired toward the steamboat. Art heard the crash of glass and when he looked up, saw that the pirate was shooting toward the wheelhouse, trying to hit the pilot and thus cause the boat to wreck. Thankfully, he'd missed the man.

Using a bale of cotton not only for cover, but also to provide a resting place for his rifle, Art fired at the pirate who had just shot, and saw him grab his chest, then fall back into the river.

That seemed to open the door, for those two single shots were followed by a rippling volley of fire as men in the skiffs and men on the boat exchanged fire with each other. The sounds of the shots, barely separated from one another, rolled back from the trees on each side of the river, thus doubling the cacophony of the battle.

The battle was brief but brutal. Realizing that they had lost the advantage, the pirates gave up the fight and started paddling hard to get away. At almost the same time, Dewey put the engine into full speed forward. The *Delta Maid* leaped forward. It was a moment before Art realized what they were doing, but once he understood, there was nothing he could do but stand by and watch.

Captain Timmons deliberately ran over one of the boats. Art rushed to the railing and saw pieces of the boat drifting away as the three men who had been in the boat were paddling hard to stay afloat. One of them slipped underwater and, caught by the severe undertow, didn't reappear. The other two swam hard for the opposite shore, chased by bullets fired at them by the angry crewmen of the *Delta Maid*.

Bullets popped into the water all around the swimmers, sending up tiny geysers as they did so. One of the two was hit and, like the unlucky man who had caught the full brunt of the collision, he went under and didn't come back up. The third man reached the sandy shore on the other side, pulled himself out of the water, then started toward the tree line.

At that moment, only Art, of all the men on board, had a rifle that was primed and ready. He raised the Hawken to his shoulder, touched his finger to the trigger, then had second thoughts. The man represented no immediate danger now, so why kill him?

Art lowered his rifle, then realized that if he didn't shoot, the others might question him. Raising his rifle, he did shoot, aiming not at the escaping pirate, but at a tree branch just above him. He pulled the trigger, there was a flash and a boom, then the tree limb exploded, just over the fleeing pirate's head.

"Ayii!!" the pirate shouted in fear, his cry of terror clearly heard by everyone on the boat.

"Good job, lad, you put the fear of God into him, that's for sure an' certain!" Dewey said, laughing.

"Too bad you ain't a better shot," one of the others said. "If you was, we would'a got 'em all."

At that moment the pirate who had made good his escape looked back toward the boat, and Art was able to see him more clearly. It was Eby.

When Eby stepped into the parlor of Etta Claire's Visitation Salon in Cape Girardeau, he was met by Etta Claire herself.

"Good evening, sir," she said. "May I get you a glass of wine while you are making up your mind which of our girls you will be visiting tonight?"

"I ain't visitin' with none of them," Eby said. "I'm Bruce Eby. I'm here to claim my girl, Jennie." He showed Etta Claire the papers proving that he owned Jennie.

"Oh, Mr. Eby," Etta Claire said. "Yes, I knew who you are, even though I've never met you. Jennie is engaged at the moment. If you will be patient for just a little longer, she'll be free, then you can go up to see her."

"I ain't here to see her. I'm here to take her out of here," Eby said.

"I've been making the deposit on a regular basis," Etta Claire said. "There is no difficulty with that, is there?"

"No, I got the money all right," Eby said.

"Then, I don't understand. If you are getting the money, then why do you want to take Jennie from here? It seems to be working out so well, and I know she is happy here."

"Happy?" Eby said. He laughed gruffly. "Woman, what the hell do I care whether or not she's happy. She's a slave. My slave. It don't make no difference to me whether she's happy or not. Now, you go upstairs and get her down here like I said. Else I'll get the sheriff on you."

"There is no need for that, Mr. Eby," Etta Claire said. "I'll bring her down to you."

"And if she's got 'ny clothes or anything that's hers, have her bring them too. We won't be comin' back."

When Etta Claire went upstairs to fetch Jennie, Eby picked up the bottle from which she had offered to pour a drink earlier. Pulling the cork with his teeth, he spat the cork out, then turned the bottle up to his lips, taking several Adam's-apple-bobbing drinks before pulling it down. Some of the wine dribbled down his chin and onto his shirt, but the shirt was so stained that it was scarcely noticeable. He ran the back of his hand across his lips, belched, then looked over toward the parlor itself, where several of the girls were looking back at him with a mixture of fright and revulsion.

"What the hell are you whores a'lookin' at?" he asked gruffly.

With a little gasp of fear, the women withdrew to the other side of the room.

"Mister, are you really going to take Jennie from us?" one of the girls asked.

"That's what I'm here for," Eby said.

"Who the hell thinks he's so important he can pull a man away from a woman before he's even finished?" a loud, angry voice said. The sound of heavy footfalls could be heard clumping down the stairs.

Eby pulled his pistol and cocked it, then held it level with the foot of the stairs.

"Where are you, you son of a bitch?" the voice declared. "Me and you are going to have . . ." At that moment the irate customer appeared at the foot of the stairs. At the same moment, he saw the pistol leveled at him and the anger left his face, to be replaced by fear. He held his hands out in front of him. "Hold it, hold it," he said.

"You goin' to make any trouble?" Eby asked.

"No, sir. Not a bit of it," the man said meekly. "Not a bit of it. You want her, you take her. She's all yours."

"Jennie!" Eby called. "Jennie, get your nigra ass down here now before I start tearin' up this place."

"Nigra?" the customer said, looking back up the stairs. "You tellin' me that girl is a nigra?"

A moment later Etta Claire and Jennie came down the stairs together. Jennie was clutching a cloth bundle. Tears were streaming down her face.

"Well, now," Eby said. "What's the cryin' about? You didn't think you'd come here to live, did you?"

Jennie didn't answer him.

"Mr. Eby, she has grown so close to the girls. Can she please tell them good-bye?" Etta Claire asked.

Eby picked up the wine bottle. "Yeah, she can tell 'em good-bye," he said. "I don't ever want it said that I'm a evil-spirited man." He drank from the bottle as, one by one, the girls came over to hug Jennie. All were crying, including Etta Claire, when Eby led her through the door.

"Mr. Eby, will I ever be comin' back here?" Jennie asked as they left the house.

"No," Eby said.

Jennie sobbed aloud.

"Ain't no sense in cryin' over it. That ain't goin' to change anything," Eby said.

Eby thought of the close call he'd had on the attempt to hold up the riverboat. Too many of his operations had taken place within fifty to sixty miles of Cape Girardeau. It was time for him to move on.

"I'm glad to see you ain't got ugly yet. Whores gets mighty ugly after a while, so iffen you're goin' to be of any use to me, I had to catch you while you was still comely."

"Yes, sir."

"Have you learned to enjoy sportin' yet?"

"Sportin'?"

"Lyin' with a man. You learned to enjoy it yet?"

"I . . . I don't enjoy it," Jennie said. "But I can do it."

Eby laughed gruffly. "Well, hell, girl, you been doin' it for what, five or six years now? I would expect you can do it. But that ain't what I ask. What I ask is, have you learned to enjoy it enough to make the man enjoy it?"

"They seem to like it."

"That's good. From time to time, maybe I'll teach you some of the things that men like," Eby said, subconsciously grabbing his crotch. "You'd like that, wouldn't you?"

In the whole time she had been with Younger, he had never been with her. She was certain it was because of Mrs. Younger, and for that she was glad. But there was no Mrs. Eby, which meant there was nothing to keep him away from her.

"I asked if you would like that," Eby repeated.

The little trick Carol had taught her, thinking of Art when she was with someone, had helped her get through some very disagreeable men. She was sure it would work with Eby as well.

"Yes, sir," she said dispiritedly. "I would like that."

"Yeah, I thought you would. Especially since I'm takin' you up to St. Louis, where you'll need to know more things. St. Louis is a fearsome big city and the men up there can't be pleased as easy as the men down here. But I figure with what I can teach you, with more men to be customers, why, you'll be makin' a lot more money in no time."

19

With a population in excess of eight thousand people, St. Louis looked particularly impressive as it was approached from the river. It spread out for some distance along the banks of the river and even back away from the river. Some of the buildings were as tall as three stories high. Art thought all of the buildings were handsome, whether they were made of brick, wood, mud, or stone. Regardless of their construction, they all glistened brightly, painted as they were by whitewash made from the limestone that was so plentiful in the area.

Even before turning toward shore, Captain Timmons signaled his presence by blowing the two-toned whistle. His whistle was answered by the firing of cannon from ashore.

Art, too recently in battle, where the firing of cannon meant more than a mere signal, jumped at the sound of the shore guns, but he recovered quickly. Sheepishly, he looked around the boat, then saw Dewey looking at him.

"Ain't nothin' to be embarrassed by, boy," Dewey said. "Only them that's actual fit in a battle knows enough to be a' feared of 'em."

Art nodded, but he didn't answer. No answer was needed.

Captain Timmons turned his boat toward the west, then ran it into the bank, putting the bow hard against the shore. A deckhand was standing at the bow, and carrying a line, he jumped down onto the riverbank as soon as the boat landed. The line was attached to a larger hawser, which he pulled off the boat, then tied around a post that was put in the ground for just that purpose.

Timmons signaled the engine room to stop the engine, and Dewey closed the throttle, then vented the steam. It was an impressive arrival.*

The landing of a steamboat was a great event in the lives of the citizens of St. Louis, and a significant number of them had come down to watch. Art's final job before reporting to the purser for his pay was to spread a tarpaulin over the remaining ricks of wood in order to keep them out of the weather. Even as he was attending to that, the gangplank went down across the front of the bow, and the stevedores came on board to begin unloading the cargo.

"Art? Art, is that you?"

Looking up toward the bald, bearded man who had called out to him, Art recognized Tony, the man he had worked with at the wagon-freight company.

"It's me, all right," Art said, smiling at his old friend.

"James! James, come look who we have here!" Tony said.

James came over and stuck out his hand. Remembering that he had once fought with James, Art was a little hesitant, but James didn't give him a chance. He grabbed his hand and pumped it enthusiastically.

"Art, m'lad, sure n' 'tis a fine thing to be seein' you. How have you been?" James asked.

"I have been fine," Art replied.

"Did you go to war?" Tony asked.

"Yes. I was at New Orleans."

---

*Although steamboats were on the Mississippi, as early as 1811, the first steamboat did not actually reach St. Louis until the *Zebulon Pike* arrived at the foot of Market Street on July 27, 1817.

"Ahh, I heard we gave the English 'what for' at the Battle of New Orleans," Tony said. "It's too bad the war was already over."

"What?" Art asked, surprised by the comment. "You mean the war is over?"

"You haven't heard? The Americans and the English signed a treaty ending the war. And, as it turns out, almost a month before the fight at New Orleans."

"Before the fight at New Orleans?"

"Yes."

"Damn," Art said. "Then that means all those men died for nothing."

"All what men? I heard we didn't have but just a few kilt," Tony said.

"That's right, we only lost a few. One of them was my friend, Mr. Harding. But I was also referring to the English. They left so many of their dead on the field you could have walked nearly half a mile on them without your feet touching the ground."

"Aye, 'tis bad all right, even though the English be black-hearts, every mother's son of them," James said.

"Here, you two! You ain't bein' paid to palaver!" Mr. Gordon said, shouting at Tony and James.

"Mr. Gordon, look who is back," Tony said.

Gordon looked toward Art, then acknowledged him with a nod. "If you plannin' on comin' back to work for me, boy, keepin' them two from their labors ain't the way to do it."

"I'm sorry, Mr. Gordon."

"Boy, what about we meet later for a beer?" Tony asked. "Irish Tavern?"

"Aye, lad. Irish Tavern, same as always."

"I'll be there," Art said as his two friends went back to work.

Before going ashore, Art and the other crewmen lined up on the afterdeck to receive their pay from the purser. Captain

Timmons stood by, smoking his pipe and watching in silence, until Art stepped up to receive his pay, which was five dollars.

"Boy, a word with you," Timmons called, beckoning with his pipe.

"Aye, Cap'n?"

Timmons had a scowl on his face. "Dewey tells me you ain't at all interested in bein' a river man, that you was just using the boat as a means of getting to St. Louis."

Sheepishly, Art looked down at his feet. "Yes, sir, I have to confess that's true. I'm sorry if I misled you."

Unexpectedly, Timmons smiled. "No need to apologize," he said. "I admit, I would like to have you stay on. You're a good hand and there's no doubt in my mind but that you would make a fine river pilot if you wanted to, and set your mind to it. But I don't believe you can push a rope. If you don't want to be a pilot, there ain't nothin' I can do to change your mind."

"Being a riverboat pilot is about as noble a profession as I can think of," Art said. "But I've got a hankering to see the creature, and I made a promise to a dead friend to do just that."

Sticking his pipe back in his mouth, Timmons nodded. "Then, boy, you do that," he said. "A promise made to a dead friend is one you ought to keep." He stuck his hand out. "Good luck to you, Art. And if there's ever anything I can do for you, you just get in touch with me."

"Thanks," Art said. "I appreciate that."

Lucas Younger was one of the many who had come from the town to stand on the riverbank and watch the boat land. He was totally shocked to see that Art was one of the boat crew. Seeing the boy renewed the anger Lucas felt. After all, it was out of the goodness of his own heart that he had taken Art in. And how did Art repay him? By taking Jennie away from him, that's how. The best moneymaking scheme he ever had was gone because of this boy's interference.

I should've left you lyin' facedown in the shit and the mud behind the tavern in New Madrid, he thought. If it weren't for you, I'd still have Jennie.

As he thought of Jennie, he rubbed himself. He had never personally taken his pleasure with the young girl. He'd wanted to, but he'd held back because he knew Bess would raise hell with him.

Well, Bess was dead now, having died of the fever during the winter. She was dead, Jennie was gone, and he was left with an empty wallet, an empty bed, and no prospects. All because of Art.

Of course Younger had managed to turn a little profit on the boy, selling him to a slave hunter. It had been amazingly easy to pull it off. All he had to do was claim that Art was his slave. The burden lay with Art, then, to prove that he wasn't.

He wondered if that would work again.

"Seamus! Look who has come back to us," James called as he, Tony, and Art entered the Irish Tavern that evening. "'Tis Art himself, a hero now he is, havin' fought the black-heart Englishmen at New Orleans."

"Welcome back, lad," Seamus said, greeting him warmly. "Find a table and it's an Irish whiskey I'll be bringin' you."

Art held his hand up. "Whiskey is still a bit too strong for my taste. Beer will do."

"Then beer 'tis, with a bit o' honey for sweetner if you need it," Seamus teased good-naturedly.

"Careful with the teasin' now, Seamus," James said. "I can tell you myself what the lad can do with a wee club."

The others laughed at James's self-deprecating humor. The three friends sat at a table in the center of the tavern, Art choosing the seat that left his back to the front door.

"So, tell us what it is like to be fightin' in a war," Tony said.

"It's noisy, frightening, noisy, cold, noisy, wet, and noisy," Art said.

"Would you be sayin' it's a bit noisy then?" James asked.

The others laughed.

"Well, guns do make noise," Tony suggested.

"Yes, but it's not only the guns," said Art. "It was a big army, and when you are around that many people all the time, half of 'em are talking, the other half are singing, coughing, belching, or farting, and no one is listening. There's never a quiet moment."

"Well, that's the way of it in civilization," Tony said. "Now you take St. Louis. It's a big, noisy city."

"True," Art said. "That's why I'm leaving."

"Leaving St. Louis? Sure'n you just got here, lad. Where would you be goin', pray tell?"

"If it's your job you're worryin' about, we've already talked to Mr. Gordon. He'll put you on if you want. Without firing James," Tony said.

"I appreciate your asking for me," Art replied. "But I figure that as soon as I put together a few things I need, I'll be headin' west."

At that moment Lucas Younger entered the tavern, accompanied by the city sheriff and his deputy. Younger pointed to Art.

"There he is, Sheriff. That's my slave boy Art."

Hearing, and recognizing, Younger's voice, Art spun around quickly. He started to reach for his Hawken rifle, which was leaning against the table.

"Easy boy," Tony said quietly, reaching out to put his hand on Art's arm. "Your rifle's not primed and their pistols are."

Tony was right. Both the sheriff and his deputy were holding charged pistols.

The sheriff got a puzzled look on his face. "What do you mean that's your slave boy?" he asked. "That boy's no nigra."

"He's Creole," Younger said. "You can't hardly tell Creoles

from white folks. And he's my slave. I got the paper right here to prove it." Younger held up a sheet of paper.

"Sheriff, I'm no slave," Art said. "I don't know what that paper is, but it's wrong. And I'm not Creole, I'm white."

"White are you? Near 'bout all white folks have last names, but you don't. You two, what's his last name?" he asked Tony and James.

"He ain't never told us," James said. "But that don't make no never mind. You can look at him and tell he's white."

"My last name is Gregory," Art said. "You can check with General Jackson. I was a lieutenant in his army at New Orleans."

The sheriff laughed out loud. "You, a lieutenant? Now I know you are a'lyin', boy. Ain't no way someone as young as you would be a lieutenant."

"Read this here runaway notice," Younger said, handing another paper to the sheriff. "It'll prove I'm tellin' the truth and the boy is lyin'."

"Keep an eye on 'im, Coy," the sheriff said to his deputy. "Iffen he tries to run, shoot 'im."

"Yes, sir, Sheriff, I'll do just that," Coy replied, licking his lips and smiling at the prospect.

The sheriff began to read. "It says here a slave boy by the name of Art, so light that he could pass, escaped from his master while working in a lime pit in Sainte Genevieve." The sheriff looked over at Younger. "I thought you told me your name was Younger."

"That's right."

"This here paper says he run away from a man named Matthews."

"That's right. After the boy run away from me, I sold him to a slave chaser. The slave chaser found him, and sold him to a man by the name of Matthews. But all that bein' said, the boy is still a slave and since Matthews ain't here to press his claim, I'm goin' to do it for 'im. Sort of a friendly arrangement between businessmen, so to speak."

The sheriff nodded, then glanced back at Art. "That true? Did you run away from Matthews?"

"Well, yes, but . . ."

"Ain't no buts to it, boy," the sheriff said. "If this be you"—he held up a piece of paper—"then you are a runaway slave. And it's my duty to take you back to your master."

"Them's my guns too," Younger said, pointing toward the table. "The pistol and the rifle, he stole 'em both from me when he run away like he done."

"Sheriff, you know he's lying now," Tony said. "If he stole them guns from Younger there, how do you suppose he still has 'em? Ain't no way this fella Matthews would let a slave boy keep guns like that."

"Ain't my job to be supposin' things like that," the sheriff replied. "Mr. Younger here is makin' all the charges. And since this boy done admitted that he run away from Matthews, well, I reckon I'll be takin' Younger's word over that of the Creole."

"I'm not Creole!" Art insisted.

"Uh-huh. And you said you wasn't no slave neither, then I got you to admit you was. All right, Mr. Younger, here he is. Now, how you goin' to hold him?"

"Don't you worry none 'bout me holdin' 'im. I got me some shackles hangin' from the saddle of my horse," Younger said. "I'll keep 'im shackled up till I get him back to his rightful owner."

"Let's go," the sheriff said, waving his pistol at Art.

"Sheriff, you're making a big mistake," Tony said. "They's too many things ain't addin' up here. I just don't believe this boy is a slave."

"Mr. Younger's got papers says he is," the sheriff said. "And the boy done admitted that he run away from Matthews down in Sainte Genevieve. 'Peers to me like that pretty much closes the case."

* * *

"Keep up, boy, keep up," Younger said, giving the shackles a jerk.

The hard yank caused Art to stumble, and he would have gone down had he not been fallen against Younger's horse. Younger was riding and Art was walking behind, pulled along by a chain that connected his shackles to the saddle of Younger's horse.

"I hear tell Matthews is a rich man," Younger said. "Ain't no tellin' what he might give me as a reward for bringin' one of his slaves back to him. What do you think, boy? You was with him. How much do you think he'll give me?"

"Whatever he gives you will be a waste of money, because I'll just run away again," Art panted. He had to pant because the brutal pace was causing him to gasp for breath.

"I reckon Mr. Matthews can break you of that. He's got hisself a big nigra with a long black snake of a whip. Slaves that runs away gets whupped by that nigra." He chuckled. "If I don't get nothin' from him but the chance to watch you get whupped, that'll be reward enough."

Art didn't answer.

"You shouldn't of come back and stole Jennie from me," he said. "You brought all this on yourself. When I let you go back in the woods, why didn't you just go your own way?"

"You didn't let me go, you tried to kill me. You left me for dead," Art gasped.

"Yeah, well, it would probably have been better for both of us if I had killed you."

Suddenly, and unexpectedly, Younger stopped his horse. "Now that I'm thinkin' on it, why am I even botherin' to take you all the way to Sainte Genevieve? You're right, Matthews probably won't give me any money a'tall." He got down from the horse. "So, what am I going to do with you now?"

"You could let me go," Art said.

"No, I don't think I can do that. I think I'll just shoot you."

"You can't just shoot me. You won't get away with that."

"Sure I will. You're a slave, remember? There won't nothin' happen to me. All I got to say is you was tryin' to run away again." He raised his pistol, glanced at it, then laughed, an evil, cackling laugh. "But it ought to make you feel a little better to know that you're goin' to be kilt with your own pistol."

Younger pulled the hammer back and aimed at Art. Art waited until Younger was about to pull the trigger. Then, timing it just right, he swung the chain. Even though the other end of the chain was attached to the saddle, there was enough slack in it to loop around the pistol in Younger's hand. Art jerked as Younger fired. As a result, the gun barrel deflected and Younger wound up shooting himself in the stomach.

"Uhnn!" he yelled in shock and pain. He looked down at his lower abdomen and saw blood pouring from the self-inflicted wound. Dropping the pistol, he put both hands over the wound, trying to stop the bleeding. It was a futile effort, for bright red blood spilled through the gaps between his fingers. "I've . . . I've kilt myself!" he said. He looked up at Art. "You!" he said. "You!" He reached toward Art with bloody palms. Staggering toward Art, he tried to grab him, but Art stepped back and watched as Younger plopped facedown into the dirt. Younger moaned a few more times, jerked once, then was still.

Art waited another moment before he knelt beside him. Turning him over, he looked down into eyes that had already glazed over with death. Then he reached into Younger's jacket pocket and found the key to his shackles.

Two minutes later, mounted on Younger's horse and armed with his own rifle and pistol, Art turned west.

20

Heading northwest from where he left Lucas Younger, Art came upon the Missouri River within a few days. Although he had never been in this part of the country before, he was now confident that he couldn't get lost. All he would have to do is follow the river, and that seemed like a simple enough task.

Shooting the turkey was easy. The bird had landed in front of him, then began pecking around in the grass as if totally unaware of Art's presence. Art could only imagine that the turkey either didn't see him, or perhaps he did see him but, never having seen a man before, didn't know enough to be frightened.

Art pulled his Hawken from its saddle sheath, hooked one leg across the saddle pommel, rested his elbow in that leg, then leaned forward to take careful aim before he fired. Nearly concurrent with the discharge of the powder and the rolling kick from the gun, feathers flew up from the turkey. The bird dropped without another twitch.

It was while Art was cleaning the bird that he came up with the idea of building an oven. He used stone and mud to make it, being careful to build it in such a way as to allow it to draw properly. After that he built a fire, and only then did he commit his turkey to the experiment.

Rather quickly, the aroma of the cooking turkey let him know that his experiment was successful. The turkey was browning nicely, the juices sealed behind the crispy skin.

"Hello the camp!"

The hail startled Art, who had been so intent on cooking his turkey that he hadn't paid enough attention to what should have been routine camp security. He was surprised a moment later to see a tall, gaunt, bearded man come into the camp. The man was dressed in buckskin and homespun. The clothes were so gray with soil and sweat that it looked as if they had become a part of his skin.

"You campin' all by yourself, are you, young feller?" the man asked, looking around the camp.

For a moment, Art contemplated telling him that there was someone with him, but he knew better than that. No doubt, this man had already made a thorough check of the area and knew the answer to his question. If Art lied to him now, it would be a sign of weakness, a sign that he was afraid to admit that he was alone.

"I am alone," Art admitted.

"Bodie is the name," the man said, sticking out a calloused hand. "How are you called?"

"Art. Art Gregory. Call me Art."

"Art, is it? Well, you got 'ny coffee, Art?"

"'Fraid not."

"Good, good. Then if I offer to share some of my coffee with you, maybe you'd see your way clear to share some of your turkey."

"I'd be happy to share my turkey with you, Mr. Bodie."

"Just Bodie, Art, no mister needed," Bodie said.

Bodie had ridden in on a mule, not a horse, and he went to the mule now and, reaching into his possibles bag, pulled out a coffeepot and a handful of coffee beans. Then, using the butt of his pistol, he began crushing the coffee beans.

"You headed anywhere in particular?" Bodie asked as he worked on grinding the beans.

"Just west," Art replied.

"Uh-huh. Goin' after the furs, are you?"

"Furs?"

"Beaver and sech. They pay good money for pelts back in St. Louis. Course, you don't have to go all the way to St. Louis to sell your season's take. Most o' the time you can sell 'em at Rendezvous."

"What is Rendezvous?"

Bodie laughed. "Boy, you are a green 'un, ain't you? Rendezvous is just about the most grandest thing they is. It's a place where all the trappers come together after a long winter up in the mountains. At Rendezvous they's whiskey, trade goods, and the like. Sometimes they's even women there. 'Course they's all whores, but whores is good enough iffen you been a long time without touchin' anythin' soft."

"You going to Rendezvous?"

Bodie shook his head. "This year's Rendezvous has done come 'n went. No, sir, I unloaded my furs an' now I'm headed back to St. Louis." He glanced over at Art's horse. "That's a good-lookin' horse you're a ridin'."

"Thanks," Art said.

"I guess you can see that I'm ridin' a mule."

"Yes, sir, I noticed that."

"Well, sir, they's a reason for that. You see, mules is a somewhat more surefooted critter than a horse. And that makes 'em good for use in the mountains. Fact is, it'd prob'ly be a good idea for you to trade that horse in and get yourself a mule."

"That a fact?" Art considered the situation. He was going to the mountains, so a mule might indeed be a better mount. Also, though he wasn't a slave, he was now technically a horse thief. And if caught with this particular horse, he might be tried for the crime.

Art started to say yes. After all, it seemed to him that the smart thing to do would be get rid of the horse. On the other hand, if Bodie got caught with the horse, he might be taken for the thief, and perhaps for a murderer, since only Art knew the truth of how Younger died. No matter how good a deal it might be for him, he couldn't leave Bodie holding the bag like that.

"There's somethin' you need to know 'bout how I come by this horse," Art said.

Bodie put the ground beans into water, then set the pot over the same fire that was cooking the turkey before he replied.

"You stole him, did you?"

"In a manner of speaking, yes," Art said.

"Then looks to me like you'd be anxious to get rid of him," said. "And to make it a better swap for you, I'll even throw in my trap line. If you're goin' after beaver, you're to be needin' a good trap line."

"There's more to it," Art said. He explained how Younger made the claim that he was a slave, how Younger was going to shoot him, but how he wound up shooting himself instead.

"All I was tryin' to do was get away from him," Art said. "But when I jerked the chain, somehow it caused him to shoot himself in the stomach. No one is going to believe that. Once they find his body, they are going to think I'm the one who killed him."

"Yeah, well, if you ask me, it served the son of a bitch right, killin' hisself like he done," Bodie said.

"Yes, sir. But I don't think anyone is going to believe me."

"I believe you, boy. If you wasn't tellin' me the truth, you wouldn't have to be tellin' me nothin' a'tall. You could'a just traded the horse for the mule and you'd be in the clear whilst I'd be the one ridin' the stole horse."

"Yes, sir," Art said.

"You got yourself a cup?"

"Right here," Art said, holding up his cup.

Bodie poured coffee into Art's cup, then into his own. "Her name is Rhoda," he said.

"Beg pardon?"

"The mule," Bodie said. "Her name is Rhoda. You'll be good to her?"

"You mean, after all I've told you, you'd still be willin' to trade?" Art asked.

"Well, I need me a horse," Bodie said. "And the one you're a'ridin' looks pretty good."

"What about the fact that it was Younger's horse?"

"From what you've told me about the bastard, I doubt he has too many friends who are crying over him. And since I know what to look out for, why, I reckon I can stay out of trouble. So, what do you say, boy? We goin' to trade?"

Art smiled broadly. "Yes, sir, we'll trade," he said.

"Listen, when you get up into the mountains, if you run into a couple o' ugly varmints—one is named Clyde, the other calls himself Pierre—why, you tell 'em that ole' Bodie says hello, will you?"

"Yes, sir. I'll do that."

"This be your first time in the mountains, boy?"

"Yes, sir."

"I thought so. Well, watch yourself up there. Winter comes early to the high country. Before too much longer you're goin' to be needin' to go to shelter. You any good with that there Hawken?"

"Tolerable," Art replied.

"Then I advise you to get you some meat shot, couple o' deer, an elk, maybe a bear. A bear would be nice 'cause you'd also have its skin to help you through the cold."

"Thanks for the advice."

* * *

Art and Bodie parted company the next morning, having changed mounts. Rhoda wasn't as comfortable a ride as Younger's horse had been; she had a more syncopated gait and Art had to get used to it. But she wasn't the first mule he had been around; back in Ohio his father had farmed with mules, so he knew how to work with them. And as mules go, Rhoda had an unusually gentle disposition.

Harding's description of the West had been accurate. He had said that you would travel for days to reach the horizon, only to see it continue to stretch out before you.

The plains had been impressive, with their wide-open spaces and the great herds of buffalo, along with deer and other game. But his pulse really quickened when he caught his first sight of the mountains, rising in the distant west.

At first, he thought it was a low-lying cloudbank. But after a day or two, he realized that it must be a mountain range, though certainly more magnificent in size and grandeur than anything he had ever seen before.

It took him nearly two weeks of hard traveling before he got close enough to make them out as individual mountains, rather than a featureless, purple rise in the distance. The closer he got, the higher and more formidable they became. He knew there was no way over them. He wondered if there was a way through them.

Perhaps he was too focused on the grandeur of the mountains, or maybe he was just careless, but for some reason he was nearly right on the bear before he saw it. Art had seen bears before, but he had never seen a bear the size of this one. This bear was at least twice, and maybe three times as large as any of the brown or black bears he had seen back east.

It was nearly time for it to hibernate, that is, assuming bears out here hibernated. Art didn't know whether these creatures hibernated or not. After all, he was in an area of the country he had never seen before. Here, everything was big, the mountains, the wide-open spaces, and this bear.

So far the bear had not seen Art, but that didn't mean he didn't know Art was here. Standing up on his hind legs, which gave him a height of at least eight or nine feet, the bear sniffed the air, trying to determine the source and direction of the scent he was picking up. Art had no doubt that once the bear located him, he would charge. Remembering Bodie's suggestion that a bear would be a good means of providing for the winter, as well as for his own self-preservation, Art decided to shoot it. Keeping a wary eye on it, he loaded his rifle, primed it, then pulled back on the hammer and aimed at the beast.

It was at precisely that moment that the bear saw him. Much faster than Art would have believed, the bear whirled around, came down on all fours, and started toward him. Art fired at the exact moment the bear turned to charge. As a result, the carefully aimed bullet that would have hit the bear in the heart, hit him in the side.

The grizzly roared in pain and rage as it lumbered toward Art at amazing speed. Art pulled his pistol and fired, hitting the bear in the throat. The bear slapped at the wound, as if driving away a mosquito, but it didn't stop its charge.

Art thought about running, but realized that he wouldn't be able to outrun the bear, and if the grizzly caught him from behind it would be all over. He had no choice now but to pull his knife, pray, and hope for the best.

The huge beast raised up as it reached Art. It tried to claw Art, but the bullet in its side had broken a couple of ribs, so it wasn't able to control the swipe. Art ducked under the bear's initial swipe, then stepped into the animal, thrusting his knife deep into where he thought the bear's heart was.

The grizzly made a second swipe with its other paw, and this time it connected. The long, sharp claws cut through Art's buckskin shirt and opened up four deep gashes in his shoulder and chest. Fortunately for Art, that was the bear's last effort, for even then it was dying. It fell on Art, knocking him down.

Pinned beneath the one-thousand-pound grizzly, Art struggled to roll out from under. The struggle was difficult, not only because of the pain of his wound, but also because the loss of blood was making him feel dizzy and weak.

Then, finally free, he stood up, staggered a few steps away from it, and collapsed.

21

When Art opened his eyes, he realized, with some surprise, that he was inside a building. He could smell smoke, and feel warmth from a fire. He could also smell something cooking.

He tried to sit up, but when he did pain and nausea overtook him, and he fell back on the bunk. He moaned.

"Bonjour, mon ami," a voice said.

Art turned his head and saw a man standing near the fireplace, in which a fire blazed. The fireplace didn't draw that well, thus accounting for the smoke Art smelled. That same smoke also filled the room with such a haze that it was difficult for him to make out the man's features.

"Who are you?" Art asked.

"I am called Pierre Garneau," the man said, speaking with a decided accent. "And you are?"

"My name is Art." Art studied his surroundings. The last thing he could remember was crawling out from under the bear. "The bear?" he said. "What happened to the bear?"

"Oh, you killed him, my young friend. It was a brave thing you did, to kill the bear with only a knife."

"I tried to shoot him, but I couldn't get the job done that way." Art looked around. "Where am I?"

"You are in the cabin of Monsieurs Pierre Garneau and Clyde Barnes."

"I've heard of you. You are Bodie's friends," Art said.

"Oui," Pierre replied, showing little surprise at Art's response. "Monsieur Barnes and I are most curious. How is it that you are riding Monsieur Bodie's Rhoda?"

"I traded my horse for Rhoda."

"I thought as much. Are you hungry? Do you wish to eat?"

"Yes."

Art tried once more to sit up, but again he was overcome by pain and nausea, so he fell back down. "I am hungry," he admitted. "But I don't think I can sit up."

"That is no problem. I will feed you," Pierre offered. "I myself made this wonderful soup. I think you will like it, and I think it will be good for you to eat."

Pierre carried a bowl of soup over, then sat on the edge of the bed and began spoon-feeding it to Art.

"Thanks," Art said after taking his first bite. "Umm, you are right, it is good soup. What kind is it?"

Pierre laughed. "Why it is soup from the bear you yourself killed," he said, holding another spoonful of the broth to Art's lips.

Art studied his benefactor. Pierre looked to be in his late forties or early fifties. He was a big man, bald, with a round face and full beard, brown but turning to gray. His eyes were blue, and one of them was drooping because of a scar that started at his hairline, then came down to the eye socket itself.

Pierre saw Art looking at the scar, and he chuckled. "My face, it is not a pretty thing to see, no?" Pierre asked, pointing to his scar with the spoon, empty between bites.

"It's all right," Art said, not sure how to respond to the question.

"You are a good boy not to hurt my feelings," Pierre said.

"I . . . I didn't mean to stare," Art apologized.

"An unfriendly Sioux left this scar," Pierre explained. "He

was angry because I had no scalp for him to take." He laughed at the self-deprecating reference to his baldness.

"Where is this cabin?" Art asked.

"It is in the mountain range called the Grand Tetons." Pierre laughed. "That is a joke, my friend. Most Americans do not know that Grand Teton means big titties." He put his hands over his chest, approximating breasts, and laughed again.

"Why would someone call mountains big titties?" Art asked.

"When you are well, look at them from a distance sometime. It looks like a woman lying down."

"Oh," Art said. He looked around the cabin. "Nice cabin," he said.

"Oui. I built this cabin myself, many years ago, when there were only a few Frenchmen and many Indians out here. At first I lived alone, then I met Monsieur Bodie. One year ago Clyde came to live with us, and this year Monsieur Bodie left, but as always I have stayed. And now you are here, so we are three again."

"Where is . . ."

"Clyde?"

"Yes."

"Clyde is collecting wood. He will be back soon, I think."

Almost as if on cue, the front door to the cabin opened and a man came in, carrying an armload of wood. This man was tall, clean-shaven except for a mustache, and with a full shock of hair that was dark brown. He was much younger than Pierre.

"Ahh, here is Monsieur Barnes," Pierre said. "Clyde, our young visitor is awake. His name is Art."

Clyde dumped the wood in the wood box, then brushed his hands together as he looked over toward Art.

"That was some deed, killin' that bear like you done," Clyde said. "Folks'll be tellin' that story for some time. Most especial you bein' someone as young as you are. How old are you anyway?"

"About sixteen, I guess," Art said. "I've sort of lost track of time."

Clyde nodded. "That'll happen to you out here. Don't happen that much to pups like you, 'cause we don't normally see folks as young as you out here. What you doin' here anyway?"

"I came to see the creature," Art said.

Clyde laughed out loud. "Come to see the creature, did you? Well, boy, that's as good an answer as any I've heard."

Finished with the soup, Pierre put the empty bowl down, then reached his hand out to touch Art's wound. Art reacted to the touch.

"Easy, *ami,*" Pierre said. "Does it hurt?"

"Not too much," Art said.

Slowly, gently, Pierre pulled the bandage off the wound so he could examine it. "I've made a poultice of bear fat and pine needles," he said. "I believe that might be helping."

"Is it putrefying?" Clyde asked.

"No," Pierre replied.

"That's a good sign. If it ain't putrefying yet, it ain't likely to do it." Clyde came over to look down at Art.

"Boy, if you ever decide to become a gambler, you ought to do well by it," Clyde said. "You are one lucky fella."

"Yes, sir," Art said. "I guess what I'm luckiest about is that you two came along when you did. I'm beholdin' to you for taking me in."

"There is no need for you to be indebted to anyone," Pierre said. "You have purchased your right to be here with the food you brought."

"Food?"

"The bear," Clyde explained. "Most likely that single critter will feed the three of us for most of the winter."

"Oui," Pierre said.

"Besides which, we ain't neither one of us been back to the States in three or four years," Clyde added. "It'll be good to have someone to talk to this winter. You can fill us in on all the latest news."

"I don't keep up with the goings-on," Art admitted.

"Tell us about the war," Pierre said. "We have heard talk of a war between the United States and England. Is that so?"

"Yeah," Clyde said. "We're sort of wonderin' now if we're Americans or English."

"Or French," Pierre added.

"You are Americans," Art said. "We all are. America won the war."

"I'll be damned," Clyde said. "Beat them Brits again, did we? Well, I reckon that'll keep 'em in their place for a while."

"If the United States won it, it was, no doubt, with the help of France," Pierre said. "In the last war with England, the war you Americans call your war of independence, you won it only with the help of the French."

"I don't think the French were involved in the war this time," Art said. "If they were, I didn't hear anything about it."

"Do you know anything about the war?" Clyde asked. "Did you read or hear anything about any of the battles?"

"I know about only one battle," Art said. "And that's the Battle of New Orleans. I can tell you everything you want to know about that battle."

"And how is it you know so much about it?" Pierre asked.

"Because I fought in it," Art answered simply.

"Glory be. You? Young as you are, you fought in the war?" Clyde asked, surprised by Art's response.

"Why are you so surprised, Clyde?" Pierre asked. "Did the boy not kill a grizzly bear, armed only with a knife? Compared to that deed, I think fighting the British could not be so much."

Thanks to the attention given his wound by Pierre, Art recovered from the bear-mauling with no aftereffects. He began helping out around the cabin, preparing meals and cleaning and pressing beaver pelts. Finally, the time that Art was waiting for came. Pierre invited Art to go out with him and Clyde to help them set the traps.

When Art left the cabin to go with them, he was surprised at how cold it was. When he commented on it, Pierre reminded him that it was getting late in the fall. He also told him that the higher one went in the mountains, the colder the weather.

"How high are we?" Art asked.

Pierre shook his head. "That I cannot tell you, for I have no way of measuring such things. I know only that it is high."

Loading traps and camping gear onto their mules, for like Art, Pierre and Clyde were also riding mules, the three started out to set their trap line.

Pierre was riding in the lead, Clyde was following, and Art was bringing up the rear. The three rode for what seemed like hours, with not a word passing between them.

Art was actually enjoying the solitude, for he was coming closer than he had yet come to seeing the creature. Never had he seen such towering peaks as these, and he looked at them with wonder and appreciation, sorry only that his friend Harding hadn't lived long enough to see the mountains with him. And Pierre was right, the Grand Tetons did look like a woman lying on her back, breasts thrusting into the air. "Big titties," he said to himself, laughing at the illusion.

"I think this may be good place," Pierre said after they had been riding for several hours. When he dismounted, Clyde and Art dismounted as well. Pierre walked over to the edge of the stream and looked around. "Yes," he said. "I was here in 1802. The beaver were many then. I think maybe they have come back to this place."

"You were here in 1802?" Art asked in surprise. "But that was before Lewis and Clark, wasn't it?"

"Lewis and Clark?" Pierre asked.

"Yes, you know, the great explorers?"

"Oh, yes, I remember them. They were nice young men. They were . . . how do you say . . . green behind the ears?"

Clyde chuckled. "Wet behind the ears," he said.

"Oui, wet behind the ears. They needed lots of help, but they were friendly enough."

"They needed help?" Art asked.

"Yes. And I did what I could to help them," Pierre said without elaboration.

"But surely they didn't need much help. They are the ones who opened the West."

Clyde laughed. "You think Lewis and Clark opened the West, do you, boy?"

"That's what I have always heard and read," Art said.

"Well, don't believe everything you hear and read," Clyde suggested. "When Mr. Lewis and Mr. Clark came West, there were already people out here, including our own Pierre Garneau. Pierre was one of their guides."

"How long have you been out here?" Art asked Pierre.

"I came out here when I was twenty-two years old," Pierre said. "That was in 1782."

Art whistled. "1782? You must've been the first one out here," he said.

Pierre laughed. "Hardly the first, my friend. And certainly not the last. Now, let us gather some traps and get to work, for we have a saying out here. *La langue n'attrape pas le castor.* That means, the tongue does not catch the beaver."

"We better get to work, Art. Else we'll have this old man to deal with," Clyde said good-naturedly.

Taking half-a-dozen traps from the back of the mule, Art threw them over his shoulder and followed his two mentors. When Pierre stepped out into the water and began wading, Art hesitated.

"What is it, boy?" Pierre asked, looking back at him. "Why do you stand there?"

"Isn't that water cold?"

"Oui, it is very cold. That's why I don't want to stand here all day."

"Then why are you standing in it?"

"You want to leave your smell for the beaver?" Clyde asked, wading out into the water behind Pierre.

"Oh, I see," Art said, understanding now that if they were careful to stay in the water, no human scent would be left. He followed the other two in the water, catching his breath sharply from the icy cold that shot up his legs when he stepped into the stream.

Pierre wandered down the stream for at least half a mile, looking for sign of fresh beaver activity. Finally, he stopped and held up his hand. Clyde and Art stopped as well.

"We will put our traps here," Pierre said. Dropping all his traps in the water, he proceeded to set them, depressing the springs by standing on them, putting one foot on each trap arm to open them up. When the traps were opened, he engaged the pan notch, holding them in the set position.

Art began setting his own traps, watching the other two in order to learn how it should be done. Once a trap was set, the trap chain was extended its full length outward to deeper water, where a trap stake was passed through the ring at the end of the chain and driven into the streambed.

Finally, the bait was placed. This was a wand of willow, cut to a length that would permit its small end to extend from the stream bank directly over the pan of the trap. Bark was scraped from the stick and castoreum was smeared on the small end of the switch, so that it hung about six inches or more above the trap. Castoreum, Art learned, was an oil taken from the glands of a beaver.

Once the trap was set, Art and the others would leave, remaining in the water until they were some distance away in order to avoid leaving their own scent to compete with that of the castoreum.

When the last trap was set, the men returned to the first group of traps. There, they found that some beavers had already been taken. They removed the beavers, then skinned them by making a slit down the belly and up each leg. After that they would cut off the feet, then peel off the skin. Once the pelt was removed from the carcass, it was scraped free of fat and flesh, the necessary first step in curing the pelts.

"Here, boy," Clyde said, lobbing off the tail of one of the beavers, and tossing it to Art. "Cook up our dinner for us."

It was the first time Art had ever eaten beaver tail, but he found it quite delicious.

The three men being hanged in St. Louis were river pirates who had terrorized the Mississippi River for several months. Their mode of operation was to wait in hiding along the banks of the river until they saw a flatboat or keelboat making its way downstream. Then they would get into a skiff, paddle quickly out to the boat, kill the unsuspecting boatmen, and take the boat's cargo.

More than fifteen boatmen had lost their lives to these same river pirates, and thousands of dollars worth of goods had been stolen. Then a group of St. Louis citizens, tired of the piracy, set a trap for them by concealing several armed men on one of the boats. The pirates were captured, brought to St. Louis, tried, and sentenced to death by hanging.

Today was the day their execution was to be carried out, and almost two thousand people had gathered along the riverbank to watch the spectacle.

Bruce Eby, thankful that he had avoided this fate, stood in the crowd and watched as the three pirates, Moses Jones, Timothy Sneed, and Ronald Wilson, were led to the gallows. Wilson was a boy, no older than fifteen, and he was weeping and wailing entreaties to God to have mercy on his soul, and by his contrition had elicited some sympathy from the crowd of onlookers who were gathered for the execution. Moses Jones remained absolutely silent, but he glared sullenly, frighteningly at the crowd. Timothy Sneed, on the other hand, shouted taunts at them.

"Hear me, all you good people of St. Louis," Sneed called out to them. "You've come to watch ole Timothy Sneed dance a little jig at the end of a rope, have you? Well, don't be bashful. Come on up close. Hold your children up so they can get a good, close look at my ugly face. When my ghost comes callin' in the middle of the night, I want all the little children to know it's me comin' to get them!" He glared at the children, then laughed maniacally.

"Mama!" a boy yelled in a frightened voice. "Is he going to get me?"

"Yes, I'm comin' for you, sonny!" Sneed said. "I'm comin' for all of you!" he added. "No more peaceful sleep in St. Louis." Again, he laughed, a cackling, hideous laugh.

"You're an evil man, Timothy Sneed, to be frightening children in such a way," someone shouted up from the crowd.

"I may be frightenin' the children, but I'm givin' the ladies a bit of a thrill, I think. You men will all be thankin' me tonight when the ladies, still warm and twitching from watching ole Timothy's eyes pop out, will be snugglin' up to you for a little lovin'."

"Shut your evil mouth, Sneed, or I will gag you before the hanging," the sheriff warned.

Sneed laughed again. "Why would you gag me, Sheriff? If I didn't play the fool for you at this hanging, what would be the pleasure in watching? Don't you know this is all part of the show?"

"Do you have no shame? Have you no sorrow for your wicked ways?" someone asked from the crowd.

"None!" Sneed replied.

"I do!" Wilson shouted. "I am sorely shamed that I left my poor old mother to seek my fortune. How she will grieve for me when she learns of my fate." Wilson was weeping now.

"Hell, boy, your mother's a bloody whore," Sneed sneered. "Grieve for you? She don't even remember you."

"Lord, I'm sorry for my sins!" Wilson shouted.

"Die like a man, Wilson," Sneed said. "Don't be givin' these psalm-singers your prayers."

"Leave the boy alone, Sneed. I'm thinkin' it might do us no harm to be goin' to meet the Lord with a prayer on our lips," Moses suggested.

"Ha!" Sneed replied. "It's not the Lord we'll be seein' when we open our eyes again. It'll be the face of Satan his ownself, and I'll not be goin' to that bloody bastard with prayers. I'll be screamin' and cussin' all the way to hell. And when I get there, I plan to kick the devil right in his rosy red ass."

A gasp came from the crowd, for never had this group of God-fearing people been so close to pure evil. Some swore they could even smell sulfur.

"It's time," the sheriff said. He nodded to his deputy, and the deputy slipped a black hood over the head of each prisoner, one at a time.

Just before he put the hood over Sneed's face, Sneed happened to see Eby standing in the crowd.

"Eby, you son of a bitch!" he yelled. "I remember when you was one of us! How is it you ain't up here getting' your neck stretched?" The last part of Sneed's shout was muffled by the hood.

For a moment, Eby was frightened that perhaps someone in the crowd would connect him with Sneed's last, agonized challenge. But it quickly became obvious that Sneed's words were a mystery to the crowd.

With the hoods in place, the deputy stepped back away from the three men, then nodded at the sheriff. The sheriff pulled a handle that opened the hinged floor under the feet of the condemned.

The door fell open with a bang, and the three men fell through the hole. They dropped no more than knee-deep into the hole before the ropes arrested their fall. The ropes gave a snap as they grew taut. The hangman's knots slammed against the backs of the now-elongated necks as the three bodies made a quarter turn to the left.

Moses Jones and Ronald Wilson died instantly, and their bodies hung still. Timothy Sneed was not killed outright, and he jerked and twitched, lifting his legs and bending at the waist as if, by that action, he could find some relief. Those in the front row could hear choking sounds coming from behind the black hood, and they watched in morbid fascination as he continued his death dance.

Not until Sneed's body was as still as the others did Bruce Eby turn away. He felt a little nauseous, not because he had watched his erstwhile friends die in such a brutal way, but because he could have been one of them. It was only by luck that he'd avoided capture during his years of piracy, as it was by luck that he'd escaped death a year earlier when he and others had attempted to rob a steamboat.

He had given up piracy after the steamboat incident, and for the last few months had been living solely on the income generated by Jennie's prostitution. But though Jennie was a favorite among St. Louis's sporting gentlemen, she wasn't the only whore in town and competition was getting stiffer. It was time to do something else, and he already had his next move planned.

22

It was a man, full-grown, who came down from the mountains three years later, riding a horse and leading a mule. His square jaw, straight nose, and steel-gray eyes staring out from under a wide-brimmed hat gave him the kind of rugged good looks that women would find handsome, if there were any women around to observe him. But for the last two years, from adolescence into young adulthood, Art had been much more apt to encounter a grizzly bear than a woman.

When he could, Art rode down the middle of a stream, thus keeping his track and scent difficult to follow. The mule behind him was packed with his share of the beaver pelts he, Pierre, and Clyde had taken over the last two years, and now he was going to Rendezvous to sell them.

This would be Art's first Rendezvous, and he was very much looking forward to it. Pierre and Clyde had told him a great deal about Rendezvous, how trappers and mountain men from all over the West would gather in one place to sell their furs and buy fresh supplies for the next year's trapping.

"They's booze there too. And gamblin'," Clyde said.

"And sometimes ladies," Pierre added.

"Whores," Clyde corrected.

"Prostitutes they may be," Pierre agreed, "but they are women nevertheless."

"What are you tellin' him about it for?" Clyde asked. "He's just a boy."

"A boy? He is bigger and stronger than either of us," Pierre said. "And I think the women might find him better-looking as well."

"Maybe so. But seein' as he's never had a woman, he's still a boy far as I'm concerned," Clyde said.

That conversation had taken place a week ago. Then, when Art announced the next morning that he would be leaving for Rendezvous before them, Clyde teased him by asking if he was going early so he could find a woman and become a man.

"I'm going because I can no longer stand the sight or smell of either of you," Art replied. It was all in good-natured fun, and though Art had already informed them that, after Rendezvous, he planned to go out on his own, the three men parted as good friends. And why not? Art knew that he owed his very life to them.

For the time being, Rendezvous on the Platte was the biggest city between the Pacific Ocean and St. Louis. Nearly a thousand people were gathered in the encampment: trappers from the mountains, fur traders from the East, Indians, explorers, mapmakers, merchants, whiskey drummers, card sharks, and whores.

Before Art left the cabin, he, Pierre, and Clyde had divided, evenly and fairly, the beaver pelts they had taken. When he arrived at Rendezvous, he was greeted by representatives from the fur traders, all wanting to make offers on his plews, as the beaver pelts were called.

"The London Fur Trading company will give you the best deal on your plews," a representative of the company said. "If you sell to anyone else, you'll regret it."

Similar offers came from half-a-dozen other traders, all anxious to take his load. Some offered "a line of credit at any merchant in Rendezvous" as their compensation.

Art sold to a dealer from St. Louis, doing so because, though the St. Louis dealer offered him less money, it was all in cash. Also, Art could remember seeing one of the company signs back in St. Louis, so he knew it was a legitimate operation.

With the money in hand, Art began wandering through the encampment grounds to see what was available.

He bought lead and powder, a new trap to replace one he lost, a new rubber slicker, and some waterproof matches. He bought some new flint, a needle and thread, a flannel shirt, and some socks. He also bought a book. When he left home, sneaking out of the house that night five years ago, the last thing he ever thought he would miss was reading. But there were times over the last couple of years when he wished he had a book, not only as a means of passing the time, but also in order to improve his reading skills.

He bought coffee, flour, and sugar. He also bought some dried peaches, thinking he might make a pie or two when he got around to it.

After he made all the necessary purchases, he began looking around the encampment to see what kind of entertainment was available. There was a tent that sold liquor, so he had a couple of beers. There were whores there too, but they were obviously whores who were no longer able to earn a living in competition with younger, more attractive whores. Every one of them was much older than he was, and all showed the ravages of their profession.

One thing that did catch his interest was a shooting contest. A hand-lettered sign offered a prize of one hundred dollars to the winner. A board was stretched across two oaken barrels, and on the board was the sign-up form for the contest. Behind the board, a man sat in a chair, paring an apple. He looked up as Art studied the entry form.

"You plannin' on enterin', mister? Or, are you just goin' to read the words offen that piece of paper there?"

"Where does the one-hundred-dollar prize come from?" Art asked.

"It comes from me," the man said.

"You are going to give one hundred dollars to the winner?"

"Yep. Crazy of me, isn't it?" the man replied. He carved off a piece of the apple and popped it into his mouth. "But that's the kind of man I am. You think you could win?"

"I don't know," Art replied. "Maybe."

"Then you ought to enter. It would be an easy one hundred dollars for a man who can handle a rifle."

"All right," Art said. He picked up the pen and started to sign the paper.

"Huh-uh," the man behind the board said, shaking his head. "First you give me ten dollars. Then you enter."

Art took ten dollars from the roll of money he had just received for his pelts.

"Sign up, young man."

As Art signed the roster, he saw that he was the twenty-seventh man to do so. He looked at the proprietor, who was carving off another piece of the apple.

"According to this, you have already taken in two hundred seventy dollars. I don't think it will be all that hard for you to give away one hundred."

"Well, well, what do we have here, a scholar? What do you care about how much money I make, as long as you get yours?"

Art thought about it for a moment, then nodded. "All right," he said. "I won't mind taking your money."

It was early afternoon and Art was waiting, with more than three dozen other shooters, for the contest to begin. Some of the shooters were cleaning their guns; others were sighting down the barrels of their rifles at the targets they would be using. Some were just standing by calmly, and Art was in that group.

"Art? Art, do you remember me?" a woman's voice asked.

Startled to hear his name spoken by a woman, Art turned to see who had called him. He saw a young woman between eighteen and twenty. She had coal-black hair, dark eyes, and olive skin. She was pretty, though there was a tiredness about her. Suddenly Art recalled the young girl who had cared for him in Younger's wagon so long ago.

"Jennie? Jennie, is that you?" he asked.

She smiled at him. "You remembered," she said.

"Yes, of course I remembered."

Spontaneously, Jennie hugged him. He hugged her back.

"Here, now, that's goin' to cost you, mister," a gruff voice said. "I ain't in the habit of lettin' my girls give away anything for free."

Quickly, Jennie pulled away from Art, and he saw the expression of fear and resignation in her face.

"Iffen you want to spend a little time with her, all you got to do is pay me five dollars," the man said.

"Eby," Art said, recognizing the man.

Eby screwed his face up in confusion. "Do I know you, mister?"

"No," Art said. "But I know you. What have you got to do with Jennie?"

"Ahh, you know Jennie, do you? Then you know she's the kind that can please any man."

Art looked at Jennie, who glanced toward the ground. "He owns me, Art," she said.

"What about it, mister?" Eby said. "Do you want her, or not?"

"Yeah," Art said. "I want her."

Eby smiled. "That'll be five dollars."

"No," Art said. "I don't want her five dollars worth, I want to buy her from you."

Eby took in a deep breath, then let it out in a long sigh. "Well, now, I don't know nothin' 'bout that. She's made me a lot of money. I don't know if I could sell her or not."

"You bought her, didn't you?"

"Yes, I bought her."

"Then you can sell her. How much?"

"One thousand dollars," Eby said without blinking an eye.

"One thousand dollars?" Art gasped.

Eby chuckled. "Well, if you can't afford her, maybe you'd better just take five dollars worth."

"No," Art said. "I reckon not."

"On the other hand, you could come back next year. I 'spec she'll be a lot older and a lot uglier then. You might be able to afford her next year."

Art looked at Jennie. For just a moment, there had been a look of anticipation and joy in her face. When she realized that her salvation was not to be, the joy had left. "I'm sorry," he said.

"Shooters, to your marks!" someone called.

Looking away from Jennie so he wouldn't have to see the disappointment mirrored there, Art picked up his rifle and walked over to the line behind which the shooters were told to stand.

Those who weren't in the shooting contest gathered round to watch those who were. There were a few favorites, men who had participated in previous shooting contests, and the onlookers began placing bets on them.

The first three rounds eliminated all but the more serious of the shooters. Now there were only ten participants left, and many were surprised to see the new young man still there.

"All right, boys, from now on it gets serious," the organizer said. "I'm putting a row of bottles on that cart there, then moving it down another one hundred yards. The bottles will be your target, but you got to call the one you're a'shootin' at before you make your shot."

As Art looked up and down the line of competitors, he saw that one of them was Eby. He wondered if anyone but him knew who Eby was, that he was a river pirate and, probably, a murderer.

Eby had the first shot. "Third from the right," he said. He aimed, fired, and the third bottle from the right exploded in a shower of glass.

This round eliminated four more, the following round eliminated two, and the round after that eliminated two. Now, only Art and Eby remained. A series of shots left them tied.

"Move the targets back another one hundred yards," the organizer ordered, and two men repositioned the cart.

By now all other activity in the Rendezvous had come to a complete halt. Everyone had come to see the shooting demonstration. Only two bottles were put up, and Eby had the first shot.

"The one on the left," Eby said quietly. He lifted the rifle to his shoulder, aimed, then fired. The bottle was cut in two by the bullet, the neck of it collapsing onto the rubble.

"All right, boy, it's your turn," the organizer said.

Art raised his rifle and aimed.

"Boy, before you shoot, how 'bout a little bet?" Eby said.

Art lowered his rifle. "What sort of bet?"

"I'll bet you five hundred dollars you miss."

Five hundred dollars was all the money Art had left. If he missed, he would leave here totally broke. Plus, he would have lost the shooting contest, so he wouldn't even have that money.

On the other hand, he had already bought and paid for everything he needed for another winter's trapping.

"Ahh, go ahead and shoot," Eby said. "I'll be content with just beating you."

"I'll take the bet," Art said.

"Let's see the color of your money."

Art took the money from his pocket, then held it until Eby also took out a sum of money. Both men handed their money over to the organizer, who counted and verified that both had put in the requisite amount.

"It's here," the organizer said.

"All right, boy, it's all up to you now," Eby said.

Once again, Art raised his rifle and took aim. He took a breath, let half of it out . . .

"Don't get nervous now," Eby said, purposely trying to make him nervous.

Art let the air out, lowered his rifle, looked over at Eby, then raised the rifle and aimed again. There was a moment of silence, then Art squeezed the trigger. There was a flash in the pan, a puff of smoke from the end of the rifle, and a loud boom. The bottle that was his target shattered. Like the other bottle, the neck remained, though only about half as much of this neck remained as had been left behind from the first bottle.

The crowd applauded as the organizer handed the money over to Art. "Looks like you won your bet, but the outcome of the shooting match is still undecided," he said. "Gentlemen, shall we go on? Or shall we declare it a tie?"

"We go on," Eby said angrily. "Put two more bottles up."

"Wait," Art said.

Eby smiled. "Givin' up, are you?"

"No," Art said. He pointed toward the cart. "We didn't finish them off. The necks of both bottles are still standing. I say we use them as our targets."

"Are you crazy? You can barely see them from here. How are we going to shoot at them?"

"I don't know about you, but I plan to use my rifle," Art said.

The others laughed, and their laughter further incensed Eby.

"What about it, Eby?" the organizer asked. "Shall we go on?"

Once more, Eby looked toward the cart. Then he saw that the neck from his bottle was considerably higher than the neck from Art's bottle. He nodded. "All right," he said. He raised his rifle, paused, then lowered it. "Only this time he goes first."

Art nodded, and raised his own rifle. "The one on the right," he said.

"No!" Eby shouted quickly. "You have to finish off the target you started. "You have to shoot at the one on the left."

"I thought we could call our own targets," Art replied.

"You can. And you already did. Like you said, we didn't finish them off. You called the bottle on the left. That's the one you've got to finish."

"I think Eby's right," one of the spectators said.

"All right," the organizer agreed. "Your target is what remains of the bottle on the left."

"A hunnert dollars he don't do it," someone said.

"Who you goin' to get to take that bet?" another asked. "Ain't no way he can do it."

"What about you, mister?" Eby asked. "You want to bet whether or not you hit it?"

"No, I'll keep my money," Art said.

"Tell you what. You wanted the girl a while ago. I'll bet her against a thousand dollars you don't hit it."

Art looked over at Jennie and saw, once more, a flash of hope in her face.

Could he hit it? It was a mighty small target and it was a long way off. He had never made a shot quite like this.

He knew he was a fool for taking the bet, but he used the same rationale he had used before. If he missed, he still had everything it would take to trap for a year. And Jennie would certainly be no worse off. On the other hand, if he hit it, she would be free.

"I don't want the girl to come to me. I want you to set her free."

"You hit that sawed-off piece of a bottleneck on the left there, and I'll set her free," Eby promised.

"All right, Eby. You've got a bet."

Everyone expected to wait for a long moment while Art aimed, but to their surprise he lifted the rifle, aimed, and fired in one smooth, continuous motion. The bottle neck shattered. The reaction from the crowd was spontaneous.

"Did you see that?"

"Hurrah for the boy!"

"Who would'a thought . . ."

"Look out!"

The last was a warning from someone who noticed that, while everyone else was cheering and applauding, Eby had raised his rifle and was aiming it, not at the target, but at Art. He came back on the hammer.

There was a loud bang, followed by a cloud of smoke. When the smoke rolled away, Eby was lying on his back with a large bullet wound in his chest. Turning quickly, Art saw Clyde Barnes.

"Mr. Barnes! Where did you come from?" Art asked.

"I decided to come on in early as well," Clyde said as he held his still-smoking rifle. "I couldn't let you have all the fun."

"Ever'one seen it," the organizer of the shooting match said. "Eby was about to shoot the boy, when this fella shot him. We ain't got no judge nor law out here, but I say it was justifiable killin'."

"Here, here!" another shouted.

"Anyone say any different?"

There were no dissenters.

"Then let's get that piece of trash buried and get on with the Rendezvous. Oh, by the way," the organizer said, looking over toward Jennie. "I reckon we also heard the bet. Girl, you're free."

Jennie smiled as the others applauded, though some got the distinct impression that she would just as soon have belonged to the young man who had come so gallantly to her rescue.

Art took his winnings, then turned to Jennie.

"Where will you go now?" he asked.

"I could stay with you," Jennie offered.

Art smiled. "Don't think the offer isn't tempting," he said. He shook his head. "But it wouldn't work. I'm not ready to leave the mountains yet. And I don't think you'd get on well here." He gave her one hundred dollars.

"What is this for?" she asked.

"I figure you can get back to civilization with one of the traders here," Art said. "But once you get back, you'll have to find some way to support yourself. Until you do, you'll need some money to live on."

"Thanks," Jennie said, taking the money.

"You have any idea where you'll be going?"

Jennie smiled. "You mean so you can find me if you ever come back?"

"Something like that," Art agreed.

"I'll be at Etta Claire's Visitation House in Cape Girardeau," she said.

"What is that? A hotel?"

Jennie laughed. "Something like that," she said.

When Art saw Clyde watching them, he introduced Jennie to him, telling how he had met her many years ago. "I tried to free her then," he said. "I stole her, but we got caught. This is the first time I've seen her since."

"You've changed, Art," Jennie said. "I called you a boy once. Now you're a man."

"Not quite a man," Art said.

"What do you . . . ?" Jennie started to ask. Then she smiled as she understood what he was saying. "Well, maybe we can do something about that," she suggested.

That night, Art left Jennie's tent, his passage into manhood complete.